WORLDS APART

THE MAFIA DAUGHTER

By

Paula Ellison Franklin

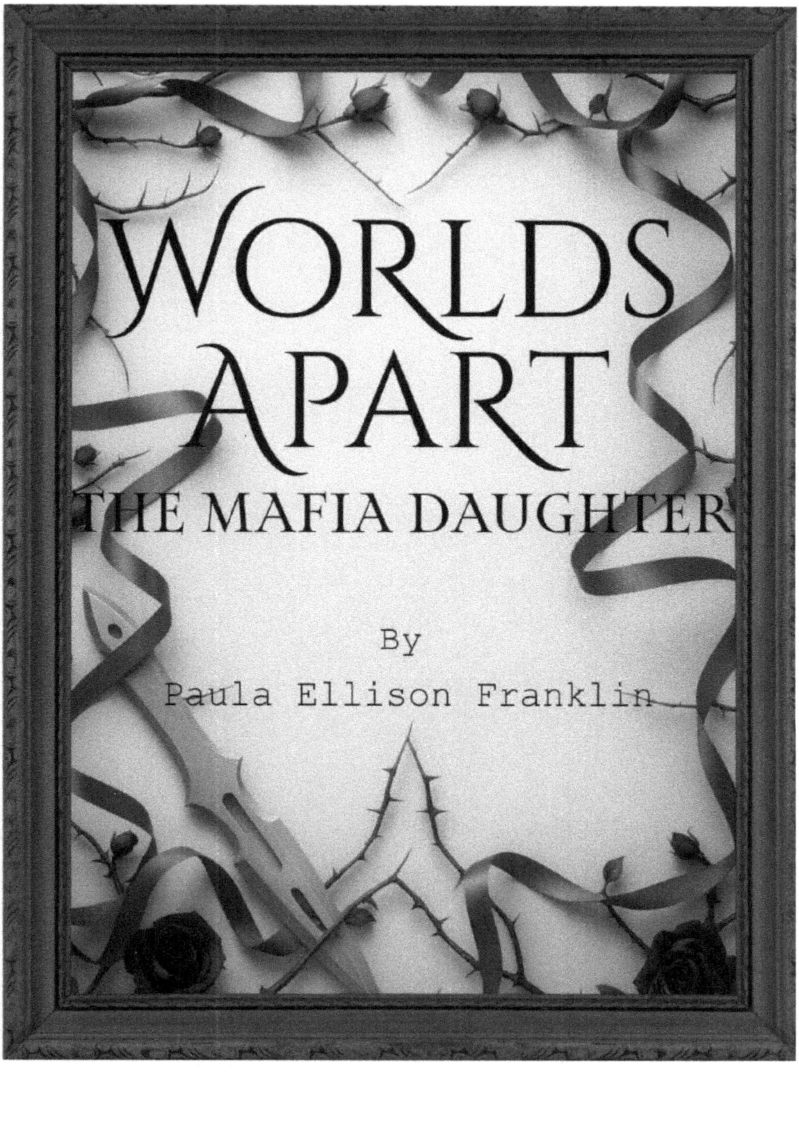

Table of Contents

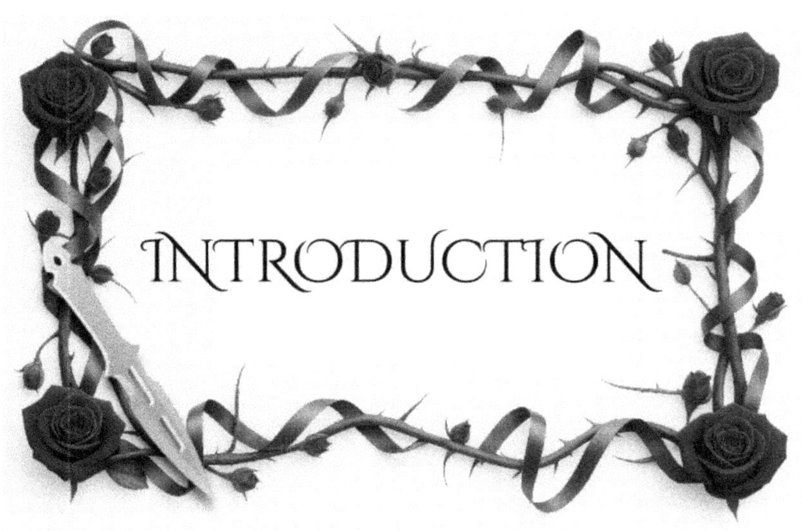

In 1845, during a significant wave of Irish immigration to the United States, the Connolly family arrived. Unlike many of their fellow countrymen, who fled Ireland to escape hunger and disease in search of a better life, the Connollys were ordered to immigrate by the head of the Irish Mafia to establish a new faction.

They landed in New York City with hopes of achieving the American Dream, intending to build businesses, acquire resources, and earn substantial profits. However, they quickly realized that this goal would not be easy, as they faced significant prejudice and inequality.

From this environment, along with their aspirations for wealth and power, the Connollys helped form the Irish gangs of New York. Initially, they made money through pickpocketing and murder-for-hire, but by the late 1800s, their activities had expanded to include counterfeiting, racketeering, and prostitution.

The arrival of Italian immigrants at the turn of the century sparked a turf war between the Irish and the Italians. Through murder and street fighting, these families fought for control over different sections of the city.

Once the turfs were established, the wars ceased until the onset of Prohibition. The millions of dollars generated through bootlegging, speakeasies, and extortion sparked a new power struggle among the families. Greed became the primary motivator to expand businesses, often crossing territorial lines. This resurgence of street violence and mafia killings peaked, resulting in the deaths of hundreds of gangsters. During this tumultuous period, two families rose above the others: the Connollys from the Irish clans and the Bianchis from the Italian Mob.

By the 1960s, the Connolly family had begun to grow in numbers and support. Their neighbors loved them, and they had a lot of public figures and politicians on their payroll. However, the Bianchi family's brutal methods were becoming increasingly unpopular in their communities. People no longer wanted to pay for protection, and the constant violence led to widespread disdain. Consequently, when the RICO Act was enacted in the 1970s, it encouraged the public to turn against the Bianchis.

As it became more difficult for the mafia to evade law enforcement, leading to many members being killed or incarcerated, the Connolly family continued to thrive. Enraged by their success, the Bianchi family declared war on the Connollys. This conflict wasn't fought publicly, like those of the 1920s during Prohibition, but rather in the shadows, with each family engaging in secretive revenge killings.

By the time James Connolly and his wife, Shannon, had their first child, they were fed up with all the death. James understood that the best way to keep his children safe was to send them to boarding school and instill some fundamental rules: always carry a weapon, never sit with your back to the door, have an alternative exit in every situation, and never be in the same place at the same time on any given day.

The feud continued back and forth until the death of James and Shannon's second child, Eileen. Eileen was married to a man named Daniel O'Brien, who came from a prominent family in a small town in West Virginia.

Daniel and Eileen met in college, married shortly after graduating and purchased a house in New Jersey to stay close to her family. Their first child, Tara, was born in the first year of their marriage, followed by their second daughter, Tennly, when Tara was three years old. Despite her father and two younger brothers, Jimmy and John, encouraging her to reconsider and send her girls to boarding school, Eileen and Daniel loved having their daughters at home and believed they could protect them.

However, as soon as Paul Bianchi learned that she took her girls to school, occasionally putting her in the same place at the same time, he ordered a hit on her.

Tara, age 8, and Tennly, age 5, waved goodbye to their mother, unaware that it would be the last time they would see her. She drove away, out of town, down the two-lane country road that led to their home, completely oblivious to the fact that she was being followed. It wasn't until she was within a quarter of a mile from the raggedy one-lane covered bridge that she noticed a car approaching from behind at an exceptionally high speed.

When they were withing feet from the bridge, they rammed into the back of her vehicle, causing her to swerve, plunging into the ravine below; the impact resulted in her instant death.

This was the final straw for James. Over the years, he had lost several family members, including two children. He no longer cared if he got caught; he simply wanted revenge. With the help of his remaining two sons and Daniel, he devised a way to kill as many members of the Bianchi family as possible in one strike.

He was counting on the fact that the Bianchis would gather on the night of Eileen's funeral, believing they would not retaliate then, so they didn't have much time.

Jimmy and John rode with Phillip, their chauffeur, in one car, while Daniel and his chauffeur, Thomas took a second vehicle. They arrived at the Italian restaurant owned by the Bianchi family, just after the restaurant closed and all the patrons had left.

Before meeting the other three men, Daniel noticed something moving in the backseat. He leaned down to look through the back passenger side window and saw Tennly sitting on the floor.

"Stay with her," Daniel instructed. "If you notice or suspect anything, get her out of here."

Despite he knew they would be down one man; Thomas understood the importance of Daniel's request and didn't question him. Daniel then approached the others, and they moved cautiously toward the restaurant.

They knew they weren't going to get out of there unscathed, but they had the element of surprise on their side. When they reached the bar's entrance, Daniel motioned for the others to take their positions, two on each side of the door. He held up his hand, counted to three, and then they charged in.

Bullets flew around the room as the men fired upon each other. Once the shooting stopped, only Daniel and his crew were left alive.

When Daniel returned to the car, he found Tennly nestled in the middle of the backseat. He climbed in beside his daughter, instructed Thomas to drive to his in-laws, and then cast a disappointed, questioning look at Tennly.

She responded with her sad, puppy-dog eyes. "I heard you were going somewhere for Mommy. I wanted to help. For Mommy."

Daniel was not an emotional man and seldom cried, but as he looked at his five-year-old daughter expressing a desire to do something for her late mother, he found it impossible to hold back his tears.

Daniel made two significant changes after that. He believed that if he had insisted the girls go to boarding school, Eileen wouldn't have been killed. So, he sold their home in New Jersey, moved back to Marinsburg, West Virginia, and sent the girls away to boarding school the very next year.

T ennly O'Brien had only one final exam left before the end of the school year. However, as she sat at her desk looking at her notes, she found herself unable to focus on studying. She spun around in her chair to take in the room that had become her second home.

Her queen-sized bed was dressed with a black and white Paris-themed comforter, complemented by pink pillows and a pink blanket neatly folded at the foot. The black and white striped curtains, held open by pink ties. A black couch adorned with pink throw pillows faced a 64-inch television mounted on the wall opposite the couch, above a chest of drawers.

She turned back to her desk and stared at her notes, reading the same passage repeatedly, struggling to focus on the content. Frustration bubbled over, as she shoved everything off the desk, sending her notes and papers flying across the room.

"Um..." Victoria paused, knocking on the doorframe. "Everything okay?"

Victoria was Tennly's first cousin on her mother's side and the oldest child of her Uncle Jimmy. She stood at 5'2", petite and cute, with long, wavy classic Irish red hair and striking green eyes. Her fair skin was dotted with tiny freckles, and she had an adorable button nose.

"I'm not ready," Tennly admitted.

"When is your meeting with Headmistress Novakova?"

"Tomorrow, after my last final."

"Have you made a decision?"

"No. I know what I want to do... or what I wanted to do... It's just different now."

"Because of your dad or Conner?"

"I could give two shits about my dad," Tennly confessed.

Despite only seeing her father a few months out of the year, Tennly used to

9

think the world of him. They shared the same interests, humor, and personality. They would spend hours together, target shooting and working out, while Tennly's older sister, Tara, wanted nothing to do with either activity.

However, when Tennly turned 13, a conflict arose between them. Daniel was away from home much more often, and his demeanor seemed different. He walked around with a distracted look, as if weighed down by burdens, and often appeared short-tempered. Tennly didn't realize until the following summer that her father's behavior was due to her maternal grandfather's deteriorating health.

She hated that her grandfather, James Connolly, was sick, but she didn't understand why they had to spend the past two summers, as well as every holiday, with him in New York instead of occasionally returning home. Both of her uncles lived within 45 minutes of her grandparents' house, so it didn't make sense to her why they couldn't take turns helping her grandmother care for him.

What she didn't know was that her mother's family, the Connollys, was the head of the Irish mafia in New York City, and her grandfather James was the boss. Upon his death, the leadership was set to pass to Tennly's mother, Eileen. However, since Eileen had been murdered when Tennly was five, they had to discuss who would take over after James's death.

Neither of Eileen's younger brothers, Jimmy nor John, wanted to become the boss. Knowing they were not natural leaders, James didn't insist they take on the role. When the discussion turned to who might be capable, only one name came to mind: Tennly.

Eileen had told Daniel and her father that there was something special about Tennly. From an early age, she had demonstrated a strong will and an ability to sense things that most kids her age could not. She was always questioning everything and was extremely resilient. While they all agreed that Tennly was destined to become a boss, they weren't expecting her to assume that role so early.

When James passed away, Tennly was just 14 years old and could not take on the position until she turned 18. Therefore, the head boss in Ireland appointed Daniel as the interim leader until Tennly came of age. Daniel spent months transferring everything into his name and making the necessary preparations.

All this work kept Daniel away from his daughters and kept Tennly away from home for the last three years. This was why she was angry; she blamed her father for keeping her away from Marinsburg. If she had been able to return home during her summer breaks instead of staying in New York, she could have resolved the issues that were making her so anxious.

"I'm sure things with Conner will work out," Victoria consoled.

Tennly's friendship with Conner was unlike any other. Even though they were from two different worlds, they shared many interests; they liked the same things, laughed at the same jokes, and enjoyed the same music and movies. They took walks, swam in the river just outside their neighborhood, got ice cream at the parlor two blocks down from Conner's house and loved causing mischief. Despite how similar they were, they both understood that no one would understand their relationship. This was why they had decided to keep their friendship a secret.

Tennly longed for the summers when she could finally be back with Conner; those were the best times of her life. However, that summer, the year Tennly turned 16, was different. She faced a significant decision.

The Connolly family gave their children the choice to stay in private school or attend a local public school in their hometown when they turned 16. Three years earlier, the decision would have been easy. However, with the uncertainties of what was going on between her and her father and her and Conner, she didn't know what to do.

Since Tennly and her father had grown distant, they were constantly arguing, and she blamed him for everything that had gone wrong. Along with that and what had happened between her and Conner the last time she saw him, made her reluctant to return home.

"If I could have gone home sooner," Tennly stated, "maybe I could have fixed it..."

"You're going home now," Victoria replied.

"It's too late," Tennly insisted.

"I'm sure it's..."

"I haven't seen him in three years," Tennly stressed, referring to Conner.

Tennly hadn't seen her father in a while either, not since Thanksgiving break in Ireland. Her family had been visiting Ireland during the American holiday for years, even before Tennly was born.

Typically, she would have seen her father two more times before the school year ended, but this year she decided to stay at boarding school instead of joining her family for Christmas and Easter. Therefore, the thought of living with him full-time was not something she looked forward to.

The next day was filled with mixed emotions. In the afternoon, after saying goodbye to the seniors, the underclassmen completed their final tests and then took some time to relax before dinner.

During this time, Tennly had a meeting with the headmistress. As she walked to the office, she couldn't help but focus on the school's intricate architectural details. The bright colors, crystal and pearl sconces, and paintings that adorned the walls, along with the white marble floors, ornate fixtures, and elaborate moldings gave it a palace-like atmosphere.

The office itself was unlike a typical school office, which often feels bland and sterile. Instead, it was spacious, decorated with vibrant gold and yellow wallpaper above a cherry wood chair rail. Below the chair rail, the walls were painted a soft red and adorned with cherry wood trim squares placed a foot apart. There were four windows, dressed in pale yellow curtains that cascaded elegantly from the ceiling to the floor. The flooring was cherry wood, and two large area rugs separated different parts of the room.

The headmistress gestured toward the seating area, which featured two leather couches and two high-backed gold velvet chairs facing each other, with a cherry wood coffee table in between. Tennly sat on the couch opposite the headmistress, who offered her a cup of tea and a plate of cookies.

Headmistress Novakova was an older lady in her 70s but appeared to be in good health and carried herself as if she were much younger. With fair skin, high cheekbones, and blue eyes, her shoulder-length hair was a beautiful white, often pulled back into a bun. As a Czech Republican citizen who was widowed and had no children, she cared for her students as if they were her own.

The headmistress didn't ask Tennly about her decision right away. Instead, she first reviewed the past year, discussing Tennly's grades and her various extracurricular activities.

"Have you made your decision?" Headmistress Novakova finally asked, in a strong Eastern European accent.

"No."

Fortunately, Tennly didn't have to make a decision right away. The headmistress allowed her until mid-July to inform her, giving Tennly time to return home and evaluate the situation.

They were half an hour into their flight to London to pick up Victoria's younger brother, Seamus and their two cousins, Johnny and Jack when Victoria looked at Tennly and asked, "Are you going to text anyone, or just stare at your phone the whole trip?"

Cell phones weren't allowed at their boarding school, so their parents made sure to have the phones ready for them when they boarded the jet. The problem was Tennly didn't get a phone until the previous summer, so she had no numbers of any of her old friends from Marinsburg.

"I haven't seen or talked to any of my friends in three years, and the O'Brien's know I'm coming home, so..."

They arrived in New York at 9:00 PM, and Phillip drove Johnny and Jack to their home in Jersey City, New Jersey. Then he took Victoria, Seamus, and Tennly to Victoria's house in Newark, New Jersey, where Tennly spent the night.

The next morning Tennly flew from New York to a small regional airport located twenty minutes away from Marinsburg, where Thomas, her father's chauffeur, was waiting for her.

Thomas was not always a chauffeur; he had originally been a hitman for the Connolly family. However, his skills in procuring things and cleaning up after them eventually moved him from the streets into their home. Over time, he became best friends with Daniel, so it made sense to go with him when they moved to West Virginia.

Thomas was in his late fifties but had the physique of a much younger man. He had a rough appearance: scruffy yet surprisingly attractive. His dark brown hair had lightened with age, and small wrinkles lined the corners of his warm brown eyes. He often looked as if he were deep in thought, always feeling like a protector. Although he had never married, he wasn't lonely. His role in the girls' lives felt more like that of an uncle than an employee.

He gave Tennly a hug and then opened the back door. "I bet you're excited to finally get back home."

"Yeah," Tennly lied as they drove to Marinsburg.

The neighborhood hadn't changed at all in the three years Tennly had been away. It was unique in that it was divided into two sections, with a row of cherry trees lining a grassy patch that separated them. The first section was the poorer part of the neighborhood, located at the front and consisting of three streets with about twenty houses on each.

Conner lived in the poorer section, at the end of the second street. His house was a light blue structure with vinyl siding, smaller than a two-car garage. As the limousine passed by, Tennly noticed that some of the siding was missing, the roof over the front porch was sagging at the right corner, and nearly all the white paint had worn off the window frames.

Flashback:

As they drove through the Marinsburg neighborhood, Tennly noticed a disheveled boy, dirty with blood on his face, sitting on an embankment in front of a light blue house. She pressed her hand against the window as if to reach out to him, but he simply stared back at her without responding. Her heart broke at how vulnerable he appeared, and she knew she had to find a way to help him.

Daniel told her she could explore the neighborhood, but only if she could convince Tara to accompany her. Tara agreed, as she was also curious about their new home and wanted to check it out. However, while Tara wanted to take her time and explore every street, Tennly was eager to find the house where the little boy was sitting.

Pretending that her quick pace was solely to reach the playground, Tennly ran straight toward it. As soon as Tennly noticed her sister chatting with some kids her age, she snuck away and dashed across the street to the boy. She slowed her pace as she approached, ensuring she wouldn't startle him, and stopped a few feet away.

"Hi," she greeted. "My name is Tennly."

"Conner," he said, suspiciously.

"I'm five. I'll be six in a couple months. How old are you?"

"Seven."

"Do you live there?" she asked, pointing at the house behind him.

"Yeah."

"I just moved here... maybe we can be friends."

Conner looked at her, intrigued by her behavior. He found the way she spoke amusing and was impressed by her confidence, though it left him feeling a bit confused. Part of him wondered if she might become a nuisance.

"Why aren't you playing with the other kids?"

"You ask a lot of questions," he replied.

"I know. My dad says it's both my strength and my weakness."

"I don't feel like playing."

"Why not?"

"I just don't."

"What happened to you?" she inquired, regarding the blood and scrapes on his face.

"Did your dad also tell you to mind your own business?"

"Yeah, but you'll find out that I don't listen very well."

"I don't either," he said, giving her a slight smile.

"Is that what happened? You didn't listen?"

"You could say that."

Tennly gazed at his house, as if she possessed the power to enter and stop whatever was causing him pain. Leaning in close, she whispered in his ear, "You don't have to worry anymore. I'm going to protect you."

Presesnt:

Tennly half-expected Conner to be in the same spot, as if waiting for her to return, but as she and Thomas drove by there was no one there.

The second half of the neighborhood, which was the wealthy section, also consisted of three streets. The first two streets had four houses on each side. Tennly's friend, Josie Wittekind, lived in a large brick house on the corner of a cul-de-sac across from the first street.

They drove past Josie's house and continued to the last street in the neighborhood. From the road, nothing was visible, other than a fifteen-foot-high dark gray granite stone wall, on the left, which featured a locked black iron gate in the middle. The wall extended the entire length of the street and surrounded the perimeter of the property.

Beyond that a quarter-mile paved driveway forked into two paths. The right passage led to a cul-de-sac that encircled the front of the 30,000 square foot mansion, while the left path ventured behind a tall grouping of trees, leading to an eight-stall garage. In the center of the cul-de-sac in front of the mansion was a magnificent garden filled with various flowers and featuring a large fountain in the center.

The exterior of the mansion was composed of the same dark grey granite as the perimeter wall, which was enhanced by black-painted window frames. Matching flower boxes hung from the windows, providing a touch of color. The mansion featured a total of six turrets. The two smaller turrets flanked the entryway, while two slightly larger ones were positioned between the entryway and the mansion's front corners. The two largest turrets were located at the back corners of the mansion.

The front door opened into a foyer adorned with a crystal chandelier hanging from the ceiling. The floor had an ivory mosaic marble design and housed a round mahogany table in the center, topped with fresh-cut flowers in a large ivory vase. Two stairways, one on each side of the foyer, led to the second floor.

Tennly ascended the right stairway slowly, her fingertips brushing against the cold, smooth black wrought iron railing as she admired the paintings that lined the walls. When she reached the top of the stairway, she walked down the right hallway to her bedroom, located two doors down on the right.

Starting from the left and moving around clockwise, the first feature was the door to the bathroom, followed by a vanity in the far-left corner. Next, there was a large antique dresser with a TV mounted above it, opposite the bed. In the far-right corner, there was a large bow window formed from the turret that featured an enclosed bench seat. To the right of that was a computer desk with a net above it, which held some of Tennly's stuffed animals. On the right wall, stood a bookshelf where seven stuffed animals lay: each a birthday gift from Conner over the years. Finally, on the back wall was Tennly's king-size bed, flanked by an end table on either side.

Her bathroom was almost as large as her bedroom. To the left was a walk-in shower featuring a glass wall with sliding glass doors. The shower itself occupied a quarter of the bathroom, equipped with two shower heads positioned on opposite sides and a stone bench against the far wall. Directly across from the bedroom door, to the right of the shower, stood an antique claw-foot bathtub; the toilet was located to the right of that. Closest to the bedroom door, was another vanity that had a sink and a place for her to sit, and to the right of the vanity was the door leading to a spacious walk-in closet.

Tennly sauntered through her bedroom, gazing at everything as if none of it belonged to her, although nothing had changed. The room was decorated in light lilac and pale greens, with murals of carousels and shelves on the walls filled with little porcelain figurines.

She picked up old belongings and rummaged through books, her eyes continually drifting to the seven stuffed animals sitting on the shelf. She grabbed the 10-inch green turtle with a brown shell and held it up to her nose, hoping to catch a whiff of Conner's scent, but it didn't smell like him. Instead, it had the fresh scent of the lemon and wildflowers that was used throughout the mansion.

Placing the turtle back, she picked up the strawberry-scented perfume bottle, on her bedroom vanity, that she used to wear, and sprayed it into the air. Although some of its fragrance had faded, it was still potent enough to make her giggle.

She looked at herself in the mirror and wondered if Conner would recognize her. She had changed so much over the past three years. The short, shoulder-length hair had grown long, reaching just above her tailbone. It was no longer as curly as it used to be; instead, it cascaded in thick, wavy locks with long layers framing her face. She started adding chestnut brown highlights to her hair, which made it appear browner than her natural dark auburn red.

Her straight, boyish figure had evolved into that of a woman, and she had grown five inches taller, reaching a height of 5'6". Despite weighing only 110 pounds, she had a curvy physique with a small, elongated waist. Thanks to her dedication to working out, she boasted a flat stomach, along with muscular arms and legs. Her once chubby cheeks had been replaced by thin, high cheekbones, and the braces on her teeth were off, adding to her new look.

She also began wearing makeup, which further enhanced her appearance. Unlike her fair-skinned sister and the rest of the Connolly family, she resembled her father's side, which had a tanner complexion and darker hair.

The only things that hadn't changed about her were her eyes and lips. Her eyes remained the same big, bright sky-blue ones they had always been, and her lips were still thick and full. However, since the addition of makeup, her eyes and mouth were almost unrecognizable. She liked to experiment with different colors of eyeshadow and eyeliner, as well as various shades of red on her lips, depending on the impression she wanted to create.

As she stared at her reflection, lost in thought, she was startled by a sudden knock on her door. Turning around, she saw Marie standing there.

Marie was a 69-year-old Irish woman who served as the nanny for Daniel and his siblings during their childhood. Marie's family had been friends with the O'Briens for many years, and she often babysat Daniel when his family visited Ireland.

After Daniel's mother gave birth to his younger brother, Donnie, Marie volunteered to move to the United States to help care for the boys. When Daniel got married, she chose to accompany him to continue as his housemaid until his children were born, at which point she became their nanny.

Marie stood 5'4" tall, had shoulder-length, thin, wavy red hair, and amber eyes. Although her physique was on the thicker side, she was not heavy. She was a soft-spoken woman who took pleasure in her household duties. She never complained but also wouldn't allow anyone to take advantage of her.

"I didn't hear you come in," Marie said with a thick Irish accent. "Thomas brought me your clothes from school. When I'm done washing them, I'll bring them up. How was your trip?"

Tennly wasn't in a hurry to get her clothes from school. Besides some pajamas, socks, and undergarments, they were all just school uniforms.

"It was fine."

"I'm sure you're excited to be back here."

"I don't really know what I feel," Tennly admitted as Marie leaned down to give her a hug.

"Ah, lass, are you and your father still not talking?"

"It's hard to talk to him when I hardly ever see him."

Marie stepped back, finding it difficult to hear someone speak poorly of her beloved Daniel, even if it was his daughter and another child she loved as her own. "Well, I know you two will figure it out. Dinner will be ready in a couple of hours. Why don't you take a shower and freshen up?"

Tennly hated to upset Marie, and she knew her advice was right. A shower was exactly what she needed. She always did her best thinking in water, whether in the pool or in the shower. There was something about the water flowing over her body that felt like it was washing away everything, creating a clean slate for her thoughts.

If only it were that easy. The longer she stayed in the shower, the more she thought about Conner. No matter how hard she scrubbed, she couldn't get him out of her mind. It wasn't until she noticed she was rubbing a bright red spot on her left arm that she realized she needed to get out.

The walk-in closet was as large as the bathroom and served as a dressing room. One wall was dedicated to shoes, another to folded clothes, and the last wall was for hanging clothes. In the far-left corner of the room stood a full-length mirror, while a five-by-five-foot leather-cushioned bench sat in the center. A shelf ran around the perimeter of the room, two feet below the ceiling, used for storing hats, purses, and various accessories.

As she stood in the walk-in closet, she realized there was no way she would fit into any of her clothes, not even the shoes. The clothes she had worn over the past three years were left at her other houses. No one, not even she, thought to ensure she had new clothes at her Marinsburg residence for when she returned.

Frustrated, she screamed as she began searching through the items until she finally found a T-shirt that was just big enough to wear. While looking for suitable bottoms, she spotted a familiar blue shoebox on the top shelf of the far wall. She hesitated for a moment but felt compelled to see if the contents she left inside were still there.

Because she and Conner had no way to communicate through the school year, they started writing letters to each other. However, unable to send them, for they were checked at the boarding school, they saved them to exchange on her first day back over the summers.

Once the letters were read, she would bundle them together and place a piece of paper indicating the year they were written, marked by Conner's grade level. There were four bundles in total, starting with Conner's 5th grade and ending with his 8th.

She grabbed the shoe box, sat down and opened it. Placed neatly on top was an old 7th grade picture of Conner. It was the only picture she had of him. He had brown hair styled in a basic short haircut. His face was soft and youthful, free of stubble or blemishes, with a light tan complexion. He had full lips that, even in the school picture, appeared to be pouting, and his eyes resembled azure, blue crystals. As she gazed into those eyes, she felt she could see beyond the fake smile, catching a glimpse of the sadness she remembered.

Flashback:

Tennly and Conner were in a neighbor's flower garden, laughing while trying to be quiet. They thought it would be fun to dig up all the flowers in Mrs. Pettroli's prized garden and replant them upside down, with the roots sticking out.

"Mrs. Pettroli is going to shit," Conner said.

"I know. These are her prized flowers. She wins an award for them every year."

"Yeah, but she's a bitch. That's why we decided to do this, remember?"

Tennly remembered. She also remembered it was Mrs. Pettroli who accused Conner of stealing some of her things that came up missing. Conner wasn't above stealing, but he never stole from the neighborhood, only stole when it was absolutely necessary, and he never lied to Tennly. She believed his innocence and agreed to help him pay their neighbor back for trying to get him in trouble for something he didn't do.

"What was it she said?" she asked jokingly. "'Kids today have no respect'. Please."

"Yeah. If she actually cared about the kids today, she'd use some of that money she has to help, instead of blaming kids for things and wasting it on all these damn flowers... I hate rich people."

Tennly stopped laughing when she heard Conner's comment. She was aware of his feelings about the wealthy, but it still bothered her. Despite their shared interests and values, this one issue created a barrier, keeping them apart in many ways. They both understood this, so they avoided discussing it as much as possible. She continued to dig without saying anything, knowing that her wealth was always going to be a sensitive topic.

Conner realized what he had said had hurt her. He kept digging too, but added, "I didn't mean to..."

"I know," she interrupted. She smiled to reassure him that everything was fine.

Often, they had to rely on body language to communicate, especially when they were around other people in the neighborhood. Over time, they became accustomed to each other's facial expressions and what they meant.

"It's just that... I keep forgetting you're rich. You don't act like it."

"And how am I supposed to act?"

"I don't know."

"Not all wealthy people are snobby, Marks. Why do you do that?"

"Do what?"

"Look, it's not my fault that I'm rich, and it's not your fault that you're poor. It's just the way things are."

"Yeah, but somewhere along the line, you got the better end of the deal."

Tennly could feel the fire rising within her. "Oh really?"

"Yeah, really. My mom left when I was four, my dad can't stand me, and I don't even have the luxury of money to make up for it like you do."

"Yeah, well, that's awful," she said sarcastically. "My mom's dead, and my dad's never home. Everything I own is superficial, and I'm barely around it anyway because I'm always away at boarding school, where everyone constantly tells me what to do, how to act, what's proper and what isn't. Most of the time, I can't even wear what I want."

They sat there uprooting Mrs. Pettroli's flowers in silence. It was as if they were reading each other's minds, as they both suddenly started to laugh at the same time. They stopped digging and looked at each other.

"We're pathetic," she admitted.

"Yeah, we sure are a pair."

Tennly picked up some dirt and threw it at him as she said, "Dig."

Present:

Tennly looked around at all the clothes that no longer fit her, along with the other material possessions she had, and realized that Conner was right. She owned more things than any young person her age should have.

She placed the stack of letters back in the box and closed it. Leaving it on the floor where she had sat, she stood up to search for a pair of bottoms that would fit. After some looking, she found a pair of elastic sweat shorts and put them on. Then, she began tossing all the clothes and shoes onto the floor.

Once she was finished, she ran to the kitchen and grabbed four large trash bags to put all the clothes and shoes in. After placing all her belongings into the bags, she stood there and looked at the bare room. The emptiness made the blue shoebox stand out more than she liked. Not wanting anyone to know about it or its contents, she hid it inside the leather bench under a pile of blankets.

The last time Tennly saw her father, they had the biggest argument they had ever had. While she recognized that she was being difficult, her anger made it hard for her to maintain a positive attitude. It was her snarky remarks that led her father to ground her for the entire week they were in Ireland, and she hadn't spoken to him since.

It was because of this that Tennly contemplated backing out of eating dinner with him that evening. She would have if she hadn't known that Marie was preparing dinner specifically for her.

The dining room table sat twenty people, and Daniel always sat at the head nearest the kitchen. Normally, Tennly would sit directly to his right, but that day, she wanted to maintain some distance and sat five seats away from him. Daniel sensed that giving her space and time to adjust was the best approach, so they remained silent for the first few minutes.

By the time they reached the halfway point of the meal, Daniel could no longer bear the tension. He hated that Tennly was so angry with him and wanted to try to mend their relationship.

"Are you getting settled?" Daniel asked as he picked up his water glass.

"Yeah." The fact that her father was pretending everything was okay between them only made her anger worse.

"I bet it's good to be back," he said, attempting to smooth things over.

"I just got back today," she retorted, with a terse tone.

Daniel put his fork down, folded his hands over his plate, and looked at her. "Tennly, let's not start out like this. I'm trying to be nice here."

"Wanting to do the fatherly thing for once?"

Daniel was about to respond, but Marie walked in and placed an apple pie on the table. She always had an uncanny knack for knowing when to interrupt. Daniel took a deep breath to avoid saying something he might regret and then thanked Marie for her effort.

He suggested that Marie take Tennly shopping to get new clothes, and after Tennly spoke out of spite that she didn't need any, Marie talked her into it.

"Then it's settled," Daniel added, taking another bite.

Tennly was determined to not let her father think he had won. After Marie walked out of the dining room, she muttered under her breath, "I'm not doing this for you."

"Tennly, we're going to be living together now, so we better find a way to get along."

She felt no inclination to respond. For one thing, she wasn't even sure she would be staying. They finished dinner in silence, and as Daniel served himself a piece of pie, he informed, "I have to go away on business for a few days. I'll be leaving on Tuesday."

Tennly couldn't help but laugh sarcastically at the irony, and then replied in a biting tone, "Live together, huh?"

"Tennly, it's business," he explained as she stood up. "I have to make a living."

"Yeah, I guess you do," she
acknowledged, before walking out of the
room.

CHAPTER 2

Tennly had been home for two days before finding the courage to walk around the neighborhood. It felt strange as she surveyed the streets. She heard screaming and laughing, and as she approached the playground, she saw several kids running around and playing on the equipment. The sight gave her a warm feeling as she reminisced about the times she used to play there.

She went by Josie's house, but no one was home, so she headed toward the field, via Conner's street. With each step, her shoulders tightened, and her legs felt heavier. As soon as she was a few feet from Conner's house, memories began racing through her mind.

She was so lost in thought that she nearly got hit by two boys on skateboards speeding out of the alley next to Conner's house. She screamed as she jumped out of the way to avoid the collision. One boy, Rick, swerved and landed on the ground as his skateboard rolled into the street. The other boy, Dougy, came to a stop right in front of her.

"Watch it!" Tennly yelled.

"You watch it!" Dougy shot back, not realizing who she was.

"I'm the one walking," Tennly pointed out.

"And not doing a very good job at it," Dougy countered.

Tennly didn't recognize Dougy even though they used to be very good friends; He had changed quite a bit. He no longer had his boyish chubby cheeks, and he had grown just shy of 6 feet tall. His dark brown, wavy hair was much shorter, and he was significantly more muscular than he used to be, as evidenced by his plain black t-shirt that showcased his well-defined left bicep tattoo.

Rick, Dougy's best friend was 5'9" tall and had straight, brown hair that reached his shoulders. Although he wasn't as muscular as Dougy or as handsome, he still had his own charm. His personality was what attracted girls the most; he was funny and had a great sense of humor, although sometimes he didn't know when to stop talking.

"Leave her alone," Rick said as he stopped beside Dougy. He gave a mock bow and added, "Let me apologize for my rude friend."

"Jesus," Dougy remarked. "Shut up."

Tennly continued to smile shyly but remained quiet.

"She looks lost," Rick noted, turning his attention back to her. "Are you lost? If you are, we can help."

"I'm not lost," she replied.

"Then you must be new," Dougy assumed.

The way Dougy smiled seemed familiar, and as he stood in front of his house, it became clear who he was.

"I'm not new," she insisted, looking at Dougy and trying to get him to recognize her.

"Well," Dougy replied, "if you're not lost and not new then..."

She shot him a look that encouraged him to think harder. As it appeared he might finally remember who she was, she smiled and nodded at him. He stepped back in disbelief, exclaiming, "Holy shit!"

"What?" Rick asked, puzzled.

"Rick," Dougy said, shaking his head in disbelief, "this is Tennly O'Brien."

"Nice to finally meet you," Tennly said, smiling.

Tennly always greeted people with either 'hey' or 'hello.' The word 'hi' was reserved exclusively for Conner, and the same was true for him. Since their first meeting, this unique salutation had become something special they only shared with each other.

"You, too," Rick replied. Although he and Tennly had seen each other around the neighborhood, they had never met in person. "Well, I hate to cut this short," Rick continued. "I was on my way home."

After Rick left, the atmosphere shifted from light and playful to serious. They both knew what Tennly wanted to discuss, but Dougy wasn't sure how to bring it up or if he should at all. They stood for a moment, waiting for the other to speak first.

"How have you been?" Dougy finally asked, giving in.

"Good," she replied, trying to hide her shaking hands behind her back. "And you?"

"Good." They stood in silence for a few seconds more before he finally asked, "Where have you been, Tennly?"

While she explained where she had been over the past two summers, he noticed that she kept glancing behind him at his house. She believed she was being more careful than she was, but her desire to see Conner didn't go unnoticed, and before she knew it, he had pointed it out.

"He's not here."

"I don't know what you're talking about," she replied. He gave her a look that indicated he knew better, to which she responded, "I'm that obvious, huh?"

"Probably not to everyone. He's hardly ever home anymore. Ever since he got back from juvy..." he paused, unsure of how much Tennly knew about the changes in Conner.

"I know. Tara mentioned it. How's he doing?"

"I don't know. It's hard to say. I don't see him that much."

"Is he seeing anyone?" she asked, immediately regretting her question.

"Are you kidding?" Dougy replied, laughing.

"What?"

"No, Conner sees girls strictly for recreational purposes."

"Oh," she uttered, a pain shooting through her chest at the thought of Conner having sex.

"I'm sorry," he apologized as soon as he saw the fake smile masking her sadness.

"It's okay."

"He's changed," he said, not sure what else to say.

There were two versions of Conner: one when he was with Tennly and another when he wasn't. He moved between the two like flipping a switch. He turned on the Conner, he wanted Tennly to see and then went back to one that had built a wall to keep everyone out when she was gone. This wall, along with drugs and alcohol, shielded him from getting hurt.

Turning the switch on was a way for him to reboot, providing him with the energy to get through the school year without losing all of who he was. However, when Tennly didn't return, Conner never switched back and became lost behind the wall he built.

Feeling the need to change the subject, he asked if she had seen anyone else. When she told him she tried to see Josie, but she wasn't home, he said she was probably at Abby's. Not knowing who Abby was, he explained that she had known Josie for several years from middle school, but they hadn't become close friends until Abby moved into the neighborhood two years ago.

"Come on," he said gesturing for her to follow him.

Dougy didn't know Abby very well and he was no longer friends with Josie. He and Josie had hung out in elementary school, but as they grew older, they drifted apart. He always sensed that Josie and her friends were afraid of him and figured it was because of who his brother was.

He took Tennly to Abby's house, which was in the affluent part of the neighborhood, and knocked on the door. Upon seeing Dougy, Abby became so nervous that she couldn't find her voice. She had been infatuated with Conner and his friends since middle school, and over the years, that infatuation had grown into an obsession.

When she moved into the neighborhood, she had hoped to run into Conner but never did. She had seen Dougy a few times but had never mustered the courage to approach him. So, having him standing on her front porch was incredibly overwhelming.

"Is Josie here?" Dougy asked when it became clear that Abby wasn't going to speak.

"Yeah," Abby mumbled quietly, still standing there and staring at him, frozen in a mixture of fear and shear reverence. Dougy looked at her, waiting for her to make the next move. When she noticed his gaze, she felt embarrassed and said, "Oh, yeah." Then she called out for Josie to come to the door.

The three of them stood in silence, Tennly standing behind Dougy, until Josie arrived and broke it. "Dougy?"

"Hey," Dougy replied.

"What are you doing here?" Josie asked.

"I brought you a gift," Dougy answered, stepping aside so she could see Tennly.

"Hey, Josie," Tennly greeted.

"Tennly?" Josie asked, surprised.

Tennly nodded, causing Josie to shriek, "Oh my gosh," and then wrapped her arms around her.

"I'm going to let you girls catch up," Dougy said and then gave Tennly a hug. "I'll talk to you later, Ten."

Abby remained quiet while Josie and Tennly caught up. She was still in shock that Conner Marks' brother had come to her house. Even more surprising was that he seemed to be close friends with the girl standing beside her.

"So," Abby finally chimed in, "you're friends with Dougy Marks?"

"Used to be, yeah," Tennly replied.

"That's cool," Abby gulped.

Josie started smiling, aware of her friend's infatuation, and said, "Don't pay any attention to her, Tennly. She's had a crush on the Marks brothers for years."

"Shut up," Abby teased. "I'm not alone in this." She looked at Tennly and asked, "You have to admit he is cute."

"He is," Tennly replied with a smile.

As they continued their conversation on their way to the ice cream parlor, Tennly's mind began to wander as they got closer to Conner's house. Although it was easier with her friends by her side, her heart raced as thoughts of Conner, fluttered through her mind like scenes on a movie screen.

Flashback:

Tennly and Conner sat on the top of a picnic table, enjoying their regular cones when Tennly noticed a car in the parking lot with its windows rolled down. She started laughing as an idea popped into her head: what if they hid one of their cones in the back of the car under the driver's seat? When she shared her idea with Conner, they both laughed while imagining the smell the cone would create after baking in a hot car for a few days and decided they had to go for it.

Looking around to ensure no one was watching, Conner carefully placed the cone under the driver's seat, hoping it wouldn't be discovered, when out of nowhere, the car's owner appeared and yanked Conner out as he began yelling, threatening to call the authorities for breaking and entering.

Thinking quickly, Tennly shouted, as she ran over, that Conner was her older, mentally impaired brother who sometimes wandered off. She gave Conner a look that urged him to play along, and he immediately started acting the part.

"I thought this was Grandma's car," Conner said, speaking slowly to mimic a delayed pattern.

"No," Tennly played along. "You know Grandma's car is red."

"Oh... yeah," Conner responded.

As soon as the man let go of him, Conner walked slowly toward Tennly, putting on a performance worthy of an Oscar. She thanked the man for being so understanding. However, as soon as they got far enough away, they turned and started running up the alley until they reached Conner's house. Despite their laughter making it hard for him to speak, he managed to say, "Holy shit! That was close."

"Yeah," she agreed. "Did you at least hide the cone?"

"All business, aren't you? No concern for my well-being?" He teased.

"I got you out of there, didn't I?" She chuckled.

He turned to her as they stopped at the front door. Dreading the thought of going inside to face his father, he said, "I wish you could help me get out of here."

Feeling a pang of sympathy for him, she vowed, "One of these days, I will. I promise."

ICE CREAM

CHAPTER 3

Everything about Daniel made him a great organized crime boss. He was tall and attractive, with a calm demeanor that, combined with his authoritative voice, was truly intimidating. His confidence was evident the moment he entered a room, and when he spoke, everyone stopped to listen. It also helped that he had built a reputation for having no reservations about doing whatever was necessary or had to be done.

Thus was the case for why he had to leave Tennly when she first got back home. One of the Connolly's accountants, Steven Garrett, was caught stealing from them. Each accountant kept three different books that they kept locked in a Connolly safehouse. One they showed the IRS of all

the legal businesses. A second book was
the ledger that held all the income from
the illegal ones. And the final book was a
combination of both with how all the
illegal money had been laundered.

What the accountants didn't know was
that Daniel had a secret accountant, that
checked all the other accountants' books
and discovered that over the past year,
Steven had skimmed more than $75,000.

When Daniel was informed, he sent out
soldiers to find Steven and soon learned
that he was staying at a friend's house in
Queens. Daniel instructed Phillip to go to
the back door in case Steven tried to
escape, while he, Jimmy, and John knocked
at the front. As soon as Steven's friend
opened the door, Daniel barged inside.
John aimed his gun at the friend while
Steven leaped over the back of the couch,
making a dash for the back door.

"That's just stupid," Daniel remarked
as he observed Steven trying to flee.

After Phillip brought him back into
the living room at gunpoint, Daniel asked
if there was anyone else in the house,
while John looked around to make sure. When
they felt the coast was clear, Daniel
motioned for Jimmy to bring Steven's
friend, who was as white as a ghost, over

to the living room and place him in the center of the couch.

Daniel then gestured for Steven to sit down while he took a seat across from him. "How long have you worked for us, Steven?"

"I..." Steven stuttered, struggling to speak out of fear for his life. "I... I think... about 12 years?"

"Fourteen, Steven," Daniel corrected, while Philip and John held down his friend as Jimmy poured a bottle of vodka down his throat. "And in those fourteen years, have I or anyone else in the Connolly family ever mistreated you?"

"No," Steven answered, trying not to focus on what was happening to his friend.

"No," Daniel repeated. "So, explain to me why you are stealing from us."

"I..." Steven stuttered again. "I'm... not..."

Daniel gave him a look of disappointment and then nodded at Phillip, who immediately punched Steven's friend in the face.

"Okay," Steven coward, then proceeded to tell Daniel about his gambling debt. "I was hoping to make enough money to pay you back, but I just kept losing."

"What do you think I should do about this?" Daniel asked, not really wanting an answer.

"I'll get you your money," Steven promised as Jimmy walked back from the kitchen holding a trash bag. "I promise."

Steven kept glancing at Jimmy's actions. In addition to the trash bag, Jimmy had grabbed a small metal trash can, placed some trash inside, and lit it on fire.

"Don't worry about what he's doing," Daniel instructed as Jimmy collected the smoke that was bellowing out of the trash can into the trash bag. "Focus on me. Do you think we should be lenient with you?"

"I have an addiction to gambling," Steven admitted.

"Shut. Up!" Daniel screamed, getting tired of his whimpering. "*You* put your friend in this situation. You were a coward and now your friend is going to have to pay for your weakness."

"What?" The friend asked as he began to show signs of being drunk.

Jimmy then took the trash bag full of smoke and put it over the friend's head and closed it off. They couldn't let the man live after everything he had seen and they had to make his death look like an accident. Not only would the plastic bag suffocate him, but the inhalation of the smoke would show up in his lungs if an autopsy was done.

After the friend stopped moving, John placed the empty vodka bottle, along with several empty bottles of beer, on the floor. Phillip then lit a cigarette and carelessly dropped it next to the trash can, which was still emitting smoke. It didn't take long for the carpet to catch fire, and the flames quickly spread to the couch, engulfing the alcohol-soaked body. The scene would appear as if the friend had gotten drunk, lit a cigarette, and passed out.

"Shit... shit..." Steven frantically exclaimed, standing and backing away from the fire.

"Now" Daniel asked, remaining extraordinarily still as the fire grew higher. "Let's go see your bookie."

Following Steven's directions to the pawn shop where his bookie was, Daniel remembered how much he despised pawn shops.

The musty smell of sweat and mildew, combined with the dim, flickering lights typical in every pawn shop he had ever visited, made his stomach churn. What he hated most, however, was the sleazy owner.

As they entered, a bell above the door jingled, signaling to someone in the back there was a customer. Daniel and Jimmy walked Steven up to the counter as a short, heavyset man waddled out wearing a cheap suit and tie.

"I hope these guys are here to bail you out," the bookie stated.

Steven started to speak, but Jimmy punched him in the stomach to silence him.

"Steven here is one of my employees," Daniel noted. "I don't like my name getting involved in any debts that could be traced back to me. How much does he owe you?"

"$10,000."

Daniel pulled out two rolls of one-hundred-dollar bills, each totaling $5,000, and handed them to the bookie. "This should cover his debt." Then he produced two more wads that added up to another $10,000 and continued, "And this is to keep your mouth shut."

T ennly had completed her tenth lap in the pool and had just turned around when she spotted Tara standing close to the entrance with a big smile on her face.

"Tara!" Tennly yelled and then swam as fast as she could to the nearest ladder. "Did you just get here?"

"Yeah, Marie told me where you were,"

They hugged and then walked over to the lounge to the left of the pool, which featured two patio furniture sets, four chaise loungers, ten bar stools in front of a full bar, and a fully equipped kitchen.

"How was your trip?" Tennly asked as she settled onto a bar stool.

"It was fun," Tara answered as she went around the other side of the bar and poured two glasses of sweet tea. "I have to admit, at first, I was reluctant to go to Myrtle, but after being there, I understand all the hype. There were kids on senior trips all over the beach. We met so many people and went to so many parties. And... I met a guy."

"What?"

"Yeah," Tara replied. "I don't know if anything will come of it, but we spent the whole week together and exchanged numbers."

Tennly was excited for her sister and listened intently as Tara recounted everything they did during her trip. After she finished, they changed the topic to how Tennly had been doing since returning home. However, before Tennly could get into it, Tara's phone rang.

"Hi, Daddy," Tara said after she answered.

Tennly rolled her eyes at hearing it was their father. She was annoyed that their conversation had been interrupted, but even more so that it was him. She thought about leaving, but didn't want to be rude to her sister.

"Hey, honey," Daniel said. "Is Tennly there?"

Tara shot Tennly a look, signaling her to behave. "Yeah," she responded, then turned on the speaker so they could both hear him.

"I just wanted to let you know that I might be a little longer than I thought, but I'll be home as soon as I can."

"Okay, Daddy," Tara said.

When Tennly remained silent, he asked if she had heard him.

"Yeah," Tennly answered curtly.

"Ten," Tara pleaded, sensing her sister's anger.

"What?" Tennly hypothetically asked. "We know what he's going to say. Right, Dad? You're so sorry... Can I bring you anything... We'll chat when I get home. How about this, dad, fu..."

"Tennly, stop it," Tara scolded. "Daddy, she's sorry."

"No, I'm not!"

Daniel didn't know what else to say. Talking over the phone to a daughter who would do the opposite of what he said wasn't the best time to discipline. "I'll be home as soon as I can," he replied and then hung up.

"I don't know what you're feeling, but whatever it is, fix it," Tara responded.

"You two have been at each other long enough. Daddy doesn't deserve to be the target of your frustration."

Even though Tennly recognized that her father wasn't the target of her frustration, he was the reason. As she contemplated her anger toward him, memories of the last night she spent with Conner resurfaced in her mind.

Flashback:

Tennly and Conner stood at the corner of Tennly's street, beneath the same light post where they had spent many nights together. It was the night before Tennly was set to leave for the school year.

Although that summer had been filled with fun, it felt different from the previous ones. They had sensed a change in their relationship but managed to ignore it. As the days passed, they continued their playful teasing, light-hearted picking, and competitive spirit just as they always had, hoping to keep their true feelings from surfacing.

Conner sat on the embankment, watching Tennly as she swung around the light post. The light illuminated her, revealing her beauty in a way he had never noticed before.

The emotions he was experiencing confused him; he never expected to feel anything more than just friendship with her. He worried that such feelings would jeopardize their relationship, which had been solid for so many years. Deep down, he believed he wasn't good enough for her. After all, she would leave the next day, disappearing from his life for another year.

Thankfully he managed to shift his focus from his feelings to their playful games when Tennly began their usual banter. "I thought you said you were getting too old to hang out with me."

Conner grinned as he responded, "Well, I figured I'd better stay in your good graces, so you'll put in a good word for me with your sister now that she'll be living here."

He couldn't help but start laughing, knowing his comment would annoy her. She stopped and looked at him, as he struggled to contain his laughter.

"My sister? You're crazy."

"Oh, I don't know. I think she has a crush on me," he said with a playful smirk.

"No offense, Marks, you're cute, but you're not all that," she shot back.

"Tell that to all the girls lined up to go out with me." He joked, though he was telling the truth.

"That's it," Tennly exclaimed as she ran over and jumped on him.

They rolled down the other side of the embankment, laughing the whole way. Conner landed on top of her, and their laughter gradually faded as they became aware of their position. She smiled, hoping to reassure him that what they were feeling was okay, but he didn't smile back. He had gone his whole life without loving anyone: not like this, anyway, and it scared him.

He wanted to get up, to end the awkward moment and return to being the normal Conner and Tennly, but he couldn't. The scent of strawberries she wore was no longer cute; it was intoxicating. As if he couldn't control himself, he took her right arm, holding it above her head, and began kissing her.

As he traced his fingers down her side, she whispered, "I love you."

Those words that Tennly spoke echoed in his mind repeatedly, and instead of pulling him closer, they pushed him away. He shook his head, giving her a cold, angry glare before returning to the street corner.

She lay there, replaying what had just happened as she placed a hand on her chest to ensure she was still breathing; It felt like she was drowning. Gaining her composure, she ran to the other side of the embankment, where he stood with his back turned toward her. Looking at him, she realized that there was no going back. Their relationship had changed.

"Did you hear me?" she asked in a sad voice laced with anger. "I said I love you."

"Jesus Christ!" he yelled, throwing his hands in the air.

"What?" she asked, trying not to cry.

He turned around, the urge to run to her nearly overtaking him. "What do you want me to say to that?"

"Something," she begged. "Anything."

He was angry with himself for not being the person she needed him to be. More than that, he was angry at her for declaring her love and jeopardizing the best thing he had ever had. Tears that Tennly fought to hold back began to stream down her face as they stared at each other, both wishing that if they could only hold the gaze long enough, time would rewind, allowing them to forget what had just happened.

"What do you want from me?" he asked.

"I don't know."

"I can't do this, Tennly."

"Why?" she replied, not understanding what was so wrong about feeling more than just friendship.

"It's not that easy."

"Why?"

"It just isn't!"

She took a step closer and tried to place her hands on his chest, believing that if she physically showed him that it was that easy, he would give in, but his fear wouldn't allow it. Instead, he grabbed her wrists and said, "Don't."

"I don't know when it happened, but it did," she pointed out. "Over the years, our friendship changed, didn't it? I love you... And I know you love me. I can feel it."

"I don't..." He stopped when he saw the look in her eyes. He had never lied to her, and it was painful. "This can't happen."

"Why?"

"We come from two different worlds. It'd never work out."

"Our friendship has."

"Yeah, in our own little world where no one is there to mess it up. Why do you think I wanted it kept secret? Ten, there is always going to be something or someone out there standing in between us. Go home. Forget about this."

"Forget about what?" she snapped, not sure if she was angry, sad, or both. "What's happening between us or our friendship altogether?"

He hated what this was doing to her and to himself. His heart was breaking, and he had to do everything in his power to hold back the tears. He didn't want her to know his true feelings; it would only *make things harder for her when she needed to forget about him.*

"Whatever is necessary," he said, forcing a callous expression.

Tennly's emotional strength prevented her from completely breaking down, but she could feel her legs begin to shake as she fought to stay upright. "Okay. I'll leave and forget about whatever... if you can look me in the eyes and tell me that you don't love me. Tell me you don't love me, and I'll go away."

He stared deep into her eyes and recognized the pain he was causing her and knew the only way to ease that pain was to lie. It would be hard on her at first, but he believed it would ultimately be better for her. Over time, he was sure she would eventually get over him.

So, he channeled the facade he presented to everyone else, leaned in and whispered, "I don't love you."

As soon as Daniel hung up the phone with his daughters, he felt a surge of anger that drove him to rush home to them. Throughout the day, he had been contemplating what to do about Steven. Steven still owed the Connollys a lot of money, which was why he hadn't killed him yet, but he didn't care.

Jimmy recognized the expression on his brother-in-law's face and shook his head at his brother, both aware that what was about to unfold might not end well. They stood up and followed Daniel into the bathroom, where they saw him approach Steven, who was hunkered down on the floor between the tub and sink.

Daniel unlocked the chains and pulled Steven up, saying, "We're leaving."

Once they reached the designated location far from any signs of civilization, Daniel yanked Steven out of the car and tossed him unceremoniously onto the ground.

Steven begged for his life, but Daniel, being done with him, callously shot him in the head. Phillip dragged his body to a hole that he previously dug that afternoon and threw him in. Daniel took out a cigarette and lit it, as Jimmy doused the body with kerosene. Then he took two puffs and threw the cigarette into the hole. Fire erupted several feet into the air getting hotter as they stood there and watched.

"When that dies out," Daniel commanded. "Bury him."

Daniel got home early the next morning, running into Marie who was preparing breakfast. She noticed how tired he looked and offered him a cup of coffee as he sat down in the breakfast nook, adjacent to the kitchen.

"Where are the girls?" Daniel asked, as Marie sat down a plate of pancakes and gave him a kiss on the forehead.

"I told them I would have breakfast ready by 9:00 AM," Marie replied. "They should be down any time now."

Tara was the first to arrive and was surprised when she saw her father. "I thought you were going to be gone a little longer?" she asked as she gave him a hug before sitting down across from him. He smiled, but his mind was occupied with thoughts of Tennly.

"I got some things moved around... Is your sister coming down?"

"Last I heard."

"Is she doing, okay? She won't talk to me."

"She's not talking to me either."

"Yeah, well, at least she likes you."

"She likes you too, Daddy. She's just upset about something and is taking it out on you." Tara hated that the two people she cared about the most were angry with each other, especially since she didn't know why. "She'll come around."

"You talking about me?" Tennly asked as she entered the nook and spotted her father sitting there.

Daniel tried to greet Tennly, but she remained silent. So, he asked, "What do you girls have planned for the day?" hoping to spark a conversation.

"I thought we would meet some of my friends at the public pool," Tara suggested.

"But we have a pool here," Daniel mentioned, looking confused.

"Yeah," Tara acknowledged. "But there are people at the public pool."

"I've never been to the public pool before," Tennly exclaimed. "I'm in."

"Just be careful, girls. I've heard some crazy things happen there," Daniel cautioned.

"It's the pool," Tennly countered, sarcastically, "not South Central."

"Jesus, Ten," Tara scoffed. "Cut it out."

Tennly didn't like upsetting her sister, but the furious scowl on her father's face made it worth it. To add to her victory, she curled her upper lip, shot a sideways glare at her father, and then asked, "What time do we leave?"

Kenneth Marks was a construction worker often called to out-of-town jobs, where he would stay gone for days at a time. This was when Conner would come home to shower, change clothes, and sometimes sleep.

Conner and his father had a troubled relationship. After his mother left, his father started drinking more, which worsened the abuse. As Conner grew older, he increasingly avoided being home to steer clear of his father, eventually only coming home when he knew his father would not be there.

When he stayed away, he occasionally crashed at a friend's place or a run-down barn outside of the city, but most of the time, he took refuge in an old, abandoned warehouse downtown.

When they were younger, the boys had shared the bedroom that was the last door on the right across from their father's room. The third bedroom across from the bathroom was used for storage. When Conner was sent away to juvenile jail, during his 10th grade year, Kenneth disposed of all of Conner's belongings, including his bed.

Dougy resented what their father did. So, while Kenneth was away on a job, Dougy worked tirelessly to clean out the storage room to ready it for when Conner came home.

The door to Conner's room was always closed, so when Dougy walked past it a few days after he first saw Tennly and noticed it was cracked open, he wondered if Conner had received his texts informing him that their father wasn't home, and he needed to talk to him. Even though Conner hated it when Dougy entered his room, Dougy slowly pushed the door open a bit more and stepped inside.

Lying on the bed, which was just a full mattress on the floor, were Conner and Shelby. Shelby was a small, abrasive girl whom Conner manipulated to get what he wanted, whether it was sex or drugs. She was a fighter: loud, obnoxious, and loved to stir up drama. Despite that, she was a cute girl with shoulder-length blond hair and the biggest brown eyes, she had lips that almost always appeared to be pouting.

Dougy hated her. He believed she was a negative influence on his brother and only contributed to Conner's downward spiral. So, when he saw her in his house, he felt his skin crawl. "Get up!" he ordered as he kicked her.

Shelby mumbled, "Go away, Dougy!" and then tried to ignore him by rolling over and pulling the covers up.

Seeing that his brother didn't wake, Dougy went around, gathered up all her clothes and then threw them at her as he yelled, "Get out!"

"I was invited here." Shelby groaned as she sat up and began to retrieve her clothes.

"I'm not going to tell you again."

"Conner wants me here and there's nothing you can do about it."

"Okay," Dougy sarcastically chuckled. "First of all, right now, Conner could give two shits who's here. Second, it's not you he wants. It's what you give him. And he gets that from anyone who offers."

"He loves me."

"You're so freaking delusional Shelby."

Shelby had good reason to be delusional when it came to Conner. She was the only girl he had slept with whom he continued to see. Although Conner didn't truly like her and was aware that he was only using her, from her perspective, it seemed as though he cared for her.

"And you're an asshole," Shelby retorted.

Dougy pulled Shelby, kicking and screaming, through the house and out the front door, locking it behind him. When he made it back to Conner, he noticed that he had vomited sometime through the night.

This wasn't the first time Dougy had to clean up after his brother; giving him a washcloth bath had become a part of their routine.

He gagged at the stench while throwing all the refuse into the trash can beside the bed. Afterward, he grabbed several towels to clean up the vomit, trying to avoid adding to the mess as he worked. Once the area was somewhat clean, he tossed the towels into the bathroom, where the stacked washer and dryer were located.

Just as he was finishing, Conner opened his eyes, took the cloth from Dougy, and slurred, "You don't have to do that."

"Why do you hang around her?" Dougy asked as Conner sat up and lit a cigarette.

"She's here," Conner replied.

"Meaning someone's not?"

Conner meant that but didn't want to admit it. "Fuck off."

"Fine," Dougy replied, knowing he needed to tell Conner that Tennly was back, but sensing he wasn't in the mood to hear it just then. "I'm going to fix some breakfast. Want any?"

"No."

While Dougy prepared breakfast, Conner took a shower, got dressed, and then met his brother in the kitchen. He grabbed a piece of bacon from a plate on the table and started to walk toward the front door.

"I need to talk to you," Dougy announced.

"Not now," Conner replied, then left the house before Dougy could say another word.

Neither Tara nor Tennly had ever been to the public pool before. It was much more crowded than they had imagined, and they weren't sure where to put their things. They finally settled on a vacant spot between the kiddy pool and the concession stand and then Tara walked off to search for her friends.

As soon as Tennly stripped down to her bathing suit, which was a tiny brown two-piece bikini, she immediately went to the diving boards. There were three springboards: the two on the sides were 3 feet high, while the one in the middle was 10 feet.

Standing beside the diving boards, about twenty feet away, were Conner and his three friends: Riley, Sam, and Joel. The four boys often hung out at the pool or in the park during the summer, just like most of the kids in the area.

While the boys discussed their plans to try and use their new fake IDs, Conner noticed Tennly walking toward them. Although she didn't look familiar, he couldn't take his eyes off her. She was beautiful and walked with an air of confidence that rivaled that of a runway model.

She stopped at the bottom of the high dive and looked up. Although she had been on several high dives before, and even some that were higher than this one, she thought it would be fun to put on a performance for the people watching. She slowly climbed up and walked to the end of the board. Pretending to be scared, she sat down on the edge and then slid off.

On her way back to the diving boards, passing Conner and his friends, she noticed they were looking at her. She couldn't help but think that all four boys were gorgeous, and their presence demanded acknowledgment, so she playfully smiled at them.

Conner's three friends, Sam Phelps, Joel Wells, and Riley Williamson, were strikingly similar in appearance. They all stood around six feet tall, with Riley being the tallest; Sam and Riley had brown eyes, while Joel's were hazel. Their physiques were muscular and well-defined, featuring impressive upper arms and chests that made all the girls swoon.

Sam and Joel had blond hair, styled differently: Sam kept his short and spiked, while Joel wore his more like a classic California surfer. Riley, on the other hand, styled his dark brown hair longer in the front than in the back, with shaved sides.

Additionally, they each had several tattoos. Sam had a wrap around the top of his left arm, one along the right side of his neck, another on the left side of his chest, two half sleeves on both forearms, and one on his lower right calf. Joel had his last name tattooed between his shoulder blades, a wrap around his right upper arm, and another tattoo around his right calf. Riley had tattoos on the left side of his chest, a wrap around his left arm, and an additional tattoo on his right shoulder blade.

While all three were undeniably attractive, it was Conner who stood out the most. Conner Marks stood at 6'2" tall and had dark brown wavy hair that fell just below his eyes and ears, giving him a perpetually disheveled look. His striking crystal blue eyes had a hypnotic quality that drew people in, making it easy for him to get them to do whatever he wanted.

His shoulders were sculpted like a fine statue, and on his right shoulder, he bore a gargoyle tattoo with wings that wrapped around his upper arm and tail that extended down to his elbow. In addition, he had the Gaelic word 'DEICH,' meaning ten, inked on his lower left arm. He also had a Celtic band tattooed around the top of his left arm, which met up with a small, hidden number ten underneath. He had an Irish knot tattooed on his left chest, featuring a Celtic symbol for the number ten in the center.

The red petals of a long-stemmed red rose peeked out above the waistband of his swim trunks as the thorned stem stretched down to just right below the left side of his pelvic bone. Over the years, he and Tennly discovered a mutual liking for similar things, but when they found out their favorite flower was the red rose, it became a symbol of their friendship. It was strong yet delicate, powerful yet fragile, wild yet safe, and despite being clichéd, the red rose was classy. It embodied everything Conner saw in Tennly, and he wanted it tattooed on his body.

The last tattoo he received was the day after he got out of juvy. It was a black and gray depiction of a tree, with the trunk starting halfway down his back. The branches wound up between his shoulder blades, circling into a Celtic triple spiral. He chose this design to represent Tennly's Irish roots, symbolizing change.

The four boys were like one thread in a tapestry, each bringing their own experiences and pasts that made them fit together perfectly.

Sam was an only child raised by a single mother who prioritized her boyfriends over him. She often chose abusive men who mistreated both her and Sam. As he grew older, he began to fight back, which led to his distrust of all women and relationships. Despite his difficult upbringing, Sam was a fun-loving and extremely outgoing person. He was always in search of a good time, constantly telling jokes or teasing his friends. He was the first to defend them and would not hesitate to start a fight or jump in to protect them when needed.

Joel, on the other hand, grew up with both parents. His mother was a waitress at the same diner where his father worked as a fry cook. He had one older sister, who was two years older than he was and had a two-year-old son. They lived with Joel and their parents since the boy's father was not around. Because of his close family, Joel often acted as a mediator among his friends. He was the one who usually talked them out of trouble. He was timid and shy, rarely speaking except when they were alone.

Riley, an only child, had a mother who was very different from Sam's. She was a nurse who dedicated herself to helping others and prioritized her son above everything else. When Riley's father died due to a sudden heart attack when Riley was thirteen, his mother never dated again.

Riley lived on the same street as Conner, in the poor section, so they had been friends since before kindergarten.

Over the years, he became very protective of Conner, often having to rescue him from his father's anger or pull him away from threatening situations.

Riley's mother instilled in him a fear of the wealthy, a sentiment that also influenced Conner. She believed that the rich were their enemies and responsible for the struggles of the poor. As a result, Riley grew to distrust anyone with wealth, convinced they could not be trusted.

Conner was the one that made the decisions and had the final say. He embodied characteristics from all three of his friends, always looking for a good time, like Sam, protective like Riley, and quiet like Joel. However, most of the time, he carried feelings of anger and sadness, but when he was with his friends, he could let go and enjoy himself, allowing for moments of fun and laughter.

Conner used sex and drugs as a means of escape. In those moments, he could forget everything, especially the things he desperately wanted to leave behind. His resentment toward women ran deep. From the day his mother left when he was four, to the ongoing abuse from his father's girlfriends and the heartache caused by

Tennly's absence, it was easier for him to harbor hate than to feel the pain of loss.

Despite his troubled past, Conner carried himself with an air of superiority, exuding confidence, speaking with authority, and possessing an overall presence that demanded respect. He was the guy every boy aspired to be, every girl wanted to date, and every parent feared.

As Tennly passed the boys on her way back to the high dive, she would have noticed Conner if she had looked directly at him. But as the boys stood together, their presence blended as a whole, rather than four individuals. So, she flirtatiously smiled and continued toward the diving boards.

As she reached the top of the highest board, she glanced back at the boys, winked, and then ran to the edge, jumped twice, and executed a stunning 1 ½ somersault with a twist into the water.

At that moment, Conner felt a strange sense of familiarity about her, but he couldn't quite place it. He had seen Tennly dive into the river when they would sneak away together, but it had never been anything like this. Over the years, she had dedicated herself to perfecting the skills from all her classes, and diving was one of them.

While the boys discussed what they had witnessed, Tennly swam underwater all the way to the shallow end near the concession stand without coming up for air once. They continued to be impressed as they watched her get out of the pool and walk to where her things were.

"Have you ever seen anything like that before?" Sam asked.

"No," Joel answered.

"Nope," Riley added.

Even though he hadn't seen anything exactly like that, Conner had seen something similar, so he remained silent, his breaths getting shallower the longer they stood there watching her.

"Okay, the quest is on," Sam declared.

"I hate to say it," Joel admitted, "but I think this one's going to be harder to get than the others."

"She's definitely way out of your league," Riley teased.

Conner wasn't going to stand and listen to them; he had to get a closer look, as if he was being called toward her. Seeing Conner walking toward the concession stand, his friends ran to catch up with him.

"What are you doing?" Riley asked after they reached Conner's side.

Conner didn't respond. He had to know. His heart raced, his mind hoping that what he was assuming was wrong, yet at the same time, desiring it to be true.

His friends were confused when Conner stopped in the concession stand line. None of them ever had a problem approaching a girl and wondered why he was behaving so strangely. They grew even more worried as he pretended to avoid her gaze like a self-conscious pre-teen boy. His coy behavior caught Tennly's attention, and she started to stare at him more than the other three.

When Riley pointed it out, Conner looked over at Tennly, their eyes locking. In that moment, they both realized who the other was. She smiled, feeling both nervous and happy to see him. Despite he was even more gorgeous than the rumors had suggested, she could still see the little boy she had once been best friends with.

Conner initially smiled, as he thought back on how this moment would be if he finally saw her again. However, his smile quickly faded as he realized he wasn't ready to confront her. He couldn't believe how much she had changed. Just looking at her sent a tingle through his whole body. The feelings he had tried to suppress over the years were bubbling to the surface, and he not only disliked it, he feared it.

"Shit," Conner whispered.

"What?" Riley asked.

Conner ignored Riley and shot Tennly a look she recognized all too well. It was the same look she had seen from him three years earlier: a mix of sadness and pain obscured by disappointment.

Even after all those years, they could still communicate without words. They understood everything each other was trying to convey simply by reading their facial expressions. Tennly realized he was going to leave when she noticed him tilt his head and push out his jaw, which made his nose curl. Her eyes pleaded with him not to do that to her again.

The last thing Conner wanted was to hurt her, but he could see in her eyes that he already was. He slowly shook his head, conveying his apology with his eyes.

"Get Dougy," Conner demanded as he gave Tennly a final look of goodbye before turning to walk away. They had seen his brother on the basketball courts earlier, so Conner knew he was somewhere in the park.

Tennly stood still while Riley chased after Conner and Sam went to find Dougy. Joel shrugged his shoulders, offering Tennly an apologetic look before following his friends out to the parking lot.

After they found Dougy and made it to Conner's car, they sat inside waiting for him to drive off, but he simply sat there, his head resting on the steering wheel. He felt like he was about to throw up, and at the same time, he was doing everything in his power to resist the urge to turn around and punch his brother in the face.

"Fuck!" Conner yelled, slamming his fist on the steering wheel. He looked at Dougy through the rearview mirror, who was sitting between Sam and Joel. "Did you know?"

"Did I know what?" Dougy replied, confused.

"Don't play dumb," Conner snapped. "Did you know she was back or not?"

"Oh shit," Dougy gulped, realizing who Conner was referring to.

"You knew?" Conner pressed.

"Yeah," Dougy admitted reluctantly.

"Who?" Sam whispered to Dougy, but he didn't respond.

"If you checked your messages every once in a while, you would have..." Dougy started.

"Don't!" Conner shouted, spinning around and pointing his finger at his brother. "You could have told me this morning."

"I tried. You said, 'not now.'"

"You should have told me," Conner said in a voice none of his friends or brother had ever heard him use before: defeat.

"It doesn't matter," Riley chimed in, "because whoever she is she's coming this way."

Conner turned around right in time to see Tennly lean down and rest her arms on the window frame. He couldn't believe how good she looked. The last time he saw her; she still had the body of a child. He tried not to stare, but from his peripheral vision, he couldn't help but notice her perfectly formed cleavage.

"Hi."

"Hi," he replied, quickly glancing at her before looking back at his steering wheel.

"We need to talk," she stated.

"So, talk," he replied, attempting to sound uninterested in what she had to say.

"In front of them?"

Conner gave her a look that clearly indicated he didn't want to, but said, "I don't care."

"You lied to me."

"How so?"

"Let me refresh your memory." She reached in and rubbed her hand over the tattoo on his chest that represented her name: Ten.

Her touch sent shivers through his body, and before it went any further, he grabbed her wrist to get her to stop. So, she leaned in up to his ear and whispered, "I don't love you."

He squeezed her wrist harder and then pushed her hand out of the car. She wasn't intimidated like others might have been. Instead of running away or getting scared, she stood her ground, and asked, regarding his tattoos, "Do they know what they mean?"

He didn't answer. For the first time in his life, he didn't know what to do. He hated the way he was feeling: the way she was making him feel, vulnerable. So, he sat there.

"Didn't think so," she said as she glanced around inside the car as if to tell the boys to ask him. Then she turned back to Conner. "I'll see you around, Marks."

Conner squealed out of the parking space as she backed up, barely missing her feet and leaving her standing there. Throughout the whole encounter, she had been strong, but as soon as it was over, she felt like she was going to collapse. She took a deep breath to steady herself, and then turned around. When she saw her sister, she knew she would have questions: questions she wasn't ready to answer.

Conner, on the other hand, wasn't quiet. He drove around, hitting the steering wheel and periodically screaming profanities.

The more Conner thought about what had happened, the more emotional he became. He kept reflecting on how nice it was to see her again. When he looked at her, all the fun times they had together rushed back into his mind: memories he had tried to forget. Yet, it took him over two years to get over her the first time, and he didn't want to go through that withdrawal again.

"Argh, damn it!" Conner exploded.

"Before you get us all killed," Riley said, "what the hell was that?"

Conner didn't answer as Sam whispered to Dougy, "Who was that?"

Dougy remained silent, giving Sam a look and shaking his head to signal he couldn't share what he knew. Conner noticed his brother's gesture, appreciating his discretion. He glanced around at the others, who were all confused and curious, and finally thought it was time to confess.

"That was Tennly O'Brien," Conner divulged.

"Are you kidding me?" Riley asked, with a surprised, yet concerned tone.

"Nope," Conner replied.

"Are you insane?" Riley exclaimed, his concern growing as he struggled to comprehend what someone like Tennly could possibly be doing with Conner. "She's an O'Brien."

Everyone knew who the O'Briens were. They were the wealthiest family in Marinsburg and one of the founding families. Daniel O'Brien had even graced the front page of Forbes Magazine eleven years earlier as the head of one of the country's top richest men.

"This is just great," Riley worried. "Please tell me you didn't sleep with her."

"Did you?" Dougy asked when Conner didn't respond.

"No," Conner assured.

"Well, that's a relief," Riley sighed, picturing Tennly's father filing a rape charge.

"Out of curiosity," Conner asked, "why would that be such a bad thing?"

"She's an O'Brien," Riley repeated, reminding him of her status. "They don't associate with people like us."

Conner thought back on the nights when at least one O'Brien had associated with someone like them. He smiled, realizing that Riley was wrong. Tennly wasn't like that. She didn't care where anyone came from or how much money they had.

"She's different," Conner said.

"How would you know?" Riley asked.

Conner thought for a moment before answering, "Because she was my best friend."

Tara confessed, "I'm sorry," as she sat down on Tennly's bed. "I should have told you about them before taking you out in public. I should have known there was a chance they could have been there."

Tennly was confused, wondering what her sister was talking about. "Why do you keep saying 'they'?"

She had heard stories about Conner from her sister over the years, and recently she had heard more from her friends, all of whom were unaware that she knew him. The stories were just gossip that they shared to keep her updated on the local teenage news. What she didn't know was that Conner and his friends had been given the name, The Untouchables. Their secluded friendship had become that of legend, giving them the power to get anything they wanted, especially girls.

"Those guys who lured you to their car," Tara explained.

Tennly began to laugh, uncertain whether it was because of her sister's reverence for Conner or the idea that her sister thought she could be easily manipulated. "Lured? Do you really think anyone could ever *lure* me anywhere?"

"I know," Tara acknowledged. "It's just that you don't know..."

"Stop," Tennly interrupted.

Although she hadn't kept her relationship with Conner a total secret, after all, she had told Victoria, it felt different sharing it with Tara.

It was difficult for her to begin, but once she did, she told her sister about her relationship with Conner, from the day they first met to their last night together.

When she finally finished, Tara lay back on the bed and stared at the ceiling. It was so much information to absorb that it nearly drained her energy. The way Tennly described Conner was completely different from how everyone else perceived him.

Tara had never heard of Conner loving anyone, and she could understand how her sister's confession might have scared him away. She sat up, spun around with her legs crossed, and pulled Tennly closer so she could look her in the eyes.

"I'm so sorry. No matter how you feel about him, you need to stay away. Saying you loved him three years ago might have scared him off then, but it would be an invitation for something else now. He doesn't know how to love, Ten. I need you to promise me you'll stay away."

Tennly looked at her sister, a comforting warmth washing over her as she recalled the look in his eyes from earlier. "If he doesn't love me, then why does he have my name tattooed all over his body?"

CHAPTER 4

Benny's was a local teen hangout, a bar for those 21 and under that didn't serve alcohol, but featured many other amenities of an adult bar. It was located just outside the city, down a long dirt road, surrounded by trees. The parking lot was situated off to the side, and behind the building was a field enclosed by a 10-foot-high barbed-wire fence.

At least once every summer, the city would use Benny's field to host the biggest music festival on tour. On that day, the venue opened to all ages, offered alcohol, and was an all-day event. People arrived early in the morning to set up blankets or chairs, as it was general admission. The stage was at the back of the field, while various vendors lined the sides.

That year, in an attempt to make peace with Tennly, Daniel gave each of his daughters four backstage passes a piece, allowing them to bring three friends each. Tara invited her three best friends: Avery, Gaylin, and Mia. And Tennly chose to bring Dougy, Josie, and Abby. Dougy almost declined the pass knowing that he would be the only guy in the group, but the desire to attend the festival was strong. He had never been able to afford the $200 ticket price, let alone a backstage pass.

Conner and his friends had been receiving tickets from the owners of Benny's for the past two summers, allowing them to attend the festival. However, having confided in his three friends about his secret relationship with Tennly, when they learned that she would be at the concert, they were concerned.

"Are you worried that you might run into her?" Riley asked as he and Conner sat down a few feet away from the stage, after Sam and Joel left to get refreshments.

"No."

"Then why are you biting the inside of your lip?"

Conner had tells. When he was angry, his jaw tensed, his upper lip curled, scrunching his nose as if he were growling, and he clenched his teeth tightly. When he was curious, he squinted his eyes and curled the left side of his mouth. When he was nervous, he would pull in his bottom lip, hold the right side with his teeth, and then slowly release it.

Conner shot Riley a look that signaled him to stop trying to read him as he let go of his lip.

"There's more to it, isn't there?" Riley pressed.

"You're not going to drop this, are you?" Conner asked.

"Are you?" Riley shot back.

Conner knew Riley was right and realized there was no point in hiding the truth from him. He took a deep breath and confessed, "I made a mistake."

"Oh shit," Riley exclaimed. "You said you didn't sleep..."

"Do you want me to tell you or not?"

"Yeah."

"Forget it," Conner dismissed. "It doesn't matter now anyway."

"Come on. I'm sorry. What happened?"

"I said to forget it."

"Fine," Riley conceded, knowing that Conner hated to be pushed.

They sat in silence for a few seconds, watching the roadies set up for the first band that was to perform.

"I fell in love with her," Conner blurted out of the blue.

Riley closed his eyes, unwilling to believe what he had just heard. It was hard enough to accept that his best friend had once been friends with a rich girl, but the thought that he had fallen in love with her was unimaginable.

"She's an O'Brien, Con."

"I know. Constantly reminding me of that doesn't help."

When the band began to play, Conner glanced at the side of the stage where his brother told them they would be and saw Tennly emerge from behind the stage.

She had her hair pulled back into a ponytail, which featured small braids with bright-colored ribbons and beads strung throughout. She wore an old black band t-shirt, torn and cut above her bellybutton. The sleeves were missing, and there were several horizontal slits running all the way down the back. The shirt complemented her tight, low-rise blue jeans, which had rips all the way up the front, and she completed the look with black Converse Chuck Taylors.

Conner was so focused on Tennly that he didn't notice when Shelby and her friend Elena sat down beside him. However, Shelby immediately saw where Conner's attention was directed: not on the band, but towards the side of the stage. It wasn't until Tennly looked over at Conner, that Shelby got upset. She tried to ask Conner who she was, but not wanting to deal with it, he left. When none of Conner's friends would tell her, she stormed over to the stage to find out for herself.

Tennly didn't think anything about Shelby walking toward her at first, thinking she was just a fan of the band and was trying to get closer. However, when she noticed Shelby scowling at her, she snuck down the stage to find out what she wanted.

"Can I help you with something?" Tennly yelled, not giving Shelby a chance to speak first as she got as close to the fence as possible.

"Yeah," Shelby threatened. "I'm going to give you a warning: stay away from him."

"Stay away from whom? You'll need to be a bit clearer; there are a lot of hims here."

Shelby smiled, as if Tennly should already know who she meant, and warned, "If you go near him, I'll kill you."

Tennly couldn't help but laugh. She had never been threatened before, and she found it amusing. Her laughter angered Shelby, prompting her to try and push through the fence. The sight of her being held back by security caused Tennly to laugh harder. She shook her head at Shelby's futile attempts and then rejoined her friends.

Tennly couldn't stop thinking about the girl who approached her at the concert. Although she found the threat amusing, she didn't like the fact that someone was out there threatening her without knowing who she was. After the concert, instead of going to bed, she snuck out of the mansion and straight to the Marks' house to speak with Dougy.

Seeing a light on in the living room, she assumed that Dougy was still awake and felt comfortable knocking. However, she was taken aback when their father opened the door.

Kenneth, in his late thirties, was very attractive. It was clear that Conner and Dougy inherited their good looks from him, having the same wavy brown hair and striking blue eyes. His good looks were deceiving though, for he was nothing but ugly on the inside.

Tennly felt nauseous as she recalled all the times she had seen him hit Conner. She had to hold her stomach to keep from vomiting, and her queasiness intensified when he stumbled into the door, the fear deepening as she realized he was drunk.

After he told her that Dougy was in his bedroom, she began walking down the hall, remembering it was the last door on the right. However, she hesitated at the first door on the left when she heard a low hum of music and noticed that the door was slightly ajar. Thinking that maybe Dougy and Conner had stopped sharing a room and that Dougy had moved to the one across from the bathroom, she opened the door and stepped inside.

Although it was dark in the room, the streetlight outside provided enough light for Tennly to see everything happening. She felt nauseous as she saw Conner lying there, on his back, with a naked Shelby, moving up and down on top of him.

Tennly wanted to leave, but she couldn't move. Her heart felt heavy as she struggled to take a breath. When she tried to turn around, she found herself in a catatonic state that left her entire body numb. She stood there, watching the horror unfold as Conner held onto Shelby's waist.

Finally, Conner turned his head and saw Tennly standing there. He was so high that he stared at her in disbelief, wondering if he was hallucinating. He closed his eyes, wishing it was her with him instead of Shelby. But when he opened them again, Tennly had vanished.

ougy woke up the next morning, unaware that Tennly had come to see him. As he entered the kitchen to prepare breakfast, his father asked him what the girl who visited him last night wanted.

Confused and afraid to ask for fear of implicating Conner, Dougy brushed it off, saying it was nothing. However, the thought that it could be Tennly, who might have accidentally gone to Conner's room, filled him with dread. He couldn't bear to think about what might have happened, knowing that his brother often used drugs or had girls in his room.

Terrified and somewhat disappointed, Dougy walked slowly back down the hall to Conner's room, trying not to alert his father to anything being wrong. When he entered, he saw Shelby sleeping while Conner sat leaning against the wall in a nearly fetal position. Dougy prepared to confront him, intending to berate him for whatever he did to upset Tennly. He quietly walked around and sat down on the mattress, bracing himself for the confrontation.

"I didn't mean for her to see this," Conner mumbled, glancing over at Shelby as if to imply that Tennly caught them in the act.

"Well," Dougy said fully intending to scold him, "she did." However, his attitude changed when Conner looked up, a slight tear forming in the corner of his eye. He now felt empathy for his brother and wanted to console him. "It wasn't your fault. She came into your room. You might want to start locking your door."

Conner managed to let out a slight chuckle and responded, "Dad broke it last year."

Dougy, laughing with his brother offered to smooth things over with Tennly. "I'll go see Ten... see how she's doing. Try to explain... I don't know. I'll think of something."

"Thanks."

"Conner, I'm going to be honest with you: you need to sober up and get your life together, or you're going to lose the best thing you ever had." Dougy stood up and added, "And get her out of here before Dad knows you're here."

Dougy had never been to the O'Brien mansion before. The security panel to the left of the gate resembled a tablet with various icons. Thankfully, it was easy to navigate. He pressed the square labeled 'visitor' and waited for something to happen. Within half a minute, the gate began to open, and a male voice came over the speaker: "Take the right at the fork."

The mansion was much farther from the road than he had expected, and it was far larger than he could have ever imagined. Standing before a dwelling that looked more like a castle than a house made him finally understand Conner's reluctance to pursue a relationship with Tennly.

As intimidating as the mansion was, it paled in comparison to the sight of Thomas. Dougy found him quite terrifying as he guided him through the foyer, directing him toward the atrium. As he walked through the halls and observed the intricate architectural details and gold-plated trim, he finally grasped just how wealthy Tennly really was. The hallway was twenty feet wide, and it took him longer to reach the atrium than it did to walk from his house to Rick's.

The atrium lay behind the mansion, nestled between the garage and the pool house. A vibrant array of flowers created a colorful canvas that served as the backdrop for everything else. Statues and fountains adorned the space, and benches lined the stone pathways that wound throughout, leading to small waterfalls and fishponds.

In the center of the atrium stood a large gazebo next to the biggest waterfall, which cascaded down into a koi pond. This was Tennly's favorite spot to sit. Dougy meandered through the pathways until he discovered one that led to the back of the gazebo. There, he found Tennly reading a book.

"Your butler guy is scary," he said as he approached the gazebo.

Tennly placed her book in her lap and chuckled, "Yeah, I can see that."

"I'm sorry you had to witness whatever you saw at my house," he apologized after sitting down beside her.

"It's okay. Who is she?"

"Shelby Torrence."

"She approached me at the concert and told me to stay away from him, or she would kill me."

"Yeah, she's a real piece of work."

"Is she... his girlfriend?"

"To be honest, I don't know what she is."

"Should I be worried?"

Dougy shrugged as he replied, "She's serious. She may not actually kill you, but if she sees you near him, she won't hesitate to hit you."

"She can try," Tennly said with a smile and then she stood up. "Come on. Let me show you around."

Flashback:

Tennly was 12 years old and had just snuck out of her house to meet up with Conner so they could watch the July 4th fireworks. Upon arriving at his house, she heard screams and the sound of shattering glass coming from inside.

Before she could run in, Conner came barging out, blood pouring from his nose, grabbing her hand and pulling her down the street. They dashed through the neighborhood, across the field, and down the trail that led to the river, only stopping when they reached the top of the hill, just in time to see the fireworks go off over the park.

The display lasted a total of 30 minutes, concluding with a breathtaking finale. As the smoke billowed toward them, they stood and began walking back to the neighborhood. The silence felt more awkward than ever, both knowing the danger that awaited him when he got home, so she tried to think of something to say.

"Wouldn't it be cool to see all the fireworks set off at the same time?" she suggested as they reached Conner's street. "Like the finale?"

He agreed but then continued to be silent until they reached his house and hesitated beside his bedroom window. Not wanting to let him go back inside, she asked him if he would be okay.

He assured her he would be fine and then right before he climbed back through his window, he stopped and said, "I hope someday you get that grand finale."

Present:

Every summer, the city set up a carnival for the entire week leading up to July 4th. There were rides, food vendors, and games throughout the park, and on the fourth, fireworks were launched over the baseball field.

When Tara mentioned that she was going to the fireworks with some friends, Tennly thought about going. She had declined to go with her friends the nights leading up to it, out of fear of running into Conner, but thought it might be easier to blend in with a larger group, so she agreed to go.

Tara and Tennly picked up Gaylin, Mia, Josie and Abby and met two of Josie and Abby's friends, Lucy and Tina: whom Tennly had met a couple of times years ago.

Seeing all the girls together made Tennly realize how different her friends were compared to Tara's. Tara's friends all looked and acted the same, blond and plastic, while hers had unique personalities and characteristics.

Josie Wittekind was a cute girl, her exotic Mediterranean heritage enhancing her appeal. She stood at an average height, had a slim build, and sported straight, shoulder-length brown hair with wispy bangs that framed her oval face, slightly covering her thick, bushy eyebrows. Josie was an only child, and her parents were still married. Because they worked a lot, she often found herself alone, a gap that she filled with her friends, growing very protective of them.

Abby Dixon was very petite with naturally dirty blond hair which she wore in a short, messy bob. Her fair skin was complemented by rosy cheeks and hazel eyes. She typically wore glasses, often coordinating them with her outfits, although occasionally she wore contacts. Being the only child of a single mother, Abby sought the attention of a father figure, which aided in her obsession with Conner and his friends.

Lucy Plant was half Japanese on her mother's side. She had porcelain skin and long, straight, dark black hair that fell just above her lower back. Her features were delicate, with a small nose and lips, and she enhanced her fair complexion by constantly wearing bright makeup. She was extremely goal orientated, leaving little room for frivolous activities.

Tina Granger was the shy and timid one among her friends. She had long, wavy blond hair that she often kept out of her face, using barrettes or headbands. Tina was the quintessential girl-next-door, standing just over 5 feet tall, making her adorably cute. She had rosy cheeks and big blue eyes framed by long eyelashes. Her makeup was minimal; usually only wearing a gloss on her lips. Tina had two younger brothers, and her parents were still happily married, which contributed to her romantic nature.

Tennly didn't want to leave the ball field, fearing she might run into Conner. However, when her friends insisted, she went along not wanting to draw attention to why she didn't want to. They strolled through the park, looking at the various food trucks, concession stands, and games that lined the closed street and parking lots. The sounds of excitement and laughter while lights flashed all around, along with the smells of buttered popcorn and greasy food, created a magical atmosphere.

While they waited in line at the cotton candy and funnel cake stand, Abby suddenly gasped, her jaw dropping open as her eyes widened in surprise.

"What?" Josie asked, intrigued.

"Look, but don't make it obvious that you're looking," Abby whispered nervously, gesturing to her right.

Conner, Riley, Sam, and Joel were walking toward them, accompanied by five girls. As they passed, Conner gave Tennly a look that lasted longer than it should have. Tennly, understanding his sucked in lower lip and lingering stare to be an apology. She secretly smiled, reassuring him that she wasn't upset, to which he responded with a subtle nod of acknowledgment.

The girls watched as the boys made their way to a picnic table on the grass nearby. Tennly didn't think it was a big deal that Conner had looked at her: at least not until Abby got all excited about it.

"He has to look somewhere," Tennly said, glancing back at the picnic table. She couldn't help but feel a pang of jealousy when she saw Conner sitting on the tabletop with a girl on his lap. While she was relieved that it wasn't Shelby, seeing him with another girl in such an intimate way made everything she had heard about him feel all too real.

"I can't believe he's looking at you," Abby marveled.

"That's not a good thing," Lucy pointed out.

"It's a great thing," Abby insisted.

"She's new, that's all," Lucy claimed.

Tennly glanced at Conner one last time. The excitement in her gaze faded, replaced by a wave of sadness as she recalled their situation. She turned away thankful that it was her turn to place an order.

They continued their conversation regarding why Conner held such a long stare in Tennly's direction, when finally, Tina chimed in, "Um, guys... I think he's walking over here."

The girls stopped what they were doing and looked toward the picnic table, seeing Conner walking toward them. He wore a pair of torn jeans and a short-sleeve button-up shirt that was unbuttoned, revealing how low his pants hung. They rested just below his pelvic bone, barely above the hairline. Emerging from the waistband of his boxers were the red rose petals, catching the attention of the girls, as if they were an invitation.

The girls ogled him as he approached Tennly, a mix of fear and anxiety washing over them. They couldn't believe he was standing just a foot away from her, causing Abby to struggle to remain upright as she grabbed Josie's hand for stability.

"I didn't mean for you..." he began, thinking she would have told her friends about their past.

"I know," Tennly interrupted, giving him a look that told him she hadn't.

"I'm sorry," Conner apologized, biting his lower lip.

Tennly smiled at him and replied, "I know."

Conner smiled back, nodded, and then before he turned to walk back to his friends he said with a mischievous grin, "Enjoy the fireworks."

Tennly couldn't wipe the smile off her face as she watched him walk away. When she turned to face her friends, she saw they were frozen like statues, completely shocked. When the concession stand employee called their names Tennly collected their orders, handed the items to each girl and then began walking back toward their designated spot on the baseball field.

"What the hell was that?" Abby asked, breaking the silence.

Tennly looked at her friends and smiled, as if she had been caught doing something she wasn't supposed to.

"You're not going to tell us?" Josie asked.

"There's nothing to tell," Tennly replied.

The four girls exchanged glances, confusion setting in, and followed Tennly to the blanket. They remained quiet as they listened to Tara and her friends. The frivolous topics drove Abby insane until she couldn't take it any longer.

"What is happening?" Abby asked, finally emerging from her comatose state. She couldn't understand how they could be discussing something as trivial as funnel cakes when one of their friends had encountered an Untouchable.

After Abby explained what had happened between Conner and Tennly, the girls sat in quiet, trying to wrap their heads around it.

"It's not a big deal," Tennly reassured, noticing their ongoing worry.

"He almost hit me with his car the other day. He was just apologizing."

Tara winced at Tennly's words, aware that it was common knowledge that Conner and his friends were never sorry. So, for her to claim he was apologizing didn't help her cover story.

"Conner never apologizes for anything," Gaylin remarked.

"That makes him apologizing to you even more suspicious," Abby added.

"He must be up to something," Gaylin suggested.

"Yeah," Abby agreed. "He wants to bag himself an O'Brien."

"He wouldn't dare," Mia interjected. "Your family is the most powerful family in town. It would ruin him."

"Okay," Abby pressed, unconvinced by Mia's reasoning. "So, what does he want?"

"Who knows?" Gaylin replied. "But whatever it is, it can't be good."

Tennly listened intently to everything they were saying, remaining quiet out of fear that if she spoke, she would reveal her secret. However, the

longer they talked, the more they
criticized him, leaving her confused. One
moment they idolized him, and the next they
painted him as an evil monster intent on
taking her virtue. She was just about ready
to tell them all to shut up and reveal the
truth, when their conversation was
interrupted by the announcer over the
speakers.

"Can I have your attention, please?...
Before the fireworks start, I have a letter
to read." He cleared his throat and then
began, "'Hi'..."

It was the 'hi' that caught Tennly's
attention, and as her heart began to
flutter faster, she started looking around
to see if she could spot Conner anywhere.

"It was good to see you," the
announcer continued in a monotoned voice
as if he didn't want to be reading the
note. "But it is what it is. Enjoy the
fireworks."

Shortly after the announcer finished
reading the letter, the fireworks started.
Instead of launching one at a time, they
all went off together in one big grand
finale.

The following morning, Tennly decided to let Josie know about her relationship with Conner. She was the one that was most neutral about him, and she felt close enough to her to be comfortable.

She found it much harder to bring up her secret than she had expected, so she let Josie steer most of the conversation, as they walked down Conner's street, seeing his car in the driveway. They were just a few feet from his house, when the front door swung open, and Conner stepped out, dragging a screaming Shelby by her shirt.

Shelby, under the influence of something, stumbled to the ground and began laughing. Even from a distance, they could see his clenched teeth as he picked her up and threw her into the car. Then he slammed the door and stormed back into the house.

As Tennly and Josie stepped from the road onto the sidewalk next to his house,

Conner emerged from the front door, coming face-to-face with Tennly. They stared at each other for a few seconds until Conner heard Shelby calling for him. He shook his head, his expression revealing his annoyance at having to deal with Shelby and then nodded before getting into his car.

Josie desperately wanted to ask Tennly what was going on but figured she would talk when she was ready. They had ordered some ice cream and were sitting at the picnic table before Tennly said anything.

"Large chocolate dipped in chocolate," Tennly described, glancing out over the parking lot at the spot where Conner had placed the ice cream cone in the back seat of a stranger's car.

"What?" Josie asked, confused.

"That's what he always orders. A large chocolate cone dipped in chocolate."

"Who?"

"Conner."

"How do you know that?"

Tennly hesitated before saying, "Because that's what he always ordered when we would come here."

"I don't understand."

"I've known Conner since I was five years old, and we started spending nearly every summer night together when I was eight, after everybody went home."

Knowing that her friend would have more questions, Tennly decided to share the details of their relationship all at once to avoid answering each question individually. However, the more Josie listened, the more it felt like she was in an alternate universe, the confusion causing even more questions to arise. Just like with Tara, Tennly's description of Conner was completely different from the persona he showed to everyone else. This worried Josie, making her think that perhaps Tennly had fallen under his spell, just another casualty of his charm. Yet, she couldn't help but notice how heartbroken she was and wanted to try and understand.

"What happened?"

"I ruined it. I told him I loved him. I guess that's one thing everyone has right about him."

"I'm so sorry. If I had known how you felt about him, I could have warned you."

Tennly attempted a smile, but it appeared forced, emerging from her sadness. "I don't think you could have warned me about how he felt."

"How do you know what he felt?"

"I could feel it, and I saw it in his eyes."

"He has a way of making all the girls feel that way, though, Ten."

"Maybe," Tennly pondered as she recalled all his new tattoos, which she recognized as representations of her, whether it was the number, Ten, or something she liked. "But then why have it written all over his body?"

"The tattoos?" Josie asked, trying to understand what she meant.

"Yeah. Have you ever looked closely at them?"

"Every chance I get," Josie professed, playfully acknowledging that she enjoyed looking at him, just like all the other girls.

After observing Josie's mix of excitement, fear, and worry about her relationship with Conner, Tennly realized that her other friends wouldn't be as understanding and supportive and would never stop hounding her about it. Not wanting to confront those worries just yet, she made Josie promise to keep their conversation a secret.

Standing over Conner as he slept, and feeling apprehensive about what they had to do, Riley tapped Conner on the side with his foot and said, "Get up... Conner, wake up. We told Ty we'd do that job for him tonight."

Ty Wheeler was a local drug dealer in his mid-thirties who ran his business out of his decrepit father's dive bar. He stood 5'10" tall, had a medium build, and sported scraggly brown hair. With a scruffy goatee and mustache, brown eyes, and a two-inch scar that ran from the corner of his right eye to the bottom of his earlobe, he was a terrorizing figure.

Ty handed them four wads of cash, totaling $8,000, and instructed them to go to the railroad bridge to meet a man underneath it to exchange for a package.

There was very little light under the bridge, but they could see four men waiting when they arrived. Conner's heart raced, and he began to doubt his decision to not allow Sam and Joel to come along. Two of the men circled around behind them, while a third stood by the hillside. Conner chuckled sarcastically at himself, realizing their escape route had just been cut off if things went sideways.

"You Ty's boys?" the leader asked, stepping forward.

"Yeah," Conner replied, recognizing the man's attire as that of a local biker gang known for being heavily feared.

The man nodded to the two behind Conner and Riley, and before they knew it, guns were pointed at their heads.

"Whoa," Conner shrieked, raising his hands defensively.

"You're not Ty's usual guys," the man observed and then gestured to the two individuals holding the guns. The cocking sound startled Conner causing him to close his eyes, convinced he was about to die.

"If that's what you think," Conner dared. Opening his eyes, he leaned his head into the barrel of the gun, exclaiming, "Then shoot me!"

"Conner," Riley stressed, attempting to encourage him to act a bit more cautiously.

"Conner?" the man asked, recognizing the name. He looked at the guy standing off to the side and inquired about it.

"Marks," the second man replied.

"You're Conner Marks?"

"Yeah," Conner responded, unsure if his admission would prompt the trigger to be pulled or cause the men to lower the guns.

"You have quite the reputation on the streets," the man stated. "What are you doing working for someone like Ty?"

"I don't," Conner replied. "Just do jobs."

The man gestured for the men behind them to lower their guns, then said, "I'm Boulder, and I could use someone like you. Stop working for Ty and come work for me."

Conner had a healthy respect for biker clubs, understanding that if he showed them the same regard, Boulder would likely return the sentiment. He informed Boulder that he would consider his proposal. Boulder nodded, then handed Conner a business card, saying, "When you're ready... But you can no longer work for Ty; it's a conflict of interest."

Conner looked at the card in his hand. He hated doing jobs for Ty, but he wasn't sure if he should get involved with the most dangerous biker gang in town. "I'll consider it. Thank you."

After completing the exchange, they dropped off the package to Ty and picked up Sam and Joel. Sensing that something significant had happened during the deal, they sat in silence, as they drove to Riley's, waiting for an explanation.

Conner suddenly started laughing, feeling relief as the tension of how close they came to death dissipated, causing Riley to teasingly say in a funny voice, "You have street cred," which made Conner laugh even harder.

"What's going on?" Sam asked.

"Are you going to do it?" Riley asked, ignoring Sam's question.

"I don't know," Conner replied. "I can handle Ty. He's the devil we know. Bikers... that's some serious shit."

"Bikers?" Sam shockingly inquired.

After Riley explained to Sam and Joel what happened he looked back at Conner. "You're going to do it, aren't you?"

"It's more money," Conner pointed out.

"And more risk," Riley countered.

As they pulled into Riley's driveway, Conner muttered, "I really hate Ty." He turned off his car, gave Riley a look that indicated he was going to accept the offer, and repeated, "And it's more money."

CANDY
CARAMEL APPLES

CHAPTER 5

Tennly was thrilled to finally have her friends over to her house for the first time. They started their visit in the game room, where the boys spent a little over an hour playing pool and darts. Afterward, they alternated between playing video games while sitting in game chairs facing two large televisions and standing in front of one of six vintage video game machines lined along the walls.

The girls sat at the bar, located on the far wall between the game and lounge areas, watching the boys play while Tennly prepared mocktails they had chosen from menus placed on the counter.

After leaving the game room, they walked through the mansion and passed by the gym. Peering inside, the boys were mesmerized to see a fully equipped fitness center filled with all the latest machines. Additionally, on the far wall, there was a salmon ladder, to the left, a complete parkour course, and in the center of the room stood an official-sized boxing ring.

Seeing the desire in the boys' eyes to run the parkour course, Tennly gave them the go-ahead. They each tried it two times before giving up, prompting Tennly to lead them to the pool house.

On the far side of the pool were a 6-foot straight slide and a 20-foot-high twisty slide. At the deep end, there were both a 3-foot and a 10-foot springboard, along with a 30-foot-high diving platform.

On the side opposite the slides, there was a hot tub located near the diving boards and a swim-up bar by the 3-foot section. The bar featured ten round concrete stools on one side and a selection of drinks and refreshments on the other.

"This place is like Disneyland," Rick marveled as they walked around the pool and stopped at the lounge area.

She guided them past the lounge to a room behind the slides. On the left side of the room was a rack filled with men's swim trunks, while on the right was a rack of women's swimsuits, each in various styles and sizes.

Immediately after putting on their chosen swimsuits, the boys raced to the slides, while the girls settled at the swim-up bar as Tennly swam around to take their drink orders.

Just like in the game room, the girls admired the fancy glasses that accompanied each drink and were impressed by how well Tennly knew which glass went with the designated drink. Tennly hadn't realized it was such a big deal until her friends started joking about it. Having grown up in homes with full bars and seeing different drinks served in various glasses, it was something she had simply become accustomed to.

"Did you learn that at boarding school?" Abby asked, laughing.

"Believe it or not," Tennly replied, laughing along with her friends, "sort of. We had classes on etiquette, and that was a part of it... but I guess I just picked it up from watching all the adults throughout my life."

"That's so weird," Lucy remarked.

"Cool, though," Josie added.

"What other things did you learn there?" Lucy asked.

"We had the same academic classes that we would have had back in our home country," Tennly explained. "That's how I earned my credits to be a sophomore this year. But our electives were different. We all had to take etiquette, Latin, as well as another foreign language of our choosing, and a physical education class every year. We also had to participate in either a sport or an art."

"What did you participate in?" Abby inquired.

"I took swimming and diving, marksmanship, and various martial arts classes," Tennly answered.

"Are you, like, some super ninja or something?" Abby asked.

"I can hold my own," Tennly said, giving her a wink as she watched Dougy swim up to them.

Although Abby was starting to feel a little less nervous around Dougy, she couldn't help but feel butterflies when he sat right next to her.

While mixing drinks and responding to Rick's shouts from the top of the diving boards, Tennly nearly missed the moment when the topic of the annual neighborhood football game came up.

Tennly remembered when the football game began; it was her and Conner who started it. So, when she heard that Conner no longer allowed girls to play, she couldn't help but think it was because of her. Feeling a need to remedy the situation, she said, "I guess we'll just have to see about that."

"He won't let you play," Josie replied.

"We'll see," Tennly stated.

"He's dangerous," Lucy disclosed. "You need to just stay away from him." Then she glanced at Dougy and said, "No offense."

"None taken," Dougy replied, perfectly understanding how his brother was.

"He won't hesitate to remove you... physically," Lucy warned.

"We'll see about that," Tennly said, feeling a surge of determination.

"On a similar note," Abby said, "has anyone ever wondered why they've never played football for school?"

Tennly knew why: at least she knew why Conner never did. But she didn't answer. Instead, she asked, "Why doesn't someone just ask them?" All the girls stopped and looked at her as if she had two heads.

"Oh my God," Lucy screeched, overwhelmingly frustrated. "You have so much to learn. You don't ask The Untouchables anything. You don't even question them."

"The Untouchables?" Tennly asked, confused at hearing the moniker for the first time.

"It's what they're called," Abby answered.

"Why?"

"It's just the way it is," Abby stated.

"Since when?"

Josie gave Tennly an apologetic look, knowing how long she had been friends with Conner, and said, "Since they were in seventh grade."

Tennly felt as if a piece of her heart had been ripped out. She was crushed that he had never told her about his friends or their status and title. The same status she had received for being wealthy, which he claimed to despise, was the exact status he had gained for being popular. And she felt betrayed.

Flashback:

Neither Conner nor Dougy was in the bedroom, when Tennly emerged through the window and immediately heard loud yelling coming from down the hall. She couldn't make out what was being said, but it didn't sound like one of Mr. Marks' violent outbursts.

Before long, Conner stormed into the bedroom and threw a wadded-up piece of paper onto his bed.

"Come on," he said, taking Tennly's hand and leading her out the window.

They walked in silence through the neighborhood until they reached the field. Tennly stood there, waiting for him to explain what had happened, but he just paced back and forth in front of her, as if he had something urgent to do.

"Grrr," he screamed, throwing his hands into the air. "I hate him so much!" Tennly just looked at him, giving him time to compose himself. "I wanted to sign up for football at school this year, but he won't sign the papers."

"Just forge them," Tennly suggested.

"Along with the papers, there's a fee," Conner replied. "He won't give it to me."

"I can give you the money," Tennly offered.

"I am not your charity case," he said angrily.

"I didn't mean..." she started to say.

"I know," Conner interrupted, realizing he had no intention of yelling at her. "I'm sorry. I know you mean well. I just get so angry that he can buy whatever he wants, but when I want something, he never seems to have the money. It's so frustrating."

"It's not fair," Tennly agreed.

"Promise me, Ten, don't let anyone tell you that you can't do something."

"I won't. I promise. But you have to promise me the same."

"I'm a lost cause. I don't have the money you do."

"So... what you're saying is that I can become something only because I have money?"

"It certainly makes things easier."

At first, it made her angry, but after reflecting on what he said, she realized he was right. She had resources and support that he didn't.

"Yeah," she replied. "I'll give you that. But you don't need money to achieve your goals, Marks. All you need is determination and creativity. I see a big field. Any ideas on what we should do with it?"

He admired how she could take something negative and turn it into a positive. He extended his hand to her as if they were sealing a deal, smiled, and said, "Let's play some football."

Present:

On the day of the annual neighborhood football game, Tennly stood in front of the mirror eyeing her appearance. She wore black sports shorts with a light pink stripe down the sides and a matching pink tank top. Her tennis shoes were black and light pink, complemented by knee-high light pink socks. She styled her hair into a high ponytail with two small braids and one larger braid, adorned with a light pink ribbon intertwined.

Once she felt she was ready, she took a deep breath to calm her nerves, gathered her sister, and headed to the field. There were way more people there than she had expected but was able to locate her friends. While they asked her if she was still planning on playing, she surveyed the field. She noticed ten boys on the left side and six boys on the right, but Conner wasn't any of them.

"He's not here yet," Dougy said as he and Rick approached.

"They're always late," Abby remarked.

"Annoyingly so," Josie added.

"Rude, if you ask me," Tennly grumbled.

Shortly after, The Untouchables showed up. Conner and Riley were dressed to play, sporting baggy sports shorts and tight t-shirts that highlighted every muscle.

Tennly had started getting used to her friends making a big deal over Conner and his friends, but when she saw everyone's reactions, she realized how much of an impact they had. Every eye was on them, and she could hear girls giggling and making comments about their looks. Even though she recognized their attractiveness, she chuckled to herself at how pathetic it all seemed, as she walked onto the field.

"This is going to be fun to watch," Dougy stated as he and Rick sat down on the grass beside Abby.

Tennly hoped to reach Conner before any of the other boys noticed her, but was intercepted by Gage Smith, an upcoming senior at their school. He was extremely tan, had short, spiky dark brown hair and blue eyes, and his height aided in his ability at being a star receiver on the high school football team.

"You need to get off the field," Gage directed.

"I want to play," Tennly replied.

"No girls allowed," Gage informed. "So, why don't you go sit on the sidelines with the other cheerleaders?"

Tennly started laughing as she taunted, "That's so cute. Are you afraid of getting beat by a girl?"

"Either get off the field," Gage threatened, upset, "or I'm going to make you get off it."

"I'd like to see you try," Tennly dared, taking a step closer to him.

Gage moved toward her, not wanting to let her have the last word, but before he could reach her, Conner appeared.

"She can play."

Tennly shot Gage an 'I told you so' look and then smiled at Conner in gratitude.

"Fine," Gage conceded, knowing better than to challenge an Untouchable. "But she's not playing on the townie side."

"She's from the neighborhood," Conner replied, gesturing with his head for her to follow him.

As the neighborhood team gathered, onlookers were astonished by what they were witnessing. Whispers filled the air as people questioned who Tennly was and why she was allowed to play.

Shelby attempted to step onto the field, assuming that Conner would let her join as well. However, he shot a look at Sam that clearly indicated he wanted him to stop her. Sam and Joel didn't participate in the game because they weren't from the neighborhood, which meant they couldn't play on Conner and Riley's team. Instead, they chose to stay on the sidelines.

When Sam refused to let her join, Shelby threw her arms up in frustration and screamed like a child throwing a temper tantrum.

It was evident that Conner hadn't changed his mind about allowing girls to participate; he was specifically giving permission to Tennly. This sparked questions among everyone about why that was the case.

"I can't believe this," Abby said, perplexed. "How did she know Conner would let her to play?"

Before anyone could respond, Shelby appeared. She kicked Dougy in the leg and asked, "Who is she?"

"If you kick me again," Dougy replied, "I'll punch you in the twat."

"Who is she?" Shelby pressed.

"Tennly O'Brien," Dougy answered.

"An O'Brien?" Shelby gasped, her voice much calmer. She felt relieved as she continued, "That makes sense."

"What?" Josie asked.

Shelby didn't answer, but they all knew what she meant. They had all thought it before; Conner wanted to have sex with an O'Brien.

The crowd quieted as the two teams got into their huddles. The game was played like a traditional football game, except there were no goal posts, and each team consisted of six players. Each team had four downs to advance twenty feet for a first down, and each touchdown was worth one point. The game lasted ninety minutes and two timekeepers indicated when the hour and a half was over. The winning team was determined by whoever was ahead at the end of the allotted time.

"You still remember how to play?" Conner asked, looking at Tennly.

"Are you still an ass?" Tennly bantered, smiling at him.

The guys huddled around them tried to suppress their laughter, unsure of how Conner would react. Conner gave Tennly a smile and said, "Okay, here's what we're going to do."

The neighborhood team always went first. They got into formation, and Riley hiked the ball to Conner, who threw it to Tennly for a first down. On the next play, Conner kept the ball and ran it in for a touchdown. However, their lead didn't last long as the townie team scored on their first possession, tying the game at 1-1. Two possessions went by without any touchdowns until the townie team scored their second, bringing the score to 1-2.

Tennly noticed that after the townie team scored their second touchdown, they didn't receive as many cheers as the neighborhood team had. She found this odd, considering that most of the onlookers weren't from the neighborhood.

Rejoining her team, they gathered in a huddle. Conner looked at Tennly and asked, "Do you still throw like crap?"

"Yep," she replied, aware that he was teasing and meant the opposite.

He instinctively shook his head to hide how impressed she still made him and called the next play. They got into formation, and Riley hiked the ball to Conner. As the townie team came rushing toward him, Conner threw the ball backward to Tennly. She dodged one tackle and threw the ball while Conner blocked another opponent from reaching her.

The ball was caught by a neighborhood boy, who ran it in for a touchdown. The crowd's joyous excitement suddenly turned to an abrupt silence as they watched what happened next. Immediately after Tennly threw the ball, Gage shoved her to the ground, shouting, "You don't belong out here!"

What followed was something no one had ever witnessed before. Conner sprinted toward Gage and punched him in the face, knocking him to the ground. He stood over Gage and yelled, "Don't touch her!"

Gage rubbed his cheek where Conner had struck him and got back to his feet. His first instinct was to retaliate, but hitting an Untouchable would be social suicide, so he settled for a hateful glare before walking back to his team. Everyone was astonished by Conner's actions. They watched as he reached down to take Tennly's hand, only to be shocked when she didn't accept it. While every other girl would have jumped at the chance to touch him, she swatted his hand away and stood up on her own.

"Why did you let me play?" Tennly fumed as she stood face to face with Conner.

"I don't know."

"Yes, you do. Why?"

He shook his head telling her she knew why, but he wasn't going to say it.

"Okay," she responded, accepting that he wasn't ready to admit his feelings, "treat me like the others, or I walk off the field right now."

Conner nodded and said, "Then let's win this game."

There was silence around the field, broken only by a few distant birds and the occasional passing car. It wasn't until they resumed playing that the sounds of whispers began to circulate through the crowd as to who Tennly was and why had Conner behaved so out of character.

Tennly's friends exchanged anxious glances, hesitant to speak for fear of being overheard, but they all shared the same concern. They worried that if she wasn't careful, she might end up with a bad reputation or worse, fall under Conner's spell and get seriously hurt.

The score was tied 2-2 with just over a minute left in the game, and the townie team had possession of the ball. After a huddle and the ball snap, Riley and two of the neighborhood boys blocked three members of the opposing team, preventing them from advancing downfield. Conner and Tennly sprinted together toward Gage, anticipating that he would be the intended receiver for the pass. A townie boy, believing Conner to be the greater threat, chose to block him, which left Tennly free to intercept the ball before it reached Gage.

Three boys, including Gage, chased after her. She outran one of them, while Conner tackled Gage, and she leaped over the third boy as he sprinted beside her, attempting to trip her. Just as the whistle blew, Tennly ran the ball in for a touchdown, securing the neighborhood team's victory with a score of 3-2.

Tennly glanced down the field as her teammates rushed toward her. She locked eyes with Conner, who smiled and nodded while she was being surrounded.

After celebrating with everyone, despite having won, when she looked back for Conner and he wasn't there, she felt a sense of loss.

"You certainly know how to make a first impression," Josie remarked after grabbing Tennly by the arm as the two of them, along with their friends, made their way back to Josie's house.

By the time they made it to Josie's bedroom, their excitement weened to concern. Lucy wouldn't stop giving examples of the bad things Conner and his friends had done, while Abby stammered with her words as she went between how fascinating the boys were to agreeing with Lucy.

Tennly could see on her friends' faces that they were all trying to warn her and since Abby wasn't doing a great job of getting out what they were trying to convey, Tennly finally said, "Get to the point."

"We think you're getting too close," Josie stated.

"To what?" Tennly asked, eyeing Josie as if to imply she should be more cautious about joining in with the others.

Josie gave Tennly an apologetic look as Lucy cautioned, "You're playing with fire, Ten. You've put yourself out there and now you're on their radar. It's only a matter of time before you get hurt."

Tennly couldn't help but chuckle as her friends exchanged glances, shrugging their shoulders as if unsure whether their intervention was effective.

"All we're saying...," Lucy continued to explain.

"Okay," Tennly interrupted. "I will heed your warning, if that makes you feel better." She believed that going along with their concerns would be the best way to get them to stop talking about it.

"That's all we're asking," Abby replied.

"It would be cool, though," Tina chimed in.

"What are you talking about?" Abby asked.

Tina shrugged and answered, "If he would end up liking her."

Tennly smiled at Tina and nodded, while Abby agreed, and Lucy threw her hands up in the air, as if exasperated. "You two are hopeless," Lucy huffed, looking between Abby and Tina.

"Whatever," Abby said. "Still... Tina has a point."

"Okay," Lucy said, giving in to the notion for the sake of argument. "Let's just say Conner can love someone, if he does then what is keeping him from acting on it?"

"He's afraid," Tina suggested.

"Nah," Abby replied. "The Untouchables aren't afraid of anything."

"Everyone is afraid of something," Tennly remarked, knowing Conner's fears.

"Not them," Abby insisted.

"Trust me, Abby," Tennly refuted. "They are."

Flashback:

Tennly was standing, looking in the direction of Conner's house, waiting for him to arrive while the neighborhood kids were choosing a seeker for Hide and Seek.

She felt relieved when she finally saw Conner walking towards the group, but her relief quickly turned to worry when she noticed he was walking with a limp. She moved around the outside of the group to where Conner was standing and positioned herself behind him.

"You look like shit," she whispered, teasing him. She knew that this approach would be more effective than outright asking how he was doing.

Conner appreciated her playful tact and, without turning around, shot back, "Yeah, well, I'm taking your beauty tips."

Tennly secretly punched him in the back, causing him to grimace from the beating he had just received from his father.

After the first seeker was chosen, she was taken by surprise when Conner grabbed her hand and asked her to hide with him. They quietly made their way to Conner's house and got into the front seat of his dad's car. As they scrunched down low enough not to be seen, Tennly sensed that the reason for hiding wasn't just to escape the seeker.

Conner reached into his pocket and pulled out a set of keys. "I'm taking the car."

"Conner, you can't! If you get in trouble one more time, they'll take you away."

"I can't stay here tonight. If he doesn't kill me, then I'm going to kill him."

"Then I'm going with you."

"You're not coming with me."

"Then why did you ask me to hide with you?"

"To say goodbye... to say..."

"I'm going with you," she insisted.

"I'm not going to get you in trouble too. You can't come."

"Then you're going to have to push me out."

He lay there, looking at her, trying to find a way to convince her to leave. But when it came down to it, he didn't want her to go. He was just about to tell her she could come with him when the door burst open, and he was yanked out by his head.

"Should have locked the damn door, dumbass," Kenneth Marks yelled as he shut the door and threw Conner to the ground, kicking him in the stomach. He seized hold of his shirt, as Conner screamed for him to let go, and pulled him toward the house.

Tennly started to breathe heavily as her body began to shake. This wasn't the first time she had seen Mr. Marks hit Conner, but it never became any easier to watch. She knew she had to do something when she saw him drag Conner by the neck into the house.

"Let him go!" she yelled as soon as she entered.

"Get... out... of... here, Ten," Conner managed to say, barely able to speak.

Kenneth tightened his grip around Conner's neck, making it harder for him to breathe. Upon seeing Conner turning blue, she stepped closer and repeated her plea for Kenneth to let him go. When Kenneth not only didn't let go of him, but threatened her, she became enraged.

"I don't think you want the neighbors to find out that you need to beat your son to feel like a man," she warned.

"You little shit," Kenneth scolded. With Conner still under his arm, he started to go after her, but she didn't budge.

"Touch me and It'll be the last thing you touch. Let him go, or I'll run to the nearest neighbor and tell them everything you do in this house."

She was determined not to back down, as their stares conveyed a sense of dominance, each waiting to see who would look away first. Her once trembling body was now completely still, poised for action, and he could see her determination in her eyes.

"Ah, I didn't want you here anyway," Kenneth grumbled, finally relenting. He threw Conner down onto the floor and added, "Get out!" Then he kicked Conner in the back and walked to the kitchen to grab a beer.

Tennly rushed over to Conner and wrapped her arms around him, pulling him up and out of the house. She helped him walk around to the back to avoid being seen, and once they felt safe, he collapsed to the ground. She sat beside him and gently placed his head on her lap.

"I told you to leave," Conner said, trying to laugh.

Tennly let out a sigh of relief. "And I told you I'm not leaving."

Once Conner regained his ability to breathe normally, he started laughing.

"What's so funny?"

"He got the keys."

Tennly couldn't help but cackle, "Jesus, Conner."

She helped him up, and they continued to walk in the shadows until they made it to Riley's house and hid in the garage. There was enough light coming in through the window from the back porch that Tennly could finally see the damage his father had done.

"You can't keep living like this, Con."

"I know."

"You've got to let me tell someone... get you some help or..."

"No! No... I'll figure it out."

"I don't know... I'm afraid that..."

"Ten, I'll figure it out. You promised..."

"I know, but..."

"You promised."

Tennly let out a sigh, knowing that she should tell someone, but she couldn't bring herself to break her promise to him. Regardless, there was no way he was going to be able to go home that night, which caused her to suggest that they meet in the field after the game was over and all the kids had gone home.

He waited for her while she walked up carrying two sleeping bags, two pillows, and a backpack, having told her father that she was spending the night with Josie. After sitting down, she opened the backpack, pulled out a bottle of water and a baggie of Tylenol.

"Are you going to sit down or not?" she asked, handing him the pain reliever and the water.

He did as she asked as she handed him an ice pack. "Here. It'll help with the swelling."

"Why do you hang out with me?" he asked, placing the ice pack over his left shoulder. "I bring you nothing but trouble."

"Yeah, well maybe I like trouble."

"Stick with me, and you're sure to run into some," he said, thinking of all *the stuff he was involved in that she didn't know about.*

She took the ice pack from him and motioned for him to turn around so she could reach the spots on his back that he couldn't get to. The sensation of her touch sent a wave of feelings through his body that he wished he weren't experiencing. He grabbed the ice pack and turned back to face her.

"I'm good," he assured.

"It's okay, I don't mind."

"I said I'm good," he snapped.

Tennly was confused by his response, considering she had often helped him heal his wounds after a beating. He had never spoken to her like that, so she raised her hands in defeat.

"I didn't mean to..."

"I'm not as innocent as you think I am," she interrupted him.

"Don't do that," he replied.

"What?"

"Don't change on me, Ten. Promise."

"I won't."

"Because I can't lose this."

"I know, me either." She felt the tension rising, so she picked up her pillow and lightly hit him with it. "Now stop being so serious. It freaks me out."

CHAPTER 6

Marinsburg's largest fundraiser was hosted by the O'Brien family every summer at the Marinsburg Inn and Conference Center downtown. This banquet was an exclusive black-tie event, with attendance limited to invited guests only. Most attendees were wealthy enough to afford tickets, but a few individuals received complimentary tickets from the O'Brien family. These included the chief of police, local law enforcement officers, parishioners, members of the board of education, and their families.

Since it was the first time in three years that Daniel and his daughters attended the banquet, Tennly was excited to dress up and see everyone, but she couldn't shake off a sense of hypocrisy as she looked at herself in the mirror. Her hair had been styled by a professional hairstylist who came to the mansion. It was arranged in an updo with thick braids on both sides that circled around in the back, forming a fan at the ends.

The formal gown she wore was violet and made from pure silk. It was floor-length with a high neckline that draped down both sides, revealing her entire back, which rested just below the dimples right above her behind. A high-cut slit on the right leg stopped at mid-thigh, showcasing a classic designer stiletto pump in the same violet color as the dress.

To complete her look, she wore a violet garter belt strapped under her gown at the top of her right leg. It was placed high on her thigh, allowing it to conceal one of her throwing knives. Besides her family, no one knew that she carried at least one knife at all times. She had started carrying a throwing knife when she was 13 years old. Her instructor had told her that while she was good at throwing them, she would become great if she treated them as extensions of her body.

Tara, on the other hand, wore a simple, form-fitting, floor-length light pink gown with spaghetti straps, complemented by a matching shawl draped over her shoulders. Unlike Tennly, who dressed in a more risqué and flamboyant style, Tara was more reserved. She had always wished she could be as bold as her sister; however, whenever she attempted to wear something provocative, she felt uncomfortable.

"Are you ready to go?" Tara asked, glancing at her sister through the mirror.

"Do you ever wonder what it's like not to know when your next meal is coming?" Tennly wondered, still focused on her reflection. "Or to go without something just to keep the heat on in your house?"

"Where is this coming from?" Tara inquired, puzzled.

"We're about to attend a banquet where people who don't have to worry about those things auction off items to help those who do," Tennly explained. She turned to look at Tara and continued, "And here we are... doing it while wearing clothes that cost more than what some people make in half a year. Doesn't that bother you?"

"Of course, but we can't help being rich. We help in any way we can. We donate our time and money, and we hold charity benefits. You're just going to have to learn to accept who you are."

Tennly remembered how she used to tell Conner that she couldn't help being rich, just as he couldn't help being poor. But she always felt guilty about it. Recently, she had started to feel comfortable with her identity and was enjoying giving her friends experiences they wouldn't normally have. So, she wasn't sure why that night was bothering her so much.

The banquet room in the Marinsburg Inn and Conference Center featured gold walls adorned with sheer golden drapes hanging over every window. The floor was covered in two-toned gold carpeting, and 24 round tables, each seating eight people, were set up ten feet apart. Each table was decorated with an ivory satin tablecloth and a lit candle in a small, elegant crystal candle holder in the center.

At the front of the banquet hall, four long rectangular tables were arranged end to end, all covered with the same color tablecloths as the round tables. On these rectangular tables were the items to be auctioned off, and behind them stood a pedestal where the speakers took their turns.

The moment Tennly stepped into the ballroom, she remembered why she disliked the banquet so much. Everywhere she looked, people were fawning over any O'Brien they could find, pretending to be just as wealthy or prestigious. Everything was meticulously organized, with nameplates on the tables and a clear flow for how people could move about. What bothered her the most, however, was the lack of carefree children; it felt like the kids were being trained to act like little adults, not allowed to speak or have fun.

Tennly maintained her composure, despite her overwhelming urge to escape, as her father introduced them to everyone. Thankfully, they finally reached their designated table, which included their cousins Patience and Prudence O'Brien.

Daniel took a moment to address everyone, encouraging them to bid generously to raise as much money as possible to support local shelters and food pantries. He also aimed to restore the old community building located downtown by the river, near the railroad bridge. His vision was to transform the building into a women's shelter.

When Daniel's brother Donnie began auctioning off items, Daniel took a seat at the table with Donnie's wife, Stella, their other brother, Sean, and his wife, Anna. Shortly after he sat down, Tennly noticed Thomas approach Daniel and whisper something in his ear. A minute later, after Thomas left, Daniel stood up from the table and walked out of the banquet room.

Feeling suspicious about her father's behavior, Tennly excused herself to go to the restroom but instead decided to follow him. She watched as he met up with Thomas, and together they walked down the long hallway, exiting through the back door at the end. Tennly waited until the door closed, then quietly peered out to see what was happening.

She shuddered when she saw her father approach a man, that her Uncle Jimmy and Uncle John were holding, and punched him in the stomach. Thomas then opened the back door of the car, while John went around to enter from the other side. Daniel grabbed the man by the hair, whispered something in his ear, and then pushed him into Thomas, who caught him and placed him in the back seat. After exchanging a few words with Jimmy, Daniel walked back toward the conference center.

Quickly closing the door to avoid being seen by her father, Tennly darted into the nearest open room. She leaned against the door, confused, waiting for him to pass as she contemplated what she had just witnessed.

The room was a small conference space, dimly lit except for light streaming in from the streetlamps and stoplights outside. Positioned near one of the windows, she had a clear view across the street. Under a light post at the corner stood Conner, his friends, and two unfamiliar guys. The longer she watched, the more she realized they were in the middle of a drug deal.

Acting on impulse, she rushed out of the room, made her way back through the hotel, and exited through the front door. After checking to ensure no one had seen her, she walked over to the corner where Conner was standing.

"Uh oh," Sam announced, being the first to notice her. "Here comes your girlfriend."

"What?" Conner replied, looking in the direction Sam was pointing. Embarrassed, he handed Riley the package and said, "Hide this."

Riley quickly tucked the package into his pocket while the two guys Tennly didn't know left. The boys couldn't help but notice how she walked with such poise and confidence, making her astonishingly beautiful. Conner felt his heart race the closer she got, and when she stopped just a couple of feet away from him, he thought for a moment that it had skipped a beat.

"Hi," she said.

"Hi," Conner replied, his three friends backing away slightly.

"Just gonna do that right out in the open, huh?" she asked.

"What do you want, Tennly?" Conner responded, annoyed that she knew exactly what he was doing.

"Oh," she replied sarcastically, "I'm sorry. I didn't mean to interrupt your little soiree. Next time the chief of police and the juvenile judge are within feet of you, I won't bother to warn you." With that, she turned and began walking back toward the conference center.

"Stop," Conner demanded, walking up to her. He gently placed his hand on her arm, prompting her to turn around. "Thank you."

She nodded, reminding him that she had promised to always be there for him, and she meant it. After she walked away, Conner turned back to see that his friends were still nearby. Sam and Joel were impressed that someone of Tennly's stature and upbringing would go out of her way to warn someone like Conner. Riley appreciated her actions, but he believed they would only bring Conner closer to her. And if that happened, he was sure it would end badly.

Daniel was eager to open the women's shelter as soon as possible, so Tara and Tennly, along with Prudence and Patience, volunteered to help paint the walls. The girls worked diligently over the course of three days, finishing by lunchtime on the third day.

As Tara and Tennly made their way to the parking lot, they heard splashing and deep voices shouting down toward the railroad bridge. When they reached Tara's car, they glanced down toward the commotion and saw Conner sitting on the bank beside Riley, while Sam and Joel were swimming in the river.

Tara noticed a look of longing on Tennly's face and realized she wasn't going to get into the car. She gave Tennly a worried glance, trying to convey her concerns and persuade her not to approach Conner, but it was futile.

"I'll be back," Tennly said.

"Ten," Tara called out, attempting one last time to keep her from going.

"I'll be fine."

As Tara got into the car, she watched her sister walk down the riverbank. It was difficult for her to let Tennly go and sit next to the most feared boy in town. Despite her concerns, Tara couldn't help but feel jealous at her sister's courageous determination.

"Hi," Tennly greeted, as the wind carried the smell of mud and dead fish toward them. Unlike her sister and cousins, it didn't disgust her; instead, it was comforting: a reminder of the summers spent at the river with Conner.

"Hi," Conner replied, which made Riley get up in abhorred displeasure and walk down to the river.

"I didn't get to thank you for letting me play in the football game," she said, ignoring Riley's departure, as she sat down.

Conner nodded and replied, "It was your idea, so..."

"You know you should really consider letting the girls play," she suggested. "That's pretty shitty."

"Well, I'm a dick... so..."

"Be that as it may," she advised with a smile, tilting her head so he had no choice but to look at her.

"Yeah, okay," he conceded, not able to resist her charms.

Riley didn't like Conner spending so much time talking to Tennly. He felt that the more time they spent together, the greater the chance Conner would let her into his life. So, he sent Sam over in an attempt to drive Tennly away.

"Hey, Con," Sam called out, stopping just a few feet away from them. "We're going to jump off the bridge. Do you want to come?"

"Nah, go ahead," Conner replied.

Sam looked over at Tennly, thinking that if he spoke to her, she might get scared and leave. "What about you?"

Tennly smiled but declined, "Thank you, but I'm good."

"I dare you," Sam challenged. "Unless you're chicken."

"What are you, like five?" Tennly retorted.

Sam's attempt at goading her backfired, causing Conner to chuckle. He found it intriguing that she wasn't scared of Sam; instead of pushing her away like Riley had asked, Sam wanted to see how far she would go.

"A bet then," Sam suggested, a mischievous grin spreading across his face.

"I wouldn't," Conner warned, knowing that Tennly had jumped off that bridge many times before and wouldn't pass up a good challenge.

"I bet you a hundred dollars that you can't jump off the bridge," Sam dared, assuming Conner's response was due to not wanting Tennly to jump, rather than a warning that she could.

Tennly gave Conner a smile that indicated she was going to have some fun, and then stood up. "You're on," she said, and began walking toward the bridge with Sam.

As they climbed up the rafters to the base of the bridge, Riley and Joel approached Conner and sat down beside him.

"What's going on?" Riley asked, wondering why Tennly was going up the bridge with Sam instead of leaving as he had wanted.

"Sam is about to lose a hundred bucks," Conner replied, a sense of contentment and pride evident in his voice.

Sam and Tennly reached the center of the bridge, hovering above the river. "It looks higher up here, doesn't it?"

"It does," she agreed.

"You don't have to jump," he added, unsure if the look on her face was pure horror or a silent challenge telling him to go first. "Okay, see you down there!"

With that, he jumped off the bridge and surfaced a few feet away from the bank.

"You can back out if you want!" he yelled up to her.

"And you can go sit down and watch!" she shouted back.

The bridge stood about ten feet higher than the diving platform at her house, making it nearly 40 feet above the water's surface. Not only did she want to win the bet, but having jumped off that bridge several times before, she wanted to make a statement.

She took a step backward and bent over, placing her hands in front of her feet. She brushed off any debris that might irritate her skin, and before the boys could fully process it, she executed a handstand at the edge.

"What is she doing?" Sam asked, impressed by what he was witnessing.

"I warned you," Conner replied, watching as Tennly kicked out into a pike position and then dove headfirst into the river.

"How did you know she would jump?" Sam asked after Joel started laughing.

"We used to come down here all the time," Conner informed.

"Well, that's great," Sam grumbled. "You could have just told me that. You owe me a hundred bucks."

"Oh no, I don't," Conner replied. "You took the bet. You owe the money."

"You saw her dive off the board at the pool," Riley added, upset that Sam hadn't done what he asked. "You didn't have to bet her."

"You're the one who told me to get her aw..." Sam started to say, but he stopped when he saw Riley signaling him to stop because Tennly was approaching.

When she stopped right in front of the boys, she looked directly at Sam. "You owe me a hundred dollars."

The boys found her statement refreshing. Given her wealth, they knew she didn't need the money and could have easily told him to forget it. However, she remembered Conner telling her never to treat him like charity and figured his friends likely felt the same way.

"I don't have it on me," Sam assured. "But I'll get it."

"I expect no less." Then she turned to Conner and added, "I'll see you around, Marks." He nodded at her, and as she began to walk away, she paused next to Riley. She looked at him and stated, "For the record, I'm not that easy to get rid of."

Conner smiled as he continued to gaze at the river, while the other boys watched her walk toward the parking lot.

"I like her," Sam professed after she had walked far enough away.

"Yeah," Conner agreed.

"She's still trouble," Riley commented.

"Yep," Conner acknowledged.

Conner was the only one of his friends who had a car, but all four of them owned motorcycles. Riley had a royal blue 1979 Harley-Davidson Shovelhead that had been passed down to him from his father.

A few years earlier, Sam's mother's boyfriend owned a garage that· bought and sold used motorcycles. He offered Sam and Joel two motorcycles if they worked for free to pay for and restore them. Sam ended up with a black and yellow Honda Chopper, while Joel chose a black Kawasaki Vulcan with dark red accents.

Similarly, Conner had to save money to buy his motorcycle. He was very particular about what he wanted and spent three years saving up for it before finally finding the right one. He purchased it just a few months before school ended that year.

The motorcycle was a 1963 Triumph Bonneville that needed restoration. Since Riley's father had built a garage for working on cars, Conner kept his motorcycle there while he worked on it. All the trim, wheel covers, and handlebars were painted black, and even the seat was black. The pipes were chrome, while the gas tank was off-white on the lower front third and dark turquoise blue on the top.

The day after Conner's bike was completely restored, he and his friends drove around and eventually found themselves at Benny's. The sound of the four bikes roaring echoed like thunder, drawing a crowd. After showing off

Conner's new ride for a few minutes, they headed inside.

An hour later, Tennly, Dougy, and their friends arrived. It was Tennly's first time at Benny's, other than during the music festival, and she felt more than excited to be there. The front door opened to a large foyer with a counter in the front left corner where an employee checked to ensure, other than chaperones, no one over 21 entered. On the side of the door were two rows of lockers available for rent, and the restrooms were located across the foyer on the far wall.

To the left of the restrooms was the door that led into the game room. Inside, there were four pool tables in the center, various arcade games in the back, counters running along the walls with bar stools for seating, and three large televisions hanging from the ceiling.

Hearing music coming from the door to the right of the restrooms made Tennly curious to see what was inside. It was more spectacular than she had expected. As soon as she stepped in, the beat of the music vibrated through her chest while the lights flickered on and off like a laser show. There were at least thirty people dancing, and she became giddy at the thought of joining them.

After dancing, the girls sat down with Dougy and Rick, enjoying the refreshments they had ordered. Before heading back to the dance floor, the girls made their way to the restroom. Tennly was impressed to find that the restroom had a vanity with a long mirror and three padded chairs in front of it.

"This is actually really nice," Tennly commented as Lucy sat down to reapply her lipstick.

"Yeah," Lucy agreed. "I was skeptical about coming my first time, but they did a good job."

"What's in the other room?" Tennly asked as Josie emerged from one of the stalls, exchanging knowing glances filled with worry with Lucy and Tina. They all knew that the only other room available was the game room, where the shadier kids, including The Untouchables, tended to hang out.

"Oh," Tennly replied, realizing from her friends' facial expressions that if Conner was around, that was where he would be. "Well, let's go have some fun."

"Ten?" Josie pleaded, hoping to deter her from going, but it was too late.

They hoped The Untouchables weren't there, but Tennly was certain they were. She had seen the four motorcycles parked out front when they arrived, remembering the exact bike Conner always vowed he would own someday.

When Josie and Lucy spotted the four boys, their anxiety grew, anticipating that Tennly would approach Conner. However, they became confused when instead she walked past him and headed straight for Sam.

"You have my money?" Tennly asked with a smile.

"Yeah," Sam replied as he reached into his pocket.

"What would you say to double or nothing?" Tennly suggested. She didn't really want to take his money; she knew the only way to get out of it was to propose another bet. There was a 50/50 chance she could win and double what he owed, but at least it would give him a chance to save face. Not to mention, she enjoyed playing and hoped it would rekindle Conner's interest in her.

Sam loved the idea but needed to get Conner's approval first. He glanced over at Conner for a moment of clarification before responding to Tennly. Conner didn't mind Sam taking on another bet with Tennly and was excited at the thought of watching her in action. He just didn't want to make it obvious, so he shrugged slightly and nodded, signaling to Sam that it was up to him.

Sam turned back to Tennly and asked, "What do you have in mind?"

"Follow me," she said.

Sam wasn't the only one who followed. As soon as everyone saw The Untouchables abruptly leave the game room, they hurried after them. Josie and Lucy dashed to the dining area to gather their friends, causing a commotion in the dance room that made nearly everyone stop what they were doing to see what was happening.

By the time Tennly and Sam reached outside, a huge crowd had gathered behind them. Tennly knew that Conner and their friends would follow, but she never expected such a swarm of onlookers. She still found it hard to accept the influence that The Untouchables had, and the absurdity of it made her laugh every time.

"Are those bikes yours?" Tennly asked, already knowing the answer.

"Yeah," Sam replied, curiosity piqued.

"If the others let me borrow one of their bikes," she continued, "we could have a race. Down to the river by the railroad bridge and back. First one back here wins."

Sam knew that Tennly was only 15 and therefore didn't have a driver's license. What he didn't know was that her father allowed her to drive often. Daniel thought it was good practice for her to learn how to navigate the laws, even if he knew it posed little risk since half the police force was on his payroll. Tennly believed it was simply because he frequently needed Thomas for something and didn't want to take the time to drive her around. Regardless of the reason, she relished the freedom and never questioned it.

Another aspect that Sam and everyone else, except for Conner, didn't know was that Tennly owned a motorcycle of her own. Her father had bought her a metallic purple Kawasaki Ninja 400 for her 13th birthday. Although she hadn't had the chance to ride it much, she had ample experience driving other family members' motorcycles.

It wasn't that Sam minded racing against someone so young, but he was concerned that Conner wouldn't support it. Although Conner was hesitant about her racing, he also didn't want anyone to know his true feelings. He shrugged his shoulders, signaling to Sam that he could proceed. Sam then turned to Riley and Joel to check if they were okay with Tennly borrowing one of their bikes. Even though Riley hated the idea of her touching his bike, he couldn't be the only one to say no. So, after Joel nodded in agreement, he too gave his permission.

"Okay," Sam said, turning back to Tennly. "I'm in. What are the rules?"

"None," Tennly replied. "The first one to get there and back wins."

"How do I know you won't cheat?" Sam questioned with a smile.

"How do I know you won't?" Tennly countered, smiling in return.

They agreed to a spotter who would be willing to drive to the railroad bridge by the river to make sure they both reached it. Once they had someone, Sam pointed out his bike and told Tennly to choose one from the other three.

Tennly walked around the three motorcycles, slowly, as if acting uncertain about which one to choose. She ran her fingers down each bike as if she were stroking a cat. The crowd held its breath, waiting to see which one she would pick. She examined Joel's first, then Conner's, and finally Riley's. It seemed she would choose Riley's, but instead, she turned around and placed both hands on Conner's seat.

"I'll take this one."

Conner smiled, aware that she knew it was his, as he reached into his front right pocket and pulled out his keys. Everyone watched as she walked over to him, anticipating what he was going to do.

"You finally got your bike," she whispered, so no one else could hear.

"Yeah," he replied, handing her the keys. "So, don't wreck."

"Are you worried about the bike or me?" she flirted.

Conner smiled the most gorgeous smile she could ever remember as he shook his head, signaling that he wasn't going to answer her question. She could see why her friends had been warning her about him; his smile nearly melted her. However, she couldn't let him know how she felt, so she stood firm and continued to look him straight in the eyes.

"Just don't wreck," was all he said.

As she walked to his bike, people were placing t-shirts over the plates and gas tanks to try to keep the motorcycles as unidentifiable as possible. She picked up Conner's helmet, just as she heard Sam start his bike and drive it to the edge of the lot where the gravel met the pavement.

She started Conner's bike and put on the helmet, but before she pulled up to the starting line, Conner ran up to her. He didn't say anything, but he ran his finger down her left hand and gave her a look that clearly told her to be careful. She nodded at him to show that she understood, then drove to where Sam was waiting.

Joel stood ten feet in front of them and announced, "On your marks, get set, go!" And they were off.

Everyone stayed, eager to see who would be the first to return. Those at the neighborhood football game found it interesting that the same girl Conner had let play was now racing on his bike against Sam, another Untouchable. Those who hadn't been at the football game were curious about who Tennly was. Despite the questions, everyone was thinking the same thing: Why did Conner look so concerned about her?

"She's not going to listen to us, is she?" Lucy stated as Tennly's friends settled down at one of the many picnic tables near the front of the building.

"Would you?" Abby replied. "I mean, if he looked at you like that."

"He looks at lots of girls like that," Lucy pointed out.

"Not like that," Abby refuted, feeling a twinge of envy.

They all took a defeated breath as they awaited the racers' return. The race from Benny's to the river and back should have taken only thirty minutes: fifteen minutes each way, give or take a minute or two. The first five minutes were easy, as it involved driving through the backwoods with hardly any traffic or street signs.

The next few minutes were a bit more challenging. They encountered three stoplights, two stop signs, and a large, sharp turn before reaching the main part of the city. The final five minutes, when they arrived downtown, proved to be the toughest. Every block was filled with stoplights and traffic was heavy.

As they raced through downtown, they were neck and neck, instinctively staying together as they heard sirens approaching. However, at the next intersection, when Tennly turned right, Sam chose to go straight. She noticed the sound of the sirens fading and looked back, realizing that Sam was no longer with her.

In hopes of reconnecting with Sam, she turned left down the first alley she could find. As she reached the end of the alley, she spotted Sam coming from her left, pursued by one police car, while another was heading straight at him.

The vehicle approaching Sam parked horizontally across the street, blocking his path and forcing him to stop. He glanced behind him and saw the other police car, realizing he was in a tight spot. Without hesitation, Tennly grabbed a medium-sized rock and dashed out of the alley. She raced down the road, past the first police car, past Sam, and hurled the rock at the rear window of the police car parked sideways.

The officer whose car had been hit raced back to his vehicle to pursue Tennly. This diversion gave Sam the opportunity he needed. He swiftly made a left turn into the alley, emerging on the street where Tennly was driving. He crossed the road right in front of her, gesturing for her to follow him to the other side.

They maneuvered in and out of alleys until they reached an abandoned warehouse. Sam honked a secret code to gain entry as the sirens intensified. As soon as the garage door opened wide enough, they hurried inside. The door closed behind them just as the sirens reached their peak volume and then faded until they were no longer audible.

Tennly's heart raced as she surveyed the warehouse. Several people were seated in different areas, and Dante, the overseer of the place, was descending the stairs from his loft.

Dante was an African American man in his mid-twenties. He kept his hair short, had big brown eyes, and was very good-looking and clean-cut. He always dressed nicely, often wearing suits, and spoke as if he were well-educated. He took pride in keeping the warehouse clean and had established rules to ensure it remained that way.

"Sam," Dante greeted as he approached them. "Is that you making all that noise out there?"

"Yeah," Sam replied. "Ran into some friends."

"Well," Dante said, "make yourself at home for as long as you need."

"Thanks," Sam responded.

"Won't they look in here?" Tennly asked.

"No," Dante answered. "They avoid facing what's in here. If they did, they'd have to actually do something about it, and they'd rather just ignore the problem of homelessness."

"All these people are homeless?" Tennly inquired, looking around.

Throughout her life, she had participated in charity fundraisers and donated time and clothes to causes that she thought her father had always exaggerated. However, after seeing all those people, whose ages ranged from pre-teen to mid-twenties, she began to wonder if her family was truly doing enough.

"I didn't catch your name," Dante said, looking at Tennly. He could tell by her designer clothes and shoes, as well as her innocence and naiveté, that she was not part of that world.

"Tennly," she replied.

"Tennly?" Dante asked, recognizing the name. "O'Brien?"

A few people, aside from Dougy, were aware of Conner's relationship with Tennly before she returned, and one of them was Dante. After she didn't come home for a year, Conner found the warehouse and felt comfortable confiding in Dante. He spent many nights crying to him about her until he eventually hardened himself enough to move on.

"Is there a problem?" Tennly asked, sensing his suspicion about her.

"Not as long as you promise to keep this place a secret," Dante replied. "You see, Tennly O'Brien, for some of these people, this is the only family they have. Here, they have a safe place to sleep, food and water, and access to a shower."

Tennly thought about Conner and the abuse he endured at the hands of his father and understanding the failed child protective system, she realized that Dante was right.

"You understand, don't you?" Dante acknowledged. Tennly gave him a look that indicated she did, but she didn't respond. He nodded to let her know he respected her privacy and then turned to Sam. "Take your time."

"Thanks," Sam replied and then escorted Tennly to a room under the loft.

"We can wait in here until the coast is clear," Sam suggested, sitting down in the chair in the corner of the room.

"How long do you think they'll search for us?" Tennly asked as she looked around.

"Not long," Sam answered, lighting a cigarette. "Thanks, by the way. What you did was really cool. You could have left me."

"I don't know what you're talking about," Tennly replied, smiling at him.

"So," Sam said, appreciating her discretion, "where does that leave us with the bet?"

"The way I see it, you still owe me a hundred bucks."

Sam laughed as he reached into his right pocket, pulled out a one-hundred-dollar bill, and handed it to her. "We good?"

"We are," she nodded, taking the money. As she put it in her pocket, she walked around the room, examining the few belongings scattered throughout. There wasn't much, but enough for her to know it belonged to Conner.

"Conner stays here, doesn't he?"

The room was nicer than Conner's bedroom at home. Placed against the off-white walls was a cot with a real mattress, sheets, and a comforter, over an area rug. There was also a dresser with a mirror on top and a matching nightstand.

"How do you know?"

"For one," she grinned, "it smells like him."

"Conner has a smell?" Sam chuckled.

"Yeah. It's a mix of cigarettes and a musky scent, combined with citrus."

"Old Spice."

"I know," she acknowledged, smiling. Lamenting, she pointed to a bracelet hanging from the lamp on the nightstand. "I made that bracelet for him when I was eleven."

"I like you, Tennly, so I'm just gonna say it. You scare me; and you scare the hell out of Riley."

Tennly was glad that Sam felt comfortable enough to share his feelings, but she wasn't sure she wanted to hear them. She was already getting advice from her friends and didn't need another source. Still, she sat down on the bed, waiting for him to continue; she felt he deserved at least that much.

"I've known Conner since the sixth grade," Sam explained, "and he's always been consistent: same guy, every time. But he's different with you; around you. I'm not saying it's good or bad, but Conner's inconsistency can be dangerous. If his head isn't clear, he might do something that will get him killed or in trouble."

"I appreciate your honesty," Tennly said, "and I like you as well. But with all due respect, Conner never got into trouble while I was with him. If anyone should be scared, it's me."

Sam nodded, then declared, "Sounds like we're at a crossroads."

"Sounds about right."

Sam extinguished his cigarette in the ashtray located on the end table and stood up. "I think the coast is clear. You ready?"

Everyone back at Benny's was beginning to feel anxious, but none more so than Conner. He had started pacing, growing increasingly concerned about why it was taking them so long. With each passing minute, his worry intensified at the thought of Tennly being hurt or in trouble. After nearly forty-five minutes of waiting, he couldn't bear it any longer.

He tried calling Sam, but there was no answer. Frustrated, he approached Riley, held out his hand, and demanded, "Give me your keys."

"Give them another couple of minutes," Riley suggested.

"Give me your goddamn keys!" Conner screamed, raising his fist in preparation for a fight if necessary.

The crowd couldn't believe what they were witnessing. They had never seen, nor heard of, their beloved Untouchables fighting among themselves, and they didn't like it. Some were angry that it was over a girl, and they hated her for it. Those who heard she was an O'Brien hated her even more.

Feeling that Tennly was coming between them, Riley shook his head, his lips pursed, and asked, "Are you really going to fight me over her?"

"I would fight..." Conner began but stopped when he heard an engine approaching.

As the sound of a motorcycle grew louder, Conner shot Riley a look that said he should feel lucky. Then, taking an anticipatory breath, he turned to see who was arriving. When he saw Tennly drive up, relief washed over him.

He walked up to her as she dismounted his bike, while everyone eagerly waited to hear why it had taken so long for her to return and why Sam wasn't with her. The silence was eerie, broken only by the rustling leaves on the trees on the other side of the lot. Tennly took off the helmet, placed it on the seat, and handed Conner his keys as she gave him Sam's message of meeting them at Riley's house.

"Are you okay?" Conner asked.

"Yeah."

He leaned in, her heartbeat getting faster, and whispered, "Don't do that again."

"What?"

Conner shook his head, not wanting her to know how scared he had been. He then motioned to Riley and Joel that it was time to go. When they arrived at Riley's house, Sam was already there, sitting on his bike and waiting for his friends. Without hesitation, Conner walked straight up to Sam and asked what had happened.

Sam explained the entire situation with enthusiasm, expressing appreciation for what Tennly had done for him. "I was a goner. She saved me."

Riley felt grateful to Tennly for helping Sam out of a tough spot, but no matter how much good he heard about her, he couldn't bring himself to trust her. After nearly getting into a fight with his best friend over her, the thought that she had somehow managed to win Sam over made him nauseous. He shook his head in disapproval and then stormed into his house.

"What's going on with him?" Sam asked.

"Conner almost hit him," Joel replied.

"What?" Sam exclaimed in surprise.

"Shit," Conner mumbled to himself, realizing he needed to apologize to Riley. "I'd better go talk to him."

"Yeah," Sam agreed, shooting Joel a look that suggested they should leave.

Riley's mother greeted Conner at the door and upon seeing her he could barely look her in the eyes. She had been like a mother to him since he was four years old and knew she wouldn't be happy about him and Riley fighting.

When Riley walked into the house, she could see etched on his face that there was conflict. She asked him what was wrong, but he ignored her, heading straight to his bedroom without a word. Seeing that Conner had the same troubled expression, she gave him a hug and whispered, "Fix this."

Conner nodded in response and then walked to Riley's room, where he was sitting on his bed, smoking a cigarette: a mix of rage and sadness exhuming from him.

Wanting to just forget about what happened, Conner asked, "Are we good?"

"I don't know."

"Riley..."

"Do you really care for her that much?"

"Yeah."

Riley took a deep breath and then asked, "What's so special about her?"

Conner smiled as he considered the question, realizing how difficult it was to answer. "She's always been there, always in the back of my mind. She understands me, and... I don't know. When I'm not with her, it feels like a part of me is dead, like I'm in a constant state of panic. I can't breathe. When she came back and I saw her, an overwhelming mix of joy and terror came over me." He paused for a moment, letting out a slight chuckle. "But I could finally breathe again."

"But she's an O'Brien, Con."

"I know."

"There's too much risk involved. Her father has a lot of influence over the police and the judicial system here. If he finds out..."

"I know," Conner interrupted. "But I don't know how much longer I can stay away from her."

ennly went home that night, worried that she had ruined her chances of reestablishing a relationship with Conner. The panic was so overwhelming that she was startled when she walked into her bedroom and saw her sister sitting on her bed, waiting for her.

"You have fun tonight?" Tara asked, as if she already knew the answer.

"Yeah," Tennly replied as she walked to her vanity and sat down.

"Anything exciting happen?"

"Nothing unusual."

"So, you didn't get into any trouble with the law?"

"Oh my gosh!" Tennly huffed, turning around to face Tara. "That just happened. How do you know already?"

"A friend's sister was there. She told my friend, and my friend told me."

"This is crazy. Now I understand why Conner wanted our friendship kept a secret. This town would never let it go."

"They're just concerned about you."

"Well, tell them I can take care of myself."

"Do you want to talk about it?"

"No."

"Tennly, Sam Phelps? Really?"

"What did you hear?"

"That you made a bet with Sam Phelps, then rode off with him and were alone together for a good half hour or more."

"That sounds about right," Tennly concurred, brushing it off as if it were nothing.

"Sam... Phelps," Tara emphasized, hoping this would make Tennly realize how dangerous he was.

"He's not as bad as people think," Tennly smiled, thinking of how kind he was to her.

"I don't know, Ten. And the worst part about it is that everyone thinks you're like some Yoko Ono."

Tennly laughed and then sarcastically replied, "What? Splitting up their beloved Untouchables?"

"Yeah," Tara admitted, trying to sound as serious as possible.

Tennly stopped laughing, grunted, "That's stupid," stood up, and said, "I'm going to bed."

Tennly had a difficult time sleeping that night. After tossing and turning for over an hour, she decided to go to the kitchen to find a snack. She discovered some cheese squares and was about to pour herself a glass of sweet tea when she heard voices approaching.

Quickly, she closed the refrigerator door and slid down behind the kitchen island. As her father and two uncles walked through the room, she overheard them discussing a package. She carefully scooted around the island to avoid being seen while trying to listen in on their conversation. Although she missed a few details, she was able to catch that a shipment was arriving at the Cass Yacht Club in Cincinnati, Ohio, on a boat named the Silver Coin.

"It will dock after midnight in six days," Jimmy informed. "Then it will

202

remain abandoned for two days to give you enough time to retrieve it before it departs. If you miss it, we won't get it, and it'll move on to the next location."

"How much do I need to leave?" Daniel asked.

"Fifty grand," Jimmy replied. "That covers the actual cost, the seller's fee, and ensures that everything is untraceable."

Tennly wanted to stay and hear more, but when the men moved over to the nook, she saw her chance to slip away unnoticed. She wasn't sure exactly what she had heard, but she knew whatever her father was into was illegal. She spent the rest of the night reflecting on everything that had seemed strange about her family: the night she saw blood all over her father when he returned to the car after handling something for her late mother, the secret meetings between her father and her uncles and how he would abruptly leave to 'take care of business,' whenever she walked into the room, the men would stop talking, and the hidden compartments behind picture frames. But the most suspicious things were the secret doors that led to different rooms and the hidden tunnels beneath the house.

Flashback:

Tennly had snuck into Daniel's office, in Marinsburg, and was hiding under his desk when Daniel, Jimmy, and John walked in and sat down in the seating area. Throughout the summer, she had been sneaking around, listening in on conversations, and had become so adept at it that most of the time, no one noticed she was there. From her hiding spot, it was hard to make out what the three men were saying, so she didn't realize when Daniel paused, held up his finger to signal Jimmy and John to be quiet, and slowly stood up, trying not to make any noise as he walked over to his desk. Before Tennly knew it, she was face to face with her father, and he did not look happy.

"Out," Daniel said, gesturing for her to leave the office.

Tennly gave him a smile, and after she left Jimmy remarked, "It's like she knows."

"I think, in a way, she does," Daniel acknowledged.

"She's only seven," John replied. "We need to be more careful. If she overhears

something she shouldn't, who's to say she won't tell someone?"

"She won't tell anyone," Daniel insisted. "I know my daughter. She'll keep it a secret and use it when it benefits her."

"And how do we know that won't be when she's a moody teenager upset because you won't let her do something?" John asked.

"I'm sure it will," Daniel admitted.

"Blackmail?" Jimmy inquired.

"Extortion," Daniel corrected with a smile on his face. He then shook his head and began to walk toward the office door.

Tennly hadn't walked away; she stayed outside the office and listened to the men talk. When she heard her father's footsteps approaching, she ran down the hall and hid around the corner. Once she was sure the coast was clear and she heard the office door close, she dashed through the atrium and headed for the door that led to the backyard.

She walked around the perimeter of the estate, searching for the tunnels she had overheard the men discussing, until *she found herself at the entrance to the front gate. It was past the time she was allowed out of the yard, and being only seven years old, she wasn't allowed to go out without her sister, anyway. So, she waited and hid behind some bushes until her uncles left. When the gate opened to allow their car through, she slipped out just in time before it closed behind her.*

She considered pushing the code to get back inside. It would have been much easier for her than trying to find another way in without being noticed, but she was committed to her adventure of finding the tunnels at that point.

She walked back and forth, examining every part of the wall until she noticed something peculiar about the pillars embedded in the wall every forty feet. The pillars were square, measuring five feet by five feet, resembling small turrets and lacking any visible doors. She had passed by them several times over the years without giving them any thought, but as she approached the nearest pillar, she wondered if there was something more to them.

Running her hands over the rough stones, she searched for any clues. The texture was rougher than she anticipated, causing her hands to scrape against the surface. It didn't take long for her to notice a tiny straight line etched into the stones, forming the outline of a large rectangle.

She began to push on each stone, but nothing happened. Glancing at the ground, she looked for a lever, a rock, or any other mechanism, but found nothing. Then she recalled overhearing her father mentioning that 'the wall is the way in.'

She ran her hands over the wall to the left of the pillar until she found a stone that felt smoother than the others. A sense of relief washed over her as she smiled. She pushed the stone, and the front of the pillar opened.

As soon as she stepped inside, the door closed behind her, leaving her in complete darkness. Her first instinct was to turn around and escape, but when she pushed on the door, it wouldn't budge. She turned around and put her hands in front of her, feeling another wall only a foot away. Panic set in as she realized she was trapped. However, she knew her father well enough to believe he would have provided a way out. She felt around until she found a small box on the left wall, about four feet above the floor. When she touched it, the center lit up, revealing a silhouette of a hand. The illuminated area was a palm reader that Daniel had programmed to recognize family and only those he trusted.

She held her breath as she placed her hand over the light and watched as the inner door opened, revealing a ladder that descended to a tunnel below. As she walked down the tunnel the lights illuminated the path ahead of her, while those behind her flickered off. She could feel the floor sloping deeper underground, below the mansion. The further she went, the colder the air became, and the musty smell intensified. The walls were cracked, with water seeping through, and every so often, she spotted insects scurrying into the crevices.

After walking several feet, she finally reached the end of the tunnel. It opened into a round room with six other tunnels branching off from it. Above each tunnel door, words were inscribed in old Gaelic, indicating where each passage led: the pool house, the garage, the great room, Daniel's office, the game room, the downstairs living room, and the one she just came from.

She took the tunnel marked 'Living Room,' since it was the closest room to her bedroom, emerging from a secret door that was hidden behind a bookshelf.

She managed to return to her bedroom without anyone noticing her absence. Over the next week, she quietly explored the mansion and discovered every hidden door it harbored. Not only did she find tunnel doors, but she also uncovered secret doors that connected various rooms.

The most significant secret door for her was the one in her own room. It was cleverly concealed in her walk-in closet, hidden behind the shoe wall. High on the top shelf, beyond her reach from the floor, was a small button protected by a plastic cover.

Using a step ladder, she reached the button, removed the protector, and pressed it. A secret door to her left swung open, revealing access to the adjacent upstairs living room that the girls had claimed as their space. This living room was situated directly above the downstairs living room, which she already knew had a tunnel leading to it. Additionally, she discovered a hidden elevator behind the upstairs living room bookshelf, connecting the two living rooms.

Her discovery became her refuge, as she found a way to see Conner without anyone discovering her secret. And that was exactly what she did.

CHAPTER 7

Every year, the third week in July was dedicated to the Marinsburg Homecoming. This event spanned three days and took place on the last two streets downtown by the river. A total of ten blocks were closed off to accommodate various food trucks, stages, exhibits, games, and rides.

Since it was easy to access from the neighborhood via the railroad bridge, every summer, Conner and Tennly would sneak down and explore the festivities. Although they remained in the shadows around the perimeter, away from the lights, fearing that being in the open would make them easily identifiable.

This year as she prepared to go with her friends to the homecoming, Tennly spent hours choosing the perfect outfit and styling her hair, wanting to appear cute yet alluring. She arranged her hair in two high pigtails, adorned with an off-white lacy ribbon in each. She wore a casual, loose-fitting, off-white gypsy-inspired mini dress that hung off her left shoulder. A tan leather necklace hung down her chest, complementing her sandals and the concealed knife thigh holster she wore underneath the skirt.

Her makeup featured a gypsy-inspired look, with thick black eyeliner and dark brown eyeshadow creating a smoky effect. In the inner corners of her eyes, she placed small adhesive white diamond rhinestones, along with three larger ones at the outer corners. Her cheeks held a light, shimmering pink hue complemented by matching pink lipstick.

Once they arrived at the Homecoming, Tara and her friends stayed at the main stage to watch a band, while Tennly and her friends wandered around. It had the same feel as the 4th of July carnival, lights flashing, music blaring, and Tennly loved it.

The street was so crowded that it was nearly impossible to see more than a few feet ahead. So, before Tennly knew what was happening Sam picked her up and swung her around. The excitement of the moment caused her friends to step back to avoid getting hit by Tennly's flailing legs.

"Tennly," Sam joyfully yelled, placing her back down on the ground.

"Sam," Tennly replied with a smile. It was great to see him, and she was pleased that he no longer seemed to fear her: in fact, he appeared to like her.

"You look as beautiful as ever," Sam complimented.

"And you, as well," Tennly responded flirtatiously.

Sam winked and cooed, "Ah. See ya."

"Goodbye, Sam," Tennly replied.

Tennly watched as Sam walked away and rejoined his friends. She glanced at Conner, who had witnessed the entire exchange, and wondered how he felt about it. She knew he wasn't the jealous type: at least, he had never been before, but she hoped there was a part of him that would want her more after seeing her flirt with someone else.

Conner was happy that his friend liked her, but his rational mind told him it wasn't enough for him to risk getting closer to her. He simply nodded to say goodbye and then walked away with his friends.

"I'm never going to get used to that," Abby remarked.

The two groups continued walking toward their destinations, unaware that Ty Wheeler was sitting on a bench just out of sight.

After Conner informed him that he and his friends would no longer be doing jobs for him, revenge filled Ty's heart. He witnessed the entire encounter between Sam and Tennly, as well as the look Conner gave her. Not knowing who Tennly was, he snapped a picture of her with his phone and made a mental note that she might be useful to him.

Needing a break from dancing, Tennly and her friends stopped by the table where the boys were sitting with drinks. After quenching their thirst, they headed to the restroom coming face-to-face with The Untouchables, Shelby, and Elena, who were walking in through the front door of Benny's.

Jealousy kicked in which caused Shelby to possessively wrap her arm around Conner. Perturbed by Shelby's gesture, Conner maneuvered himself to get away and as Sam greeted Tennly in his usual cheerful fashion, Shelby let out an angry huff before storming to the game room.

Conner nodded at Tennly as the two groups parted ways, but within half an hour, his desire to see Tennly overcame him, and he found himself in the dance room ordering a drink. Leaning back, he searched the floor until he spotted her. The way she moved was mesmerizing; as she swayed back and forth, her blouse flirted with showing more than he wanted, yet it always seemed to flow back just in time.

Tennly wore a 1970s-inspired white satin spaghetti strap tank top that sagged slightly, making it somewhat revealing. Her outfit included a tight black mini skirt that hugged her figure just below her bottom, and she completed the look with black Christian Louboutin pumps featuring white heels and toes. Her hair was down, styled in teased beach waves, and her eye makeup featured a 1970s-inspired cat eye, complemented by shiny light pink lipstick.

At just the right moment, Tennly turned and noticed Conner watching her. Encouraged by his gaze, she danced even more provocatively. She felt relieved when the song ended, knowing that although he was inviting her over, she didn't want to seem overly eager.

"I'll be back," Tennly told her friends.

They watched as she walked toward the bar and saw who was sitting there. Exchanging worried glances, they knew there was nothing they could do, so they returned to their table to watch. Tennly wedged herself between Conner and another patron and ordered a Shirley Temple. She then turned around, resting her elbows on the bar to present herself confidently to Conner.

"Don't you think you're wearing a bit too much makeup and not enough fabric?" Conner taunted, not looking at her.

Tennly smiled as the bartender placed her drink on the bar behind her. She picked up the glass, stirred it, and took a sip as if sucking on a lollipop. "Doesn't seem to be bothering anyone," she countered, taking another drink.

"You look like a slut," he smirked, half-teasing.

Turning sideways to meet his gaze, she retorted, "I guess you would know, since that's who you like to hang around with these days. The only difference, sluts don't wear $900 pair of shoes."

"No," he replied with a smile. He then slammed the rest of his Coke, leaned in closer, and teased, "But whores do." Then he winked and walked away.

Tennly took a deep breath to steady herself, trying to keep from falling off the stool. They had exchanged some playful banter over the summer, but this was the first time they both felt a charged sexual tension. When she was finally able to stand without feeling dizzy, she began walking back to her table. She got halfway there when she was stopped by Shelby, who had witnessed the interaction between them.

"I thought I told you to stay away from him," Shelby scolded.

"I'm sorry," Tennly replied sarcastically. "Shelby, is it?"

"Yeah, I'm Conner's girlfriend."

Tennly couldn't help but let out a loud laugh as she responded, "Oh, okay."

"So, stay away from him."

"Okay," Tennly repeated, still laughing.

Tennly tried to walk away, but Shelby placed her hand on her shoulder and pulled her back to face her. "I'm serious..."

Before Shelby could finish speaking, Tennly grabbed her arm and bent it painfully behind her back. As she pulled it up into an extremely uncomfortable position, she warned, "Here's the thing, Shelby: you and I both know that Conner will do whatever he wants. Your idle threats at me will not aid in your keeping him. He's not yours to keep. He never was and never will be. So, threaten me again and you'll get your fight. Understood?"

Shelby didn't say anything, so Tennly forced her arm up further, nearly at the breaking point, which caused Shelby to scream out, "Okay!"

Tennly gently lowered Shelby's arm, letting her go as she noticed a crowd forming around them. Among the crowd were not only her friends but also Conner. She shot him a look that clearly conveyed her need for him to keep Shelby away, and then turned to walk back to the table where she and her friends had been sitting. She grabbed her small clutch purse, and as she made her way through the foyer, the crowd began to disperse. Her friends followed closely behind, unsure of how to feel about what they had just witnessed, and occasionally glancing over their shoulders, worried that Shelby might suddenly appear.

"That was awesome!" Abby exclaimed excitedly as they caught up to Tennly by the limousine.

Josie and Lucy looked at Abby, as if to convey that it wasn't awesome but rather dangerous. Then Josie said, "No one has ever talked to Shelby like that."

"She touched me," Tennly remarked.

You need to be careful, Ten," Josie advised. "Shelby doesn't fight fair."

"She can fight however she wants," Tennly nonchalantly replied as she unlocked the limousine. "She'll regret it." Then she gestured for Dougy and Rick to get in. "I'll see you all tomorrow."

T ennly had managed to talk her father into getting tickets for her, Tara, and their friends to see a musical in Cincinnati, on the night the Silver Coin was set to arrive. Relieved to have a reason to be in Cincinnati, Daniel agreed to take the kids to the musical.

Since he was not a well-known individual in Cincinnati, Daniel could not gain access to the Cass Yacht Club unless he had a vessel docked there. So, to accommodate his true reason for needing to be in Cincinnati, specifically the yacht club, Daniel suggested making the trip an overnight one and take the yacht. Tennly, aware of his hidden motive and eager to reach the Silver Coin herself, loved the idea and played along, pretending it would be an enjoyable trip with her friends.

The O'Brien yacht, named, Chéadsearc, a term from old Irish meaning 'my one true love', was dedicated to Daniel's wife. It measured 75 feet and featured three levels.

The top level included an open-air seating area with lounge chairs for sunbathing and a semi-circular couch facing a sliding glass door that led to a smaller indoor seating space with a full bar. The second story, situated at sea level, showcased a spacious garage for four jet skis and a small dinghy, a wide swimming platform, the main living room, a generous dining area, a kitchen, and the master estate room with a full bath. The lower level contained four family bedrooms, a full bath, and at the very end were the staff quarters and a staff bathroom.

All the woodwork was crafted from mahogany, the flooring done in beige marble tiles, and the fixtures were made of brass. The cushions were light beige leather adorned with navy blue and beige throw pillows. Crystal chandeliers hung in the indoor dining rooms, and Persian rugs were placed under every seating area.

By the time the yacht docked at the Cass Yacht Club, everyone was dressed and ready, arriving just in time for dinner. They piled into the limousine that Daniel had rented for the night and arrived at the restaurant with plenty of time to relax and enjoy their meal. It was a French restaurant that Tennly and her family had visited a couple of times and found to be authentic.

Although most of Tennly and Tara's friends came from wealthy families, none of them had ever dined in such a fancy restaurant before. They were all excited about experiencing a Michelin Star restaurant, but Dougy and Rick felt out of place. Their discomfort grew when the waitress approached their table and asked for their drink orders in French.

What was even more surprising was when Tara and Tennly responded to the waitress in the foreign language, having no idea they could speak it. After their drinks were ordered and they began to look at the menus, they noticed that the menus were also in French. Tara and Tennly laughed at their friends' confused expressions as they tried to decipher what to order.

Daniel smiled as he watched his daughters translate the menu for the others. He found it amusing that they had overlooked mentioning that the restaurant they were dining at was owned and operated by French immigrants, who employed staff that also had limited English proficiency.

Feeling his face blush as he tried to find the cost of each item, Dougy leaned over to Abby and whispered, "There's no prices listed."

"That's because anyone who comes here doesn't have to worry about the cost," Abby whispered back.

Tennly overheard them and chimed in, "Just order what you want. It's on us."

Dougy stared back at his menu, nervous and couldn't help but think about his brother in a situation like this. He started to worry that perhaps it would be best if he and Tennly never got together; he could easily imagine his brother getting frustrated and embarrassed enough to storm out.

As uncomfortable as Dougy felt in the restaurant, he surprisingly did not feel the same at the musical. Despite his initial doubts, he ended up enjoying it, wondering if it would be the same for Conner.

They returned to the yacht a little after 11:00 PM. Daniel excused himself to his stateroom while the kids changed into their casual clothes and met up on different levels. Tara and her friends went to the second level, while Tennly and her friends gathered on the upper deck; Tennly wanted to get a better view of the Silver Coin's arrival.

The Silver Coin docked around 12:30 AM, just as Josie and Abby were feeling tired and wanted to go to bed. Tennly informed the boys that she would be back and then accompanied the girls to her room. However, instead of returning to the boys, she took the set of stairs closest to the garage. Carefully, she snuck off the yacht, making sure no one from the Chéadsearc had seen her before moving further away.

She maneuvered her way to the Silver Coin, a small two-level, 25-foot houseboat, without being seen. The interior was filthy, with piles of clothes and trash scattered everywhere. The smell of week-old, spoiled food combined with body odor nearly made her gag. Not wanting to stay any longer than necessary, she quickly scanned every room. Finally, she discovered a large, faded tan duffle bag hidden in the cockpit under the captain's chair.

Upon seeing several guns inside the bag, everything began to make sense. Over the years, her father's and uncles' strange behaviors, combined with the discovery of tunnels under the mansion that led to secret doors, heightened her suspicions about her family's involvement in illegal activities.

After returning the bag to its place, Tennly quietly made her way back to the Chéadsearc just as the boys informed her, they were tired. She escorted them to their cabin and then snuck back up to the top level to watch for her father as he made his way over to the Silver Coin. As soon as Daniel left the yacht, Tennly headed to his stateroom, sat down on one of the chairs facing his door, and waited for his return.

"Tennly," Daniel exclaimed as he walked in and placed the duffle bag in his closet, as if he had just come from the gym. "Did you need something?"

Tennly had rehearsed in her mind exactly what she wanted to say to her father when he arrived. She was going to inform him that she knew he was involved in something illegal, but at the last minute, something told her it wasn't the right time. She had only had speculations about him and the family, but now she had solid proof that she could hold over him if necessary.

"I just wanted to thank you for today," she said as she stood up.

"You're welcome," Daniel replied, sensing that she wasn't being completely honest. "It was my pleasure."

The tension between them was detectable, as they both knew that the other was hiding something. She thought she could keep her thoughts to herself to avoid revealing her suspicions, but when he said it was his pleasure, she felt compelled to respond. She glanced quickly back at the duffle bag and then looked at her father, nodding slightly to indicate that she knew its contents.

"It's nice to know you can spend time with your girls without an ulterior motive," she said sarcastically, before leaving the room.

Tennly's relationship with her father changed after the trip to Cincinnati. Instead of anger causing tension between them, it was replaced by suspicion and distrust. Tara could sense the difference but was unsure whether it was better or worse. The cruel jabs that had become commonplace from Tennly to their father were now replaced with cryptic comments that Tara didn't understand.

Whatever was happening between her father and her sister, Tara knew there was nothing she could do about it. The two of them were remarkably similar, and they were both just as stubborn. The only thing Tara could do was spend time with them individually and hope that eventually, they would work out their issues.

"You ready?" Tara asked as she walked into Tennly's room.

"Yeah," Tennly answered, finishing putting on her shoes.

They were meeting Tara's friends at the park to play a game of mini golf. They took Tara's gunmetal grey Bentley GT convertible and picked up Josie along the way. By the time they arrived at the park, crowds had already gathered at every location.

They parked in the lot beside the pool and walked to the miniature golf course, where Gaylin, Avery, and Mia were already waiting. It took longer to play a round of mini golf than usual due to the large crowd, but they didn't mind, especially Tennly. It was nice to take her mind off Conner and her father and have a good time with the girls. However, it didn't take long before that changed.

As they walked from the miniature golf course to the go-kart track, they heard whispers that The Untouchables were at the basketball court. Tara and Josie hoped they could get to the track before the other girls insisted on going to find the boys, but that wasn't the case. There was no way they would miss an opportunity to see The Untouchables play.

When they arrived at the courts, several kids were already vying for a spot to watch the basketball game. Tara, Tennly, and their friends squeezed into the last available seats on the bottom two benches of a set of bleachers. Other kids were left to sit on the ground so that those behind could see, or they perched on top of the picnic tables surrounding the perimeter.

It was The Untouchables facing off against four other boys, all of whom were going to be seniors that year. As Tennly glanced around the crowd at the many girls with longing expressions, watching The Untouchables race up and down the court, she found it hard to understand the popularity and blatant adoration that Conner had gained over the years.

She was laughing to herself while observing the crowd and didn't notice the basketball soaring through the air in her direction, barely missing her.

Everyone watched as Sam went to retrieve the ball. However, upon seeing Tennly, he approached her instead. He stopped in front of her, held out his hand, and when she took it, he kissed the back of it, saying, "Tennly."

"Sam," Tennly replied, smiling and then someone through him the ball.

As the game continued, Ty, who had witnessed the encounter, walked over to Tennly. He stood beside the bleachers, close to her and her friends, in an intimidating way, and watched the game. He didn't plan to say anything; he simply wanted to see how Sam would react to him being so close to her. To Ty's surprise, it wasn't Sam who stopped playing to come over, but Conner.

"You need to move," Conner threatened.

Ty shrugged and said, "It's a free country."

Conner got in Ty's face, causing everyone nearby to take steps back to get out of the way. "I'm not going to tell you again," Conner demanded. "Move."

Ty held up his hands, laughed, and said, "Okay, okay," then pretended to walk away. Believing that Ty was going to listen, Conner glanced at Tennly as if to warn her to be careful around Ty and started to walk back toward the court.

"I'll just wait to talk to her when you're not around," Ty goaded, turning back to Conner. "If you won't work for me anymore, maybe she will."

A fire raced through Conner's veins at the thought of Ty hurting Tennly in any way. Without hesitation, he spun around, ran to Ty, and punched him in the face. The kids nearby backed up and formed a circle around the two boys as they fought. After exchanging punches, Conner finally got Ty down on his back, banged his head against the ground, and began punching him repeatedly in the face and stomach.

Conner's friends rushed over, trying to push through the crowd to reach him, but nothing they did got him to stop. When Riley attempted to pull Conner away, Conner instinctively swung his arm back and elbowed Riley across the face. They tried again to intervene, but Conner was lost in his rage.

Tennly knew she had to do something. It was because of her that Conner was fighting, and unless she showed him she was okay, he wouldn't stop. As she stepped toward the boys, she heard her sister say, "Ten, don't."

Tennly shot Tara a look that conveyed she had no choice. Pushing through the crowd, she approached until she was just a couple of feet away from Conner, stopping right beside Riley. Riley looked at her, confused and unsure what she could do about

it. She held out her hand to signal him to
be quiet so she could try.

"Conner," Tennly said softly. "It's
okay. Conner... Marks!... Look at me..."
The more Tennly spoke, the less rage Conner
felt, slowing down until he finally
stopped and looked at her. It was as if
they had stepped back into the past to the
days when she was there to ensure his
safety or prevent his anger from
escalating, and he missed that. He missed
her.

She smiled at him as she continued to
say, "That's it... Just look at me, okay?...
I'm right here..."

Conner got off Ty and moved so close
to her that she could feel the heat
radiating from his body. His chest was
rapidly rising and falling as he tried to
calm his breathing. There was some blood
on his knuckles and splatter on his face.
But instead of being scared by his primal
state, which often terrified other girls,
she found him even more desirable.

"Hi," she said softly, smiling at him
as she placed her hand on his left cheek.

He didn't say anything in response.
He was still breathing heavily but managed

to express his gratitude with his eyes, giving her a silent 'thank you.'

She could see the regret, a clear indication that he was sorry she had to see that side of him. She shook her head, signaling that it was okay and that it didn't bother her. Then she used her thumbs to wipe the sweat from his brows before it could roll into his eyes. He grabbed her hands and stepped closer, tears beginning to form in hers. At that moment, they felt a sense of peace in each other's presence, though they were uncertain if it was the right thing to feel. He placed his hands gently on either side of her face, resting his forehead against hers.

They stared into each other's eyes while everyone around them watched, unsure of what was happening. Seeing them together, they looked like poetry; their silent communication revealed the deep love they shared. He lifted his head and gently wiped away a tear that had rolled down her cheek. Everyone waited to see what would happen next. Unfortunately, their moment was interrupted by the sound of approaching sirens.

"Conner, we have to go, man," Riley said, relieved to hear the sirens, as they provided a perfect excuse to pull Conner away from Tennly.

Despite the sirens growing louder, Conner couldn't tear his gaze away from her. They were in a place they hadn't been for a long time, and they feared that if they stopped now, it would be over, but Riley was right. The sirens were getting closer, and if the police caught him there, he would be sent away.

"Go," she urged.

Conner's final look conveyed his love for her, and she smiled back, her expression echoing the same sentiment. But as her tears began to flow more freely, Conner shook his head, indicating he wasn't going to leave her. She placed her hands on his cheeks and insisted, "Go."

He took her hands in his, gave her a nod, and then turned to run off with his friends. Tennly stood there watching him leave, but she couldn't remain idle for long. She still had to protect him, and part of that responsibility was taking care of Ty.

She walked over to Ty, who was resting on his elbows. Leaning over him, she noticed he was bleeding and could hardly move or breathe, but Tennly felt no sympathy. Her only concern was keeping Conner out of trouble.

"Get up," she commanded. When he didn't respond, something dark stirred within her. "Get up!" she screamed, and with that, she struck him across the face with the back of her hand.

Sounds of disbelief echoed through the crowd, accompanied by screams of fear from her sister and Josie. However, Tennly remained composed. She stood her ground, hovering over Ty like an assassin ready to strike.

Ty moaned as a friend of his ran aggressively toward her. She moved out of his way, using her hands to push off from him, grabbed the knife that she had hidden in a belt holster and threw it at the man. With remarkable precision, the knife went through the man's left shoe and imbedded into his foot.

Without any remorse, Tennly marched over to the screaming man, put her left hand on his chest, bent down, and pulled out her knife. Before anyone knew what was happening, she had it held up to his throat as she warned, "Come after me and this goes into your heart."

She stormed back over to Ty, crouched down, and whispered sternly, "I don't think you know who you're dealing with." She swiped both sides of the knife over Ty's shoulder, wiping off the blood from the other man, while also ensuring the blade nicked the side of his neck. "Everyone here may be afraid of you, but I'm not. Who do you think those cops that are coming will believe? Me and everyone else here, or you? So, if I were you, I'd leave before they arrive, or you'll be the one getting sent away."

Seeing Tennly act like that scared everyone present, but none more than her sister and the girls who knew her. It was not the Tennly they knew; it was as if a switch had been flipped, transforming her from caring and compassionate to hateful and vengeful. More troubling was their concern that she was messing with the wrong person. Everyone knew Ty wouldn't hesitate to seek revenge, patiently biding his time until the opportune moment.

Josie and Tara couldn't stop thinking about what had happened at the park. They understood why Tennly felt the need to protect Conner, but they couldn't comprehend how she could throw a knife at someone and not care. They wanted to talk to her about it, but Josie had a sleepover planned for the night after the incident, leaving them little time for a conversation. Their only opportunity to speak with Tennly was the next morning, just hours before the sleepover.

Both girls felt uneasy about confronting Tennly, especially after witnessing her violent tendencies, but they felt they had no choice. Josie arrived at the mansion at 10:00 AM to meet Tara in her room so they could go together for their makeshift intervention.

"Should we wait?" Josie suggested, after hearing that Tennly was in the gym, working out. "Maybe we can get her in a more relaxed environment?"

"When she's working out, she is relaxed."

When they arrived at the gym, Tennly was on the fifth rung from the bottom of the Salmon ladder. They watched as she took a deep breath and pushed herself up to the next rung. They knew not to interrupt her at that moment because it was the furthest, she had ever gotten, and they didn't want to be the reason she couldn't go further. They stood back, remained quiet, and watched her attempt to go from the sixth rung to the seventh. She almost made it, but the left side of the pole hit the top of the rung, and before they knew it, she was on the floor, yelling profanities.

Josie leaned in close to Tara and whispered so Tennly wouldn't hear, "She doesn't sound relaxed."

Tara smiled and nudged Josie to follow her through the gym. Sensing someone behind her, Tennly placed the pole back into the bottom rung and turned around.

Upon seeing her sister and Josie together, she knew they weren't there for a friendly visit. "If this is about last night, I have nothing to say."

"Well," Tara said, "then listen, because we do."

Tennly walked past them over to the boxing ring and grabbed the towel hanging from the bottom rope to wipe the sweat from her face. She wanted to leave the gym and head to her room for a shower, so the fact that they were just standing there in silence was upsetting her.

"Can't listen if you're not speaking," Tennly said, perturbed.

"It's not easy for us, Ten," Tara replied.

"And it's easy for me?" Tennly shot back.

"We know it isn't," Tara acknowledged. "But... it just seems to us that... well... when it comes to Conner, you're not making the best decisions."

"Like throwing knives at people, you mean?" Tennly mentioned.

"For one, yes," Tara replied.

Tennly reassured them that she had no choice and that she wouldn't have thrown the knife if she hadn't felt her life was in danger. Seeing that they weren't going to get anywhere with warning her, Josie cautioned, "Just... be careful. Ty isn't someone you want to mess with, let alone get on his bad side."

"Who is he anyway?" Tennly asked. "And why does he have it out for Conner?"

"He's a drug dealer," Josie explained. "One that The Untouchables have worked for. Based on what he said, it seems they no longer work for him, and he's angry about it. He probably thinks he can get revenge on them by targeting you."

"That's why you need to be cautious," Tara added. "We both know how you feel about Conner... But it's not that simple. Conner has a lot of baggage, and Ty is just one part of it."

"Yeah, I met another one at Benny's a few weeks ago," Tennly acknowledged.

Tara looked at Josie, confused because she didn't understand what Tennly meant.

"Shelby," Josie clarified.

"Jesus, Tennly," Tara exclaimed. "You've only been home for a little over two months, and you already have two of the most dangerous people in town after you."

"They're not the most dangerous in town," Tennly disputed.

"You're right," Tara responded. "Conner is."

"No!" Tennly screamed. "I am!" She noticed the concern and doubt on their faces, so she felt it was necessary to explain herself further. "Neither of you has been around me for the past three years, so you don't really know what I'm capable of..."

Seeing that her explanation scared them even more, she calmed down. "Josie, if I wanted to, I could have thrown that knife in that guy's chest and killed him instantly. What the two of you fail to realize is I am not the one who should be afraid of Conner... or Ty... they should be afraid of me."

The first thing the girls did after arriving at Josie's house for her sleepover was make individual pizzas, which they then carried to Josie's room. They spread out their sleeping bags in a circle on the floor around her bed and sat down to eat.

Tennly and Josie weren't surprised when the conversation quickly turned to the events that had taken place at the park the night before. They exchanged a look that seemed to say, 'Here we go,' and prepared themselves for the discussion.

As Abby and Lucy recounted what had happened, the girls gained a clearer understanding of the situation. However, they were still uncertain about the reasons behind it and the identity of the girl involved.

"So," Tina sighed, "there is a girl?"

"Looks like," Abby replied, just as excited as Tina was about the prospect of Conner being in love.

Fearing that there might be some evidence circulating about what happened that night, Tennly asked, "Wouldn't there be some video or something that could show who the girl is?"

They looked at Tennly as if she should already know the answer as Abby explained, "A few years back a guy posted a video of Conner, and when Conner found out, he beat the living daylights out of him. Since then, no one has posted any videos of The Untouchables."

"But I've seen pictures," Tennly countered.

"Pictures are okay," Abby clarified. "As long as they don't show them doing anything illegal or stupid. But never videos."

Tennly felt a sense of comfort knowing that Conner wielded that much power, enough to make people go against the very culture of posting everything on social media. She couldn't help but wonder what they could accomplish if they ever combined their abilities.

"Weren't you guys at the park last night?" Lucy asked, glancing between Tennly and Josie.

"Yeah," Tennly replied before Josie could respond. "But we didn't see anything.

"There's got to be a way to find out who this girl is," Abby pondered.

The girls discussed possible identities for the mystery girl for a few more minutes, unaware that she was sitting right next to them. After exhausting all possibilities, they shifted to other topics. Finally, they decided to sneak out some alcohol and shot glasses that Abby had managed to swipe from her mother's liquor cabinet and had given them to Josie the previous day to hide.

"It's time to bring out the big guns," Abby announced as she pulled out her overnight bag.

"What's she talking about?" Tennly chuckled.

"The game," Josie answered, giving Tennly a look to prepare for what was coming. "She always gets out the game."

"What game?" Tennly inquired.

They proceeded to tell her about a game they made up a couple of years ago while playing Truth or Dare. When it turned out to be all Truth, they decided to change it to just asking questions. They worked tirelessly during every free time they had writing down any question they could think of on pieces of paper until they couldn't think of anymore. They bought two draw string bags, placed all the pieces of paper in one and left the other for the discarded questions. If someone didn't want to answer the question, they didn't have to but there was a consequence, which they all agreed to be to run around the house, naked.

"Everyone get your shot glasses ready," Abby announced as she passed out disposable plastic shot glasses. Then she looked at Tennly and explained, "Before we start the game, we take a shot. The person who puts their glass down last goes first. After that, we go around the circle clockwise."

Abby counted down to start the game, and they all took their shots, leading to Tennly putting hers down first and Josie last.

"Who was the first person you went to first base with?" Josie read. The girls laughed as Josie reluctantly replied, "Tommy Hendge. You guys know that already."

"Your turn," Abby said, nudging Tennly.

Hesitantly, Tennly reached into the bag and pulled out a piece of paper. "Would you make out with another girl for money?" she read, bursting into laughter. "What kind of question is this?"

"You don't have to answer it," Abby reminded her. "You could always take a stroll around the house."

"Nah, I'll answer it," Tennly said. "I wouldn't kiss a girl for money, shock value... sure."

All the girls busted out in laughter as Tennly passed the bag to Tina. When asked if she had ever stolen anything, Tina shook her head. Lucy commented that the question was directed to the wrong person, as Tina never got into any trouble. The only time she risked it was during sleepovers, and even then, she was very careful.

Lucy's question was if she would make out with a friend's boyfriend which was a good question for her, as she had started dating her boyfriend, Randy, while he was still dating an old friend of hers. After a few questions about Lucy's relationship, Abby looked at Tennly and asked her if she had ever been in love.

Tennly smiled and replied, "I don't have the bag." Then she motioned for Abby to take a question.

They finished the round with similar questions, and thankfully none that led to The Untouchables. Josie was relieved and hoped the rest of the game went as smoothly. The next round began, with Tennly again being the first to lower her glass, but Abby being the last.

"Name a fantasy you have," Abby read after pulling a question from the bag.

Everyone knew what Abby's fantasy was, leading Lucy to grumble, "Just say it and pass the bags."

"Oh no," Abby delightfully responded. "I'm going to cherish this moment and appreciate the game gods for giving me this question... And there is nothing any of you can do about it."

"Fine," Lucy conceded, while the other girls stifled their giggles.

"I want to date an Untouchable," Abby declared. "I don't care which one. They're going to see me from across the room and know right then that I'm meant to be with them. They'll..."

"Aagh," Lucy moaned, interrupting her. "You really need to get a new fantasy. You know none of them are good for you."

Josie sat back, saying nothing. She was relieved Lucy had made that comment, which shifted the conversation to how bad The Untouchables were showing Tennly why she should stay away from them without her having to say it directly.

"It's a fantasy," Abby corrected, her tone shifting to one of sadness. "Because in reality, I know none of them would ever want to be with me."

"Why do you say that?" Tennly inquired.

"That they're not any good?" Lucy chimed in, thinking she was talking about what she said.

Ignoring Lucy, Tennly looked at Abby and clarified, "That they would never want to be with you?"

"Because look at them," Abby responded. "Compared to them, I'm nobody."

"You listen to me," Tennly instructed. "You're just as good as they are. Don't let anyone make you feel lesser."

The third round started off great, and there were no mentions of The Untouchables until it was Tennly's turn. She took a deep breath after reading her question silently to herself. She hesitated to read it aloud, out of fear that she knew what would happen, but didn't want to be the first to quit the game. "If you could date anyone, who would it be?"

Josie shot Tennly a look of concern, while Lucy reminded her of the consequence if she didn't want to answer it. Tennly glanced around at all the girls, considering the options. Then she looked back at Josie, who's expression indicated that she was tired of keeping secrets and believed it was time to tell their friends.

Despite she knew how her friends would react, a mixture of judgment and concern, she knew it was only a matter of time before they found out the truth. The encounters with Conner were happening more frequently, and each time, Conner and Tennly seemed to get a little closer.

So, she shrugged her shoulders and confessed, "I can't keep this a secret much longer anyway." Taking a deep breath, she continued, "Conner Marks."

"Ha!" Abby squealed in a loud, triumphant tone. "Who doesn't?"

"Abby, shut up," Josie interjected, reminding everyone that this was a serious conversation.

"Conner Marks?" Lucy asked, her tone incredulous. "Really, Ten? I thought we warned you about this."

"You did," Tennly admitted.

"Trust me," Abby cautioned. "As much as I talk about them and idolize them, they scare me. It's wise to stay away from them."

"I'm not interested in them," Tennly replied. "I'm only interested in Conner."

"But you don't even know him," Abby pointed out.

"I know him," Tennly responded, annoyed that she had to defend their relationship.

"How do you know him?" Lucy asked, clearly skeptical.

"From the neighborhood," Tennly answered, struggling to tell the full truth. "Over the years."

"But how? You haven't even been here for the last three years," Abby pressed.

"I know him," Tennly insisted.

"But how well could you know him?" Lucy challenged.

"Pretty well," Tennly replied, trying to avoid a deeper argument.

"Then you know he's been to juvy?" Lucy asked.

"Yeah," Tennly confirmed.

"That he's a damn womanizer who treats women like crap?" Lucy continued.

"Yeah."

"Did you know he almost killed a guy?" Lucy went on.

"Yeah."

"That he does drugs?" Lucy imparted.

As the relentless questioning continued, something inside of Tennly built up to a breaking point, and she couldn't take it anymore. Once she started talking, it was as if she had opened a pressure cooker, and all the steam came pouring out.

"Yeah," Tennly thwarted. "Did you know his favorite color is navy blue? Favorite season is fall. He's not afraid to die, he thinks it'd be better than living sometimes.

"He always wanted a dog; said he would name it Steve because it's not a typical dog name. His birthday is April 4th, not April 1st like everyone thinks. He thought it would be funny, given how close his birthday is to April Fool's Day, to play the ultimate prank and change it. He loves pranks.

"He hates people and calls them plastic, which explains his solitude and limited number of friends. He also can't stand authority, but not for the reason most think. It's that authority follows rules without questioning them.

"He loves to read. He enjoys biographies mostly, but he'll read anything. The only thing he truly lives for, his only dream, is to have fun at any cost. He's loyal and honest, sometimes brutally so. He would die for those he loves... and he does love. I've seen it.

"He doesn't like board games or cards, except for poker. He dreams of living on the beach, even though he's never been there. He does have fears, things that scare him: Dougy's future being one."

She glanced around at all the girls, who displayed looks of disbelief and heartache. Their wide eyes and dropped jaws made her smile as she slowed her speech to a finish.

"His favorite tv show is M*A*S*H, favorite food is Mexican, favorite music is heavy metal, though when no one is watching, he listens to classical. His favorite pizza is pepperoni, sausage, and mushrooms. He loves brownies, but they can't have icing on them, and nuts are a must. His favorite action hero is Ironman. His favorite car is a black 1969 Pontiac GTO, and his favorite motorcycle is a Triumph Bonneville: which is how I knew which one was his at Benny's. His favorite movie is Trainspotting, which is ironic when you think about it... And three years ago, he fell in love with a rich girl from the neighborhood. Did you know all that?"

As she felt tears starting to form, she added, "You see, I don't have a crush on Conner. I know all those things because... I'm the girl." She wiped her eyes, stood up, excused herself, and left the bedroom, a huge knot in her throat, and headed outside.

Sitting on top of the picnic table on the side patio, Tennly watched as her friends creeped toward her and sit down as Josie nervously asked if she was okay.

"I don't know. I'm sorry. I just had to get some air."

"We should be the ones apologizing," Lucy acknowledged. "Especially me."

"It's okay," Tennly reassured her.

"How do you know all that stuff about him?" Abby asked.

"He was my best friend," Tennly replied and then told them about her relationship with him.

"So romantic," Tina cooed.

Lucy threw a seat cushion at Tina, as the other girls laughed, which was exactly what they needed to lighten the mood. The only thing was, now that Tennly was able to talk to her friends about Conner, she wanted to learn more about his friends.

She asked them about The Untouchables and what the big deal was with them. Abby did most of the talking, since she considered herself The Untouchable expert. She explained from the first time she ever saw them she saw something different. How they disregarded authority and did whatever they wanted to do. That their confidence was not haughty like most people who with high self-esteem had, and even though they embraced their elevated status, they never reveled in it.

She described how they became known as The Untouchables. How they stick together as a group of four, not allowing others in, and are untouched by anyone, and unfazed by anything.

"They are what we wish we could be but don't have the guts to become," Abby finished. "Just once, I wish I could do something daring... something dangerous. I wish I could stand up and cuss someone out instead of holding it in. The Untouchables are a fantasy: everyone's fantasy. Not only because they're gorgeous but also because they represent the rebellious side of us that we suppress to please everyone else. They don't think about the consequences. Like you said, fun at any cost. Who wouldn't want that?"

"I get it," Tennly said as she felt something inside her pocket vibrate. "It's Dougy. He wants to know what I'm doing."

"Oh, oh!" Abby gushed excitedly. "Tell him to come over."

Josie shot Abby a disapproving look and raised her hands as if to question her about inviting him over so late at night. Abby shrugged her shoulders while Tennly typed a response about where she was and what she was doing.

The girls waited in anticipation for Dougy's response as Tennly read it silently, a scared look on her face.

"Is he coming over?" Abby asked, not able to wait any longer.

"No," Tennly gasped, taking a deep breath. "But Conner is."

"What?" Josie exclaimed. "I can't have Conner Marks come to my house!"

"Why is Conner Marks coming here?" Lucy asked, her expression resembling that of someone who had just seen a ghost.

"I'm in pajamas," Abby fretted. "I can't let Conner Marks see me in my pajamas."

"I don't know," Tennly replied. "Dougy just said he wanted to see me, and he warned that he's drunk."

"We should probably go inside and avoid him," Lucy suggested.

The girls debated about whether they should stay outside or go back in. They realized they had taken too long with the decision when Tina chimed in that it was too late because he was already walking toward them. He was wearing a pair of jeans that hung low, resting just above his pelvic area. His hair was disheveled as if he had just gotten out of bed, and he had a determined look on his face.

"Holy shit," Abby swooned, before he reached them, feeling a wave of nausea from her nervousness.

The closer he got, the more tense the girls became. When he got right in front of Tennly, he wedged himself between her legs, and placed his hands on the table, one on each side of her hips. Tennly felt a tingling sensation all over but kept her composure, sitting as still as a statue as they stared at each other.

"Hi," he said.

"Hi."

"We need to talk," he stated.

"Yeah."

The girls watched as he took Tennly's hand and gently pulled her off the table. His hand was warm to the touch and brought back memories of the safety it always made her feel. However, it also had a feeling of uncertainty, as they walked hand in hand across the yard toward the wooded area at the corner.

"He's holding her hand," Abby said awestruck.

"We see that, Abby," Lucy huffed after she and Tina turned around to watch.

Tennly could sense confliction within him. The tension between them, as she waited for him to explain why he was there, hurt too much, so even though she didn't want to, she pulled her hand away from his.

"You look like shit," Tennly pointed out.

"I don't feel like playing, Ten."

"I wasn't playing," she replied, wanting him to know she could tell he was under the influence of something.

"Why do you do that?" he asked.

"Do what?"

"Blow me off?"

"Me?" she shot back with a sarcastic laugh. "You've got to be kidding me."

"You're the one who left," he finally addressed.

"You're the one who said you didn't love me."

In his drunken state, as if trying to convince himself that he needed to stay away from her, he blurted out, "You're like a goddamn parasite. Or, better yet, one of those viruses that consumes everything."

"Well," she grumbled, taken aback by where their conversation was heading, "if that's how you see me, then we have nothing further to say."

Turning to walk away, he grabbed her arm and pleaded, "Don't."

"What?" she snapped, turning back to look at him and pulling her arm out of his grip.

Unable to hold back any longer, he picked her up, his hands cradling her bottom as her legs automatically wrapped around his waist and her arms around his neck as if they were meant to be there. Before either of them could stop it, their passion took over and they began kissing.

"Oh my gosh," Lucy exclaimed.

"That's it," Abby declared with a defeated tone. "How do you come back from that?"

"I don't think you can come back from something like that," Josie added.

Just when they thought everything was going one way, it took a sharp turn in the opposite direction. He let her go, pushed her away, and then spun around as if he didn't know what to do. she stood there, feeling her chest getting tighter, unsure whether to walk away or ask him what was happening between them.

Suddenly, he stopped spinning as if he had an epiphany and looked at her with the same expression he had given her three years before. "My life is really fucked up right now. You don't want to be a part of it."

"That's my decision."

"I don't want you to be a part of it." He noticed tears forming in her eyes and felt she needed a clearer explanation. "It took me over two years to finally get over you. I was fine until you came back. Now I'm second-guessing everything I do... And in my life, second-guessing can get people killed... God damn it! I can't do this again. So... just stay away from me!"

He didn't give her a chance to reply; leaving her standing there with tears streaming down her cheeks, feeling as if her legs were about to buckle as she held back her desire to chase after him. She looked up at her friends, who were all staring at her in silence. Unable to face them, knowing she would only receive pity, she walked up to them and said, "I'll get my things later. I just... I can't."

CHAPTER 9

After Josie's sleepover, Tennly shut herself off from everyone. She wasn't answering texts or calls and refused to go anywhere. Every time Tara tried to talk to her, Tennly would either walk away or yell at her to leave her alone. Tara had called Josie, who explained everything to her, and yet she still didn't know what to do to help her.

After three days of Tennly's moping, Tara knew she had to do something. She marched into Tennly's bedroom, where she was laying curled up in a fetal position, and sat down beside her.

"You can't stay in bed forever. And as much as I hate to say this, if this is how it's going to be with you here, then maybe you should go back to boarding school."

As soon as she was alone, Tennly stomped to the bathroom and, in a fit of rage, stripped off the clothes she had been wearing since Josie's sleepover and stepped into the shower. When she finally emerged, she had a newfound perspective, determined to show Conner that she wasn't as innocent and fragile as he believed.

For the next two weeks, partying became her salvation. It felt good to numb her emotions; the more dead she felt, the more drugs and alcohol she used. She slept all day and stayed out late at night, until one night, she didn't come home at all.

Worried sick and hoping that Conner might know where she was, Tara grabbed Josie so she wouldn't have to go alone and headed to the Marks' house.

As they sat in Tara's car, they exchanged uncertain glances, silently questioning whether they were really about to knock on his door. After a slight hesitation, they nodded reluctantly, knowing they had no choice, and nervously walked onto the porch and knocked. Holding their breath, they waited.

Conner opened the door wearing only a pair of shorts, sweat pouring down his chest that made it clear that there was no air conditioning in the house. He stared, waiting for them to speak, but they were momentarily tongue-tied.

"Yeah?" he coaxed, hoping to break the silence.

"Do you know where Tennly is?" Tara finally managed to ask after exhaling.

"No," he yawned, rubbing his eyes, clearly having just woken up. "What time is it?"

"It's almost 11:00 AM," Tara answered.

"Maybe she's with a friend," he suggested, his speech slightly slurred.

"She's not," Tara said, growing more nervous the longer she stood in front of him. "We've checked everywhere we can think of."

"Well, I don't know where she is," he shrugged.

"No one knows where she is," Tara informed. "She's been coming home late and under the influence for the last two weeks, but last night she didn't come home at all.

Please, if you care... or cared about her, help me find her."

Conner shook his head as if he wasn't going to help, then went inside. The girls shrugged their shoulders, both thinking he wouldn't come back out, so they started walking toward the car. Just as they stepped off the porch, they heard the door open again. They turned to see that he had put on a shirt, jeans, and shoes.

He walked past them and said, "Go home," before continuing to his car.

He checked the warehouse first to see if anyone had seen her or knew of any parties that had taken place the night before. Learning of one party, where she was spotted, he drove to the house to see if she was still there. By the time he arrived at the house only a handful of kids remained. The person whose house it was, told him she was there but had left earlier that morning.

Conner frantically darted in and out of every street he could think of, asking anyone he saw. Having no success, he reluctantly returned home. When he stepped inside, Dougy was sitting on the living room couch.

"You left your phone here. Tara texted me. Tennly's home and is asleep now."

Conner nodded, feeling relieved, but said nothing as he went back to his bedroom. He sat down on the bed and ran his fingers through his hair, pondering why Tennly would have stayed out all night and what had happened to her.

Tennly had spent the night drinking with Gage Smith at a party, but when they started kissing, Gage pulled back, worried about what Conner might do if things progressed further. Frustrated by Conner's influence over her life and feeling drunk, she left the party. Not wanting to go home and having nowhere else to go, she parked down a dark country road and cried herself to sleep.

When she woke the next day, she sped home and ran to her room, passing Tara along the way. She screamed for her to leave her alone and slammed the door behind her.

Tennly slept all day, waking up just in time to have dinner with her father and sister before taking a shower to get ready for another night out. Unbeknownst to her, Tara had texted Josie to ask if she and Abby could come to the mansion after dinner.

They thought that if they were there when Tennly was ready to leave, they could convince her to go with them and keep an eye on her.

As soon as they got into the limousine, however, they began to second-guess their decision. They realized they wouldn't have ridden with Tennly if they had known she would start drinking the moment they left the estate.

"Ten," Josie said. "Do you really think you should be drinking while driving? You don't even have your license."

"I've been driving since I was nine," Tennly stated. "I'm fine."

Josie looked back at Abby, who shrugged letting her know she didn't know what to do, so they decided to hope for the best and drove in silence all the way to Benny's. Inside they immediately spotted Lucy and Tina at a table in the dance room. Believing they were successful, they were surprised when instead of dancing, as she usually would have, Tennly snubbed their friends and marched off to the game room.

As she wandered around, she spotted a couple of guys from a recent party.

Approaching them, she hoped to find something to help her relax. They handed her a couple of sedatives and mentioned a party they were planning to attend. When she offered to drive them in her limousine, they eagerly accepted.

On their way out, they encountered Josie, who recognized one of the guys, Lucas Spencer. Lucas had a reputation like that of The Untouchables; he was charming and attractive. At one point, he had hung out with them until Conner discovered that Lucas liked to drug his dates to ensure they would have sex with him. Conner didn't tolerate that behavior, and their friendship ended.

Josie pleaded with Tennly to stop so she could warn her about Lucas, but Tennly ignored her and left with the guys anyway. Josie frantically returned to her friends, telling them what had happened, and immediately called Tara for help.

While they were outside waiting on Tara, Conner and his friends arrived. Josie looked at the girls, and they all understood what she was thinking. Taking a deep breath, Josie approached The Untouchables before they could enter and informed them that Tennly had left with Lucas. The news caused Conner to feel as if he had been punched in the stomach. Knowing who Lucas was, his friends didn't hesitate to go with him to find her.

Unsure of where to look, Conner drove while the other three guys texted everyone they could think of to see if anyone had seen Tennly or Lucas. Within seconds, Sam received a tip, and they sped straight to the house party. Conner rushed through the house and up the stairs, desperately shoving people out of the way and throwing open every door. Finally, he found Lucas and Tennly in the master bedroom at the end of the hall.

"Get off her!" Conner screamed as he threw Lucas onto the floor. When he looked at Tennly, she was reaching for her shirt at the bottom of the bed.

"Who do you think you are?" Tennly slurred angrily as she tried to put on her shirt.

"Are you okay?" Conner asked, watching as she finally managed to get her arms in the sleeves.

"She's fine," Lucas said.

"Get out!" Conner shouted at Lucas as he aggressively moved toward him.

However, before he could get too close, Tennly ran over and shoved Conner back a few steps with surprising strength. "Leave him alone!" Then she stumbled out of the bedroom and staggered down the hall.

Conner shot Lucas a threatening look before going after her. Seeing the state she was in, he grabbed her arm and yelled, "Stop!"

She swung around, pulling her arm from his grasp, and hit him across the face as she screamed, "Wha you care? You din't wan me anway, member?"

Conner stared at her, unsure of what to say. He did want her and hated seeing her like this. When he told her to stay away, he truly believed he was doing what was best for her; he just didn't realize how difficult it would be for them both. As she tried to walk away, she stumbled, the effects of the alcohol and drugs she had taken worsening. When Conner reached out to catch her, she pushed him away and screamed for him not to touch her.

The commotion grew louder, drawing a crowd outside the bedrooms and at the bottom of the stairs. The sight of so many people watching her intensified her anger and reminded her of how much he had changed.

She turned around to look at him and goaded, "You car bout me? Then say it." He just stood there. She gave him a maniacal smile and cried, "You no want me cause I'm too precious for you? I... I'm not... precious..." She started to feel dizzy as all her surroundings began to spin.

When Conner saw what was happening, he quickly grabbed her to prevent her from falling down the stairs. However, feeling his touch only made her angrier, and she punched him in the chest while barking, "You don know me!" She attempted to hit him again, but he managed to grab her wrist, turned her around to get a better hold on her, and held her arms to help guide her down the stairs safely.

As they reached the last four steps, she reared her head back just as he reached down to get a better grip on her and struck him in the nose. The impact caused him to let go and combined with the loss of her peripheral vision, she fell down the remaining steps, landing on her back.

She didn't know what came over her other than wanting to prove to Conner that she wasn't as innocent as he thought. She reached into her sock and pulled out her throwing knife. However, as she went to throw it, she saw three of everything and wondered if she would be able to aim accurately.

She could feel herself drifting off as he got closer, and she knew that if she didn't act in that moment, she wouldn't be able to. She focused on the target in the middle and threw the knife. Everyone around gasped in disbelief at the sight of her throwing a knife at an Untouchable. The knife narrowly missed Conner's left foot as he stepped down off the last step, prompting sighs of relief before falling into a heavy silence.

Conner and Tennly stared at each other, realizing how close they had come to seriously hurting one another. He reached down, pulled the knife from the step, and walked over to her. He then placed the knife in his back pocket and extended his hand. Everyone expected her to swat it away, but instead, she accepted it, allowing him to help her up.

Their breaths heavy, Tennly tried to wipe away the blood that was running down his nose. He brushed a strand of hair away from her face and tucked it behind her ear, then ran his thumb across her lips. As he held her chin in his hand, her eyes rolled back, and she passed out. Instinctually, Conner quickly wrapped his arms around her back to keep her from falling and picked her up.

"Find out what he gave her," Conner ordered looking at Sam and then carried her out of the house.

They had just stepped off the front porch when Tara and the girls pulled up. Terrified, they got out and ran toward them, asking if she was okay.

"I don't know," Conner replied.

"What do you mean...?" Tara began, but her question was interrupted by Sam running up to them.

"GHB," Sam informed.

Knowing Lucas's reputation, Tara's concern got worse. "He didn't...?"

"No," Conner reassured.

"Is she going to be okay?" Tara inquired anxiously.

"I don't know," Conner repeated. "She's breathing fine, but she's cold. I won't be able to tell for a couple of hours."

"Shouldn't we take her to the hospital?" Josie suggested.

"I've seen people in worse shape," Conner divulged. "But that's your call."

"Does she need to go to the hospital, Conner?" Tara pressed with a strength in her voice that she and the other girls could hardly believe she used on an Untouchable.

"If you know what to watch for," Conner began, but hesitated as he realized what needed to happen; he could take her home with him.

It was as if they both thought the same thing, recognizing it in each other's eyes, although Tara couldn't believe she was about to say it out loud. However, with her father likely to find out if Tennly went home and the tension that would follow between them, along with her instinct that Conner would know exactly what to do, she felt she had no choice. She took a deep breath at the thought that she was going to allow her sister to go home in a drunken and drugged state with an Untouchable and asked, "Will you keep her safe?"

He nodded and swore, "On my life."

Tara nodded in agreement to show her trust in him and then Conner laid Tennly down across the bench seat in the back of the limousine. He ordered Tara to drive while he settled into the back with Tennly, gently resting her head on his lap. Josie, Abby, and Tina squeezed in across from them, while Lucy, not wanting to be near an Untouchable, chose to sit beside Tara.

They drove to Conner's house in silence as all the girls watched him. He kept running his fingers gently down Tennly's cheek, as if reassuring her that everything was going to be okay. They could see the depth of his love for her in his eyes, but when he looked away as if looking at her hurt too much, they noticed how sad he was.

Despite her nerves, Josie grabbed the box of tissues that was beside her and reached across the limousine to hand it to him. She touched her nose to indicate that he still had blood on his.

Conner had been so focused on Tennly that he had forgotten about his own injury. He took the box of tissues and said, "Thanks," then cleaned up the blood as best he could. "She has a hard head."

"Yeah," Josie replied, even though none of the girls knew what happened.

He glanced back down at Tennly as she started to move and again brushed his hand across her cheek, trying to soothe her.

The girls found it interesting to see an Untouchable exhibiting nurturing tendencies, and they smiled as they continued to watch him.

When they reached Conner's house, Tara stopped him before he carried Tennly inside. "Please, take care of her."

"You mean don't do anything to her," he clarified.

Tara felt guilty for thinking that way, but it was still so hard for her to shake off his Untouchable persona. When she remained silent, he gave her a look that conveyed he understood.

"I'll get Dougy," he said. "He can go with you to get your car."

"Thanks," Tara replied.

He carried Tennly into the house and immediately ran into Dougy, who was sitting in the living room watching television. "Tara's outside. I need you to go with her to get her car."

"What's going on?" Dougy asked, concerned.

"Just go," Conner commanded, as he continued through the living room.

No sooner had he laid her down on his mattress when she started gagging, albeit a good sign that she was going to be fine, it was still a warning that she was about to vomit. The GHB she was given wouldn't allow her to move, so he got on his knees, position her mouth over the side of the bed. When he felt she was finished, he ran to get a couple of wet washcloths and a dry towel to clean her.

By the time Dougy returned home, Conner was confident Tennly would be okay. He told his brother to watch over her for the rest of the night; seeing her like that was too hard for him, but he also didn't want to be there when she woke up. He was afraid that if he were present, it would only make it more difficult to stay away from her.

"This is your mess," Dougy insinuated. "Not mine."

"She's your friend," Conner countered.

"She'll want to see you."

"I can't."

"Why? Because you know why she's doing this? And it's too hard for you to see?"

"Just watch her," Conner pleaded.

Conner left, thinking about how they kept doing dangerous things just to get each other's attention or to forget about one another. What he wanted was for her to move on and live the life she was meant to live. At least that's what he thought he wanted as he found himself returning to the party and engaging in the very same behavior, he had just prevented Tennly from doing.

Tennly woke up the next morning with a pounding headache and had no idea where she was. Once she managed to fully open her eyes, she recognized the room but struggled to remember how she had ended up there. Sitting up, she felt as though her body had been run over by a truck. She placed her feet on the floor and massaged her forehead and temples, hoping it would alleviate the headache. As she looked around the room, she spotted Dougy asleep on the floor against the far wall. She grabbed a pillow and threw it at him; the impact jolting him awake.

"I'd ask how you're feeling, but I know the answer," he yawned.

She groaned as she asked, "How did I get here?"

"Conner."

"He had no right to..."

"Just stop," Dougy interrupted, frustration evident in his voice. "Do you know how close you came to being assaulted last night?"

"What are you talking about?"

"I talked with your sister," Dougy continued, ignoring her question. "She told me you were hanging out with Lucas Spencer."

"So?"

"Lucas Spencer is known for drugging girls. It's practically guaranteed." Tennly stared at him, trying to make sense of what he was saying. "He gave you GHB, Ten. If Conner hadn't shown up, you would have passed out, and Lucas would have raped you."

Tennly could feel her stomach turn as nausea began to wash over her. She ran her hands through her hair and leaned down to rest her head on her knees, as her legs began to shake. Dougy stood up, walked over to her, and sat down on the mattress. He placed his hand on her back as she rocked back and forth, struggling to process everything that had happened.

"I know what you're trying to do, but you will never fit into his world. If you try, it will consume you and eventually devour you."

"But he lives in it," she rationalized.

"Yeah, and it devoured him. You're not going to win him over by entering his world. That world will destroy both of you. If you want my brother, you have to find a way to draw him into your world."

Tara gave her sister a day to regroup alone before going in to check on her. She expected to find her laying in her bed, but when she walked in, she wasn't there. She went to her bathroom, and upon seeing the closet door open, she looked inside and saw her sitting on the floor with a blue shoebox on her lap and holding a piece of paper.

"What are you doing?" Tara asked.

Tennly looked up at her sister, tears streaming down her cheeks. Instead of responding, she glanced down and began reading one of Conner's letters.

"Tennly, I don't know how I'm going to get through this year without you. You've only been gone for a week, but it feels like a month. I have some friends who help, but it's not like having you here. I love my friends, but they don't really understand me like you do. Anyway, I just had a bad night and missed you. Always, Conner."

She dropped the letter and then dumped the rest onto her lap to show her sister just how many there were. Then she reached down, picking a few up and then dropping them back down.

"I am not a giddy teenage girl with a crush on the most popular guy in school. This," she said as she repeated the action of picking up and dropping the letters, "this is real. So, how do you make the love go away? How do you make it go away, Tara? Can you tell me that? Just tell me, and I'll be happy to forget him."

"I don't know," Tara answered, feeling her heart break for her sister.

Tennly wasn't sure if she was ready to go out, but she knew she couldn't hide in her house forever. After a couple of days of rest and meditation, she agreed to meet Josie, Abby, and Tina at the mall.

They did a little shopping before taking a break in the food court. They were halfway through their food, when a couple of boys from school, Nick and Blake, came over to say hello. Tennly started to sense her friends were up to something and her suspicions were confirmed when one by one they started making excuses to leave until she and Blake were left alone.

"Why do I feel like we were just set up?" Blake asked, having no idea about the plan.

Blake Sheridan was in the grade above Tennly and her friends. He was a football player and very attractive, with short dirty blond hair shaved on the sides and big dark brown eyes. He had a youthful face that all the girls loved and came from a wealthy family that parents would approve of. He was the perfect match for someone like Tennly, and her friends thought it was time for them to meet.

"Because I think we were," Tennly said, blushing, not just from embarrassment, but also from anger. "Remind me to kill my friends. I'm sorry about this."

"I have a feeling my friend is just as guilty," Blake remarked. "Well, since they went to all this trouble... I didn't catch where you're from?"

"I'm originally from New York, but I've lived here since I was five."

"I haven't seen you at school. Do you go to North?"

"No, until this year I was going to a private school."

"So how do you know Josie and the others?"

"I've known Josie since I was about eight, I think. I live in her neighborhood."

Blake thought for a moment before inquiring, "I was pretty sure I knew everyone in that neighborhood. Which house is yours?"

"The one on the last street," she answered hesitantly, knowing that would reveal her identity.

"But that's the... Oh," Blake realized, piecing it together.

"Yeah," Tennly apologized. Over the years, she had grown accustomed to feeling sorry for being wealthy; it had become a habit. "I'd understand if you wanted to walk away."

"It doesn't bother me," Blake comforted.

Tennly smiled. Even though she didn't feel an instant connection, it was nice to have a boy interested in her who wasn't intimidated by her or her family. So, when he asked her if she would like to go out on a date, she agreed.

They went on three dates before
Tennly realized that given how quickly
gossip spread in Marinsburg, it was only a
matter of time before her father would find
out. So, she decided to tell him, and, as
she had suspected, he requested to meet
Blake before they went out again.

Blake arrived an hour before Daniel
was due home for dinner, allowing Tennly
to show him around. He was just as
captivated by the mansion's extravagance
as anyone else but wasn't intimidated by
it. After Tennly finished giving him the
tour, they settled down in the game room
until it was time for dinner, in the main
dining room.

The aroma of Marie's roast wafted out
of the kitchen as Daniel offered to pour
each of them a glass of water. Tennly knew
her father's gesture wasn't out of
kindness, as he never poured drinks at the
table: Marie always did. It was his way of
signaling to Blake that he was in charge.
She shot her father a look that conveyed
she wasn't nervous about the inquisition
he was about to subject Blake to, but he
smiled back, suggesting she should be.

The questioning began right after
Marie brought in all the food and left the
room. Daniel asked standard questions any

father would pose to a potential suitor and by the fourth question, Blake started to feel calmer and successfully answered without issue. Tennly listened to their conversation, unable to shake the feeling that all of Blake's responses were mundane, as if he were reading them from a script. In that moment, she found him boring.

Blake was the perfect boyfriend, and she hated it. Yet as much as every answer made her skin crawl, she realized that keeping Blake as her boyfriend was necessary. He served as a buffer, allowing her to divert her father's attention away from Conner. If Daniel believed she genuinely liked Blake and that he was her boyfriend, then perhaps any interactions she had with Conner would go unnoticed.

After they finished dinner, Tennly and Blake went out to a movie while Daniel retreated to his office to handle a few business matters. The most pressing issue concerned some news about a few corrupt cops in a small town in New Jersey.

"This couldn't have come at a better time," Jimmy proclaimed over video chat. "With the new route going right through that area, it'll be crucial to have employees we can depend on." He waited for Daniel to respond, but noticed he was staring off into space. "Dan... Daniel, can you hear me?"

"Yeah," Daniel replied as he refocused on his laptop screen.

"Everything okay?" Jimmy asked.

"I don't know," Daniel pondered.

"Is it Tennly?"

"Yeah. I met her new boyfriend tonight."

"And? What's he like?"

"He's perfect."

"That's good."

"No... no, it isn't."

"So... perfect isn't good?"

"Tennly doesn't like perfect."

"Maybe this means she's getting on the right track."

"Tennly knows what she's doing. Her dating him is a smokescreen."

"For what?"

"Doesn't matter," Daniel said, shifting the topic. There was no need to disclose anything about Conner to his brother-in-law. "About the new employees...

it'll be good to have some we can trust.
You know what to do."

"Of course. What are you going to do about Tennly?"

"Nothing... for now."

THEATER
Pizzeria

CHAPTER 10

Out of all the spectacular birthday parties Tennly had experienced, she was most excited about her upcoming 16th birthday. It surpassed even the time her father rented an amusement park, hosted a carnival at their home, or took her to Disneyland. This year, she was looking forward to having a simple birthday party with just her friends.

However, turning 16 was a significant milestone, which meant she had to include both sides of her family in the celebration. To compromise, she spent the day with both the O'Briens and the Connollys so they could celebrate with her and watch her open their gifts.

Among all the presents she received, Tennly liked the one from her father the best. Daniel surprised her with a fully restored mint-condition 1969 International Scout in a vibrant hugger orange. Tennly had first seen an International Scout when she was eight years old while on a trip in Mexico and had always dreamed of owning one.

Despite her excitement about the car, she couldn't shake the feeling that it might be a bribe. Since their trip to Cincinnati, Tennly and her father had been tiptoeing around each other, as if both were waiting for the other to break the silence about unspoken issues.

Regardless of her conflicted feelings about her father, Tennly enjoyed her time with both families and appreciated all the gifts she had received. Although, she felt a sense of relief when her friends started to arrive. Once everyone was gathered, Daniel gave a heartfelt toast celebrating friendship and supporting Tennly as she embarked on a new adventure: starting public school. He then dismissed the young people to the pool room for the main party.

The food was catered from one of the O'Brien restaurants, featuring sliced flank steak, butterfly shrimp, dinner rolls, and a fully stocked baked potato bar. Additionally, Marie had prepared an array of finger foods and baked two cakes: one white cake with raspberry filling and raspberry buttercream, and a three-layer German chocolate cake, which was Tennly's favorite.

They ate first and then swam for a couple of hours before returning to eat cake and open gifts. Her friends insisted on giving her presents, even though she had told them not to and mentioned that she didn't need anything. Nonetheless, they bought her gifts anyway. Josie got her a t-shirt from her favorite department store, Abby chose a cute pair of sandals, Tina bought her several different colored ribbons she could use for her hair, Lucy, having the same idea as Tina, gave her assorted hair ties in various shapes, colors, and themes, and Blake gifted her a delicate gold bracelet with a small gold letter 'T' on it.

After finishing the planned activities in the pool house, everyone went to their designated rooms to change out of their swimsuits. All Tennly's four friends and her cousins, Victoria and Patience, were staying in her room. Marie had Thomas set up six cots around Tennly's bed, forming a large circle.

Down the hall and around the corner
from Tennly's room were the guest rooms.
Dougy and Rick shared one room, while Blake
and Randy, Lucy's boyfriend, occupied
another. They all understood that the
girls would take much longer to get dressed
than the boys, so Tennly told them they
could head to the game room and wait for
the girls there.

When the boys arrived in the game room,
Marie rolled in carts filled with small
desserts and bite-sized hors d'oeuvres.
She placed them next to the bar and told
the boys to help themselves before she
left.

Giddy about having more food, the
boys fixed their plates before settling
down in the seating area. It didn't take
the girls as long as expected. They all
managed to shower, put on their loungewear,
and join the boys within an hour. As soon
as Tennly told everyone they could play
with anything they wanted, the boys jumped
off the couches and sped to the video games,
knocking each other over as they went.

Soon after, Dougy asked Tennly where
the nearest restroom was. Being a good
hostess, she escorted him out of the game
room and pointed him toward the restroom
down the hallway. Dougy didn't actually

need to use the restroom although he thanked her and went inside. After a moment of waiting for Tennly to walk away, he snuck up to the room he was sharing with Rick.

Once in the guest room, he went straight to his backpack sitting on one of the beds. He opened it and pulled out a box wrapped in brown paper. Unbeknownst to him, the cameras placed throughout the mansion were capturing his every move, and Daniel and Thomas, seated in the office of Thomas's apartment, noticed his actions on one of the monitors.

"Should we do anything?" Thomas asked after they saw Dougy sneaking around upstairs.

"No," Daniel replied, looking at the monitors. "Let him go. Just keep an eye on him for the rest of the night. I have to go to the Inn."

Due to Tennly's party, the Connolly families, who were in town, did not stay at the O'Brien mansion as they typically would. Instead, they chose to stay at the O'Brien owned, Appalachian Inn. Daniel didn't plan to be there for long, but he needed to discuss a few things with Jimmy and John.

After an hour of playing in the game room, they ended the night by watching a movie in the theater. It was a small theater with five rows, each containing five yellow plush recliner seats on the left side of the room and a four-foot-wide walkway was located on the right. It was decorated with pale yellow walls and gold pillars. Scarlet red curtains adorned either side of the 30 feet by 25 feet movie screen, complete with gold tassel tiebacks.

When the movie was over, Tennly walked the boys to their rooms, while the girls went to her room. Busy in Tennly's bathroom, the girls were doing their nightly routines and didn't notice the brown package on Tennly's bed until they settled down on their cots.

"What is that?" Patience asked, being the first to mention it.

"I don't know," Josie replied. "Maybe her dad or someone left a gift for her."

"No," Victoria informed. "She opened all the gifts from family earlier."

"Wonder what it could be then," Abby inquired.

Tennly walked into her room, laughing and saying, "I swear, boys are idiots. This is..." But her smile faded, and she halted when she noticed the brown package.

The girls could tell that the sight of the package stirred up feelings in Tennly that they thought had faded since she started dating Blake. They watched her closely as she sauntered anxiously toward her bed and sat down. She eyed the box with trepidation, as if it were a bomb waiting to explode, afraid to touch it.

"I can't believe it," Tennly whispered, loud enough for everyone to hear.

"What is it?" Josie asked.

Tennly knew what it was and who it was from. But how could he do that to her? It had been almost three weeks since she had last seen Conner, and she had finally started to feel normal again without him. Her friends had even stopped discussing him and warning her about him, and she wasn't sure if she was ready to face it all again. His gift only made things more confusing than they already were. By giving her a gift, he had extended an invitation without having to admit his true feelings.

"Ten," Josie said, getting Tennly's focus back on them.

"It's from Conner," Tennly answered.

Hearing that brought back all the feelings her friends once had about Tennly and Conner. Josie felt an instant surge of worry. Abby got excited about the possibility that maybe Tennly and Conner weren't over each other and she could still have a chance at becoming a friend to an Untouchable. Lucy couldn't help but feel scared, while Tina smiled at the potential for romance.

"How do you know?" Abby asked after realizing that no one was saying anything.

"See those?" Tennly replied, pointing to the seven stuffed animals. "They all came in the same brown paper wrapping."

"Those are all from Conner Marks?" Abby blurted out in disbelief.

"Yeah. Every year on my birthday, Conner gave me a gift wrapped in the same brown paper. I think it's from brown paper grocery bags or something... He never forgot my birthday: not once."

"Not gonna lie," Lucy confessed. "This is freaking me out."

"If you think you're freaking out," Tennly countered with a smile, "you should be inside my head right now."

Josie hated that Conner had done this. She knew his gift would only make Tennly question everything, from Conner's intentions to her relationship with Blake. She had hoped that Tennly had moved on from Conner enough that something like this wouldn't affect her, but the look on Tennly's face told Josie that she wasn't over him.

"I wonder how it got in here?" Victoria asked, breaking the silence.

"Dougy," Tennly assumed. "It's the only thing that makes sense."

"Are you going to open it?" Abby asked.

Tennly smiled, nodded and then slowly opened the package, half savoring it and half afraid of it. Delight finally befell her as she pulled out a 10-inch stuffed gargoyle.

"How cute," Tina remarked, as delightful 'ahs' could be heard around the room.

"What you fail to realize, Tina," Victoria pointed out, "is that Tennly loves gargoyles. Just look at all her figurines."

"Does Conner know that?" Lucy questioned as the others glanced around the room.

"Yeah," Tennly replied, tears of joy forming in her eyes.

"Doesn't he have a gargoyle tattooed on his right arm?" Patience inquired.

"Yeah," Tennly answered, giving them a knowing look that implied there was only one reason he would have gotten it.

"Wait a minute," Patience said. "Doesn't he also have a red rose tattoo?"

"Yup," Tennly answered, aware of where her cousin was headed with that information.

"So?" Abby replied.

"Tennly's favorite flower is the red rose," Victoria explained, smiling at Patience for bringing it to their attention.

"Unbelievable," Lucy muttered.

Tennly smiled at her friends as she placed the stuffed animal on her lap and peeked back into the box. Inside, she discovered one more item: a stack of letters wrapped with a rubber band, topped with a piece of paper. She carefully put the stuffed gargoyle back into the package, choosing not to mention the letters to her friends. After placing the box underneath her pillow, she spent the rest of the evening chatting about anything except Conner. Once everyone had fallen asleep, curiosity got the better of her. She pulled out the letters and began to read them by the light of her phone's flashlight.

Ten,

I went by your house to see if you had left yet, but you were already gone. Man, I wish you were here so we could talk.

Always, Conner

Ten,

You're never going to guess what happened at school today. I wish you could have been there to see it. I think we made quite an impression, especially since we're new to high school this year. The cockroaches were everywhere! You would have loved it!

Always, Conner

Ten,

Jesus. Why aren't you here? I can handle my father much better when you're here. Hurry up and get home, will you?

Always, Conner

Ten,

I've been staying away from the house for a few weeks. I had found this place a little while ago but never stayed there. The guy who runs the place is really nice and has given me a room. So, I don't have to be home when dad's there. Anyway, I'm going to go. I need to find something to eat. That's the hard part about staying at this place, finding money. Talk to you soon,

Always, Conner

Ten, I got the keys.

Conner

Ten,

Well, you're coming home tomorrow. To be honest, for the first time, I'm a little nervous. This year has been so shitty. The whole car thing got me on probation. Which sucks because I have this community service thing I have to do, along with all this stupid counseling. But you're going to be here tomorrow, so I'll bitch about it then.

Always, Conner

Ten,

Where the hell are you? I hope you're not mad about what happened last year. Maybe you're as nervous as I am. Hopefully, I'll see you tomorrow.

Always, Conner

Ten,

Well, Summer has started, and it doesn't feel the same without you.

Always, Conner

Ten,

Guess you're not coming back. Going to be at that place for a while. Dad's project is done, and I can't be home with him. So, not sure when I'll be able to write again.

Conner

Ten,

I can't believe you're being such a bitch...'

Ten,

I'm in some trouble. I mean some really bad trouble this time. I don't know what happened. I just catch myself being so angry at you but conflicted and some guy... it doesn't matter. I have my hearing next month, so I don't even know why I'm still writing to you. It's obvious that you don't care. So much for always being here...

Tennly paused after reading the letter and carefully folded it, as if it were a special document that required gentle handling. Tears streamed down her face, and she struggled to hold back a full-on cry.

She placed the letters back into the box while the girls remained asleep. Lying there, she reflected on everything she had read. She wanted to run to him, but she knew she shouldn't. She was dating Blake, a nice guy who never made her cry, but was that enough? She liked Blake, but deep down, she knew she didn't love him. Even as she tried to justify her relationship with Blake, thoughts of Conner consumed her.

Quietly, she navigated her way through the cots, careful not to wake her friends, and slipped into the dressing room where she had hidden the letters she had written to Conner. Then she opened the secret door and made her way to Conner's through the tunnel.

The window to his room was open, and she could hear music coming from inside. She climbed in and saw him asleep on his stomach, wearing only a pair of blue boxers. Feeling her heart pound harder, her hands shaking, she considered leaving, but instead, she slid down the wall onto the floor and watched him. She barely noticed when he opened his eyes since the only light in the room came from a streetlight outside.

"Thanks for the gift," she said.

"I don't know what you're talking about," he denied, giving her a wink.

"Thanks anyway."

He smiled, nodded, and asked, "What are you doing over here so late? Won't you get in trouble?"

"I snuck out," she joked as she stood up.

"You snuck out?" he asked, chuckling as he remembered her stories of sneaking out of the boarding school. "I guess some things never change."

"Shut up," she teased with a smile.

"But why are you here?"

"I wanted to say thanks."

"You could have done that tomorrow," he pointed out.

"I wanted to tonight."

"Well, you said it. Now you can go."

"You're an ass, Marks."

"You came here. I didn't ask you to."

"No, you didn't," she replied. "You just sent me the invitation."

"Is that what you're calling it?"

"Isn't that what it was?"

"What do you want now, Tennly? Ice cream? We're not kids anymore."

"Then why did you send it?"

"I had it from two years ago. I thought I might as well give it to you."

"No... you could have given it to me another time. You could have kept it. You could have even thrown it away... But you gave it to me *tonight*..."

"You're making a bigger deal out of this than it is," he claimed, reaching for his pack of cigarettes that was on the crate beside his mattress.

His shift in positions, revealed fresh bruises on his upper body, arms, and the right side of his face.

"What happened?" She asked after she got closer to him.

"Nothing," he lied, pushing her away. He leaned back into the darkness, making it harder for her to see him.

"Is it your dad? Is he still hitting you?"

"Get out, Tennly."

"Is he?"

Even though it was difficult for him to lie to her, he couldn't reveal the truth. He received the beating during a drug deal for Boulder, and despite everyone knowing how he made money, he wasn't ready to admit it to her. So, he did the only thing he could think of to make her leave: he scared her. He leaped over, grabbed her arms, and slammed her against the wall.

"Look at me. Do you see this?" he screamed, showing her the new bruises and cuts on his body. "I can't get you involved in my life."

"I'm already involved," she exclaimed, feeling as though her breath was being stolen as she struggled to take in more air.

"Not anymore," he replied, letting go of her. "Get out."

"I'll stay out of your life if you stay out of mine."

He brushed back the strand of hair that was always in her face and, with an apologetic look, said, "It's the way it has to be."

"Then stop sending me things. It hurts too much," she nodded and then left through the window.

To resist the urge to go after her, he sat down on his bed and stared at the spot where she had just been sitting. Placed there were the letters she had written to him, stacked as if intentionally left behind to signal that their relationship wasn't over.

Every year, on the Saturday night before the first day of school, local kids threw a back-to-school party on the outskirts of the city. It took place in a large clearing in the middle of a wooded area, and the only way to reach it was via a winding, one-lane gravel road. At the end of the road, there was a piece of land where everyone parked their cars before walking down a gentle slope to sit around a small lake.

All around the lake, there were various bonfires, blankets, and makeshift seats made from logs and crates positioned for everyone to sit. It was a bring-your-own-beverage party, though some people also brought kegs to share.

Tennly's friends had never gone to the party before, and even though they were worried Tennly might see Conner, they were excited about the prospect of attending. The moment they arrived, they navigated through the crowd of partygoers to a bonfire on the right side of the lake, while enjoying music playing from loudspeakers.

Conner immediately spotted Tennly from across the lake. Unbeknownst to him, she had started dating Blake and seeing him with his arm around her ignited a wave of uncertainty and jealousy within him that he had never felt before. In response, he instinctively leaned towards the girl sitting next to him, wrapped his arm around her, and began making out with her. When he realized that, due to the direction of the car headlights gleaming over the lake, he could see Tennly, but she couldn't see him, he abruptly shoved the girl away, causing her to fall to the ground.

He was about to walk back up the hill, to leave, unable to bear watching her being so intimate with another guy, when he saw her stand up, pulling the other girls to follow her.

Curious as to where she was going, he made his way toward the same direction. She had noticed several partygoers starting to jump into the lake and even though they didn't bring their swimsuits, Tennly didn't care and convinced her friends it would be okay.

At the far end of the lake, there was a deck that stretched the entire width, equipped with four pool ladders bolted 20 feet apart. In the center of the lake was a small dock measuring 10 feet by 10 feet, which also had two ladders leading up to it.

Conner watched from just behind the trees, as Tennly and her friends took turns diving off the small dock. They didn't swim much longer because Abby and Lucy wanted to return to the bonfire and back to the guys. Tennly had no desire to return to Blake; she had other intentions.

As the girls retrieved their clothes, Tennly told them she needed to use the restroom and would meet them back at the bonfire. Instead of heading to the designated restroom area, Tennly walked toward the woods, meandering her way to the spot where Conner was lurking.

"For someone who is trying to stay away from me, you're not doing a very good job," she attested, causing him to emerge from behind the tree.

The soft glow of the headlights illuminated over them, allowing him to see every part of her body. The shear wet fabric of her bra and panties left little to the imagination. She noticed his eyes moving up and down, clearly focused on more than just her face.

"Do you like what you see?" she flirted.

He not only liked what he saw, but he wanted it. It frustrated him that despite every logical part of his brain urging him to stay away, he couldn't help but feel drawn to her. He took a step closer, hoping to scare her, and threatened, "You don't want me to like what I see."

She smiled at him and countered with, "I'm not afraid of you, Marks."

He leaned in closer until their lips were almost touching and said in a serious tone, "You should be."

He hoped that between her knowledge of his reputation and the undeniable sexual tension between them, she would feel nervous enough to back away. But she didn't. The recent discovery of her family's possible illegal activities, coupled with her suspicion that her skills in throwing knives and martial arts were more than just hobbies, led her to believe that he wasn't the dangerous one. So, instead of backing away, she trailed her finger down the front of his chest, gliding between the two open flaps of his shirt.

"Maybe it's you who should be afraid of me."

He grabbed her wrist to prevent her from touching him: out of fear stepping back, releasing her.

"Next time you don't want to be seen, don't smoke," she advised. "You can spot the cherry from a mile away."

Conner smiled as he watched her leave, retreating to the deck to gather her clothes. His heart fluttered in admiration at how she toyed with him and how confident she was. Once she was out of his sight, he turned and rejoined his friends. "Let's go," he demanded as he walked past.

They were just about to reach their motorcycles when Conner felt a tap on his left shoulder and saw Blake standing there.

"She's too good for you," Blake informed.

Blake didn't know that Tennly was the girl everyone was talking about. He didn't socialize at the local hangouts where other teens gathered, and he ignored anything related to The Untouchables, believing they were beneath him. Instead, he spent the entire summer at the country club and on vacations. He assumed that

Conner viewed her as just another conquest. So, when he spotted them together, he left his friends behind and marched up the hill to confront him.

"Go away," Conner ordered, continuing to walk away with his friends.

"I just thought you should know," Blake insisted, as Tennly's friends and many other onlookers gathered around them. "So, stay away from her."

Conner had repeatedly told himself that he needed to stay away from Tennly, that he wasn't good for her. But hearing someone else say it, especially a rich, pretentious punk, made him furious. He stopped walking, turned around, and got in Blake's face.

"And you're going to stop me?" Conner threatened.

Blake knew there was no way he could physically stand up to Conner, and they both understood that. However, he felt a strong obligation to defend Tennly's honor. "I don't have to," Blake replied. "She wouldn't want anything to do with you anyway."

"Doesn't seem that way, does it?" Conner taunted, realizing the only reason for Blake's confrontation was if he had seen them by the lake.

Blake felt anger boiling inside him at Conner's words, partly because they were true, so when Conner started to walk away, he ran after him and shoved him from behind. He wasn't thinking about his own safety or the very real possibility of getting hurt. All that occupied his mind was his frustration with The Untouchables, who always got what they wanted without any regard for others.

Conner turned around and warned, "You don't want to fight me, Blake. Go away!"

"I just want to make sure you understand," Blake stated, getting in Conner's face.

"You have no idea how much I understand!" Conner screamed. "Get the fuck out of my face!"

Tennly finally made her way through the crowd just in time to see Conner about to punch Blake. "Stop!" She yelled as she gave Conner a look that told him he should know better and then turned back to Blake, saying, "Blake, come on. It's not worth it. How about we go back to my place, okay?"

Tennly's words stung Conner, and the thought of Blake going home with her created an aching feeling in his chest. He had been struggling to suppress his feelings for her since she returned and had never considered the implications of his actions. He leaned in getting within an inch of her face, causing them both to breathe heavily. His gaze was so captivating that at one point, she forgot that Blake or anyone else was there.

Blake couldn't stand Conner's arrogance any longer, so he stepped around Tennly, intending to hit Conner, which snapped Tennly back to reality. She quickly stopped Blake and motioned for him to step back. Her eyes pleaded with both boys to stop. Then she turned back to Conner.

"Don't do this," she softly whispered.

The pain in her eyes made Conner want to tell her he loved her, but he couldn't. Instead, he leaned in as if he was going to kiss her. In that moment, lost in a trance and oblivious to everyone around her, she wanted him to. Her heart pounding in her chest, the tips of her fingers tingling as their eyes locked. She was ready, but instead of kissing her, he leaned in and whispered in her ear, "Keep him away from me."

She caught herself, as her legs began to buckle beneath her, hoping no one noticed as she watched Conner and his friends drive away. When she turned around, she noticed that everyone was looking at her. At that moment, she realized that Blake was gone, and she felt terrible about what happened.

As she drove home, she wondered if someone had told Blake about her being Conner's girl and if that was the reason for their confrontation. She had no idea that Blake or anyone else had seen them by the lake. She noticed that her friends weren't speaking, which was unusual. She had gotten used to them chatting about Conner after every encounter, so the silence indicated there was more going on.

"What do you want us to say?" Josie asked.

"Anything," Tennly replied.

"How about discussing how you acted tonight?" Josie suggested, a disgusted tone in her voice.

"I didn't think I handled it that badly," Tennly said. "I got them to stop fighting. Granted, I probably got a little too close to Conner, but... I was able to keep him from beating up Blake."

"Tennly, you're trying to live two separate lives," Josie mentioned. "Pick one. We are your friends, and we'll support you 100%. But you can't toy with people like you did tonight."

"What are you talking about?" Tennly asked.

"Blake saw you and Conner by the lake," Josie answered.

"Everyone saw you and Conner by the lake," Abby added.

Tennly anticipated feeling nervous about her first day of school, especially with the uncertainty surrounding her relationship with Conner and the added pressure of needing to resolve things with Blake didn't help. She had tried to call Blake all weekend, but he wouldn't answer.

Deciding to give him some space, planning to talk to him at school, she got up early on the first day to give herself plenty of time. She tried on several different outfits, but none felt quite right, so she settled on her favorite, a white, lacy boho-style blouse with bell sleeves that hung off one shoulder. Her skirt was a ¾-length designer rag skirt made of denim, decorated with various shades of white fabric swatches. On her feet, she had white sandals made of braided denim fabric that wrapped around her calves and tied in the back.

She let her hair hang long in messy waves, a couple braids with added beads, ribbons, and the same denim material intertwined. Wanting to keep her makeup subtle, she chose a soft 'girl-next-door' look, wearing light pink on her cheeks and lips, along with soft blue eyeshadow, black eyeliner, and mascara.

She arrived at the school parking lot ten minutes later than planned. As she nervously walked from her Scout to where her friends were standing, she noticed people staring at her. She expected some attention because she was new, but what she was witnessing seemed a bit over the top.

As she meandered through the halls, she noticed just how different public school was from her boarding school. Students were loud, and profanity was heard all over. She had to dodge students as they ran past her, and occasionally she caught a whiff of cigarettes or weed. Surprisingly, she didn't hate it, finding a certain calmness in the chaos.

What she disliked most was seeing Blake hunched leaning into a locker as she walked down the hall. She knew she had to confront him to apologize, but she wasn't looking forward to it, especially since she could feel the stares, as if she were some kind of pariah.

"I'm sorry," Tennly said, after Blake closed the locker door and turned around.

"You're her, aren't you?" he replied, not addressing her apology.

"Yeah."

"I can't compete with an Untouchable."

"You don't have to."

"It doesn't seem that way."

"I have a past with Conner," she explained. "That's all it is. A past. He's not my future."

"Am I?"

"I don't know," she answered honestly, however she knew she needed him. "But I'd like to find out if you'll still have me."

He genuinely liked her, and even though he sensed that she didn't feel the same way, he wanted to give their relationship another chance. She was thankful, and when he took her hand and led her to her first-period class, she felt relieved.

Lunch was just as exciting as navigating the halls. Tennly's friends had told her they would meet her in the quad, so she looked around until she found the right door: through the cafeteria. To her pleasant surprise, the quad was nicer than she had expected. Three walls were formed by the school building, while the fourth consisted of a dense row of trees that seemed impassable.

A sidewalk ran from the cafeteria door around the perimeter of the quad, as well as down the middle, separating the two rows of tables. What she found most interesting was that there were no teachers present in the quad at all.

She spotted her friends, Josie, Tina, Rick, and Dougy, who had first lunch with her, sitting at the fourth table down on the left. She hated that Abby and Lucy wouldn't be able to eat with her but was comforted with the fact that Blake had second lunch. In case she had the same lunch as Conner, she didn't want to feel stifled.

"Hey guys," Tennly greeted as she sat down with her back to the cafeteria door.

"Hey girl," Josie replied. "What took you so long?"

"I couldn't get that darn lock on my locker to open," Tennly giggled.

Tennly enjoyed hearing how everyone's first day was going and particularly liked when Dougy's intelligence came up. She had always assumed that the Marks' brothers were smart, but it was nice to have it verified.

Their conversation was quickly halted when everyone turned in unison to look back toward the door. She braced herself as Conner and Riley came into view and stopped a few feet away from her table. Riley stayed back while Conner approached and told Dougy he couldn't take him home after school and then met back up with Riley.

"Where are they going?" Tennly asked, after seeing them disappear behind the trees.

"The Path," Dougy answered, still annoyed with his brother.

"What do you mean, the Path?" Tennly pressed.

"All the students call it the Path of Freedom," Rick explained.

The students had created a path through the trees that was nearly impossible to see. There was a green ribbon hanging from a branch that was hard to notice from a distance, which kept the few teachers who occasionally peeked out into the quad from discovering it. Once through the opening, the path led to a landing. Beyond that was another path that led to the old part of town, filled with abandoned factories and empty, condemned houses.

"What do they do down there?" Tennly questioned.

"He's either going to smoke a cigarette or skip the rest of the day," Dougy replied.

After school, Tennly was still exceptionally hyper from her first day, that she decided to go to Josie's. While they walked down the second street in the affluent section to the field, they discussed the day's events. Unsure whether it was instinct or an underlying desire to see Conner, instead of returning to Josie's the same way, they found themselves on Conner's street.

Conner was alone; his friends having left a few minutes earlier. Josie hoped they could pass by him without being noticed or without Tennly feeling compelled to walk over. However, seeing him leaning over the hood of his car, wearing nothing but jeans, Josie knew Tennly wouldn't be able to resist.

Before Tennly could make any move toward him, they watched in fascination as he straightened up, grabbed the beer that had been resting on the fender, and took a drink: resembling a tantalizing beer commercial. When he set it back down, his gaze shifted towards the girls as they walked by. Without signaling any interest, he bent back over the engine, pretending to work on it.

"I'll see you later," Tennly said and then walked over to him.

She lingered beside him for a few seconds, inhaling the scent of oil and gas, and feeling the overwhelming masculinity that surrounded him which made him even more alluring.

"Why didn't you tell me?"

He set the wrench he was holding down on the car and replied, "Tell you what?"

"All of it... any of it."

"There's a lot to tell, Ten."

"About the drugs, The Untouchables?"

"Jesus, Tennly." He grunted, half disgusted, half embarrassed. He grabbed his beer and walked over to sit on the front porch steps. As she sat down beside him, he lit a cigarette and said, "The nomenclature was still new back then... I kept the rest from you because... I didn't want you to hate me."

"There's nothing you could have done to make me hate you."

"Could've?" he asked, looking at her with a sideways glare.

"Isn't," she corrected, smiling as they both began to feel more comfortable.

"Are you sure about that?"

"I don't know. Maybe I didn't really know you at all."

"Maybe you didn't."

"It saddens me to think you didn't trust me," she admitted.

"It wasn't a matter of trust, Ten. What's the point of this? Does it even matter anymore? Aren't you dating Blake?"

"Aren't you dating every girl in town?" she retorted, a snarky undertone evident in her voice.

"That's not the same, and you know it," he shot back.

"So, you and I can't talk because I'm dating someone?" she challenged.

"No."

"Why not?"

Not wanting to give her false hope about their potential relationship, he said, "Just forget it."

"Yeah, you're right," she surrendered, standing up to leave. "What's the point in trying to salvage what we had?"

As she started to walk away, he grabbed her arm to stop her. "We were there for each other when we both needed it. I'll always love you for that."

"But...?" She stared at him, dreading his answer. "You don't need me anymore?"

He shook his head, needing her more than ever, but said, "You don't need me."

"But I..." A tear formed in her eye, and she struggled to find the words.

"Sh, no," he consoled, standing up and cradling her face in his hands as he wiped the tear away with his thumb.

She shook her head, signaling that she was going to find a way to be together. "I'll see you around, Marks."

CHAPTER 11

Conner realized that with every encounter he had with Tennly, it was becoming increasingly difficult for him to stay away from her. The only way he knew he could forget about her was to become completely numb.

It was easy for him to maintain this numbness during the first few days of school because his father was out of town, allowing him to stay home. He would go to school during the day and then return home at night to get so high that he would pass out and forget about Tennly. By the fourth day, he had established such a routine with his cocktail of drugs that when Dougy informed him he wouldn't be home that night, Conner felt completely relaxed.

When he awoke to excruciating pain in his back shortly after midnight, he didn't understand what was happening. As he attempted to get up, he felt the same pain radiating across his left shoulder and into his left rib cage. He managed to roll onto the floor between his mattress and the wall, just as he heard his father, who had come home a day early, yelling at him.

"I told you never touch my tools," Kenneth screamed as he ran around the bed and pulled on Conner's legs to get him out and into the center of the room.

Frightened, Conner tried to escape through his window, but Kenneth took his bat and hit him across the legs three times until his left knee popped, and he screamed out in agony. Kenneth then pulled him out of his bedroom yelling the entire time.

He got Conner into the hall, where he kicked him repeatedly in the stomach and face. When Conner stopped moving, he dragged him into the living room, where he had his toolbox sitting on the coffee table. He dropped Conner's legs right beside it and then grabbed a screwdriver from the toolbox.

"You want to use my tools," Kenneth fumed as he thrusted the screwdriver into

Conner's right shoulder. "Here, you can have this one."

Conner screamed as the pain brought him back into awareness. He lay there, trying to think of what to do, knowing that if he didn't find a way to escape, his father was going to kill him. He pulled the screwdriver out of his body, and just as his father was about to use another tool on him, he thrust the screwdriver into his father's Achilles tendon, causing him to fall to the floor, writhing in pain.

Quickly, he shoved the toolbox off the coffee table and onto his father, hitting him in the chest. With little time to escape, he used the coffee table for leverage to stand up and hobbled over to the door, while his father threw tools at him. He opened the door as quickly as he could, stumbled onto the porch, and slammed the door behind him. Unsteadily, he walked toward the steps, but due to his dislocated knee, he buckled and rolled onto the ground.

As he lay at the base of the porch, he heard the front door open. After that, there was only a loud ringing in his ears, accompanied by an intense pain in his upper back and the base of his head. Kenneth had thrown the toolbox with all his strength, striking the bottom of Conner's head, as he screamed for him not to come back inside.

Conner lay there for several minutes before finally becoming conscious. His vision was blurry, and it was difficult for him to keep his eyes open. Somehow, he managed to crawl to his car, open the front door, and pull himself into the driver's seat.

It was difficult for him to drive. Between the drugs, the beating, and his blurred vision, he kept drifting in and out of consciousness. Suddenly, his body was thrusted into the steering wheel as he came to an abrupt stop. Coming to, he realized he had crashed into the gate of the O'Brien Estate.

The impact left a slight opening in the gate, just large enough for him to squeeze through. Before he fully registered what was happening, he found himself halfway down the driveway. Thinking his vision was blurring again, he rubbed his eyes in an attempt to clear his sight. When he opened them, he noticed two men approaching him.

By the time Daniel and Thomas reached the cul-de-sac, Conner could barely breathe. As he saw the men running toward him, panic set in. He began yelling that he would leave, but his mumbling made it difficult for them to understand. When they grabbed him, his screams transformed into pleas for them to let him go. He struggled to break free but kept stumbling to the ground. Each time, they hoisted him back up by his arms.

Tennly was awakened by the commotion outside her open window. Rushing over to see what was happening, she spotted Conner being held by Thomas and her father. Afraid of what they might do to him, she sprinted through the mansion and burst out the front door.

"Get off him," she demanded as she pushed her father away and wrapped her arms around Conner.

"Hi, Ten," Conner mumbled.

"Hi," she responded as tears formed in her eyes.

"I done... look ery... good... do I?" He slurred as his breathing became raspier.

"No," Tennly answered trying to smile.

"Tennly," Daniel warned. "You take him in the mansion, and I will call the police."

She looked at her father, feeling grateful that she had saved all the information she had collected on him to use at just the right moment. A maniacal smile spread across her face as she threatened, "I *am* going to take him inside, and you're not going to do a damn thing about it... If you do, I'll call the police and sing like a fucking canary."

She struggled to get Conner up to her room. He collapsed multiple times, and she had to keep begging him to stay awake and help her support him. The noise and bumping against the walls woke Tara, and by the time she poked her head out of her door, she saw them disappear.

Tara ran to Tennly's door just as Tennly managed to get Conner onto her bed. "Oh my gosh... Ten... What's going on?"

"Get some wet towels."

Conner was covered in blood. His white T-shirt was mostly stained red, except for the lower left side. Where his jeans were torn, the blood seeping through, matted together with the fringe of the fabric. If it weren't for the fact that they knew it was Conner, they wouldn't have been able to recognize him, lacerations covered his swollen face and jaw.

Tara rushed into Tennly's bathroom just as Tennly was sliding off Conner's jeans, revealing fresh bruises and several bloody gashes. His left knee appeared swollen and likely dislocated. Lifting his T-shirt, she saw that his entire left side was covered in a large blue bruise that extended from under his arm down to his hip. He moaned when she took off his shirt and as she tried to comfort him, she noticed the stab wound just below his right shoulder.

"Oh my gosh," Tara gasped, handing the towels to Tennly. "What happened to him?"

She didn't respond to her sister at that moment; the night she had always feared had finally arrived, and she needed to focus on caring for him. She cleaned up as much of the blood as she could and then pulled the bed sheet over him to make him as comfortable as possible. After laying the blood-soaked towels on the floor, she sat beside him, trying to think of what else she could do to help. As she contemplated finding a way to get a doctor, Conner temporarily became conscious. He attempted to move, but she gently calmed him down and told him to rest.

He looked at her and slurred, "He id... it good... dis time, huh?"

Tennly immediately knew what had happened and had to keep herself from acting on her anger. She wanted to leave right then, grab one of her father's illegal guns, walk to Conner's house, and shoot Mr. Marks in the head.

Conner reached up and softly touched her face with the back of his hand. "I love you, Ten," he whispered before passing out again.

Tears streamed down her face as she glanced at her sister, who had mixed emotions about the situation and couldn't believe what she had just heard. She had seen the love on Conner's face the night they found Tennly at the party but hearing him say it out loud made it even more real.

"Watch him," Tennly instructed, knowing she had no choice but to seek help from the only resource she had.

Ignoring her sister's pleas to not leave her alone with an Untouchable, Tennly rushed through the mansion and straight to her father's office. As soon as Daniel and Thomas saw her dash out of her room and down the hall, they knew where she was headed and quickly turned off the monitors to prevent her from realizing they had been watching.

"Get me a doctor!" Tennly demanded as she burst into the office.

"Get him out of the mansion, and I'll call an ambulance," Daniel countered.

Tennly remained calm but became firm as she approached his desk. Daniel wondered what she was doing while he and Thomas watched her intently. She reached in front of him, pushed a button under his desk, and then stepped back as the far wall opened to reveal a secret room filled with weapons.

"Get me a doctor," she repeated as she stared at him.

Daniel nodded and said, "It'll take at least an hour to get a hold of him and for him to get here."

"Then you have an hour," she warned. "One minute over that and I call the police."

"I own the police," Daniel informed, in a tone that told her he was one step ahead of her.

She smiled, thinking that was valuable information for her to keep in mind. Leaning in closer to him, she made it clear that she wasn't afraid of him; in fact, he should be afraid of her. "Test me, Father, and you will lose. You have an hour."

Daniel didn't respond as he watched her run out of the office. But as soon as she was gone, Thomas spoke up. "She could be dangerous. You should send her back to Prague before she does something that could hurt this entire family."

"No," Daniel replied, a slight proud smile on his face. "She's perfect."

"She's threatening to call the police."

"She's discovering her power and strength. She's going to need it."

"I hope you're right."

"She won't hurt this family. Can't you see what she's doing to protect someone she loves? This is what she's been training for her whole life. Get Jimmy on the phone. I need to tell him she's ready."

D r. Pratt was an older gentleman in his seventies. He was petite, with a thick head of silver hair and bushy eyebrows to match. Despite his slim physique, he had a round face with rosy, chubby cheeks that stood out above his grey mustache and goatee. The only elements of his attire that hinted at his profession were the stethoscope around his neck, the medical bag he was carrying, and the large case he was pulling behind him.

Tennly was impressed by the efficiency of the doctor. He worked quickly yet thoroughly, completing all the procedures in just under an hour. Once he finished, he packed up his supplies and searched through his bag until he found three prescription bottles.

"He has a concussion," Dr. Pratt informed, "but that's not the main concern. The dangerous issue is the trauma to the back of his head. I relieved the swelling by draining the fluid, which should allow the hematoma to expand without causing any damage to the brain. The incision needed two sutures. I reset his dislocated knee and wrapped it. I'm surprised it wasn't broken. He needs to stay off it for at least three days.

"He has two broken ribs. They're wrapped... just have to wait for them to heal. The puncture on his left shoulder barely missed his lung, so that wound should heal just fine. It required 3 sutures. His jaw isn't broken, just bruised. He has some defensive wounds on his hands, and his left pinky is broken. I put a splint on it. It should take about three weeks to heal. He also has several lacerations all over his body, but only three required stitches: one above his right knee, one on his left elbow, and one above his right eye. All the stitches are dissolvable."

He handed her the first prescription bottle and explained, "This is an antibiotic. It's intended to prevent infection and is also what's in the IV bag. I'll stay here until the bag is empty, which will take about an hour. After that, I'll return to remove it. He needs to take the antibiotic pills three times a day for seven days."

Next, he handed her the second bottle and instructed, "This is an antiseizure medication. Given the brain swelling, there's a chance he could have a seizure. If he doesn't have one within the next 72 hours, he should be fine, but I want him to take these for two weeks just to be safe."

He then handed her the third bottle and continued, "This is a pain medication. From what I can tell, he has been able to obtain these on his own. It's likely what kept him alive."

"What do you mean?" she asked.

"He's high as a kite. All the instructions are on the medicine bottles." He then pulled out a business card and handed it to her. "If you ever need me, call me. I've been hired by your father to handle cases like this with complete discretion."

"Thank you."

Conner woke up at seven the next morning while Tennly was still asleep. He opened and closed his eyes several times, but his right eye was swollen shut, making it difficult. With every breath, pain shot through his chest, a pounding headache throbbed with each heartbeat, and when he attempted to move, it felt as if cinder blocks were weighing him down.

Lying there and staring at the ceiling, he tried to remember where he was. The last thing he recalled was seeing Tennly. He licked his dry lips and turned his head to the right. When he saw her sleeping peacefully, facing him, a wave of regret washed over him as he wondered what he might have said or done.

As he sat up, it felt like a knife piercing through his ribs. He held his breath to stifle a scream as he placed his hand over the bandage wrapped around his chest. After bracing himself, he stood up, grabbed his jeans and shirt folded on the nightstand, and quietly slipped out of Tennly's room.

He wasn't sure which way to go; He guessed and turn left. He used the wall for support to relieve some pressure off his left leg as he walked down the hallway. When he reached the top of the stairs, he paused to brace himself before descending. Leaning on the banister for support, he successfully made his way down to the foyer and out the front door.

Outside, next to the Mercedes sedan, stood Thomas, who had the back passenger door open and was waiting for Conner to approach.

"Get in," Thomas commanded.

"I have my car..." Conner said pointing in the direction of the front gate.

"No, you don't," Thomas refuted, causing confusion on Conner's face. "It's at your house."

Conner gave him a questionable look as if to ask if he was going to kill him. "If I was going to kill you, I would have done it while you slept. I'm just getting you away from here as quick as possible."

Conner reluctantly got into the car and remained quiet, feeling uneasy about the whole situation, while Thomas continued to speak. "I shouldn't have to remind you; never show up here again."

"No," Conner replied as they drove down the driveway.

Upon seeing the busted gate, Conner remembered crashing into it. A flood of emotions washed over him, with embarrassment being the strongest. He considered offering to cover the repair costs but quickly realized he wouldn't have enough money, so he chose to stay silent.

The day arrived when it was time to take Tara to school and Daniel had insisted that Tennly go with them. She wanted to stay home in hopes of running into Conner to make sure he was okay and taking the medicines she had placed in his jean's pockets, but she also felt obligated to see her sister's college.

In hopes of finding out why Daniel was insisting she go to Boston, Tennly went to see Marie. "Do you know why dad's making me go to take Tara to school?"

"If I were to guess," Marie said as she grabbed an oven mit, "I would say he's going to show you some things that you need to understand. You can't threaten the family and expect it to go unnoticed, Tennly."

"He told you?"

Marie reached into the stove, pulled out the tray of chicken, and placed it on the counter. "He did."

"It's not that big of a deal," Tennly insisted. "Conner was injured, I helped him... That's it."

"I can see the torment and love in your eyes every time you talk about him. Love isn't the only thing needed in a relationship. Your heart can lead you down the wrong path. You're the smartest kid I know. Use your brain and be careful."

Out of everything Marie tried to convey, the only thing Tennly focused on was the fact that she mentioned every time she spoke about him. There was no way Marie could have known about any conversations regarding Conner unless she had been eavesdropping. However, she couldn't imagine Marie or her father hiding in closets or around corners to overhear conversations.

Tennly slowly walked through the mansion, looking around, focusing on every corner, crevice, and architectural detail to see if there was anything out of the ordinary. To her surprise, she noticed small half-inch black shiny holes spaced every so many feet. They were in inconspicuous locations, like in the corners of picture frames or on the newel post of the steps. Spotting them helped her know what to look for when she got to her room. She found one of the holes in the crown molding in the corner beside her bedroom door and became outraged.

The thought of being watched in her bedroom made Tennly angrier than she had ever been with her father. She felt violated and was determined not to let him get away with it, especially if he was listening in.

She dashed to her father's office, but the door was shut and locked. Laughing at his attempt to keep her out, she quickly ran to the nearest room with a tunnel and made her way into the office.

He had one computer monitor on the front desk and three behind it against the wall. Scanning around the room, she noticed a small hole to the right of the painting behind the desk. It dawned on her that her father might be watching her from somewhere else.

"Set it up," Daniel instructed Jimmy over the phone while watching Tennly through a monitor in his bedroom.

"I still don't think this is a good idea," Jimmy replied.

"She's in my office and smiling maniacally at me through the camera," Daniel said, unfazed.

"Our lives will be in her hands," Jimmy apprised. "What if she can't do it?"

"I told you; she's ready," Daniel insisted, keeping his eyes fixed on Tennly as she left the office.

After settling Tara into her private dorm room, Daniel and Tennly said their goodbyes and flew into New York. Phillip was there to pick them up and drove them to Jimmy's estate. It felt strange being there without any of the other kids, who were all away at school. The mansion was quiet, lacking the usual sounds of the boys running around.

They met up with Jimmy and John in the parlor, their hugs feeling different than normal. Each embrace carried a finality, as if they were saying their goodbyes to her. She remained quiet and listened to her father explain her mother's family history.

Then they informed her that her grandfather became the boss after her great grandfather died. More importantly, this advancement made her mother the second-in-command, since her older brother had been killed in a mafia-related drive-by shooting. Tennly found it remarkable that if her mother hadn't died, she would have been one of only a few female mafia bosses in history: the first female boss in the Irish mafia.

However, it was disheartening to learn that her mother's death wasn't an accident. As she listened to their words, her chest tightened, struggling to concentrate as she imagined her mother's fear while plummeting over the ravine.

The men explained how organized crime had evolved over the years and emphasized that it was much harder to get away with illegal activities due to modern technology, and the existence of electronic paper trails. As a result, operations had to be conducted the old-fashioned way, without any correspondence or record-keeping on computers or cell phones. The families had soldiers positioned everywhere, and their main role was to gather intelligence. To minimize risks, Daniel, Jimmy, and John took on most of the jobs themselves, but they also had a few trusted employees they could call upon if necessary.

"That's why I'm away a lot," Daniel concluded.

Her father's explanation helped her understand his absence, and she found the history of her family to be fascinating, and instead of feeling shame, she felt a sense of pride. However, one thing did anger her: her father's hypocrisy. All this time, she had been led to believe that she and Conner came from two different worlds. In reality, their worlds were not that far apart, and as she had suspected, her own world was far more dangerous than his.

She wanted to confront her father about this, but just like before, she put it aside in the back of her mind to use as she needed. Instead, she decided to focus on the family and consider what her role would be within it. She asked about the O'Briens, to which he explained all the businesses and income from his side of the family were legitimate.

"Then why do I feel like you are the boss?"

"Our sister was second in command," Jimmy explained. "When she died, it passed to me. I'm not a leader."

"Nor am I," John added.

"And your father was just a natural at it," Jimmy continued.

"But those aren't the real reasons," Daniel interjected. "I'm not of Connolly blood and therefore can't be the boss... permanently anyway... I'm just holding it, like a regent does for a king."

"For whom?" she asked, her intuition telling her she already knew the answer.

"Your mother left strict instructions in her will," Jimmy declared. "It goes to you."

"She knew, as we all do," Daniel clarified. "That Tara and Vicki won't be able to handle it, and the boys haven't shown any characteristics of a leader. But you, she knew by the time you were two."

"You sensed things that the other kids didn't," Jimmy included. "And you still do, from what your father tells us."

"As soon as your mother died," Daniel added, "I knew what I had to do, and I've been training you this whole time."

"School," she acknowledged, confirming her suspicions that her extracurricular classes were more than just fun. They had all involved some form of fighting or self-defense, strength training, or manipulation techniques.

"Yes," Daniel confessed. "I could have sent you to any school anywhere. I chose that one because it has been used in the family for years for training purposes."

"Am I an assassin?" Tennly contemplated, knowing how skilled she was with a gun and her knives.

"You're a weapon," Daniel corrected. "At least until you take over, and then you will need those skills to keep your throne."

"Do I get a say?" she inquired. It wasn't that she didn't want to be the leader: she did. To her surprise, she felt an innate sense that she was meant for the role. She asked the question because knowing she could choose not to accept it meant that if she did, her word would be law, and her father would no longer have control over her.

"Of course," Daniel answered. "But if you decide not to take it, we need to know before you turn 18 so we can prepare."

"Prepare for what?" she asked.

"We don't need to worry about that right now," Daniel replied.

"Prepare for what?" she demanded, as she tested her authority.

"Who will take over in your place," Daniel replied. "If you don't take the reign, it will be up for grabs."

They continued to tell her that Tara nor any of the other kids knew about the family due to the rule that kids can't know until they turn 18 and made her promise to keep their secret.

"Now, get some sleep," Daniel said. "You're going on your first job tomorrow. Be ready by 7:00 AM; we head out at nine."

Two weeks ago, Jimmy received information from one of their street soldiers indicating that a small group of employees was planning to betray them. This group felt they weren't being adequately compensated for their work and intended to ambush Daniel and Tennly's uncles during their next drop-off. Daniel, Jimmy, and John were uncertain about how many additional men might participate in the coup. In addition to needing to assess Tennly's performance on a job, they believed her extra firepower would be beneficial.

The exchange was scheduled to take place at an abandoned airfield in upstate New York, where the only structure was the airport terminal featuring a control tower.

The next morning, they drove Tennly to the airfield six hours before the meeting time and escorted her to the terminal. Daniel handed her a pair of binoculars, a bag filled with snacks and water, a book to read, a Beretta .50 caliber handgun, and her 10-round competition sniper rifle. He also provided her with an earpiece and a small, wired microphone to attach to her shirt. Since he had made her leave her cell phone at Jimmy's house in New Jersey to prevent tracking, this was their only means of communication.

"If our suspicions are correct, a couple of hours before our meeting, some men should show up to hide around the perimeter. You'll be able to see everything from the tower. All you need to do is let us know where they are."

"I can do more than that," Tennly suggested as she looked down at her rifle.

"The gun is there only for your protection," Daniel clarified.

"If that were true," she countered. "You wouldn't have given me my sniper rifle."

Daniel nodded knowing she understood why she had the rifle and said, "I don't want you to do anything you are not comfortable with, but it's there if we need it."

"Are you sure about this?" Jimmy asked. "You don't have..."

"I'm good, Uncle Jimmy."

"If you need anything," Daniel instructed, "or you sense any danger to you, find a way to get out and run as far as you can."

"Okay," she replied.

"And you're sure you want to do this?" Daniel asked.

"If I don't, it puts you at risk."

"We'll find another way, Tennly," Jimmy added.

"I'm your best bet," she reminded. "You can't let them get away with this, right?"

The three men smiled as the memory came to them of what she had said about taking care of her mother's killers when she was just five years old. Although they were impressed by her strength and bravery, they couldn't shake their reservations about leaving her alone.

Her reassurance was enough for the three men to leave her, and as soon as they were gone, she began to scan the surroundings. The tower was filled with a strong, dusty smell, and as she walked past the windows with broken glass, she caught a whiff of jet fuel. Every corner was covered in dust or cobwebs, making it difficult for her to find a place to sit.

She pulled a rolling desk chair over to the window that overlooked the landing strip, where her father had said they would meet. She laid her rifle on the control panel, along with a pair of binoculars and her book. Brushing her hand over the chair to remove some dust, she finally sat down.

For the first two hours, she read her book, being confident that nothing was going to happen during that period. By the beginning of the third hour, she was starting to feel a bit bored and longed for some excitement. Although she knew she shouldn't, she picked up her pistol and walked out of the tower.

She made her way through the terminal, carefully paying attention to her surroundings, and then went outside to check out the landing strip and the hangar. There was nothing of interest on the landing strip, but the hangar was impressive. Inside, she saw three old World War II biplanes, along with two 20mm cannons resting on the ground beside them. Compelled to investigate the planes, she climbed up onto the wing of the first one she approached and noticed small bullet holes in a straight line along the body. Before she could sit down, a chilling wind blew into the hangar, as if the spirits of the pilots were warning her to leave.

A cold shiver ran down her spine, and she immediately heeded the omen, hurrying back up to her post in the tower. She picked up the binoculars just in time to see two cars pulling onto the landing strip. Five men got out of the first car, and four exited the second. They retrieved several guns from the trunks of the vehicles, and after a few minutes, the drivers climbed back into the cars and drove away.

"Dad, are you there?" Tennly asked into her communication system.

"Yeah," Daniel responded. "Are you okay?"

"I'm fine, but two cars just pulled up and dropped off seven men."

"What do they have and where are they going?" Daniel inquired.

"It looks like they have two .22 rifles... two AR-15s, three MAC-10 machine guns... and some smaller handguns. They may have a couple of grenades as well. I saw them put something in their pockets; that's what it looked like," Tennly explained as she scanned through her scope.

"They mean business, don't they?" Daniel joked with a nervous laugh.

"I suppose they do," Tennly chuckled, then her expression turned serious. "Um... Dad, there are two of them heading into the terminal."

"Tennly," Daniel fretted, growing worried that they might be heading up to the tower. "Hide."

"I love you, Dad," Tennly replied, shifting her focus away from the outside. She quietly placed her rifle on the control panel, picked up her pistol, and aimed it at the door. "But that's not going to happen."

"Tennly, get out of there," Daniel insisted.

"And go where?" Tennly whispered. "If they're on their way up here, it's already too late."

"Tennly..." Daniel urged.

Tennly removed her earpiece so she couldn't hear him. It was stressful enough waiting for the door to open; she didn't need her father's voice adding to her anxiety. She held still, aiming the gun at the door, feeling her heart race and her breaths grow heavier. She had never been this scared in her entire life, but she knew she had to stay focused and be ready for when the men appeared.

Time passed, and the men still hadn't reached her. Just as she was about to open the door to see where they were, she heard voices from outside the window. She turned and peered out to see the two men standing just below her on the terminal roof. A wave of relief washed over her as she sat down in the chair, taking a few seconds to calm down enough to put the earpiece back in.

"I'm fine," she whispered, stopping her father, who was repeatedly calling her name and asking if she was okay. "Dad, I'm fine."

"Oh, thank God," Daniel sighed, taking a deep breath.

"They're on the roof below me," she continued to whisper.

"Where are the others?" Daniel asked.

She scanned the perimeter of the field using the scope of her rifle. "There are two hiding in the grass opposite me... one to the left of them... another on the right behind a large jet engine. And...," She paused, until she spotted the seventh, "there's one hiding inside the crashed Cessna between the road and the terminal."

"Good job, Ten," Daniel praised.

Finally, when the time arrived, two black cars emerged on the horizon. The first car carried her father and uncles, while the second was occupied by three men. A part of her felt guilty for not being closer to the action, and she promised herself that when the moment came, she wouldn't hesitate to take a shot.

The men approached each other and shook hands, as was customary during a transaction. Daniel made sure he and his two brothers-in-law stayed as close to the vehicles as possible without appearing obvious, in case they needed to use them as shields when the bullets started to fly.

John took a large black duffle bag from one of the men, while Daniel asked, "Was it hard to get?"

"Not at all," replied the man in the middle.

"That's good," Daniel said. "Here is your payment."

Tennly noticed movement on the roof and looked through her scope for a closer look. The two men were lying on their stomachs, rifles aimed down toward her father. Tennly glanced at her father, realizing what the men were about to do.

She took aim at the man on the right, and said to her father, "get ready," then pulled the trigger, hitting the man in the head. Before the other man could react, she shot him dead as well.

The two gunshots echoed across the airfield, which caused the battle to begin. Using the cars as barricades, and Tennly in the tower, the enemy fell one by one. After the shooting stopped, Tennly ran down the tower to check on her father. When she reached him, she hugged him tightly, holding on like she hadn't in a long time. The thought that he could have died made her realize how much she loved him, and she couldn't imagine what she would do if something happened to him.

Her uncles rushed over, thrilled that she had successfully completed what they needed her to do. It was because of her they had minimal injuries; John being shot in the left arm. While Tennly was gathering her things, Daniel, Jimmy, and John collected all the deceased bodies and placed them in the back seat and trunk of the employee's car, then called a cleaner to get rid of any DNA.

After finishing her shower, she went through the motions, feeling numb as she got dressed, pulled her hair into a ponytail, and walked back to the main sitting area of the jet, where her father was still waiting for Jimmy and John to return from disposing the bodies.

"You did well today," Daniel said as he took a sip of whiskey. "It could have turned out much worse if you hadn't been there."

Instead of addressing her father's comment, she blurted out, "Am I a sociopath?"

"Oh honey," he comforted, putting his arm around her. "No, of course not."

"I killed five people, and I feel nothing for them."

"You killed five people who were going to kill us. There's nothing wrong with that."

Before she had a chance to consider anything her father said, Jimmy and John barged into the jet, "We have a problem," Jimmy blurted out and then threw the large black duffle bag on the coffee table.

After seeing the contents of the package, small bright yellow pills with a pressed beetle on each, Daniel explained to Tennly that it was ecstasy, and it was stolen. They rarely stole any merchandise; It was too risky, and when they did, it was only from lower-ranking suppliers who didn't have the manpower to retaliate. The ecstasy sitting in front of them came from a ruthless family that wouldn't take any excuse. They manufactured and produced their own supply and would recognize it if any of it ever reached them.

"We have to destroy it," Jimmy suggested.

"And lose all that money?" John asked.

"We can't sell it," Jimmy mentioned. "It'll get traced back to us and they'll find out."

"Then we have to crush it, divide it and put it all in individual baggies," Daniel recommended. "Half a gram a bag. And then sell it in small rural areas where no one knows about this brand."

"We've done that before," John pointed out. "Should work."

"Yeah," Jimmy agreed. "But there's too much. A gram bag would be quicker to sell."

"But not as safe," Daniel countered. "The bigger the quantity, the more chance of someone being able to recognize it."

They discussed how many employees they had and how many would be needed to sell the product as quickly and discreetly as possible. If they divided the bags into ½ gram portions, they would need ten different locations across the United States. Currently, they only had nine employees living close enough to rural areas to cover these locations. They could operate in those nine locations using 1-gram baggies, but this would take longer to sell and involve significantly higher risks.

"Put it in the ½ gram bags," Tennly said after listening quietly to the men. They looked at her with question in their eyes as she continued, "I know someone who can sell the tenth supply."

"Hanging out with drug dealers, Ten?" Jimmy asked, half-teasing.

"No more than you," Tennly retaliated with a smile.

"It's too risky," Daniel said. "It's too close to home."

"Is that really the reason?" Tennly questioned, knowing the truth.

"Can you trust this person?" Jimmy asked.

"Yeah."

"Enough to know they won't tell anyone where they got it?" Daniel pressed.

"I trust them with my life."

"It's worth a shot," Jimmy remarked.

"Well, you don't know him," Daniel replied, fully aware of who Tennly was referring to.

"And neither do you," she snapped. However, instead of getting angry as she normally would, she tapped into her inner leader. "It's not a question of whether you trust him. If I'm going to be running this family one day, you're going to have to trust me."

She locked eyes with her father until he finally gave in. "Okay. Set it up. But if he fails or gets us caught, I will kill him."

The first place Tennly checked for Conner was the warehouse. Dante informed her that Conner had been there but left that morning after he could move better.

"Can I offer you some words of wisdom?" Dante said.

"Please do."

"Conner's a honey badger." Tennly looked at him with confusion. "Honey badgers are fearless and passionate. Their aggression makes them some of the most formidable animals in the wild. They care deeply about their family, and they'll fight fiercely to protect those they love, without regard for the consequences."

"That sounds like him."

"Yeah, but a honey badger can't be tamed. No matter how many times people try to capture them, they never stop attacking their captors. As long as you try to tame Conner, he'll keep running away from you. Instead, you need to find a way to let him stay wild, and then he'll come to you."

"Thank you," she said, understanding exactly what Dante meant.

Feeling defeated and having nowhere else to search, she headed home, passing by Conner's place and then Riley's. As she drew closer, she spotted him sitting in Riley's garage with Sam, Joel, Riley, Shelby, and Elena. Tennly noticed how beaten up he still looked. Although his injured eye was open, it remained swollen, and the visible stitches above it were a stark reminder of his injury.

When Conner saw her step off her motorcycle at the end of the driveway, a knot formed in his stomach. The feeling intensifying the closer she got to him.

"I need to talk to you," Tennly said. "It's important."

Seeing the grave urgency in her eyes caused him to begin to worry. Without hesitation he got up and followed her back to her motorcycle.

"Are you ok?" He asked before she could speak.

"I need a favor... No questions asked."

"What is it?"

"I need to get rid of some drugs."

"What?" Conner couldn't believe what he heard. For years he had tried to keep things like that from her and he hoped he heard wrong.

"Can you help me or not?"

"What is it? How much do you have?"

"Four Hundred, ½ gram bags of ecstasy."

"Jesus," he sighed, worried about what she had gotten herself involved in. "How did you get it?"

She couldn't help but think of the honey badger and how accurate Dante was comparing Conner to the animal. She knew he asked not because he cared about how she got it, but more concerned about the person putting her in harm's way and could see in his eyes that he wanted to kill the people responsible.

"No questions," she reminded. "And it must be people who you can trust... with minimal exposure and in low populated areas, spread it out... that would be best."

"That's a little harder," he stated, getting even more worried.

"I know."

"I'd have to ask a few people but yeah I think so."

"When will you know?"

"Maybe by Friday?"

"Okay."

With the impending sell looming over them, Conner didn't want to leave her; this intense desire to protect her overpowered his thoughts. She felt the same, as if she was about to send him into the lion's den.

"Are you feeling better?" She asked, hoping to alleviate the tension.

"Yeah," he answered. "Thank you for..."

She held up her hand to stop him. "You don't need to..."

"And you don't need to take care of me anymore."

Tennly patted his chest and then got on her bike. He put his hands on the handlebars as if trying to keep her from leaving and asked, "Tennly, is it your dad?"

"Be careful," she stressed, not answering his question, which told him it was her father, and then she drove away before he could say anything.

CHAPTER 12

It was Friday, three days after Tennly had asked Conner for help, and as she sat in the quad during lunch, watching him and Riley walk by on their way back from the landing, Conner gave her a look that indicated he wanted to talk to her.

She waited until the boys entered the cafeteria before excusing herself, unsure of her feelings about what he had said. If he couldn't sell the product, it wouldn't look good for him in the eyes of her father. She nervously glanced around finally spotting him walking toward her.

"I found three people to take it," he whispered. "That'll make it more difficult to trace. Two of them live hours away, and the one who lives close has a way of distributing it that won't get traced back to you... or here."

"Thank you. Can you meet me at the ice cream parlor after school?"

"Yeah."

She rushed home immediately after school and went straight to her father's office. She couldn't wait to see her father's reaction when she told him that Conner had found three buyers. Expecting impressive gratitude, her heart sank when he showed no signs of how he felt about it.

He handed a blue backpack to her and instructed, "When he gets the money, have him put it back in the backpack and place it in the mail slot at the front gate."

"Okay," she responded, draping the strap over her shoulder as she stood up.

"Be careful."

"Always."

If she was honest with herself, she would admit that she felt more than nervous driving her motorcycle through the neighborhood with a backpack full of ecstasy. But it was that very nervousness that exhilarated her. By the time she got in line at the ice cream parlor, she was so filled with adrenaline that she couldn't hold still.

"Is it still a small vanilla dipped in crunchies?" Crunchies was a mix of sprinkles and finely chopped nuts.

"Yeah," Tennly replied, smiling as they stood in line. "And you are a large chocolate dipped in chocolate?"

"Yeah." He smiled back at her.

After they got their cones, they walked over and sat at the same table they always chose. They ate their cones in silence, both acutely aware of the thrill that stemmed from the contents of the backpack between them. They had always felt comfortable in silence together, but as they sat in anticipation of getting caught, the infatuation between them intensified.

To ease the tension, she assured, "I promise I won't bother you again after this is over."

"You don't bother me Ten."

"I'm sorry I put you in this situation. I wouldn't have asked if..."

"If I didn't want to help," he interrupted. "I wouldn't."

She tilted her head in a shy, seductive manner and said, "I know."

He reached over and brushed the strand of hair that had fallen across her face behind her ear. He enjoyed their closeness but withdrew his hand as she shook her head, letting out a lighthearted laugh as if to convey that they were a step closer to rekindling their relationship.

They finished their ice cream cones in silence, occasionally stealing playful glances at each other and sharing joyful giggles. Once they were done, she slid the backpack closer to him.

"When you get the money," she directed, "put it back in here and drop it off at the mail slot in the front gate of the estate."

"Your place? So, it is your father..." he began.

"No questions," she interrupted, giving him a look that he was right.

It wasn't until the following week that Tennly heard anything else about the package. She was working on homework when she was called into her father's office. Daniel and Thomas were sitting on the couches, sipping bourbon. She walked in uncertain of what to expect. Had Conner sold it? Did he sell it for enough? Was it not enough? The anticipation was almost too much to handle.

"We just received the money," Daniel informed.

"That's good," she sighed, relieved that Conner had managed to do it.

"Yes, it is," Daniel affirmed. "What's even better is that he sold it for nearly double what we wanted." A sense of pride began to surface within Tennly as Daniel continued. "Not sure if he's really smart, really lucky, or just really good at selling drugs." He then picked up the envelope that was lying on the coffee table and handed it to her. "Whichever it is, here's his fee."

"What do you mean?" she asked, confused.

"Everyone who does a job for me gets paid a percentage," Daniel explained. When he noticed her curiosity about the envelope, he added, "There's $50,000 in there."

"He won't take it," she stated, trying to hand the envelope back to him.

"He doesn't have a choice," Daniel objected. "If word gets out that I didn't pay someone, my reputation, and possibly my life, are on the line. That's just something you need to learn. Make sure he gets it."

She nodded, then started to leave the office when Daniel commanded, "And after that, I don't want you seeing him again."

She closed her eyes and took a deep breath to calm her anger as she walked to her bedroom. She reflected on her father's words and found them to be senseless. She had genuinely believed that if Conner sold the drugs, her father would see him as trustworthy and finally allow her to have a relationship with him. For her father to tell her to stay away from Conner felt like the most hypocritical thing he could do.

She had a hard time sleeping that night, worrying about the possibility that what her father said was a threat. As she lay there, it became clear that what she had previously thought, that their two worlds had swapped, wasn't just a notion but a reality. As soon as morning arrived, she rushed to her father's room, hoping to catch him before he left for the day.

"I just wanted to clear something up," she started. "Most of my threats to report you and this family have been just words. But there is one time when it won't be, and that's regarding Conner. Don't think I didn't notice that what you said last night was a threat. I may not fully understand how this works yet but let me warn you... if he turns up dead or missing, I will not accept the leadership of this family... I will want nothing to do with it... or you."

"I'm only trying to keep you safe."

"Yet I have a family that puts my life in danger just for being part of it."

"He's going to amount to nothing and could drag you down with him. You are too important, and we can't risk anything..."

Tennly laughed and interrupted her father, saying, "Heed my warning, Father.

I'm not lying." She then got up and walked out.

She felt a little better after speaking to her father, even though she wasn't sure if it had worked. Not seeing Conner's car in the neighborhood, she drove to the warehouse. It was still early, so when she arrived, most people inside were still asleep.

She cautiously opened his door and found him lying on the bed, asleep, with a naked girl beside him. He was on his back, wearing only a pair of boxers, while the girl lay on her stomach, her right arm draped over his chest. Her long black hair cascaded over her back, and the wrinkled sheet barely covered her behind.

A lump formed in Tennly's throat at seeing him, yet again, with another girl, especially in that way. She tried to swallow her feelings, but as she walked over to him and noticed a needle and a bottle of pills on the end table, her sadness turned to anger.

She kicked him in the stomach, disregarding his injuries, and firmly yelled, "Wake up!"

He moaned, placed his hand on his stomach, and replied, "Go away, Dougy."

She couldn't believe how pathetic he was being, so she kicked him again. "It's not Dougy, Conner. Wake up!"

"Gawd!" he grunted, as he sat up and placed his feet on the floor.

His eyes were still closed as he ran his hands over them to help wake himself up. When he finally became conscious enough to understand that Tennly was standing there, he initially felt happy to see her, but that smile quickly faded when he noticed the disappointed look on her face. He suddenly remembered the drug paraphernalia on the nightstand and the naked girl in his bed.

"What are you doing here?" he slurred.

Before she could respond, the girl sat up, pulling the sheet over her chest. Tennly glanced at the girl and then back at Conner, her glare making it clear that the girl was a problem, and that she wouldn't continue as long as she was there. Conner opened his mouth to tell the girl to leave, but before he could say anything, she stood up.

"What's going on?" the girl asked.

"Get out!" Conner and Tennly shouted in unison, recognizing their similarities.

"Fine," the girl huffed. With that, she dropped the sheet and gathered her clothes.

Afterward, Tennly shook her head and let out a sarcastic chuckle, rolling her eyes at the entire situation. She pulled out the envelope containing the money and handed it to him, explaining, "Here's your payment for helping me out."

"I didn't do it for the money," he replied as he stood up.

Tennly noticed that he was still favoring his knee, barely putting any weight on it. His chest was still bruised and black and blue, and the puncture wound on his shoulder was healing; though it remained red with a bright purple circle around it. The bruises above his eye and at the base of his jaw still lingered and he was no longer wearing the wrap around his chest or the splint on his pinky.

"He pays everyone who works for him," she said, trying to hand the envelope back. "So, just take it."

"I'm not taking it," he maintained, pushing it back towards her.

"It isn't a choice," she insisted. "He won't take it back."

"Then you keep it... Buy yourself a new dress or something."

There it was again, the same issue that always came between them: her wealth. She was tired of defending her financial situation to him. If he wanted to play that game, she could too. She walked past him and placed the envelope on the nightstand, then turned to look at him.

"I don't need that money to buy me a dress, Conner. I get that amount in allowance every month. So, why don't you take it and buy dresses for all your whores."

He wasn't sure if it was because she had brought up how wealthy she really was or because she had pointed out that he slept around, but he could feel his entire body grow warm as if lava was being pumped through his veins. To relieve the pain, he screamed and punched the cement block wall with his right hand; Tennly jumped.

"Fuck!" he screamed, flexing his fingers to make sure they weren't broken.

He grabbed the envelope off the nightstand with his other hand and crumpled it up, throwing it across the room, but before he could say anything, Dante came running in.

"Everything alright in here?" Dante asked, looking between the two of them.

"Yeah," Conner claimed.

Then Dante turned his attention to Tennly. "Are you okay?"

"I'm fine," she responded. "Thank you."

Dante gave Conner a look that indicated he should keep it down, and then he left the room, closing the door behind him. They stood there in silence, unsure of what to say or do. Tennly needed to find a way to convince him to keep the money, so she grabbed the crumpled envelope and straightened it out.

"You are the most stubborn person I know, Marks. I don't care what you do with it, but I can't take it back." She laid the envelope on the bed behind him and then gave him the saddest look he had ever seen from her. "Shoot it up, snort it, or swallow it, but you have to take it."

Disheartened and embarrassed, he just stood there, watching her walk out. Although he told himself he wasn't going to open it, curiosity got the better of him and wanted to know how much she received every month for her allowance. When he pulled out the stack of money and counted $50,000, he couldn't believe his eyes. There was so much he could do with that kind of money, but he didn't want to feel indebted to her father.

He was uncertain about what to do until he went to put the money back in the envelope and noticed a small piece of paper inside. This is what was written:

Rules for Your Payment

1. Don't buy any high-priced items.

2. Don't spend it all in one place.

3. Don't put it in the bank.

4. Don't invest it in stocks or any other investments.

5. Don't flaunt it around or tell anyone about it.

6. DON'T GO NEAR TENNLY AGAIN!

Daniel didn't think much about the payment he made to Conner. He truly believed that someone of Conner's socioeconomic status and reputation wouldn't hesitate to keep the money. However, when Thomas came into Daniel's office holding an envelope, confusion set in.

"Tenly said he wouldn't take it," Daniel replied as Thomas handed it to him.

"View it as free labor," Thomas suggested.

"No," Daniel said, shaking his head and realizing Conner had issued a challenge, as he opened the envelope. "He is intriguing, I'll give him that."

Wrapped around the top of the stack was a new piece of paper; It read:

Rules That You Can Shove Up Your Ass

1. Take the money and shove it up your ass.

2. Take the envelope and shove it up your ass.

3. Take the note and shove it up your ass.

4. Take your job and shove it up your ass.

5. SHOVE YOUR RULE ABOUT STAYING AWAY FROM TENNLY UP YOUR ASS!

After he handed the note to Thomas he admitted, "I don't know whether to kill him or take him out for a beer."

"He is colorful," Thomas agreed.

"He's a problem."

"Want me to take care of him?"

"As much as I want to tell you, yes... there's something that keeps me from doing it."

"Tennly?"

"Maybe."

"What do you want me to do?"

Daniel kept the piece of paper, put the money back into the envelope and then slid it across the desk over to Thomas and told him to tell Tennly to either find a way to get Conner to keep the money or he would send her back to Prague.

Thomas met Tennly at the breakfast nook the next morning, after Daniel left for work. She found it strange that Thomas sat down at the table and knew something was wrong. She took a drink of her orange juice and then gave him a suspicious look.

"Don't tell me," she played as she held up her hands in a stopping motion.

"Let me guess... um..." Then rhetorically and in a sarcastic tone she joked, "You ran out of food in your apartment?... no no no... you're secretly in love with my father and need to find a way to tell him?... no..." Then she got serious. "He doesn't have the courage to face me himself, so he sent you. What does he want?"

Thomas had remained quiet through Tennly's rant. He knew she needed to get it off her chest but also found her wit and snarkiness amusing and enjoyed listening to it. After she was finished, he told her what the outcome would be if she couldn't get Conner to keep the money. Then he walked away, leaving the envelope on the table.

She struggled to find a way to convince Conner to keep the money. All she could think about was how stubborn both he and her father were being, which made her realize just how similar the two of them were. She repeated, 'They're so much alike... They're so much alike.'

She felt a surge of satisfaction for coming up with the perfect plan and shot up to Thomas's apartment located above the garage for help. Since she rarely visited, Thomas immediately knew she wanted something.

"Wait," Thomas mocked, raising his hands in the same manner she had done with him earlier. "Don't tell me..."

Tennly smiled, waiting for him to finish.

"You're here because you're secretly in love with Marie and need help finding a way to tell her... no, um... no, no, no... Marie is on strike and is no longer catering to your every whim..."

"Okay," she interjected, showing that she enjoyed his teasing but prompting him to stop.

"What do you need?" Thomas asked, opening the door wider and gesturing for her to come inside.

"You can procure things, right?"

"I can," he replied.

She handed him the envelope with the money and said, "I need you to buy a black 1969 Pontiac GTO in mint condition. Black interior, if possible, but dark gray will suffice."

"That's a very specific order, and not one that will be easy to fulfill."

"Can you do it?"

"For $50,000? I don't know. Maybe. I have some contacts who owe me favors. I'll see what I can do, but it'll take a few days."

"Thank you," Tennly said, giving him a hug before leaving.

Once she was gone, Thomas exited his apartment through the door that led upstairs, minimizing the chance of running into her again. When he reached Daniel's office, he found Daniel on the phone, so he paused at the door to wait.

"What do you need?" Daniel asked after finally getting off the phone.

"I told Tennly to find a way to get Conner to keep the money."

"Good. Did she understand?"

"She did. She came to me for help with it, but I thought I better check with you first."

"What is it?"

"She wants me to get a black 1969 Pontiac GTO in mint condition... black or gray interior."

Daniel smiled and said, "She's smart."

"Dan, if he starts driving around in a car like that, everyone will be curious about how he got the money. It's a high-priced item."

"It's a gift. That means she either thought it through or instinctively knows how this works."

"I don't see how..." Thomas trailed off.

"If people start asking questions, it can easily be explained. Like I said, it's a gift."

"So...?"

"Get the car."

Thanks to some connections, Thomas was able to acquire the car for exactly $50,000. The problem Tennly faced now was how to not only get it to Conner but how to get him to keep it. She couldn't take it to any of Conner's friends or drive it to school because that would raise too many questions. She hesitated to bring it to Conner's house, unsure of how his father would react and knew he would never come to the mansion to pick it up. Which left the warehouse.

She honked the secret code and hoped it was still the same from when she was there with Sam. Relieved upon seeing the garage door open, she pulled the GTO inside. The thunderous roar of the engine created such a commotion that several people gathered around the car. As Tennly placed the ignition key, the door key, and a slip of paper into an envelope and sealed it shut, she noticed the crowd forming, among it was Dante.

"What a sweet ride," Dante said as he stopped beside her.

"Thank you," Tennly replied. "Is Conner here?"

"I haven't seen him," Dante answered, as he continued to encircle the car.

She appreciated a nice vehicle, she loved her Scout, but it always amused her how men could spend hours just staring at a car. It wasn't like the car would transform into something different right before their eyes; after all, the engine was the same as it had been twenty minutes ago.

"Could you do me a favor?" Tennly asked after Dante stopped beside her, still focused on the GTO.

"Depends on the favor."

"Would it be okay if I left the car here for a few days?"

"Sure," he replied with confused expression.

She handed him the envelope and said, "Can you give this to Conner? The next time you see him?"

"Yeah." He wasn't trying to pry, but he could tell there were keys inside the envelope, which left him puzzled. He gave her a knowing look.

"Sh," she grinned, signaling him to keep her secret. "Goodbye, Dante."

The following night Conner showed up at the warehouse, immediately noticing the black Pontiac GTO. It felt extremely coincidental that the exact car he had always wanted was there and knew it had something to do with Tennly.

"Beautiful, isn't it?" Dante asked standing beside Conner. "She's a strange girl. Here." Handing him the envelope he added, "Told me to give you this."

Conner opened the sealed envelope and poured its contents into his hand. The piece of paper reading:

Try to stick this in the mail slot.

"Shit." He then tucked the note into his front right jeans pocket. He walked around the car, tracing the curves with his fingers as if he were caressing the contours of a woman. Out of sheer curiosity and admiration, he opened the hood. Inside was a RAM Air IV engine with 370 horsepower, featuring round exhaust ports, special cylinder heads, and unique camshafts: making it the ultimate muscle car.

Shutting the hood, he moved on to the inside and was immediately enveloped by the smell of new leather; it felt like heaven. His body melted into the seat as if it had been custom-built for him, most captivated by the dashboard. It looked as if he had just stepped back in time, complete with a vintage radio and speakers.

More than anything, he wanted to take it for a spin, but he refused to give Tennly the satisfaction. He shook his head, as he really wanted the car, but the thought that Tennly was using what she knew about him made him reluctant to keep it. Besides, he knew this was her way of making him accept the $50,000. Not to mention, after sending the money and note back to her father, he didn't want to appear hypocritical or allow him to win.

After asking Dante if he would watch the car, he got into his old car and drove away. He thought about marching right up to the O'Brien estate and demanding to see Tennly, but remembering Thomas's warning to stay away from there, figuring he would be shot on sight. Instead, he called his brother. When Dougy told him he was with Tennly at Benny's, he hung up and immediately drove to see her.

He pushed through the crowd, which was exceptionally large that night, as he made his way to the dance area. He had to walk up and down the dance floor, a task he disliked, until he finally spotted her.

Seeing her beauty momentarily distracted him from why he was there. Her hair hung in wavy ringlets that framed her face, swaying as if blown by an artificial wind. She wore a little black backless mini dress with spaghetti straps. The skirt being so short that one wrong move could reveal more than he wanted.

He stormed over to her, grabbed her arm to get her to turn around and yelled, "We need to talk!"

Tennly glanced at her friends and told them she would be right back before walking off with him. They walked across the dance floor, as if escaping a fire, and into the foyer, where it was quieter.

"I'm not keeping it," he stated.

"And I told you, I can't take it back."

"Well, I'm not taking it. If you insist on it, I'll drive it to a cliff and push it off."

"You really are stubborn, Marks."

"Maybe." He tried to hand the keys to her, but she refused to take them.

"How about we make a bet?" she suggested.

"What are you talking about?" he asked, intrigued with the idea.

"A game of pool," she proposed. "If I win, you keep the car. If you win, I'll personally push it off a cliff for you."

He paused for a moment, considering how to respond. He genuinely wanted to keep the car, and making a bet would give him a valid reason to do so.

"I would really hate to see such a beautiful car pushed over a cliff," he confessed, even though they both knew he would never actually do it.

"Then just take it."

"But... I can't play your dad's game. So... I'll agree to the bet on one condition."

"What's that?"

"A secondary wager." After further consideration, he realized he didn't want to engage in a bet where there was no real sacrifice on her part. Plus, he wanted to demonstrate that when she played games with him, he wouldn't make it easy for her. "To be determined after we each get a turn."

"Why?"

"Take it or leave it, Ten."

She knew too many suspicions would be raised playing Conner a game of pool for nothing and they could make the secondary bet look like the only one, so she agreed.

Conner dismissed the two players currently at one of the tables, insisting they leave so they could play. Tennly wasn't bothered by his disregard for the other players; in fact, she found it appealing. There was a certain comfort in knowing that when he wanted something, he had the power to get it.

Once all the balls were on the table, he pulled out a coin and asked, "Heads or tails?"

"Tails," she replied.

As he flipped the coin, whispers of their upcoming game spread throughout the establishment and reached Tennly's friends. Immediately they ran to the game room, followed by several others, eager to watch Conner and Tennly play.

"Tails it is."

"You break," she responded. "You need the advantage."

"I thought for sure you would want to since you're used to breaking balls," he teased.

Tennly's friends arrived at the pool room just in time to hear Conner's comment. They squeezed through the crowd to get as close as possible, laughter echoing around them.

"Yeah," Tennly bantered. "But the balls I'm used to breaking aren't that big."

The crowd was unsure whether to laugh or remain silent, resulting in a mix of reactions. No one typically spoke to Conner like that other than his friends, leaving onlookers uncertain about what to think.

"Just rack," Conner chuckled.

Two striped balls went in on the break, and he pocketed a third before missing. She made two shots but couldn't make a third because the cue was behind a striped ball, missing the shot. Conner had four balls left while Tennly had five when he reminded her it was time to place the second bet.

"Ladies first."

She had been contemplating what to wager ever since he suggested it. Knowing him like she did she knew that whatever his second bet was going to be, she wouldn't like it, so she had to come up with something just as intolerable.

"If I win, you have to attend school for 30 consecutive days without missing a single day or class."

Conner heard the 'oohs' and 'ahs', the giggles and cheers, along with some loud bursts of laughter, and instead of feeling embarrassed or angry, he felt enjoyment. She had thrown down the gauntlet, and he wasn't going to back down.

Giving her a challenging look, he asked, "Are you sure you're ready to play this game, Ten?"

"I've been ready for three years," she countered, knowing he wasn't referring to the pool game.

He stepped up, leaning into her in a seductive manner. "If I win," he insinuated, placing his right forefinger in the middle of her chest, just above her cleavage, "You," he pointed at himself, "and me... in the back seat of your limo for a half-hour."

The crowd fell silent, with only gasps and whispers breaking the stillness, as Tennly didn't hesitate to respond. "That's all the time it takes you?" More 'oohs' and 'ahs', snickers, and laughter erupted as she concluded with, "Tsk... I guess all those rumors are just to stroke your ego."

He gave her a look that indicated he had made that bet for a reason. She could see the mischievous intent on his face as she followed his gaze behind her and then back to her, signaling her to turn around.

Even before she turned, she knew what she would see. In the excitement and thrill of the bet, she had forgotten that Blake was supposed to meet her there after finishing dinner with his family. She closed her eyes, then opened them as she turned around and saw Blake standing there. Feeling terrible about what he had overheard, she gave him an apologetic look. But it didn't matter; it was too late. He shook his head before leaving.

She looked at her friends with an apologetic expression, unsure if she truly felt sorry and then turned back to Conner.

"You're a dick, Marks."

"Yeah," he replied seriously, leaning closer to her. "You need to learn not to play so close to the fire."

Just as seriously, she retorted, "I am the fire."

He curiously nodded, not knowing what she meant, and then turned back to the game. He made three shots before he missed, leaving him with one ball and the eight ball. He stepped back to give her room for her turn.

As she leaned over to line up her shot, he teasingly said, "Don't *fuck* up." She recognized it as a play on words and gave him an annoyingly disgruntled, yet flirtatious look.

She had five balls left on the table, plus the eight ball, so it wouldn't be easy, and everyone thought it looked dismal, except for her. All the balls were laid out perfectly, which allowed her to make them all, one by one, causing the crowd to erupt in cheer.

Without hesitation, she laid the cue stick down on the table and put her hand on Conner's chest. "I'll see you at school on Monday."

Having no desire to confront Blake and after multiple attempts to contact him, Tennly finally gathered the courage to go to his house. She was greeted at the door by his sister, Bridget, who shot her a furious glance.

Bridget was going to be a senior that year and knew The Untouchables all too well. Tennly's friends had informed her that the year before, she had fallen prey to Conner, and after sleeping with him, he never called her again.

"What do you want?" Bridget asked, making it clear that Blake had told her about what happened at Benny's.

"Is Blake here?" Tennly replied, trying to keep her anger in check.

"What do you want?" Bridget repeated.

"Is he here or not?" Tennly snapped.

Bridget stepped aside to let Tennly in and said, "You don't deserve him."

"You're right," Tennly agreed as she walked past Bridget and straight to Blake's room.

The door was open, and he was sitting at his desk working on homework. She hadn't paid much attention to his room before; She couldn't help but notice how perfectly ordered it was. Everything was in its place, as if it were a display room in a furniture store. In that moment, she realized she wasn't there to repair their relationship; she was there to end it.

"I'm sorry," she apologized as she sat down on his bed.

He sat down beside her, feeling a tinge of sadness, but mostly disappointment. "I really like you, and I thought we were having a good time. But I told you I can't compete with Conner."

"I never meant to hurt you," she confessed, not bothering to correct him.

"I know," he replied. He leaned over and gave her a hug, then added, "Just be careful, okay? He's not known for long-lasting relationships. Or any relationship for that matter."

"So, I've heard. Thank you for everything. You're a great guy, and you make the perfect boyfriend... but..."

"I'm not Conner..."

She smiled and corrected, "I'm not the perfect girlfriend... Goodbye, Blake."

"Goodbye, Tennly."

When Tennly arrived at school on Monday, she saw the GTO in the parking lot. A sense of joy washed over her, knowing that she had played a part in helping him achieve something he had always wanted.

However, the joy faded as she noticed the usual stares she had grown accustomed to appeared different. She could see, by the expressions on her friends' faces as she approached her locker, that they knew why and told her everyone thought that she and Conner had sex in her limousine the night at Benny's.

"You're kidding?" Tennly laughed, finding the rumor amusing.

"Nope," Josie confirmed.

"Well, this is going to be an interesting day, then, isn't it?" Tennly alluded with a hint of sarcasm.

Interesting wasn't even close to how the day unfolded. As she watched Conner and Riley walk through the quad toward the path, an overwhelming urge to follow them took hold of her.

The path looked different than she had expected. It was clean and well-maintained, with trees arching overhead like a canopy. Looking like the Jurassic Period, with vines and branches cascading down the trunks. The path sloped downward and opened into a landing that was almost a perfect thirty-foot oval. Several cut tree trunks surrounded the perimeter, providing seats for the kids.

The air was filled with the pungent smell of damp moss and pine, mingled with undertones of marijuana and cigarette smoke. Tennly was surprised to see so many students in the landing and right in the middle were Conner and Riley.

Riley wasn't pleased to see her; it felt like she was invading their territory. However, he realized there was nothing he could do to prevent what was about to happen. He took a final puff from his cigarette, and then stomped it out as he said, "I'll see you later."

Conner was already on edge, so seeing Riley stop in front of Tennly made him feel nauseous. His first instinct was to go over and intervene, but he knew Riley needed to express whatever feelings he had to her.

"He's more fragile than he looks," Riley declared.

"I know," Tennly replied with a soft, reassuring tone.

"Just don't hurt him," he warned, as if he understood he could no longer keep the two of them apart.

"I won't," she said. Then after Riley passed, she walked over to where Conner was standing. "Hi."

"Hi," he replied while taking a puff from his cigarette.

He smiled at how adorable she looked. She was wearing a cute pink lacy swing dress with flared sleeves, paired with lacy knee socks and white Chuck Taylor Converse shoes. Her hair was down in the back while up on the sides in little buns, with strands of hair sticking out from each.

"Only twenty-nine more days to go," she mentioned as she felt her stomach do somersaults. The uncertainty of what would happen next was more stressful than when she had given up hope of becoming friends altogether.

"Yeah," he grunted.

Afraid that if she stayed much longer, it would cause more damage, she said, "Well, I'll just leave you to..."

"Don't," he interrupted her.

"What?"

"Come down here and then leave. Don't."

"Okay... What did you tell your friends about the car?"

"That I'd been saving, did a job for someone, and stole some money from my dad."

"And they believed you?"

He chuckled a little and admitted, "Yeah, but they didn't believe I had the ability to get it. So... I told them you helped me. With your resources or whatever..."

"You always said I had resources."

"You got the car, so...," he replied.

They had never had trouble coming up with conversation topics in the past. So, as they stood there in silence, it felt different to them, causing the tension to grow.

"Riley doesn't like me very much, does he?" she asked, knowing she had to find a topic before it got too awkward.

"He'll get over it."

"I really should go... I'm sure there's another rumor brewing as we speak."

"You heard that, huh?"

"Yeah."

"Sorry, that's just collateral damage when you hang out with me."

"I can handle collateral damage." She said as they heard the bell to end lunch ring. "What should we do about the rumors?"

"Want to give them something to talk about?"

"Hell yeah," she enthusiastically exclaimed.

He reached out his arm to her and said, "Then, shall we?"

"We shall," she replied, putting her arm through his.

Several gazing eyes fell upon them as they strolled through the quad. Most of the kids were happy to see the two of them together, but Josie and Tina, weren't sure how to feel. The idea of an Untouchable getting close to one of their friends was exciting but also frightening.

"This is going to be a long year, isn't it?" Josie worried, glancing at Dougy.

"Yep," Dougy replied. "But if it's anything like it used to be, it's going to be fun."

CHAPTER 13

Tennly and Conner quickly became comfortable around each other again, and they both knew what that meant: it was only a matter of time before the pranks started. After pondering the best way to kick off their antics, Tennly finally settled on one that she believed would be the most benign.

On the fourth day of their renewed friendship, she arrived at school early enough to sneak into Conner's first-period classroom before he got there. After asking them which seat was Conner's, she poured a small puddle of water on it from the water bottle she was carrying.

She felt jumpy through all her morning classes, her anticipation for lunch building higher than it had all week.

As soon as the lunch bell rang, she dashed out of her class, dropped her books in her locker, and quickly walked to the quad. Normally, she would wait for Riley to return from the landing before heading down, but that day, she raced to reach the landing first.

In a way, she was hoping that by sharing a fun moment with Conner, Riley would finally accept her. However, as soon as Riley saw her, he told Conner he would see him later and walked down the other side of the path, away from the school. The disappointment she felt from Riley's blunt dismissal nearly overshadowed her excitement about the prank. She really wanted him to like her, if only to make things easier for Conner.

Conner walked up to her, lighting a cigarette. "Nice try."

"What?" she asked, pretending not to understand.

"The water on my seat. If it wasn't for the person behind me who warned me, I would have sat in it."

"Don't people like to have fun around here?" she pouted.

"I do," he claimed.

"Mm," she skepticized, squinting her eyes at him. "Are you sure about that?"

"Are you?" he asked with a mischievous grin.

That was all it took for them both to know that their games had begun. By the end of the day, Conner had already decided to retaliate. Tennly was surprised when she opened her locker after classes and found it completely empty.

Staring at the vacant locker, Josie asked, "Where do you think he put everything?"

Tennly let out a deep breath, shut her locker, and leaned back to think. After a moment, she realized that what he had done wasn't just a prank; it was another invitation.

"Home," Tennly replied.

Conner often used to leave or take something to get her to come and visit him. She couldn't wait to get to his house, but a part of her felt scared about her true feelings for him. She hoped she could keep their playful banter in line with their friendship and suppress her love for him.

"You have my stuff," she probed as soon as he opened his front door.

His 'you caught me' smile melted her heart as he replied, "Come in." For a split second, she pondered if it was a good idea to enter. The last thing she wanted was to react on her feelings and ruin their relationship, just as it was finally flourishing.

They made their way to his bedroom in silence where she saw all the items from her locker laid out on his bed. She gathered everything, stuffing it all in her backpack, and then turned around to see Conner leaning against the doorframe, almost as if he were blocking her way out.

He looked absolutely enticing. His eyes locked onto hers with an intensity that made her feel weak in the knees. She had to clench her fists to ground herself, knowing that if she didn't get out of there, she might end up doing something she wasn't sure he was ready for.

"I have to go. My father will see my car parked here, and..."

He nodded, feeling exactly as she did. He stepped aside to let her pass and followed her through the house to the front door, thinking she was truly about to leave. However, she suddenly turned around and asked, "Are you hungry?"

"Yeah," he answered, relieved because he didn't want her to go.

"Would you like to go to dinner with me?"

"Yeah."

As she drove them toward downtown, where most of the restaurants were located, she realized she couldn't take him to any of them. Inevitably someone would see them together and report it to her father: she laughed.

"You wouldn't happen to know a place we could eat, would you? There are too many eyes down here."

He directed her to a dive bar thirty minutes out of town in the next county over. The area was extremely rural, with only three stoplights and no major city. The bar was located on the main street of the biggest town in the county, situated between a small post office and the only bank.

When Tennly stepped out of her car, she did a full 360-degree turn to take in her surroundings. There wasn't much to see; the area was surrounded by mountains. Across the street from the bar, there was a laundromat, a convenience store, a small diner, and a barbershop. Behind these four buildings flowed a creek with an old-fashioned swinging bridge crossing it.

As soon as she noticed the swinging bridge, she became giddy as her eyes conveyed her desire to cross it. They walked down the cracked, uneven sidewalk, with patches of grass sprouting up through the concrete, until they reached the swinging bridge.

The bridge consisted of wooden planks measuring 4 inches by 3 feet, spaced 3 inches apart, firmly secured to two ropes that spanned its entire length. At each corner of the planks were vertical ropes connected to the handrail ropes.

She looked down and realized it was higher than she had expected, but instead of feeling frightened, she felt a wave of excitement. With childlike enthusiasm, she placed her foot on the first plank. The plank shifted beneath her, prompting her to grip the rope handrails tightly. With careful steps, she started her way across, finally reaching the tenth plank. It was at this point that the bridge started to sway considerably. She burst into laughter as she heard Conner behind her, making grunting sounds as he desperately held on for dear life.

She turned to check on him and saw he was clinging to the handrails. Shaking her head and laughing, she decided to walk back to him and help put him out of his misery.

"Come on, big baby."

"You tell anyone about this, and I will kill you," he teased back.

She laughed as they walked back slowly, trying to ensure that the bridge didn't sway more than necessary with each step. However, when they reached the third-to-last plank, she couldn't resist. She took a giant jump, landing hard on the first plank, nearly causing Conner to lose his balance.

"That's it," he threatened, leaping over the remaining two planks and darting after her.

He caught up to her just before they reached the bar, picking her up and swinging her around as she playfully squealed for him to put her down. When he finally released her, his hands brushed against her lower back while she wrapped her arms around his neck.

Feeling the rapid beating of each other's hearts, she said, "I'm really hungry."

"Yeah," he said, grateful for the diversion.

Inside the bar, the atmosphere was dark, illuminated only by a few lamps in the corners and small candles on each table. The wooden paneling on the walls was decorated with neon beer signs and mounted animal heads. Booths lined the center and outer walls, with the bar situated at the back.

A waitress approached, greeted Conner, and then led them to a booth off to the side. As they crossed the room, their feet stuck to the floor with a swooshing sound with every step. The booth was upholstered in dark green, shiny vinyl that squeaked as they slid into it.

After the waitress placed the menus on the table, she asked Tennly what she wanted to drink. Tennly requested a sweet tea and waited for the waitress to take Conner's order. However, the waitress walked away without asking him, prompting Tennly to look at him questioningly.

"I've been here a few times," he admitted, his expression suggesting that it was much more than just a few.

"A few?" she asked, raising an eyebrow.

He held his forefinger an inch away from his thumb and confessed, "Maybe a little more than a few."

She shook her head, laughing as she grabbed a menu and began browsing through it. He watched her skim through each menu item as if she were at a fancy restaurant. It struck him as strange to see her in such a place, and he wondered how many people of her financial status would ever be caught dead in a bar like this.

Unsure of what to get, she told the waitress that she would have the same thing Conner ordered. It took a few minutes for them to find their rhythm and come up with topics to discuss, but by the time their food arrived, they were laughing as they reminisced about childhood memories.

They had just finished eating when the waitress returned with the check. Tennly offered to pay since it was her idea to go out to dinner, but Conner refused to let her.

Her wealth had always come between them, lingering in the back of his mind. As they walked back to her car, unable to shake off the thought, he asked her how she managed to pay for things, as he had never inquired about it before.

"I sell my body," she joked as they got in the car.

He laughed and said, "Seriously. I know you get an allowance, but do you carry cash...?"

"A little, but not that much," she explained as they pulled away. "I have my own bank account, so most of the time I use a debit card."

"I don't have a bank account," he divulged, staring out the side window and wondering what it would be like to have enough money to warrant needing one. "What's it like?"

"What?"

"Never having to worry about how you're going to pay for something... Or being able to buy whatever you want whenever you want?"

"You've never asked me that before," she stated. "Why now?"

"I don't know... I guess... for years I worried that money would be what separates us. Bringing it up was just a reminder of that."

"You're no longer worried about it?"

"No... I don't know... maybe I'm just trying to understand your world a little better."

"I guess I don't think about it," she replied, answering his original question. She reflected on their two worlds and how she had recently discovered how closely related they were.

"The fact that you don't have to think about it says a lot."

"I don't know about money, Conner, but I do know what it's like to want something and not be able to have it," she countered, giving him a quick glance to let him know she was referring to him.

When Tennly arrived at school the next day, she was frustrated to find that her locker wouldn't open. After trying three times without success, she examined it more closely and realized it wasn't her lock. She had completely forgotten about the pranks and hadn't planned one against Conner that day. She noticed Josie laughing with the other girls and asked if she could use her locker.

All morning, Tennly thought about how she would retaliate, but by lunchtime, she still had no idea what to do. She was tempted to skip going down to the landing to meet Conner because she didn't want to give him the satisfaction of having outsmarted her. However, when she sat at the table in the quad with her friends and saw Riley walking out from the path without Conner, she knew he was waiting for her.

She walked down to the landing, immediately regretting her decision to go. Just seeing the smirk on Conner's face was irritating enough, but when he goaded, "Having a hard time carrying all your books today?" she realized that if she didn't come up with something soon, he would never let her live it down.

"No," she replied. "No trouble at all."

"I knew I should have changed your friends' locks too," he realized, clearly aware of why she wasn't struggling.

"Speaking of friends," she said. "I'm surprised the *infamous* Untouchables, who are inseparable, don't have lunch together."

He explained to her that Sam and Joel were in the auto shop classes that were in the morning and went through first lunch and that Riley was in the EMT program that was only offered in the afternoon, so he had to eat first lunch.

"Riley wants to be an EMT?"

"No. He wants to be a doctor, the EMT program is the closest thing to that."

"He's going to need to work on his bedside manner," she remarked, half teasing.

She spent the rest of the day contemplating how she could get back at Conner. She had hoped to come up with a plan before school ended, but nothing came to mind. It wasn't until she was driving home that an idea struck her. Knowing she had limited time to execute it before Conner returned home, she drove to Conner's house and climbed into his room through the window. She rummaged through his drawers and closet, gathering every piece of clothing she could find. She placed them into a clean trash bag she had grabbed from the kitchen and then took the bag to the yacht in anticipation for the next day.

In the morning, when Conner got out of the shower and discovered that all his clothes were gone, he immediately understood what had happened. At first, he felt a rush of excitement, thinking Tennly was enjoying the pranks just as much as he was. At least until he stood there wrapped in a towel, realizing he literally had nothing to wear to school.

Conner went through the first half of the day as if nothing was different. He thought about confronting Tennly a couple of times between classes but knew that doing so would mean admitting she had gotten to him. So, he patiently waited for lunch to see how things would unfold.

"Nice shirt," Tennly teased with a smile, noticing it was Dougy's, as she stopped in front of him on the landing.

"I'll tell you what," he offered. "You give me back my clothes, and I'll give you back your lock."

"Mm... I'm doing just fine without my lock," she grinned.

"And you call me stubborn," he responded.

"Okay, how about this: a do-over...
I'll give you your clothes back if you let
me take you out to dinner tonight."

Realizing the pranks were meant to
help them spend more time together, he was
glad she felt the same way. He lit another
cigarette and recalled, "Didn't think
there was anywhere we could go."

"I thought of a place."

The yacht was far from his thoughts
as he wondered where she might take him.
He used to daydream about it in their
younger years, wondering what it was like
to have such luxuries, always thinking
that he would feel insignificant or
unworthy upon seeing its extravagance;
however, as he stood on the deck, he became
confused when not only wasn't he feeling
unworthy, but felt completely
comfortable.

Conner's first-period teacher, Mr. Nowell, was a veteran educator in his mid-forties. Students liked him for his fun and understanding nature, yet he was also firm and fair. He had a pleasant appearance, with a full head of curly brown hair and warm brown eyes. He wore thick, dark-rimmed glasses and always sported a pair of Converse Chuck Taylors, regardless of what he was wearing.

Rumor had it that Mr. Nowell was the only teacher who liked The Untouchables, which was why he agreed to help Tennly with her next prank.

"Okay, but you do know he will retaliate," Mr. Nowell warned.

"I'm looking forward to it," she said with a smile. "Thank you!"

Tennly made her way to her first period class and as soon as she placed her things on her desk, the desktop came tumbling down into a loud crash, prompting her to let out a surprised scream.

The commotion caught the teacher's attention, who turned around and shouted, "Cheese and rice!" as all the students began to laugh. Tennly rolled her eyes, fully aware of what had happened, prompting her to move to a different seat.

Meanwhile, Conner struggled to focus as he replayed the image of her falling to the floor in his mind. He couldn't wait for lunch so he could see her acting upset as she acknowledged his perfect execution of dismantling her desk. So consumed by his prank and his belief that he had outsmarted her, he didn't hear Mr. Nowell call him up to his desk to give him a pass to go to the office.

It always worried him when he was called to the office. Usually, he had done something that warranted disciplinary action. But as he walked down the hall, he couldn't think of anything he had done that would lead to an office referral. When he approached the secretary, she looked at him with a confused expression but told him to wait while she called to see if the principal was waiting for him.

Principal Stevens informed his secretary that he hadn't called for Conner and asked her to check with another office. She contacted both the attendance office and the principal in charge of discipline, but neither had called for him. By this time, Conner knew what was going on. As she began to call the counseling center, he told her not to worry about it.

For Conner, being called into the office was a step above the pranks they had been playing, and he wasn't going to wait for lunch to let Tennly know. He marched right into Tennly's class, ignoring the teacher as she tried to tell him to leave, while all the students stopped what they were doing to watch him.

Walking straight up to Tennly, he rested his hands on her desktop, and warned, "My turn."

She smiled at him and countered, "Bring it."

During lunch, Conner asked her to go to the movies with him after school. At first, she suspected he was planning another prank, but as she walked out to the parking lot after school and saw him leaning against his motorcycle, she didn't mind. Regardless of his intentions, she wanted to spend as much time with him as possible, willing to endure any prank he might have set in motion.

She felt somewhat relieved when they arrived at the mall and walked into the theater without any signs of a prank. However, she couldn't help but wonder what it would be like to sit in a dark room so close to him.

They bought some popcorn and drinks, then settled into their seats just as the previews began. As they reclined and watched the movie, other than little tingles of excitement each time they laughed or jumped at the same moments, she was grateful for the comfort they shared. It felt as though they were kids again at the height of their friendship, as if no time had passed.

She was shocked when after the movie ended, Conner asked her if she wanted to see another one. Not wanting the night to end, she agreed to it.

He led her out of the theater they were in and down the hall to another one. "We don't have tickets," Tennly mentioned as Conner reached for the door.

"Sh," he replied, winking at her and gesturing for her to go inside.

They found seats halfway back, just as the movie began. Like clockwork, five minutes into the movie, the cinema employee walked down the aisle, to the screen, and back up again. At first, Tennly thought they had gotten away with it, but then the employee walked back down the aisle. On his way up, he stopped at each group of people and asked for their tickets.

When the employee approached them and asked for theirs, Conner replied, "You don't need to see our tickets."

"I'm going to have…" the employee began, shining his flashlight at Conner. Upon recognizing him, he quickly corrected, "I'm sorry. Enjoy the movie." Then he moved on without checking anyone else.

"That was like some weird Jedi mind trick," Tennly chuckled.

"Being who I am... sometimes has its perks."

"I suppose so," she replied, realizing that this was just another aspect that made them more alike than they had once thought.

Caught up in the excitement of the movie and all the popcorn they had consumed, by the time Tennly got home she was hungry.

She found a leftover plate with a grilled salmon steak over rice, a side of asparagus, and a piece of baguette in the refrigerator. Not wanting to carry the plate to her room and then back down, after warming it up, she sat down at the bar.

When she was almost done, shoveling in the food, she heard Marie's voice coming from the door on the left, which led to Marie's bedroom and the laundry room.

"Thanks for dinner," Tennly replied. "You didn't have to make me a plate."

"Your father told me not to."

"Then you deserve more than a thank you," Tennly admitted, wondering why her father had told her that.

"Do you want anything to drink?"

"I'll get some water when I'm done."

Marie poured a mug of coffee that looked freshly brewed and then stood across the counter, directly in front of Tennly. After taking a sip, she said, "Would you like to talk about where you were this evening?"

"No, I would not."

"Hm... Well, your father wanted me to ask you."

"Why doesn't he just ask me?"

"To be honest, I think he's afraid of you."

Tennly wasn't sure if she felt happy or sad about that. It felt strange to know that her father was scared of her, but at the same time, his fear could be advantageous.

"Why?"

"That is something you need to ask him."

"You know about the family, don't you?" Tennly inquired, aware that her father's fear had something to do with the business and her role in it.

"Aye,"

"Do you know what they expect me to do?"

"Aye."

"Do you think I can do it?"

"Be a weapon or a leader?" Marie asked.

"Both."

"I've worked for this family for years, and I have heard and seen a lot. So, I'm going to give you some words of wisdom.

Being a woman in this business isn't going to be easy. It is a man's world, Tennly. They will speak over you, ignore you, and try everything in their power to undermine you. If you truly want to become the first female boss, you will have to learn how to be both the weapon and the leader."

The first half of the next day was uneventful. Everyone walked around, moving from class to class, anticipating another escapade between Tennly and Conner, but nothing happened.

"Halfway through the day," Conner mentioned after he stopped by the picnic table before heading down to the landing. "Scared yet?"

"Are you?" Tennly challenged.

Conner gave her a look that communicated there was no way she could outdo him and then informed, "I'll be home while you're still figuring out what to do."

Tennly laughed maniacally and countered, "That is if you can even get home."

At that moment, they both realized they had done something to the other's mode of transportation. Their smiles and haughty attitudes slowly faded, and then before anyone knew it, Tennly jumped up, and she and Conner raced through the quad to the parking lot.

Tennly circled around her Scout and quickly noticed a wheel clamp on her front passenger side wheel. Meanwhile, Conner rushed over to where his motorcycle had been parked, only to find it gone.

"You put a boot on my car?" she asked, surprised.

"Where's my bike?" he responded, frustration evident in his voice.

She had snuck out during second period, moved his motorcycle behind her car, and called a tow company to report that it was blocking her way. In her haste, she hadn't noticed that he had already put a clamp on her wheel.

"It's safe," she insisted. "Take the boot off, and I'll tell you where it is."

"Tell me where my bike is, and I'll take the boot off."

"Seems like we've reached a conundrum," she said playfully.

Knowing neither would yield easily, they returned to the quad. By the end of the day, word had spread around the school, which caused a large crowd to form around Tennly's car as they walked to the parking lot. Everyone who could stick around did, eager to find out who would give in first.

As the hours passed, the crowd began to thin out and by 6:00 PM, only a few students remained. Riley was willing to stay as long as it took but when Sam and Joel said they were hungry the three of them left.

Once they were alone, Tennly and Conner climbed into the front seats of Tennly's Scout. They glanced at each other, as Conner suddenly burst into laughter.

"What's so funny?"

"Nothing," he replied, still chuckling. "It's just that I don't have to be home. I can do this all night."

Tennly shot him a look that suggested he should know her better as she pulled out her phone. She called her father to tell him she was going to Josie's to finish a lab write-up and would keep Marie informed, since he was out of town.

Once they realized they could be there for the duration of the night, they ordered a large pepperoni, sausage, and mushroom pizza and had it delivered to the school parking lot. Instead of eating it in the Scout, Conner led Tennly to the back of the school to an alcove that went down a flight of stairs to a door.

They were met by a tall man in his fifties, Henry Sargent, the head custodian at the high school. He had long, thick white hair tied in a ponytail. His big bushy white eyebrows contrasted with his dark brown eyes over a smoothly shaven face. He had a friendly demeanor that made it easy to feel comfortable around, looking more like a member of a hippie band than a school janitor.

"Conner," Henry greeted, gesturing for them to come inside.

"Henry, this is Tennly."

"I'm aware," Henry acknowledged as he shook Tennly's hand. "Nice to meet you in person, Ms. O'Brien."

"And you as well," Tennly reciprocated.

Half of the room was filled with storage items like brooms, mops, and cleaning supplies. The other half was the custodians' lounge, which featured two couches, a table with six chairs, and a full kitchen. There were no dirty dishes in the sink, very little trash, and an overall tidy atmosphere, with a pleasant aroma of lemon.

Conner and Tennly settled onto one of the couches while Henry grabbed three mugs from the dish drainer and pulled out a bottle of whiskey from the cabinet.

Noticing the surprised expression on Tennly's face, Henry offered, "I have water or pop if you would prefer."

"No," Conner replied, looking at Tennly with curiosity. She shook her head to indicate she was okay with the whiskey.

Through the evening, laughter ensued as the three of them exchanged stories. Conner and Tennly shared how they had ended up in their current situation, reminiscing about the pranks they played in their youth. In turn, Henry explained how he and Conner became friends. When Conner was in ninth grade, he witnessed a couple of kids mocking Henry for being a janitor. Conner's disapproval was all it took to get the kids to stop.

As Tennly listened to Henry recount the incident, her eyes beamed with pride and admiration for Conner. It didn't surprise her that he would stand up for someone like Henry, and it only made her love him more.

When they finally made it back to the Scout Tennly texted Marie and told her that she was staying the night at Josie's. Then she leaned her seat back as she turned to Conner, yawning. It was close to 11:00 PM and, between the late hour and the alcohol, she was groggy.

"Your bed would be more comfortable," he stated.

"Yes, it would. Do you want to take the boot off so I can go home?"

"Tell me where my bike is."

"You're infuriating, Marks," she said, sluggishly. She fell asleep so quickly that she startled awake to see Conner staring at her. She smiled and asked, "Aren't you sleepy?"

"I'm used to staying up late," he replied.

She didn't say anything else before closing her eyes again. Conner reclined his seat back, but after a few minutes he found it difficult to be that close to her and not touch her. So, he quietly crawled into the back seat, where he had more room to lie down, and soon fell asleep.

Tennly woke a couple of hours later, feeling numb on her right side. When she saw that Conner was in the back seat, looking more comfortable than she was, she crawled back and lay down beside him. He instinctively wrapped his arm around her, savoring the touch he both craved and feared. Resting his chin on the top of her head, he closed his eyes.

He was awakened the next morning by a gentle tapping on the back passenger window. He had enjoyed their time together so much the night before that he had forgotten the consequences of being caught in such a compromising position. He knew it wouldn't take long for rumors to spread that they had been intimate, and he regretted putting her in that situation.

"Ten," he said, trying to wake her. She opened her eyes after he called her name a second time and looked up at him. "We have an audience."

"Crap," she blushed, burying her head into his chest.

"I think we should call a truce... Before we go too far?" He suggested.

"Probably," she agreed, recognizing the disappointment and fear in his voice; it was the same tone he had used three years earlier.

"I'll have the boot off by the end of the school day," he promised, holding onto her to prevent her from falling as he sat up.

"I had your bike towed. I'll pay for it and have them take it to Riley's."

He nodded and then opened the door, leaving without another word. Taking a deep breath, she wondered if she hadn't already gone too far, pushing him away. As she leaned her head back, Josie climbed in on one side, and Abby on the other.

"You, okay?" Josie asked.

When Tennly didn't respond right away, Abby inquired, "Did you have..."

"No," Tennly interrupted, stopping her from finishing. Before her friends could ask anything else, she grumbled, "I'll see you at lunch."

By the time lunch arrived, whispers and curious looks followed Tennly around every corner. However, instead of feeling embarrassed, she was angry at herself for not taking things slower.

As she sat down at their table in the quad, she noticed the concerned looks on her friends' faces, though none of them brought it up. She appreciated their discretion and efforts to change the subject, knowing if they had addressed the issue, she would likely have snapped at them.

When Tennly sensed Conner entering the quad, she could feel the reactions of those around her, and her heart began to pound like a jackhammer.

It was incredible how, in one moment, Tennly felt like her whole world was crumbling, and in the next, it seemed to mend with great jubilation. Her mood shifted dramatically when, instead of walking with Riley to the path, he approached her and gave her a reassuring look that communicated everything would be okay. Then, extending his hand, he asked, "Are you coming?"

When Shelby heard that Conner and Tennly had spent the night together, she became so furious that she could no longer contain herself. As soon as she spotted Tennly on her way to her seventh period class, she followed her, gradually closing the distance until she was right behind her.

Before Tennly realized what was happening, Shelby quickly slammed her head into the concrete wall just a few feet away from the classroom door. Blood dripped down her forehead as nausea set in from the pain. Her peripheral vision faded in and out, making her feel unsteady. Before she could regain her balance, she felt a hand gripping the back of her hair, pulling her head backwards.

Before Shelby could thrust her against the wall again, Tennly quickly reached back, grabbed Shelby's head and twisted her body so that she was able to get Shelby into choke hold.

A crowd began to form around the two girls as Tennly contemplated her next move. She wanted to kill her and likely would have if she hadn't noticed the onlookers staring and the cameras throughout the entire school.

"You're not worth it," Tennly scoffed, letting her go.

As the adrenaline began to fade, Tennly stumbled and grabbed onto the wall for support. She was considering heading to the nurse when someone from the crowd shouted for her to turn around. Thanks to the warning, Tennly managed to move out of Shelby's path, punching Shelby in the face. Tennly got in another punch before Shelby screamed and attempted to hit her back. In response, Tennly swatted Shelby's arm aside and then kicked her in the stomach, causing Shelby to fall backward.

Tennly was about to move toward Shelby for another punch when two teachers finally stepped in and escorted them to the office, where they were made to sit on opposite sides of the room. The principal called in Shelby first and suspended her from school for five days, while he sent Tennly to the nurse. The nurse cleaned the cut on her forehead, placed a large bandage over it, and then sent her back to the main office.

"Have a seat," Principal Stevens gestured, pointing across from him. "Why does a good girl like you associate with someone like Shelby Torrence?"

"It doesn't look like we have anything to do with each other, does it?" Tennly refuted, finding it humorous that everyone assumed she was a good girl.

Because he watched the video and due to who her father was, she was only suspended for the next day. She thanked him as he handed her a form that needed her father's signature before she could return to school, and then she was instructed to wait in the lobby until someone from her house arrived to pick her up.

As she stood up, she had to brace herself, feeling a bit wobbly as she made her way to the lobby. While she waited, she texted her friends and Conner to explain what happened, hoping to prevent them from hearing any false rumors.

She expected Thomas to come for her since Daniel was out of town. So, she was surprised when her father walked into the office to sign her out. She feared he might discipline her; not primarily for being in a fight but for the embarrassment she had caused him.

"Are you okay?" Daniel asked as he placed his hands on her shoulders and examined her forehead. A hint of red was seeping through the gauze, a bruise had formed around the bump, and she appeared nauseous.

"I'm fine," she replied. "I thought you were going out of town."

"Just for last night. I made it back a couple of hours ago."

On the way to the hospital, he asked her what had happened. She lied and told him that Shelby was just one of those girls who hated rich people and was jealous of her money. When he didn't believe her, she said, "Well, I have a big mouth... so..." Her lie worked and she could feel her shoulders relax knowing her father wasn't angry.

She ended up with two stitches right at her hairline, making them easy to hide, and the brain scan showed no signs of damage, aside from a concussion. Daniel was proud of her for standing up for herself but felt obligated as a parent to impose some sort of punishment, so he grounded her for just a day.

When Tennly got home, she rested, drifting in and out of sleep for several hours. Then as soon as night fell, she quietly snuck through the tunnels to Conner's house. She climbed through his bedroom window and found him sitting on his bed, smoking a cigarette.

"I suppose it's a good thing you have a hard head," he joked.

"Shut up," she teased as she laid down across the foot of his bed. "I wish it were harder than it is. It's killing me."

"I'm sorry she did that."

"I can take care of Shelby."

"Yeah, but the fact that you have to..."

"Stop," she interrupted, sensing that he was blaming himself for what had happened to her. "I'm fine."

"I can't believe you got suspended."

"Just for tomorrow."

"That's cool."

Noticing a picture sticking out from beneath the lamp, she crawled across the bed to look at it. It was a photo of her, at 12 years old, on Conner's back with her legs and arms wrapped around him. He was standing and had his right hand on her face and his left hand on her wrist, both donning joyful expressions.

"Do you remember this day?" she asked.

"Yeah."

"What happened to us?... We were so happy."

"We grew up."

Tennly placed the picture on the end table, wishing that someday they could find their way back. Being able to understand her facial expressions, he knew what she was thinking. They both felt the growing desire between them and knew that if she stayed there another moment longer, they would end up giving in to it.

She buried her head down into his mattress, then shyly looked back. "I should go."

"Yeah."

Covering her mouth with the back of her fingers, she playfully shook her head and rolled her eyes to let him know she didn't want to leave.

"Are you scared?" she asked, wondering how much longer their relationship would last.

"Terrified."

"I don't want this to end," she sighed. "Do you?"

"No."

"So how do we keep that from happening?"

"We'll figure it out," he assured.

She noticed him biting his lower lip, which was a sign he was worried. She didn't think he was lying to her; rather, it seemed more like a concern that they would eventually give in to their desires and weren't sure what would happen next.

"Promise me, Conner. Promise me that this won't end."

He leaned over, resting his forehead against hers. "We'll figure it out."

52

CHAPTER 14

Since Tennly was suspended from school, Daniel decided it would be a good time to take her to New York City to meet the other families affiliated with the New York Irish Mafia. There were three: the MacFaddens, the O'Gradys, and the Sweenys.

The meeting took place at a safe house located an hour north of Manhattan. The house was a well-maintained, century-old farmhouse with a wraparound porch. The living room was furnished with two adjacent couches, a love seat, and four straight-backed wooden chairs, all arranged to face one another. Daniel took a seat in one of the straight-backed chairs facing the group and gestured for Tennly to sit in the wooden chair to his right.

Tennly was the only person under the age of thirty and the only female present. While it seemed strange for her to be in a room full of grown men, it was even stranger for them. They all knew that after Eileen's death Daniel was given the interim position until Tennly turned eighteen, but they still believed that when the time came, they would choose someone they considered more suitable.

"Now that we're all here," Daniel began, gesturing for everyone to take a seat. "Let us..."

"With all due respect," Peter O'Grady, the head of the O'Grady clan, interrupted. "Should we be speaking in front of your daughter?"

"I agree," Tyler Sweeny, the head of the Sweeny family, added. "I don't like it."

"It's a rule that our children should not know until they are adults," Mikey MacFadden, the head of the MacFadden family, chimed in.

"Not that I need to defend myself," Daniel replied, "but I didn't tell her. She found out on her own."

"Again," Peter interjected, "with all due respect, that suggests you weren't careful enough."

"As you already know, someday Tennly will take over. That's why I brought her here today to show her how things are done and how we run our businesses. I want you to know that she is our newest soldier... at least until she turns 18 and is old enough to become the boss."

The men fell silent, exchanging glances, before Peter remarked, "She's tiny. What kind of soldier could she be?"

Daniel told them not to worry about it and then proceeded with the biannual meeting. Tennly sat and listened as the men discussed finances, assets, and losses. They talked about employees who no longer worked for them, upcoming events and jobs, and any concerns or threats that had arisen. She found it fascinating how similar it was to a real business meeting.

"Now to answer your question," Daniel said, as Thomas snuck behind Tennly and abruptly grabbed her by the neck, pulling her up and over the back of the chair.

Shocked and confused, Tennly reacted quickly. She leaned down, spun around, and before Thomas realized what was happening, she had twisted his arm behind his back. In one swift motion, she kicked him in the stomach, causing him to fall backward. At the same time, she threw a throwing knife at her father, barely missing his left shoulder by two inches.

Daniel pulled the knife out of the chair while Tennly glanced over at Thomas and asked if he was okay. After Thomas nodded, she shot an angry look at her father. When he smiled at her, she understood what he had done. Not only had he showcased her abilities to the men, but he was also signaling to her that she had complete control over them and should not hold back.

"Impressive," Peter finally commented, breaking the silence. "But she did miss."

"I wasn't going to actually stab my father," Tennly barked as she walked over to Daniel to get her knife back. "A heads up would have been nice."

"It wouldn't have been as dramatic," Daniel stated handing her the knife.

"You didn't know?" Tyler asked.

"No," she answered, giving her father an icy glare.

"How accurate are you with that knife?" Mikey inquired.

If her father wanted drama, she was going to give it. So instead of answering, she threw the knife at Mikey, hitting the chair in between his legs, missing his pelvic region by one inch. "Pretty accurate."

The empowerment and pride she felt when she left the meeting quickly faded as she reflected on everything during her journey home. She began to feel as though she were being used, almost as if she were programmed to fulfill the expectations of her father and the other men around her.

On the jet, Daniel noticed that she was deep in thought, brooding in silence, so when she showed up in his office after they got home, he wasn't surprised.

"I know I threw a lot at you today, but..."

"Here's what's going to happen," she interrupted. "I want to work for this family. To be honest I enjoy it. The thrill it gives me. But I will not be paraded around like a circus monkey."

"I apologize."

"I'm not done," she continued. "If I'm old enough to work for this family and kill people, then I'm old enough to be considered and treated like an adult. And as long as I stay out of trouble and keep you abreast of what I'm doing, you will have no further say in what I do."

"Tennly, I don't think..."

"This is not a negotiation," she snapped with an authoritative tone he had never heard from her before. It wasn't the anger or frustration she usually displayed; this was the voice of a leader. "If you say you're just worried, that excuse went out the window the moment you took me on my first job. If you had me trained as well as you claim, you know I can take care of myself."

Before leaving, she turned around and disclosed, "And I will no longer be sneaking out through the tunnels. Instead, I'll be walking out the front door."

Tara had been away from Marinsburg for more than a month and a half, and her boyfriend, Joey, noticed that she was feeling homesick, so he offered to take her home to visit.

They reached the estate shortly before dinner and found Marie in the kitchen. Overjoyed, Marie dropped the knife and potato, rushed over to Tara, and gave her a warm hug. After Tara introduced Joey to Marie and got caught up on her schooling, Tara and Joey went to the gym to see Tennly.

When they got there Tennly was hanging upside down on one of the bars doing inverted sit-ups. She was dressed in a small black sports bra and matching tight spandex shorts that showcased her bellybutton.

Joey was amazed by Tennly and found her to be completely different from what he had envisioned. He thought she would be like Tara: more reserved. Aside from their looks, they were nothing alike. Tennly's outfit was much more revealing than what Tara would ever wear, and Tennly was far from timid or shy. So, when she ran up to them without any inhibitions, it startled him.

"What are you doing here?" Tennly joyfully asked, hugging her sister.

"Not happy to see me?" Tara teased.

"Don't be stupid," Tennly replied.

They had just enough time for introductions before they had to get ready for dinner, but Tara managed to sneak away and meet up with Tennly after she got a shower. She wanted to know what she thought about Joey and if she thought their dad would approve.

"You don't think he'll notice that he's Italian, do you?" Tara asked as the girls sat in Tennly's bedroom.

"He exudes Italian, Tara. He'll notice. But... stand your ground if he says anything. Most Italians are good people."

"Easier said than done."

"You seem happy. If you're happy, Dad will be happy."

"I am. On another note, how are things with Blake?"

"We broke up."

"What happened? He seemed so perfect."

"Yeah," Tennly sighed, glancing at the little hole in her wall where she knew a camera was hidden. "But I'm not."

"What are you talking about? You're as perfect as anyone could be."

"I guess he didn't think so."

"Well, his loss. I hate to ask, but... how are things with Conner?"

Tennly looked up at the camera again before turning back to her sister and lying, "They're not."

"Oh, I'm sorry. I thought maybe..."

"No," Tennly interrupted. "It's okay, though. We come from two different worlds, so..."

They met Daniel at one of their family's restaurants for dinner. Throughout the meal, Tennly noticed that he was avoiding eye contact with Joey and kept glancing at his watch. Additionally, his fidgeting and constant readjusting in his seat made it clear to Tennly that he was not entirely comfortable with Joey's presence.

Watching how her father interacted with Joey made Tennly think about how he would react if he ever found out about her relationship with Conner. So, as soon as they got home, she removed the camera hidden in her bedroom wall and cut the cord. To emphasize how serious she was, she marched straight to his bedroom.

"I fixed the camera in my room," Tennly announced.

"I didn't know it was broken," he responded as he walked to his vanity chair and started taking off his shoes.

"It wasn't," she said. She was glad he didn't even try to hide the fact that there was a camera in her room.

He nodded and asked, "What do you want?"

"I just wanted to make sure you knew that there will be no more watching my room or listening in on it."

"It's for your safety, Tennly."

"It's disturbing... And I thought we had a deal?"

"At least tell me if you're seeing him."

"That's none of your business and definitely not part of the deal."

"Tennly, you know how I fee..."

"He's not part of the deal... Keep your eavesdropping out of my bedroom."

For the first time since becoming the family boss, Daniel felt lost. Frustrated and unsure of himself, he needed a drink and a friend.

"She's sneaking out to see him," Daniel briefed as he and Thomas sat in Thomas's apartment above the garage.

"That would be my guess," Thomas replied.

"I have one daughter who sneaks out to see a thug and another who is dating an Italian. Where did I go wrong?"

Thomas smiled and then suggested, "It would be easier just to kill them."

"Yeah... I'm leaving for California tomorrow. I'll be gone for a week. Follow Conner around for a couple of days... to see where he goes and who he hangs out with."

Conner had been neglecting his friends recently to spend time with Tennly, so he felt obligated to attend a party with them. Since it was a school night, he had no intention of staying long. He simply wanted to make an appearance, spend some time with his friends, and then leave. However, before he knew it, he was extremely drunk and high. With his inhibitions lowered, he eventually started making out with a girl who was sitting next to him on the couch.

Overwhelmed by guilt and flooded with thoughts of how much he loved Tennly, he pushed the girl away. However, just before she turned to leave, a realization struck him: his actions were proof that he and Tennly were edging closer to taking their friendship to a romantic level, and that frightened him. Believing the only way to ensure that didn't happen and to make sure Tennly understood they couldn't act on their true feelings, he stood up, grabbed the girl's arm, and led her upstairs to one of the bedrooms.

He woke up the next morning, still slightly high and extremely hungover. Rubbing his eyes, he sat up and felt movement beside him on the bed. Although he had woken in similar situations many times before, this time felt different.

Not only was the guilt heavy on his heart, as if it were slowly chiseling away at it piece by piece, but as he began to think clearly, he also felt anger towards himself for the pain his decision would cause Tennly when she found out.

He tried to clear his mind before standing up. That's when he noticed the girl he had gone upstairs with, wearing only her panties, asleep on the floor at the foot of the bed, as he heard another girl beside him groan and shift around.

"Where are you going?" The girl asked.

Conner nearly stopped breathing when he recognized the voice. Lying on her side, with the sheet pulled down to her waist was Shelby. She had seen Conner, and the other girl walk up the stairs and saw an opportunity to win him back.

"Come back to bed," Shelby pleaded. "I missed you." Ignoring her, he finished getting dressed as she screamed, "You're going to her, aren't you?"

Conner pointed a finger at her, struggling to find the right words. When nothing came to mind, he turned to leave as Shelby wailed, "She'll never accept you like I do!"

Stumbling to the living room, he found Sam asleep on the couch and nudged his shoulder to wake him up.

"What?" Sam mumbled, still groggy and unaware of who it was. When he opened his eyes and saw Conner, he groaned, "Riley took Joel home last night."

"I drove," Conner reminded him.

"Oh," Sam replied, sitting up. "Then... I don't know."

"Jesus," Conner exclaimed. "When's he coming back?"

"I don't know..."

"Great," Conner groaned. "I'm not staying here. Tell him I'll pick up my car later."

"Okay."

Conner walked for an hour and a half, finally reaching downtown Marinsburg shortly after noon. He was exhausted, hungover, and burdened by guilt over his actions. Eventually, he arrived at the warehouse, where he collapsed and slept for the rest of the day.

As Tennly and her friends approached her car after school, they noticed a large crowd gathered around it, with Shelby right in the middle. Tennly wished that, just once, Shelby would confront her in private so she could throw one of her knives into her neck and watch her bleed out.

After getting the image out of her head, Tennly asked, "What do you want, Shelby?"

Shelby smirked widely as she boasted, "I'm just here to tell you where Conner was today."

Tennly felt her body heat up as she noticed how giddy and excited Shelby was to share this information. She dug her fingernails into her palms to suppress any urge to react aggressively or escalate the situation.

"He spent the night with me," Shelby divulged with a triumphant tone. "Unlike you and your prudish lifestyle, I can share him. We had the best time with another girl." Then, taking a step closer, she disclosed, "He likes threesomes. Would you be willing to do that if that's what he wanted?"

"Get out of my way, Shelby," Tennly warned, maintaining a firm stance even though she felt as if she might collapse.

"Or what?" Shelby challenged.

Tennly shoved Shelby aside to reach the door. The force of her push sent Shelby stumbling back before she regained her balance. Just as Tennly was about to get into her car, Shelby steadied herself and pushed Tennly against the open door. Tennly braced herself and quickly turned just in time to dodge a punch. She grabbed Shelby's right arm as she swung and slammed her against the car.

Shelby started laughing, knowing she had gotten on Tennly's last nerve. She was enjoying the moment, aiming to get under Tennly's skin as much as possible. Even though she knew that she couldn't win in a fair fight, making Tennly angry was worth the risk of any beating she might receive.

Tennly slowly released her grip, as she maniacally smiled at her. "I feel sorry for you. If I were Conner's girlfriend, as you claim to be, he wouldn't want anyone else. So, you need to ask yourself, Shelby: if you truly are his girlfriend... and he truly loved you... why aren't you enough?"

Shelby screamed and attempted to hit Tennly, but Tennly blocked her punch with her arms. She kneed Shelby in the stomach, then, while holding onto her head, kneed her in the face and pushed her to the side.

Before Shelby could get up, Tennly quickly drove away.

Tennly was so fired up that by the time she reached her bedroom she couldn't think straight. She felt frustrated with herself for expecting more from Conner than he could give. She understood the implications of choosing to be friends with him. Everyone had warned her about his behavior and suggested that he might not be the same as she remembered.

Even though she thought she wanted to be alone, when Josie and Abby showed up asking if she wanted to go for a walk, she felt a sense of relief.

Along the way, she asked them if they thought Shelby was telling the truth about the threesome and was saddened to hear there were several stories about it.

"Do you think underneath," Tennly asked, "he really likes her?"

"Shelby?" Josie blurted out as if the thought was humorous.

"Yeah."

"No," Abby reassured. "She's familiar. Convenient."

"And to be honest," Josie continued. "Willing and available."

"Not to mention, safe," Abby added.

"What do you mean?" Tennly inquired, interested in Abby's perspective.

"Familiarity is safety," Abby answered. "Plus, she comes from the same background. He feels safe with her. That would be my guess."

"She's got a point," Josie agreed. "Your wealth and reputation in this town is intimidating. For someone like Conner I can see how being friends with you could be scary. Let alone anything more."

"So, he's sabotaging us?" Tennly wondered.

"Maybe," Josie shrugged.

Conner had sabotaged them, believing it was the right choice. However, later that night, as he read the messages Tennly had sent him that day, he realized he had made a big mistake.

Her first message wished him a good time with his friends. The next asked if he was okay because he wasn't at school. The last message told him not to worry about texting her back since Shelby had already informed her where he was and what he was doing.

"Shit," he muttered, feeling his stomach churn.

Unsure of what to do, he contemplated calling her but couldn't bring himself to do it. Instead, he decided to respond to Riley, informing him that he was at the warehouse and to pick him up as soon as possible.

Conner's exaggerated slouch and silent glare out the side window as they drove to their neighborhood were signs to Riley that he shouldn't leave his friend alone. So, as they got out of the car, Ri asked if he wanted a beer.

"Sure," Conner murmured, relieved not to have to go home.

Riley handed him a beer, from the garage fridge, and asked, "You feeling okay?"

"Yeah," Conner woefully answered.

"You going to feel okay when Tennly finds out about Shelby?"

Conner rolled his eyes and shook his head at hearing the news about him sleeping with Shelby had already spread. "Tennly and I are just friends."

"Then it shouldn't bother her then."

"She already knows."

"I figured. Rumor has it, Shelby confronted her after school. Told her everything." The boys took a large swig of their beer and then Riley asked, "Are you sure Tennly is worth all this trouble?"

"It's not a matter of if she's worth it. The question is if I'm willing to put her through all this."

"If you don't want to hurt her, did it ever cross your mind, to just stop doing things with her?"

"You think I should stop hanging around her?"

"You know how I feel about her. I think you should kick her to the curb. But, if truth be known... and I'm only going to say this once, she makes you happy. I've seen it. Shit, everyone sees it. I hate to admit it, but she just might be good for you."

Conner gave his friend a strange, confused look and then with a chuckle asked, "Are you high right now?"

"Maybe," Riley answered laughing.

CHAPTER 15

As Tennly and her friends walked down Riley's street, heading back to Josie's house, they noticed Conner and Riley sitting in lawn chairs in the yard. As they passed by, the boys could see the scowl on Tennly's face, her lips pursed with an unmistakable expression of disappointment and sadness.

"Nope," Riley said sarcastically. "She's not angry at all."

"Shut up," Conner responded. He chugged the rest of his beer and set the empty can on the ground beside him. "I got to go."

"Conner...?" Riley asked, concerned he might head in Tennly's direction.

"I have that thing I have to do at the school," Conner reminded, trying to reassure him that he was okay.

"Oh yeah," Riley recalled, remembering it was that time again. "Want me to go with you?"

"Nah," Conner said, a determined look crossing his face. "I'm going to see if someone else wants to go."

"You're a glutton for punishment."

"Yep," Conner sighed. "I'll see ya."

Conner slowly pulled up next to the girls, an uneasy wave of guilt settling in his stomach like a heavy rock. Rolling down his window, he called out Tennly's name. She ignored him, linking her arm through Josie's, and continued walking without stopping.

"Get in the car, Ten," he requested in a polite tone. When he saw she wasn't going to respond, he swallowed his pride, got out of his car and stepped in front of the girls.

"Get out of my way, Conner," Tennly urged, her two friends becoming even more nervous with an Untouchable so close to them.

"Just like that?" he appealed. "I don't get an explanation?"

"Then explain," Tennly pressed, crossing her arms and giving him a look that indicated she doubted he could offer a good reason for his actions.

He glanced at Josie and then at Abby before looking back at Tennly, as if to let her know he didn't want to speak in front of them. "Get in the car," he pleaded. "Please..."

She took a deep breath, shook her head, upset with herself for giving in to him. Then turned to her friends, who were signaling her not to go. "I'll talk to you later."

Every time he tried to speak, his throat tightened as he felt himself holding back his sadness. She wanted to say something, but the conflicting emotions she was experiencing prevented her from addressing the strongest one. So, they drove in silence.

When they reached the end of the street, Tennly realized they were leaving the neighborhood and wasn't sure she wanted to go that far away with him. "Well? Say what you want to say and then take me home."

"This is why I didn't want to start a relationship with you," he spat out, perturbed, yet conflicted.

"Because you want to sleep around?" she shot back with an angry chuckle. "Is that why we can't be friends?"

"You're the one who's mad."

"I know," she snapped because she wasn't sure whether to admit he was right or to stay angry.

"You knew about my life before you got involved," he pointed out.

"I know," she admitted in a calmer tone. "I'm not angry that you slept with someone... I mean... maybe... but... I'm more angry that you slept with her. Why her?"

"I don't know." He glanced at her, then back at the road. Taking a deep breath, he confessed, "When you left and didn't come back, she was there. When I'm with her, she helps me forget about you."

"You want to forget about me?"

"No... Not anymore. I didn't even know it was her until this morning. Ten... this isn't easy."

"I know... So, you didn't mean to sleep with her, specifically?"

"No... I don't know. She brings me back down to reality," he declared as he pulled into the school parking lot. "She reminds me of where I'm from, who I am."

"Do you love her?"

He chuckled and said, "No. I can't stand her."

"That makes a lot of sense," she said sarcastically.

"Yeah," he replied as he parked the car. "Are you still mad at me?"

"Yeah," she maintained. Then she smiled at him upon seeing his pleading puppy dog eyes. "You are so infuriating, Marks."

"So, you tell me."

She shook her head and then relented, "Just... please... not her, okay?"

"Okay."

"Promise?"

"I promise."

"So, are you going to tell me why we're at school?"

He led her back down to the custodian's lounge and knocked on the door. She didn't mind seeing Henry again but was confused about why they were there. Conner was acting as if he was on a mission and not just there to visit Henry.

"You're still hanging around this guy, huh?" Henry asked, glancing at Tennly.

"I tried not to, but he forced me into his car," she replied. Then she looked at Conner, who shrugged and gave Henry a look that confirmed she was right.

Henry smiled and then started going over instructions for Conner to follow, as well as reminding him the cameras were off and would be back on at six in the morning. After Henry left, Conner grabbed a set of keys before heading to the main office. Once there he sat down at the administration secretary's desk.

The dim lighting made the school appear more ominous than Tennly had anticipated at night. It was remarkably quiet compared to during the day, with only the low hum of the emergency light audible. Shivers went up her spine not able to shake the feeling that the scene reminded her of a bad horror movie.

She turned her attention back to Conner, to ignore her fear as he said, "We miss a lot of school... I fix our attendance, so truancy doesn't get us."

"How did you get the login?"

"I slept with the..." He stopped abruptly, realizing what he was about to say. "Sorry."

"You slept... with the secretary?" Tennly blurted out, raising an eyebrow.

"No," he replied with a sly grin. "The assistant principal... and then I blackmailed her into giving me her login info."

"Oh," Surprisingly, she wasn't angry, hurt, or disappointed. For some reason, she found his ingenuity inspirational.

"I needed a way..." he started.

"Stop," she interrupted. "I get it."

Relieved, he brought up Riley's screen first. He fixed ten absences and checked his grades to ensure he was passing all his classes. Riley had mostly 'B's, one A, and one C, so there wasn't anything else he needed to address.

Next, Conner moved on to Joel's records. He corrected Joel's absences and

changed the F he had in English class to a
C. Then he proceeded to Sam's profile.
Sam's needed a lot of work; in addition to
fixing his attendance, Conner changed
Sam's 'F's in his four core classes to 'C's
in English and Social Studies and 'D's in
Science and Math.

"Sam is really smart," Conner
defended. "He's just... well, he's more
street smart than book smart."

Tennly laughed as he went to his own
attendance screen, but she became curious
when he started to turn off the computer
without changing his grades.

"What about your grades?"

"I don't change mine," He confessed
with a melancholy undertone.

"Just going to throw caution to the
wind, huh?" she asked, half teasingly and
half seriously.

"I don't need to change mine," he
corrected.

"I want to see," she pressed, trying
to grab the mouse. He swatted her hand away,
prompting her to beg for a glimpse.

"Fine," he relented.

Reluctantly, he opened his grade page and scooted back so she could get a good look. She froze at what she saw. While she knew Conner was intelligent, she also understood that he typically didn't care enough about school to study or complete homework, so when she saw straight 'A's, her jaw dropped. What was even more surprising was that his 'A's weren't just in regular classes but higher-level ones. She looked at him with a mix of bewilderment and pride, but his expression was not what she expected, feeling embarrassed and ashamed.

"Con," she gasped.

"It's no big deal."

"This is a huge deal!" she exclaimed. "You said you never study, and you miss a lot of classes. How...?"

"It just comes naturally to me, I guess... and sometimes when I'm bored," he admitted, as he crinkled his nose and narrowed his eyes, "I do homework for fun."

"You do homework for fun?"

"Tell anyone and I'll kill ya."

"This changes everything," she proclaimed. "With those grades, you can get into any college you want."

"I'm not going to college."

"Why not?"

"Because."

"But this could mean we can be together."

"We are together."

"You know what I mean."

"If it takes me going to college for your father to like me, then we might as well end this friendship now."

He shut down the computer, violently pushed the chair away from the desk and stormed away. Feeling terrible about making him think he was unworthy, she approached him, and clarified, "You know I don't care what my father thinks. It would just make things easier, that's all."

"I know," he agreed, giving her an apologetic look.

On their way back to the custodian's lounge, they passed one of the trophy cases. Tennly stopped and gazed at the contents inside. Some of the trophies dated back fifty years, accompanied by old pictures of the teams. Since her return, she had never considered joining any sports, even though she could have excelled in several.

"Thinking of becoming a cheerleader?" he teased, hoping to repair their previous argument.

"Do I look peppy to you?" she laughed, appreciating his banter. "Do you have keys to every door in the school?"

"Yeah, why...?"

"What do you say we have some fun?"

When Tennly and her friends got to school the next day, they were met by large crowds in every corner and hallway. They stopped near the largest crowd that was closest to the main administration office, on their way to their lockers. Upon further investigation of the trophy case, they saw several lab frogs displayed in various poses.

Conner and Tennly had arranged the frogs in entertaining scenarios, including one frog holding a scalpel with ketchup dripping from it over another frog that had ketchup smeared on its stomach, and a few others posed in dance moves and sexual positions. In addition to the trophy cases, they had placed the frogs in stairwells, the gymnasium, cafeteria, and several bathrooms.

Seeing Tennly's eyes raised and a slight smirk on her face that screamed she was guilty, Josie looked at her and whispered, "Did you do this?"

Tennly tilted her head, but before she could answer, the assistant principal ordered the crowd to disperse. Shortly after Principal Stevens came over the intercom, telling everyone to head to their first-period class. He warned that anyone found in the halls would receive detention and mentioned that they would be investigating the prank.

The week progressed, and Conner and Tennly decided it would be best to avoid being seen together at school. They wanted to ensure they could navigate the aftermath of The Great Frog Debacle without drawing attention to themselves.

It was during this time apart that Conner realized he couldn't live without her. He loved her and despite the obstacles that worried him, he felt confident they could face anything together.

Tennly was excited for the annual Halloween party at Benny's. She dressed in steampunk attire, featuring a black corset top with buckles, pockets, and satchels, over a white off the shoulder peasant blouse. The bottom of her outfit consisted of tight black short shorts paired with a black and brown, lacy layered skirt, that was open in the front and long in the back. Thigh-high black stockings adorned with garter clips complemented the lacy black and brown high-heeled ankle boots.

Her eyes were shaded with shiny brown eyeshadow on the top and white glimmer around the perimeter. On the side of her right temple, she placed gold and bronze gear stick-ons that started at the corner of her eye and trailed up to her forehead.

To complete her look, their on-call hairstylist came to the mansion to create an authentic steampunk hairstyle. On the right side of her head were three small cornrow braids, which merged into a larger, messy braid on the left side and gathered in a ponytail, adorned with ribbons. Atop her head, she wore a pair of steampunk goggles positioned perfectly like a headband.

She picked up Josie first, who was dressed as a sexy vampire, then Abby, who wore an 80s outfit and finally Dougy and Rick, who were dressed like 1950s greasers; a look that Tennly thought didn't differ much from their usual style. They then picked up Tina, who was dressed as a baby doll, and Lucy, who went as a ballerina.

Benny's foyer was transformed into a haunted house maze with jump scares that popped out and flashing lights accompanied by the loud sounds of chainsaws and screams. Inside the dance room, orange, purple, and black balloons were scattered across the floor, and bouquets of helium balloons decorated each table. The walls were adorned with Halloween decorations and even the food at the bar had a Halloween theme.

Somehow, Conner talked his friends in to stopping at Benny's before going to a party. Knowing where Tennly would be when he got there, they headed straight to the dance room. Sam ran over to Tennly, picked her up, swung her around, and shouted, "Tennly!"

"Sam," Tennly greeted, smiling after he let her go.

"Wow," Sam exclaimed. "You look great!"

"Thank you, kind sir," Tennly replied playfully. "So do you."

"I don't have a costume on," Sam informed, looking confused.

"I know," Tennly teased, giving him a wink.

"Ah," Sam exclaimed as he stumbled. "I'll see you later."

Abby looked at Tennly and said, perplexed, "I can't believe they came."

"Why?" Tennly asked.

"They never come to this party," Abby answered.

"I think it's cool," Tina said.

"Shut up, Tina," Lucy huffed realizing Tina was referring to The Untouchables being there because Conner wanted to see Tennly.

Tennly felt a surge of joy, and a warm smile spread across her face at the thought of Conner being there to see her. His friends noticed her approaching and reminded him he had a few minutes before they needed to leave.

"Hi," Tennly greeted once they were alone.

"Hi," he replied.

"Rumor has it you guys never come to this thing," she announced, holding her hand over her mouth to try and hide her smile.

"Well," he replied, face flushed. "I had a reason to this year."

He gave her a seductive look that made her wonder whether it was intentional or just a natural reaction. She had grown accustomed to his looks, even the more seductive ones, but that night it felt different: a look of resolution.

He wanted to stay with her. He wanted to tell her he couldn't live without her, but seeing Riley walking toward him reminded him that it wasn't the right time.

"If you don't go, you'll hate me," she said after she saw the expression on his face that he didn't want to leave. Then she whispered, "He'll hate me," referring to Riley. "Go."

"I'll text you later?" Conner replied.

"You better."

The next morning, Tennly woke up to find a text from Conner, asking her to go to a party with him and his friends later that night. When she told him she was going to Josie's for a sleepover, he suggested she bring them along and told her that he would be waiting at the end of her street at 9:00 PM.

She could tell that he wasn't going to take no for an answer, so she agreed to meet him. All she needed to do was convince her friends to come along.

While Josie's parents were at a Halloween party, the girls ordered pizza and handed out candy to the trick-or-treaters before retreating to Josie's bedroom for the night. As they settled into their usual spots, and Abby pulled out the dare game, Tennly became restless.

"I have to tell you guys something," Tennly started.

"What is it?" Abby inquired.

Tennly took a deep breath and then blurted out, "We've been invited to a party with The Untouchables, and Conner is picking us up at nine!"

The girls fell silent, momentarily frozen in place; the idea of going anywhere with The Untouchables terrified them.

"Hear me out," Tennly continued. "Your parents will pass out as soon as they get home, so, it wouldn't be hard to sneak out."

Once they could find their voices, they began discussing the pros and cons of Tennly's plan. When it was looking as if they weren't going to go, Tennly pleaded, "Come on, Jose, you're always saying how you want to be more adventurous. And Abby, you're constantly saying how you would die to spend even a minute with them."

The girls continued to go back and forth, concerned with having nothing to wear, being afraid to sneak out, and worried about what The Untouchables could do to them.

"I have an idea," Tina chimed in. Shocked, they looked at her expectantly. "Something that might ease all of our minds." Her pause caused them to motion for her to continue. "Why don't we just tell Josie's parents that we want to go to Tennly's house to watch a movie on the big screen?"

They all understood where she was going with this and smiled as she added, "That way, Josie wouldn't have to technically sneak out... And if it's okay with Tennly, those of us without proper attire..."

"It's perfect," Tennly interrupted. "And of course, you can borrow my clothes." Then, she looked at Josie and asked, "What do you say, Jose?"

Josie felt a bit better knowing she didn't have to sneak out, but she glanced at Lucy, who still maintained fear in her eyes. "Luce?"

Lucy put her head down, ran her hands through her hair, then looked at her friends with a defeated look on her face. "Fine."

Abby started screaming and jumping up and down, while Tennly looked at Tina and mouthed a thank you. As soon as Josie told the girls her parents approved it, they rushed to Tennly's bedroom.

They enjoyed trying on Tennly's clothes, parading around like they were in a fashion show. They were having so much fun that they lost track of time, forgetting the whole reason for getting ready in the first place. When Tennly announced they had fifteen minutes to finalize their looks, the girls stopped what they were doing and stared at her, wide-eyed.

Abby sank down onto the floor, burying her head in her knees as the reality of going out with The Untouchables loomed over her. "I can't do this."

Tennly placed a hand on Abby's shoulder and spoke in a firm yet supportive tone. "Abby, if you don't go, you will always regret it. Now get up."

Abby looked at her, fear evident in her eyes. "What if I embarrass myself, or they don't like me?"

"That's impossible. You're an amazing person, and they're going to love you," Tennly assured her. Then, with a smile, she added, "And if they're mean to you in any way, they'll have to deal with me. Okay?"

Abby had admired Tennly since the day they met, but at that moment, she realized Tennly was not just a fun person to hang out with; she was a true friend. "Thank you," Abby said, feeling encouraged. "What are we waiting for?

MHS
PRESENTED BY THE CLASS OF 1990

CHAPTER 16

When the girls reached the end of Tennly's street, Conner was leaning back against his car, smoking a cigarette. Abby grabbed hold of Josie's hand and squeezed it as they approached, while Lucy and Tina stayed a little behind, as if Josie could keep them safe.

"I was beginning to think you weren't coming," Conner said, as he stomped out the cigarette.

"We're girls," Tennly replied. "We do things on our time." She then poked his chest and added, "And you're going to be okay with that."

"Yes, ma'am," he yielded with the cutest smile, which made the other girls swoon.

He opened the back door behind the driver's seat and motioned for the girls to get in, while Tennly got in the front. His gesture confused them; they didn't understand how someone like Conner Marks could be so chivalrous. Mesmerized, they stood frozen, unable to believe they were about to get into an Untouchable's car.

"I really don't bite," he assured with the same cute smile. "Despite what you've heard."

The girls felt their stomachs turn as if a thousand butterflies were trying to escape. Lucy avoided the situation altogether, running around to the other side to sit behind Tennly. Josie was closest to Conner, so she got in first, followed by Tina. They scooted all the way across the bench seat until they reached Lucy, making room for Abby, who was still too awestruck to get in.

When Conner noticed Abby's hesitation, he smiled at her and suggested, "What do you say we get going, huh?" and then winked.

"Okay," she trembled, and then melted into the car. The look she gave the other girls reflected a delightful insanity. She thought that if nothing else happened for the rest of the night, at least she would have an unforgettable story to tell.

As strange as it was for the girls to see him opening the door for them, it was even more unusual to watch him engage in a normal conversation. They had always viewed Conner as sullen and brooding but seeing him laughing and talking as freely with Tennly as she was with him made him seem more common.

The house where the party was being hosted was set back on a private road, nestled among several rows of trees. Cars were parked haphazardly in the yard beside the house, leaving little space for Conner to park.

The living room was where the music blared, and the dancing took place. The kitchen was filled with kegs and snacks, while the dining room had a beer pong game set up on the table.

They made their way from the foyer to the kitchen, grabbing cups of beer before heading to the living room. The whole way, Tennly's friends walked so close behind Conner and Tennly that it seemed they were using the pair as shields.

Once in the living room, they spotted Riley and Joel sitting on the couch, surrounded by a group of girls. Conner dismissed the girls and invited Tennly's friends to sit down in their place.

"Where's Sam?" Conner asked as he directed Tennly down upon his lap and then wrapped his arms around her.

Riley cringed at the sight but replied, "Where do you think?"

Conner nodded, knowing Sam was likely upstairs in one of the bedrooms. "Anything happening?"

"Not really," Riley replied, taking a drink. "We have to smoke outside. Want to come?"

"Sure," Conner said, glancing at Tennly as if to ask for her permission, which irritated Riley even more.

"Go," Tennly said. "We'll be fine."

He gave her a kiss on the forehead, gently lifted her, and set her back down on the coffee table. "I'll be right back."

"I won't get into too much trouble while you're gone," Tennly claimed, flashing him a mischievous grin.

As soon as the boys were gone, Tennly's friends gave her questioning expressions. She understood their curiosity, as she was contemplating the same thing. Conner was treating her differently, almost as if she were more than just a friend.

"You guys see it too, right?" Tennly inquired.

"Oh yeah," Abby affirmed. "What are you going to do?"

"Nothing," Tennly replied. "Or... um... pretend I don't notice anything."

"Yeah, like that'll work," Abby said.

"What do you mean?" Tennly asked.

"Everyone can see how he's treating you," Abby pointed out.

"It's about time," Tina mumbled.

"Shut up, Tina," Lucy huffed.

"I'm just saying..." Tina continued, "maybe he wants you to notice... because it's too hard for him to make the first move."

"No," Tennly said, although she found Tina's comment intriguing and wished it were true. "Conner does things on his own time. He can't be rushed or pushed. I just wait."

"I don't know how you're not going crazy right now," Abby admitted.

"Who's to say I'm not," Tennly declared. "I just can't let him know that."

"The thrill of the hunt," Abby teased.

"Yep," Tennly said as she stood up. "Come on. Let's see what trouble we can find."

They ended up in the dining room where they watched the end of the current beer pong game and then Tennly asked to play against the winner. Conner, Riley, and Joel arrived just in time to hear the crowd cheer to Tennly's victory.

"I get the next game," Sam demanded as he strolled in.

"Of course, you do," Tennly replied with three light, playful taps on his right cheek.

Her playful banter with Conner had become something everyone looked forward to, but seeing her share that same dynamic with Sam made them all realize that The Untouchables had gained a new member. Which meant everyone felt comfortable cheering for her when she successfully defeated Sam.

"I am forever in your service, milady," Sam bowed, thus solidifying Tennly's new status.

Holding a ping pong ball in her right hand, Tennly tapped his left shoulder and then his right as she commanded, "You may rise, Sir Sam."

After their small theatrical exchange, they moved off to the side to let two different players take their place. However, before they were out of the dining room, they heard a familiar voice.

"What about me?" Shelby asked.

Tennly agreed to play her if they placed wagers on it. To which Shelby agreed and with a haughty attitude said, "If I win, you go back to wherever it was you came from."

"My house?" Tennly laughed, knowing what Shelby really meant.

Shelby smiled sarcastically but explained, "You leave Marinsburg High and go back to whatever fancy private school you came from."

"Fine," Tennly agreed.

Worried, Conner whispered to Tennly that no matter what Shelby bet, she wouldn't abide by it. Tennly gave him a look that told him she knew what she was doing and to trust her.

"If I win," Tennly responded, "you can never have anything to do with Conner... ever again. And I mean, nothing... And if you don't follow those rules, I'm sure everyone here will make sure you do."

A rigid glare came over Shelby's face as her jaw clenched. She could feel her muscles tightening as she stifled the urge to scream. Even though she wanted to get rid of Tennly, she didn't want the whole student body to be against her. So, with a huff, she stormed out of the room.

Not wanting to stay at the party, yet not wanting to end the night, Tennly, Conner and their friends deliberated where they could go.

"I have a place," Tennly mentioned.

The boys were excited, when they arrived at the yacht club, having never been through the gate before, but cautiously walked down the long sidewalk, past the boathouse, and to the docks. There were seven smaller speedboats, four pontoon boats, three houseboats, one very small yacht, and at the end of the docks was the Chéadsearc.

The girls boarded immediately, but the boys hesitated for a moment. As they looked down at the boys, the girls noticed a shift in dynamics; instead of the girls feeling nervous, it was the boys who appeared intimidated, clearly being out of their element.

Tennly looked at the boys and mentioned, "There's a lot of alcohol on the yacht."

"That's all I need," Sam replied before stepping aboard.

Tennly guided them on a tour, showing them around every level before settling down in the bar area on the top deck. After grabbing two six-packs of beer, Tennly instructed everyone to switch places so that they were alternating boys and girls for a game of Truth or Dare.

They didn't understand why she was making them move, especially the girls. It was already nerve-wracking enough to be sitting across from The Untouchables, let alone in between them. "It's hard to get to know each other when you're sitting in your own groups. Now move it!"

Conner found it amusing that his friends were following her instructions. Her friends couldn't believe that The Untouchables were still present and cooperating with her, making the situation feel surreal to everyone.

To ensure that no one was picked more than others, they started going clockwise and worked their way around. Due to a random draw, Tina was picked to go first. She chose Truth and could feel her nerves prickling all over her skin as she waited for Josie to ask her the question.

"Are you nervous?" Josie asked, starting with an easy one.

"Yes," Tina replied, causing everyone to laugh.

Next was Sam, who was sitting to the left of Tina. Not wanting to reveal anything about himself, he chose dare. Tina, usually shy and timid, surprised everyone by daring Sam to kiss Abby. She knew how much Abby would love to be kissed by an Untouchable and wanted to give her a memorable story.

Abby's eyes widened and her jaw dropped as every nerve in her body began to tingle, while Sam asked, "What kind of kiss?"

"I don't care," Tina replied.

"My choice?" Sam said mischievously. He then turned to face Abby, cupped her face in his hands and softly kissed her on the lips.

Abby felt a rush of heat surge through her as her entire body trembled. The kiss surprised her; it was more gentlemanly than she had anticipated, contrasting sharply with what she knew of Sam's reputation.

"You, okay?" Sam asked, noticing that Abby looked frozen in shock. The fact that he still had his fingers caressing her chin made her feel anything but okay, but she nodded. He eventually let go of her chin and said, "It's your turn. You ready?"

"Yeah," Abby barely managed to reply.

"Truth or dare?" Sam asked.

"Um," Abby moaned, unsure if she could handle another dare. "Truth."

Sam looked at her seductively and asked, "Do you want another kiss?"

Abby swallowed to gain what composure she could muster, but all she managed to do was nod.

Sam gently used his lips to open hers and then ran his tongue around the inside of her mouth. He finished the kiss by closing her mouth with his and giving her a light peck.

While Tennly, Josie and Tina were delighted for Abby, Lucy felt increasingly anxious. Seeing Sam behave in such a tantalizing manner caused her to believe that this was The Untouchables' way of getting girls to sleep with them.

It was Abby's turn and between feeling nervous and still reveling from the kiss, she had a hard time coming up with a dare for Riley.

"Dare him to eat a banana," Conner chuckled.

"You suck," Riley said to Conner as everyone laughed. When Tennly returned, from the kitchen, Riley shoved the entire banana into his mouth, letting out a disgusting sound and then turned to Tennly, not missing a beat, "Truth or dare?"

"Dare," Tennly replied.

"Afraid of the truth?" Riley goaded, causing an awkward environment.

Tennly knew he was provoking her. She just didn't know if he was trying to hurt her or prove to Conner that she wasn't right for him. No matter what she did, she couldn't get him to accept her. So, she thought she would at least show him that she wasn't afraid of him.

"Fine," Tennly conceded. "What do you want to know?"

"Are you using Conner?" Riley interrogated.

Tennly and Riley locked eyes in a tense stare as Conner yelled sternly, "Riley!"

Tennly reassured Conner that it was ok and answered his question with a no. Then without giving Riley the opportunity to say another word, she looked at Conner and asked if he wanted Truth or Dare. Conner declined the dare to give Sam a lap dance and took the consequence, a drink of beer.

The game continued around the group and when Lucy was asked why she feared them, the conversations that Tennly had hoped for were finally starting. She wanted her friends and Conner's friends to be able to get together without fears or preconceived notions about each other.

They went around the circle two more times, with the girls always asking for truth and the boys asking for dares. By the time the third round ended, Tennly's plan had worked, and they all felt relaxed, even Lucy.

While Tennly was getting out a bottle of whiskey and some glasses, Conner walked over to her. "Thanks."

"For what?" she asked.

"Just being you," he said, brushing her cheek with his thumb as the others broke into smaller groups.

Sam and Joel stepped outside to smoke a cigarette and Tina, Abby, and Lucy scooted over to sit together, leaving Josie and Riley on the other side, facing Tennly and Conner.

Seeing Riley's discomfort with the situation, visible by his furrowed brow, glaring eyes, and pursed lips, Josie politely noted, "You know it's only a matter of time."

"What?" Riley asked.

"Before they get together." When he remained silent, she added, "Why does it bother you so much?"

"Why doesn't it bother you?"

"I didn't say it didn't."

"She's not the one who's going to get hurt."

"You're worried she's going to hurt him?"

"When she's done playing with him, she'll move on."

"You don't believe that she really loves him?"

"I don't know her."

"Well," Josie said as she stood up, "maybe you should try to get to."

Her words created a weight in his heart as he watched Tennly take another drink, laugh, and then rest her head on Conner's shoulder, knowing that Josie was right. Over the past two months, Conner had appeared happier than he had in years. Just as he was about to approach, Tennly to give her a chance, an alarm went off on Josie's phone.

"We've got to go, Ten," Josie informed.

After cleaning up their mess, Conner dropped the girls off at the corner of Tennly's street and told her he would see her later. By the time the girls arrived at Josie's house, it was clear that Tennly wasn't planning to go inside.

"I have to," Tennly insisted.

"We know," Josie conceded. Even Lucy nodded in agreement, prompting Josie to say, "I'll just tell mom you stayed home."

"Thank you," Tennly said. After hugging her friends, who reminded her to be careful and expected a full report in the morning, she ran to Conner's house.

Conner had just turned on the television when he heard a knock at the door. As soon as he saw her, an electrifying warmth washed over them both. He immediately started kissing her as he picked her up, her legs wrapping around his waist, and carried her to his bedroom. Gently laying her down on the mattress, he kissed his way down her neck.

The desire to have him was so strong, that she flipped him over, so she was on top. As he helped her take off her shirt, he could tell that she was drunk. He groaned, wanting more than anything to make love to her, but instead he sat up and gently placed her beside him.

"What's wrong?" she asked, worried that she had pushed him too soon.

"Nothing."

"Then...?"

"You've been drinking... and I've been drinking..."

"I'm perfectly aware of my actions, Conner," she said as she leaned in to kiss him again.

Holding her back, he said, "Not like this. I've dreamed of this day for a long time, and when it happens, I want to be sober."

He had had sex many times before, and almost every time he was either drunk, stoned, or both. There was no way he was going to start a physical relationship with the love of his life in the same way as all the others. Despite wanting him more than anything, Tennly appreciated what he said; it made her feel special, and she respected him for it.

"Okay," she conceded and then buried her head into his chest and intertwined her legs through his. "But if you change your mind... I'm right here."

"Grr," he moaned as he could feel her pelvic region rub up against his. "You drive me absolutely crazy."

She looked up at him and licked her lips in a tantalizing way. "I'll make it easier on you." She then put her shirt back on and wiggled herself against him in a spooning position. She took his arm and draped it over her, as if it were a blanket she was using to keep warm.

"This isn't easier," he whispered into her ear.

"Would a pillow between us help?" she giggled.

"Yeah, it would," he replied playfully.

She quickly turned back around, ensuring there was at least half a foot between them. "You know that I'm a... I've never had..."

"I get it," he interrupted gently.

"And since you're kind of a professional at this," she teased, "if you think we should wait... then we'll wait."

"A professional?" he asked with a playful smile.

She shrugged her shoulders and smiled back, "I thought 'man-whore' would be too harsh."

She knew that the only way to make them pause was to start their playful banter. He understood her intentions and was grateful because if the atmosphere between them didn't shift, he would eventually give in.

Tennly woke up the next morning, with only five minutes left before she had promised Marie she would be home from Josie's. The last thing she needed was for Marie to question her whereabouts, even though every bone in her body screamed for her to stay. Feeling her confliction, he gave her a kiss, reassuring her that when the time was right, they would know. The last thing either of them wanted was to be rushed.

With less time than she initially thought, she ran down the street, unaware that Thomas had seen her. Daniel was furious when he learned that his daughter had spent the night with Conner, and he ordered Thomas to drive him to Conner's house immediately.

Hoping it was Tennly changing her mind about leaving, he was startled to see Thomas. After being told Daniel wanted to speak with him, Conner hesitated briefly, but didn't want Daniel to think he was scared. He followed Thomas to the back passenger side door and gingerly looked inside.

Daniel leaned across the back seat and commanded, "Get in." Conner gave him a suspicious look to which Daniel added, "I'm not going to kill you, get in."

Conner got in, unable to shake the feeling that it was reminiscent of a scene from Goodfellas.

"I'm not going to sugarcoat anything," Daniel said, as Thomas drove. "I've made it perfectly clear that I don't want you seeing my daughter."

"I think that's up to her," Conner countered.

"Tennly is special," Daniel responded ignoring Conner's comment. "She approaches everything with complete devotion. She pours her heart and soul into whatever she does. That means if she develops feelings for you, she won't be able to think about anything else. She will set aside her family, her friends, her school, and even her own life for you..."

Conner understood what Daniel was saying; he had witnessed it firsthand. Whenever Tennly became passionate about something, she dedicated herself fully until she felt it was perfect. If she thought she could help him, he knew she would sacrifice everything to do so, even at the expense of her own needs.

"Someday, she will take over all my businesses and be worth billions. Your involvement with her jeopardizes all that. Are you willing to risk her success and future for just a few nights of pleasure?... Now, I could easily get rid of you, and I haven't completely ruled that out. However, I'd prefer to end your relationship in a somewhat less messy way."

Daniel reached down to the floor and picked up a large dark blue duffle bag, placing it between them. "To make your decision easier..." he tempted, patting the bag. "Go ahead, open it."

Conner knew what was inside and despised the idea that Daniel thought he could be bought. He glanced at Daniel, intending to refuse the offer, but Daniel pushed the bag toward him and demanded that he look inside. Swallowing his pride, Conner did as he was ordered.

"There's half a million dollars. You and I both know she's meant for something better. So, take the money. It'll make things a little easier: a sort of compensation for your loss."

By the time Daniel finished speaking, Thomas had made his way back and was in front of Conner's house. Before Conner could figure out what to do, he suddenly found himself standing outside of the car with the bag in his hand.

"Oh," Daniel added. "And one more thing. I know a lot of people in this town. If I find out that you take my money but still see her, I will kill you, your brother, and anyone else that I need to."

Conner stood there, his body heavy and unable to move, trying to process everything that had happened in the last 24 hours. Not sure how he made it to the kitchen, he walked around, staring at the duffel bag in the center of the table. He hated the fact that Daniel was able to get him to do something he never thought he would ever do. But half a million dollars was not a small amount.

With $500,000, he could finally build a small house on the property that his grandfather had given him and escape from his father for good. He could help his friends, donate some to the warehouse, and, most importantly, assist Dougy in paying for college. However, what made him consider taking it wasn't the money. Daniel presented a strong argument for why she would be better off without him; it was the same thing he had always told himself.

He continued to stare at the duffle bag as if it were a magic ball that could tell him what to do. He knew he had made up his mind to stay away from her, but he wasn't sure if he should keep the money. He had started the day poor, and every ounce of his body urged him to take it. He just wished it didn't hurt so much.

CHAPTER 17

Conner avoided everyone for the rest of the weekend. To ease his anxiety about potentially keeping the money, he took the duffle bag to the property his grandfather had given him and hid it in a secret wall compartment in the loft of the barn.

He lay down on a small futon mattress that he had received from Riley's mother and covered himself with blankets that Dante had given him. The morning alarm on his phone woke him just in time to head home for a shower and make it to school. The thought of seeing Tennly nearly made him want to skip, but he knew he would eventually have to face her. As he prepared to leave, his nerves were so tight that his entire body was shaking.

He slumped down on his bed, trying to catch his breath. The more he focused on his breathing, the faster his heartbeat raced, and the more nauseous he felt. The only thing that he knew would help was to become numb. He thought if he could just get a small hit, he might be able to make it through the day.

Tennly sensed that something was wrong. She had texted Conner a couple of times on Sunday, but he hadn't replied. When she didn't see him that morning, her biggest fear began to materialize; she had done something to push him too far, and now he was avoiding her.

Her fears intensified when she reached the landing at lunch and saw no one there. She considered texting him again but couldn't bring herself to do it, her anger boiling within her.

Just as she was about to head back to the cafeteria, she noticed Conner walking down the path. Something seemed off about him; he staggered down the hill, his legs wobbly, nearly falling twice. By the time he reached her, his eyes rolled back into his head, and he collapsed to the ground.

"Conner!" she screamed as she slapped him in the face. "Wake up!"

She thought she knew what fear was when faced with the possibility of being killed on her first job for the family. However, that fear paled in comparison to what she felt as she watched Conner's twitches escalate. Grabbing her phone while holding Conner's head, she called Dougy.

When Dougy reached the landing, he dropped down beside them and pulled Conner onto his lap. He quickly turned Conner onto his side and tried to get him to vomit by putting his finger down his throat.

By the time Riley arrived, Conner was not moving and was barely breathing. Riley pushed Dougy out of the way and checked Conner's pulse then leaned down, placing his ear against Conner's nose to make sure he could feel his breath.

"Conner!" Riley shouted as he slapped his face. "Wake up!" He then ordered Dougy to help him get him down the path.

Tennly followed as they dragged Conner to an old, abandoned hotel at the bottom of the hill. The front door to the lobby had been kicked in, breaking the frame and the lock. Most of the windows were shattered and covered with tattered blankets. With no furniture left, Riley laid Conner on the floor while Dougy

rummaged through the boxes on the desk to
find a couple of blankets, a first aid kit,
and a large bag.

"Grab that bucket," Riley said,
pointing to the corner next to a back door.
"Take it out back. There's a stream there.
Get some water and bring it back...
Hurry!"

Tennly dashed to retrieve the bucket,
scurrying to the stream. She knew the water
was freezing, but as she dipped the bucket
into it, she felt nothing. It wasn't until
after she gave Riley the bucket and pulled
out her phone that she saw how red her
hands were. Ignoring it, she called Dr.
Pratt, who agreed to meet her there.

"I have a doctor coming in a half
hour," Tennly informed.

"He doesn't have a half hour," Riley
implied. Using a measuring cup from the
first aid kit, he scooped out black powder
from the bag, dumped it into a pitcher,
and added some water from the bucket.

"What is that?" Tennly asked, trying
to focus on what Riley was doing and not
think about Conner only having a half hour
left.

"Charcoal," Riley replied. He then
pulled out a beer bong tube from the bag,

that he had previously modified to the exact length needed.

Tennly watched as Riley attempted to insert the tube deep into Conner's throat; her body tensing as Conner started flailing his arms, trying to push it away. Dougy pinned Conner's arms down with his legs while Riley shouted at him to hold Conner's head still. It became clear to Tennly that they knew what to do because they had gone through this before.

Seeing the fear in Tennly's eyes, Dougy said, "Hopefully, he stayed true to form and took pills. If he did, the charcoal will bind to whatever he swallowed."

Riley looked at him and asked if he was ready. He then poured the charcoal mixture down the funnel and into Conner's mouth. Once all the liquid was flushed down Conner's throat, Riley removed the tube and scooted back to wait.

"What now?" Tennly asked.

"We wait," Dougy said.

The waiting felt like hours, even though it was only a few minutes before Conner started gagging. Dougy rolled him onto his side just in time for him to vomit. When he was finished, Dougy wiped his face with one of the blankets as Tennly asked if he was going to be okay.

"Yeah," Dougy replied. "He'll definitely feel it when he wakes up, and he'll probably shit bricks for a couple of days, but he should be fine."

Riley told Dougy to go back to school and tried to get Tennly to go with him, but she refused. She moved over to Conner and began caressing his face as she placed his head on her lap. Riley watched as she removed her coat and laid it across Conner's chest to keep him warm.

"How often does he do this?" she asked.

"He gets bad every other month or so... But, like this, only a handful of times."

She wondered if the reason for this time was because they were getting close again, and it overwhelmed him. Before she could ask what Riley thought, Dr. Pratt walked in. Without saying a word to either of them, he knelt beside Conner and opened his bag.

"What did he take?" Dr. Pratt asked as he started the IV.

"I don't know," Tennly replied.

"Probably oxy or some other benzodiazepine," Riley suggested.

"I noticed charcoal," Dr. Pratt said. "Whoever did that saved his life. Is this the same boy I treated at your house?"

"Yeah," Tennly answered.

"He's tempting fate," the doctor continued. "If he keeps this up, he won't live much longer." He rechecked his vitals and added, "He should be fine."

Dr. Pratt left, only after Riley assured him, he knew how to take out the IV. Followed shortly by Sam and Joel rushing in, bellowing if he was okay. After Riley told them he would be fine, Sam asked, clearly intrigued, "You have a doctor on call?"

"Yeah," Tennly confirmed.

"That's not suspicious at all," Sam suggested with a grin.

Riley wasn't in the mood for Sam's lighthearted banter with Tennly. He wanted her gone, so out of the blue he looked at her and goaded, "Did you ever stop to think this is your fault?"

"Riley," Sam barked, feeling bad for her

Tennly nodded and in a sullen voice wept, "Yeah."

"Tennly," Sam gently said, "you don't have to go."

"It's okay, Sam," she said, patting him on the shoulder as she walked out of the building.

Tennly spent the entire day waiting for Conner to text her, but he never did. The only messages she received were a couple from friends checking on her and one from Dougy saying that Conner was home and doing fine. By the time the next day arrived, she was so depressed that she couldn't get out of bed. She managed to take another sick day by faking symptoms, but by the third, Marie was onto her.

"If you don't have a fever, Tennly, you need to go to school. It's 7:00 AM. You still have time to shower and get there."

"Go away!" Tennly screamed, pulling the blankets over her head and rolling onto her side.

onner spent the next two days at the barn, wrestling with the decision of whether to keep the money or return it. He was guilt-ridden about keeping it, but he finally had a chance to help his brother escape poverty. The only obstacle in his way was Tennly.

By the end of the second day, Conner realized he needed someone to dissuade him from returning the money. Knowing that Riley would challenge him and play devil's advocate, he went to see him.

Riley knew about Conner's land but had never been there before. As he followed Conner down a path to the barn, he marveled at the beauty: the breathtaking view of the purple mountains behind the luxurious green flowing valley. Once in the loft, Conner pulled the duffle bag out from the wall and laid it down on the floor beside Riley's feet. Riley looked at him, wondering if he had gotten involved with something dangerous.

"Just open it," Conner ordered.

"Jesus," Riley exclaimed upon seeing all the money. "How much is here?"

"Half a mil."

"Holy shit. Where did you get it?"

"Tennly's dad. If I stay away from her, I get to keep it."

Riley felt conflicted about Conner's answer. He was angered that Tennly's father could think Conner was that easy to buy off, and he was saddened to see his friend in such turmoil. Yet, at the same time, the money could give Conner a chance at a better life and help him break away from Tennly.

"I need you to talk me into keeping it."

"Of course, you have to keep it. That's a lot of money. Is that why you...?"

Conner gave him a look that told him it was. "Look, yes, I think you should keep it... but I also know you. You have to be able to live with yourself. So..." He watched as Conner took the bag and hid it back in the wall. "What are you going to do about Tennly until you decide?"

"Stay away from her."

"You haven't been very successful at that so far."

"I know."

When Daniel returned home from a four-day business trip, Marie confronted him about Tennly not going to school. He went to her room and found her curled up in bed, holding a pillow and hiding under the covers.

"Marie tells me you're not feeling well," Daniel said as he sat at the foot of her bed. Tennly didn't respond. "Do you want to talk about it?"

"No."

He wasn't sure if she was aware of Conner taking the money, but he suspected it was connected to him ending their relationship. It angered him to see his daughter, who was strong and set to become the future leader of the family, in such a vulnerable state. If she couldn't handle the emotional fallout from a boy, how could she possibly manage a crime syndicate?

"You need to pull yourself together," Daniel asserted. "Get up, take a shower, and go work out or something. And you're going to school tomorrow." When Tennly remained still and silent, his frustration grew. "No boy is worth this!" he yelled. "Especially one who can be bought!"

As she lay there, wrestling with his words, the pain in her chest intensified. She got out of bed, but as she made her way to the bathroom, she collapsed on the floor, unable to breath. The thought that Conner might have taken money to stay away from her was unbearable.

The next morning, she went to school, only to confront Conner and ask him if her father's claims were accurate. Various rumors had spread about why Conner had overdosed and why she had been absent, but she paid no attention to any of them. Even when her friends tried to tell her about the rumor where she was pregnant, she shut them down.

She went to her morning classes going through the motions, waiting for lunch so she could speak to him. When she saw him walk into the cafeteria, she stormed over to him, as Riley continued to the quad.

Conner stopped to await her, seeing the look on her face and knew what she wanted. He bit his lower lip, a sign of his nervousness, but the most telling indication of his guilt was his reluctance to make eye contact.

She pushed him hard enough in the chest to make him take a couple of steps back as she yelled, "How much?" When he didn't respond, she shoved him again and demanded, "How much does it cost to buy me?"

He shook his head, unable to answer her, as the cafeteria fell silent, as if in mourning. That silence reflected Tennly's feelings; the loss of her friendship with Conner felt like a death. It was ironic that money, something he despised about her, was what ultimately separated them. The disappointment on her face caused Conner to feel such deep anguish that, for the first time in his life, he genuinely wished he was dead.

"You broke my heart," she cried before running out of the cafeteria.

She didn't stay at school, instead she went home and marched straight into her father's office. An overwhelming urge to punch him in the face crept over her. She fully intended to act on her feelings, but by the time she reached his desk, she realized there was no point in expressing her anger; it wouldn't accomplish anything. Her mind was made up.

Calmly, yet feeling defeated, she said, "You win. Get the jet ready. I want to leave tomorrow for Prague."

She started to walk away, but Daniel called after her, "Is that necessary?"

She couldn't believe that, after what he had done, he had the nerve to ask her to stay. She ran back over to his desk, slammed her hands down furiously, and screamed, "Get the jet ready!"

Conner had the same thought as Tennly, to get as far away from her as possible. However, he didn't have a private jet to escape on. His only option was to get arrested, hoping to do something drastic enough to be sent away. After downing a bottle of vodka, he got on his motorcycle and sped through the downtown streets until the police started chasing him.

He turned down a dead-end alley with nowhere to go, only to find two police cars parked behind him. As the officers aimed their guns at him, he thought for a split second to pretend to have a weapon. The only thing that kept him from it, was the thought of Dougy, so he held up his hands.

Because Conner was only 17 years old, a parent needed to be contacted. Kenneth told them to keep him, as he could no longer control him. Dougy was home and overheard and immediately ran to Riley's house to share what had happened and then texted Tennly to inform her.

It was late, and she wasn't sure what she could do, but despite what had happened between them, she had to do something. She looked around the mansion for her father, finally finding him sitting at the breakfast nook, working on his laptop and eating a piece of pie.

"Our plane will be ready at 11 tomorrow morning to take you to New York," Daniel said, after she sat down. "Are you sure this is what you want to do?"

"I need the name of one of your police officers: one who can get things done."

"Why?"

"Conner was arrested."

Daniel anticipated what Tennly was planning, so he firmly said, "No."

Tennly placed her hands down on the table, striving to remain calm. "You owe me this. I'm leaving tomorrow and will never see him again. He doesn't deserve to be sent away for something you did." She looked at him, her eyes pleading. "Please."

Daniel nodded and replied, "Follow me."

When they got to his office, he opened a drawer in his desk and pulled out a three-ring binder. Flipping through the pages, he found what he was looking for and extracted a sheet of paper.

Handing it to her he said, "If you're going to do what I think you are, you'll need this."

Tennly looked at the sheet and saw that it contained detailed information on Officer Taylor, including where he lived, his phone number, his family, and even the church he attended. She looked up at her father, nodded in gratitude, and then turned to walk toward her bedroom.

She reviewed the information until she felt she had memorized everything and then blocked her number to call the officer. Using the threat of releasing derogatory information she had on him; he agreed to meet her at the big gazebo in the park.

"What do you want?" Officer Taylor asked after he took a seat beside her.

"You arrested someone today and I want them cleared."

"I want the information first."

"I know you work for Daniel O'Brien... and..."

He laughed and said, "Whatever you think you have, there's no way Daniel will let you get away with it." Then he stood up and started to walk away.

Frustrated, she drew a knife from her belt holster and threw it at him. It grazed his right arm before embedding itself in the far gazebo post as he screamed in fear. Remaining silent and steadfast, she observed as he violently charged toward her; her only motion was lowering her hoodie.

"Who is it?" He shivered, recognizing her.

"Conner Marks."

With nervous laughter, he said, "That's impossible."

"For the sake of your family I hope it's not."

"You wouldn't."

"Are you willing to risk that? If Conner isn't exonerated from everything, I will kill you and your entire family. Get him cleared! It's a simple request. Don't ruin your life over it."

"Have someone at the jail to pick him up first thing in the morning."

Feeling a sense of pride in having successfully completed her first blackmail, there was still one more thing to do.

"Haven't you done enough?" Riley asked when he opened the door and saw her standing there.

"You won't have to worry about me after today. I'm leaving for Prague in the morning. I just need you to be at the jail first thing tomorrow... Conner will need a ride home."

As she walked back toward her car, he called out, "Wait." She turned back to face him. "What do you mean?"

"I took care of it. Just be there to get him, okay?"

He nodded, giving her a look of apology, to which she acknowledged, "Just take care of him."

The next morning, while Conner waited to hear from an attorney regarding his indictment, an officer came to his cell, opened the door and told him he was free to go. Confused, he followed the officer out to the main desk, struggling to believe that all his hard work in getting there was for nothing. He retrieved all his belongings and signed a paper acknowledging that they were returned.

Standing beside his old car was Riley, who was waiting for him; neither one speaking until they left the downtown area.

"Take me to the school," Conner said. "I need to see her and tell her I'm not keeping the money."

Riley hated to tell him the truth, but he had no choice. "She's not there. She left for Prague this morning."

Conner closed his eyes to gather himself, but it didn't help. Anger surged through him, and he started punching the glove compartment until his knuckles bled.

When Tennly arrived at the boarding school she met with Headmistress Novakova. She told her she would be staying with Victoria since her room was given away. She didn't mind; she wasn't there to matriculate anyway. Other than getting away from Conner, she was only there to train.

"I already have your training scheduled to start tomorrow morning," Headmistress Novakova informed, "but if I understood your request correctly, it will be brutal. Are you ready for that?"

"Not only am I ready, but I welcome it," Tennly replied firmly.

Tennly's first training class began at 6:00 AM the next morning. She was told to go to the building across campus, which was the original school before they renovated the current one. It was a two-story stone structure with a large, heavy, bright red iron front door. The exterior had vines growing up the walls and through the cracks, making it look more like a run-down prison.

She was relieved to discover that, despite the building's appearance, it had all the amenities, heat and electricity, allowing her to turn on the lights. However, a pungent odor overwhelmed her: an unpleasant mix of old socks, sweat, and pine soap. The smell became understandable when she discovered a large gymnasium to her right, complete with two locker rooms behind it.

To the left of the foyer was the kitchen. Which was completely furnished. There were pots hanging above the island, a butcher block beside the sink, and when she looked in the refrigerator, she saw bottles of water and ingredients to make sandwiches.

Still not seeing anyone, she went back to the foyer and up the stairs, running her hands over the railing, just as she did at home. Besides the kitchen, every inch of the building was coated in dust, and the railing was no exception.

Glancing at the watch on her wrist, one that all the students received upon arriving at the school, she saw that it was twenty minutes passed the time she was told to be there. She disliked being snubbed by someone she didn't know and hated having her time wasted.

Determined to inform the Headmistress that whoever was supposed to train her didn't show, she furiously entered her office, with no regard that she was in a meeting with someone.

"May I help you, Tennly?" Headmistress Novakova asked, her tone perturbed.

"You told me that it started at 6 this morning," Tennly responded. "No one was there."

"Really?" Headmistress Novakova asked. "How do you know?"

"I checked."

"You went into the building?" asked the man in the room, speaking with a very British accent. He appeared to be in his mid-30s and was quite attractive. He had short wavy dark hair that was tapered in the back. His brown eyes sat beneath thick eyebrows and long eyelashes. A five o'clock shadow covered his chiseled chin and high cheekbones. He wore an all-black suit, as if he was on his way to a formal event. Tennly couldn't help but find him mysterious and wondered why he was there.

She shot him a look as if to say it wasn't his business, then turned to address Headmistress Novakova. "I'm not here to matriculate like the others. If you're going to waste my time, then there's no reason for me to be here."

"Oh," Headmistress Novakova noted. "I was under the impression that you were here because you didn't want to be home."

"When am I starting my training?" Tennly demanded, ignoring her comment.

"You already did," the man chimed in. "And you failed."

"What are you talking about?"

"I'm sorry," the man replied as he stood up and extended his hand. "I should introduce myself. My name is Nigel, and I'm your trainer."

Tennly looked at him with confusion as she shook his hand. "How could I have failed if we never did anything?"

"Everything is a test or a trial," Nigel explained. "Don't go inside anywhere if you don't know what's in there... unless you want to end up dead."

Tennly closed her eyes, recalling the job she did with her father. She remembered him saying that he never met anyone inside for exactly that reason. Nigel told her to report to class and he would meet her at the building as soon as school was over.

She followed the orders she was given, but once school ended, her excitement to start training overwhelmed her common sense. When she returned to the building, believing it was safe, she stepped inside. Suddenly, an attacker approached from behind, pulling a large sack over her head and restraining her arms. As she struggled to escape, a second assailant punched her in the stomach. Bent over from the pain, she was kneed in the face.

Having no other options, she dropped to the floor, causing the person holding her to stumble. Once she felt his grip loosen, she kicked his kneecap, giving her time to wriggle out of the sack, only to get a punch in the chest, causing her to fall backward. Seeing there were two men, she believed she had no choice. She threw one of her knives, landing it in the right thigh of the man closest to her.

"That's enough!" Nigel screamed from the top of the stairs.

The man pulled out the knife from his leg, as if it were nothing, and handed it to her. Extending his hand to help her up, she gave him a look as if he was superhuman.

"I told you," Nigel said, getting her attention as the two men left the foyer. "Never go into a building where there could be dangers." Tennly licked her lips, feeling the blood flowing down her face. "Meet me in the gym."

She tilted her head clearly communicating she wasn't going to fall for his tactics again and stood her ground. "No."

"You either meet me in the gym now," Nigel commanded, "or I won't train you."

Instead of following behind, she chose to walk up the stairs to the second floor. Quietly, she continued down the hallway until she reached a door that led behind the top of the bleachers in the gym.

She saw two men positioned to ambush her. One was hiding just inside the door behind a tall basketball shelf, while the other was crouched in the opposite bleachers, aiming an air soft rifle at the entrance.

Quietly, she crawled over the bleachers to where she was right behind Nigel. "Call them off," she ordered.

Nigel smiled, as he turned around and saw her preparing to throw her knife at him. He called the men off and then gestured for her to sit down on the bleacher seat. "I don't train many people. Those I do train are chosen very carefully.

I've never trained anyone as young as you... So why push yourself this hard?"

"I've mastered everything I've ever done," she replied. "It just comes naturally to me. This seems like the next step."

"Bullshit."

Shocked by his response, she thought for a moment before admitting, "I want to be the best I can be, and I never want to be taken advantage of. I want to walk into a room knowing I have earned everyone's respect; not just because I'm rich or because I'm my father's daughter, or a Connolly. I want it to be because they fear me."

"I'll train you," he nodded. "However, this training isn't easy. I will do everything in my power to keep you as safe as I can, but there is a chance of serious injury or even death. So, how badly do you want this, Tennly?"

The thought of possibly dying didn't scare her; instead, it emphasized the dangers of being the first female mafia boss, and figured it was probably the reason her father was okay with it. This realization only fueled her determination,

motivating her to prove to the men that
women were just as formidable.

"More than anything."

554

CHAPTER 18

Tennly began her morning routine, the following day, by swimming laps in the natatorium. She loved swimming and was eager to get started, but she wasn't sure what she would be learning beyond getting some exercise. As she approached the natatorium, memories of her first encounter with Nigel flooded her mind, and she became cautious. Once she arrived, she checked everywhere for anyone who might be waiting to ambush her. When she didn't see anyone, she stripped down to her bathing suit and dove into the deep end.

Before she had a chance to swim up to the surface, she suddenly felt a tug on her right leg, pulling her down to the bottom of the pool. Panic set in as she frantically tried to swim upward. In defeat, she looked down and realized there was a steel cuff locked around her ankle, attached to a five-foot metal chain. As she tried desperately to unlatch it, she began to feel herself rise. She looked up, anticipating the moment when her head would break the surface of the water, hoping it would before she ran out of breath.

"How many times do I have to tell you, never go in anywhere unless you check it first?" Nigel asked, as she let out a scream, inhaling as much air as she could.

"Okay... okay," she pleaded. "I've learned my lesson. I won't do it..."

"Hold your breath," he interrupted as she felt the platform start to go back down.

She inhaled enough air just as she went under and quickly reached down to remove the cuff from her ankle, but it wouldn't budge. She examined her ankle more closely and noticed that the chain was attached to a large metal ball. She looked for a way to disconnect the chain from the ball but found none. Just as she started to investigate further, she felt the platform begin to rise again.

"It's impossible," she let out after she took in a deep breath.

"Nothing is impossible, Tennly. Look..."

Before she could say anything, he lowered her again. As she leaned over, she noticed that the ball was not connected to the platform. She placed her hands around the ball and tried to lift it, but it wouldn't budge. However, she realized that if she pulled the chain sideways, the ball would move. Knowing she wouldn't have enough time to pull the ball off the platform and to the shallow end of the pool before running out of breath, she decided to wait for Nigel to raise her back up.

He could see the determination on her face, indicating that she had figured out a solution. "Let's get this over with," she said, perturbed.

He lowered her back down, and she immediately began walking toward the shallow end, pulling the ball behind her. It became heavier as she felt the incline; her first thought was that she was in trouble. But then an idea struck her: she wrapped the chain around her back and used her body to pull the ball until her head was above water.

Nigel nodded as she expected praise or some sort of acknowledgement for her ingenuity, but he left without saying a word.

For her next session, Nigel wanted to see what she could do and where she needed improvement, so he had her spar with a couple of his men. She fought well, but the men were too strong for her and eventually, she found herself in a precarious situation. Unable to get loose from the man holding her from behind, another man coming toward her, she reared her knife back, thrusting it into the man's knee.

The man coming at her glance at Nigel, silently asking him what to do, in which Nigel signaled for him to continue. Without hesitation, the man ran over to Tennly, while she was gaining her energy, and slapped her across the face with the back of his hand. He hit her so forcefully that it knocked her off balance, as blood sprayed out onto the gym floor. Catching her breath, she quickly rolled out of his way just as he attempted to kick her.

In a swift move, she grabbed his foot and pulled him to the ground before getting back on her feet. They sparred back and forth, until she suddenly felt a sharp sting on the right side of her waist, as if someone had lashed her with barbed wire. She screamed in pain while gripping her side, realizing that the man she stabbed, used her knife against her.

"Stop!" Nigel yelled, knowing that if they continued, someone would get seriously hurt.

He released the men to go get treated by the doctor waiting on campus and then called Tennly over to him. She was so bloody that there was no way she could walk through the school. She had a cut above her left eye, a busted nose, a split upper lip, and a gash on the bottom of her chin. Blood had drenched her shirt, making it look as if it had been dipped in red paint.

"Let me take a look at that," Nigel said, pointing to her side.

"I'm fine," she replied, unaware of how bad her injuries really were.

"Okay, but you can't be caught looking like this."

"Okay," she accepted, continuing to hold her hand over her right side.

"If you get caught," Nigel warned, "this training is over. Understood."

Tennly nodded and walked out of the gym and into the foyer, where she stumbled into the wall beside the front door. It felt as if her body was being sawed in half. She raised her shirt and saw a three-inch gash on the right side of her torso, located about four inches above her pelvic bone. It was gaping open half an inch, revealing the muscle, and was bleeding profusely.

She thought about heading back to the dorms, thinking it was another test, but as she opened the door, she collapsed. Hearing the commotion, Nigel came running into the foyer, just in time to see her pulling herself back up.

She looked at him, white as a ghost, as blood flowed down her side. She raised her shirt, pointed at the gash and moaned, "I think I need this fixed... a doctor..."

"Next lesson then," he replied, trying not to sound concerned despite that he was. He carried her back into the gym and laid her down on the lowest bleacher seat. He then gestured to one of his employees, who went out and returned with a doctor carrying a large medical bag.

"When you're out in the field and get injured, you can't call a doctor," he explained as the employee handed him the bag.

He pulled out a bottle of whiskey, a wooden ruler, and a suture kit. "You have to learn to stitch yourself up."

"Are you kidding me?" she muttered as he uncapped the whiskey.

"Drink up," he suggested. Then he pointed to her side and added, "And then pour some on that."

Tennly looked at him as if he were crazy but complied with his request. She took two swigs from the bottle, poured a little over her wound, and then chugged a quarter more. She placed the ruler between her teeth as Nigel threaded the needle with silk. Demonstrating how to do it, he sewed the first stitch. She moaned as she bit down hard, feeling as though she might break her teeth. When he handed her the needle, she took the ruler out of her mouth, swallowed another quarter of the bottle of whiskey, and then placed the ruler back.

Taking a deep breath, she inserted the needle into her skin. Despite the cold temperature in the building, sweat poured down her face as her peripheral vision became dark. With each pass she made through her skin, her nausea intensified.

Somehow, she managed to keep her stomach contents down and completed three stitches before she dropped the needle.

"I'm just going to lie down now," she slurred and then passed out.

Nigel had the doctor finish the remaining four stitches that she needed as Nigel took off his coat, folded it, and placed it under her head.

"Have you ever seen anything like this?" the doctor asked.

"Not at her age," Nigel replied, impressed. "And not on the first attempt."

Once it was quiet and he knew no students would be walking the halls, Nigel drove her to Headmistress Novakova's office. He laid her down on the couch that had a sheet over it and then covered her with a blanket.

"Will she be okay?" Headmistress Novakova asked.

"Aye," Nigel replied.

"Did the doctor give her antibiotics?"

"Aye".

"Are you sure you're not being too aggressive with her?"

"She can handle it. She needs to handle it... You like her."

"I like all my students."

"No, this one you're particularly fond of. Why?"

"She's special... and the family needs her."

Nigel allowed Tennly to rest for the next two days before resuming training. They informed Victoria and the other students that she was sick and staying in the infirmary to prevent any contagion. Once her energy returned and could walk without staggering, she was permitted to return to Victoria's room and attend classes. Although her faux flu had passed, she still wasn't ready for anything physically demanding. Instead of engaging in fights, Nigel taught her skills that wouldn't require much exertion.

She learned how to read body language and facial expressions, a valuable tool to know when someone is lying. He had her work on her listening skills; listening to music blindfolded to use her hearing and not rely on vision. They practiced lock picking, survival skills, and how to get out of escape rooms.

Then on the fifth day, with fighting still deemed too risky, he began training her in surveillance. His first lesson took her off campus to downtown Prague. They walked the streets until they arrived at a coffee shop, where they sat by the window to observe their environment around them.

"What did you see?" Nigel asked after the waitress brought them their coffees and departed. "On our walk?"

"People," Tennly said, trying to recall what she had noticed. "Cars, several shops, brick roads, streetlights, a..."

"No, that's what's on the surface. What did you really see?" Tennly was unsure of what he meant. "Close your eyes. What do you feel? What do you hear?"

Tennly gave him a skeptical look but closed her eyes anyway. Then it came to her. "It's cold, yet there was a man wearing shorts and a short-sleeved shirt."

"Good. What does that tell you?"

"That he left his place in a hurry."

"And why is that important?"

"He's running from something."

"Good."

"Or he just finished going for a jog," Tennly added with a smile.

He smiled back and then said, "What else?"

She closed and opened her eyes again. "There was a couple, a man and a woman, arguing on the corner."

"What's the importance of that?"

"Maybe nothing. It could just be a lover's quarrel."

"Maybe."

"There was also a smell. Like burnt bread. It could mean someone was too busy to attend to it... or preoccupied. And there's a black sedan parked across the street that has been there the whole time."

He smiled again and took a sip of his coffee. "They're with me. My lookouts."

"Good to know."

"What else?"

She thought for a moment and tried to retrace her steps, but nothing else stood out to her. When she didn't respond, he continued, "There's been a motorcycle that has driven down this street five times since we started this. Miss something like that and you could be gunned down before you know it."

The motorcycle passed by just as Nigel finished, and after seeing it, Tennly couldn't believe how easily it could be missed.

"You've got to know and see everything in any location that you're in," he instructed. "At all times. You've got to notice what looks out of place or if anyone looks nervous. How long someone has been there or if they are alone or with someone. You need to know everything that is in a room, from the people to objects that appear asinine."

Totally taking in everything Nigel was telling her, feeling an overabundance of desire to learn, she pleaded, "Teach me."

After two weeks of non-violent training, her injury had healed enough for the doctor to remove the stitches and declare it safe enough for her to engage in physical activities. She began her training in the gym with some low-impact boxing and calisthenics to see how she would do. From there, Nigel moved the training to a house on the outskirts of town.

"A situation isn't going to happen in an open practice ring," Nigel noted . "It'll occur when you least expect it. You need to be prepared everywhere you go."

She nodded and then began to fight two men, taking them on one at a time. Nigel watched for nearly ten minutes, but he had to intervene when Tennly was struck hard in the stomach and screamed as she placed her hand on her previously injured side.

He gently placed his hand under her chin and lifted her head to meet her gaze. "Are you okay?"

"Yeah."

He despised seeing her in so much pain
but understood that he had to push her. If
she was going to take over the entire
Connolly crime family, she needed to learn
how to take a punch. He resumed the
fighting, intervening only when Tennly was
on the verge of collapsing.

"Enough," Nigel ordered as Tennly
knelt on the floor, her head resting on
the nearby couch as she tried to catch her
breath. He dismissed the two men, who were
just as bloody as she was, and then sat
down beside her on the couch.

"You're a great fighter," Nigel
praised. "Probably one of the best at your
age I've ever seen. And you got some good
punches in... and are amazing with those
knives. But as you've discovered between
this time and the first, despite you hit
your target every time, knives don't come
back. Which leaves you with no weapons.
You're strong, Tennly, but you weigh,
what? 110 pounds, maybe? Those men have a
hundred pounds on you, each. You will not
win using traditional hand to hand combat
methods. Look around... Everything in here
can be used as a weapon. Remember what
you've learned so far. When you have no
more knives left, you need to find
something else."

He stood up and walked over to the fireplace, saying, "You instinctively knew to find the poker and were able to use it until it was taken from you. But you didn't go back to get the spade." He pointed at the candlestick and pointed out, "A heavy candlestick can become a great weapon." He then walked over to the wall and removed a picture frame and continued, "Picture frames are perfect, especially if they have glass." He broke the frame and showed her the triangular shard of glass that she knew she could easily throw or stab someone with.

"Use your imagination. A toothbrush, or any other long thin object can be used to gouge an eye." He walked further to a side table, reached down and picked up a cord and explained, "A lamp cord, hairdryer cord, even a long enough phone charger cord can be used to strangle someone."

He made it back to the couch and sat down beside her and finished his lesson by saying, "You must learn to use your whole body as well. It is instinct to just throw a punch, but you will not be able to throw one harder than a man who is twice your size. Put your whole body behind it. Use your legs, they are the strongest part of your body. Use the walls, furniture and anything else you can find to give you momentum to make that punch stronger."

He pulled out two large marbles from his pocket and placed them on the coffee table. "You have to look at it like this." Then he explained that one marble was her and the other someone she was fighting. He hit one marble into the other at an inch away. "I used as much strength as I could, but as you see it didn't go that far. Now watch." He placed the marbles back in their original positions, an inch apart, but instead of hitting one against the other at that distance, he pulled one back to over a foot away and hit the other one again, causing the marble to fly across the room. "By getting a run, or using a wall, couch, or whatever for leverage you will be able to make your impact stronger."

Tennly reflected on everything Nigel had said while she was in the shower in the farm house. It all made sense, and she felt frustrated with herself for not coming to these realizations on her own.

Before he let her go for the night, he gave her some homework. He asked her to find ten different rooms at the school and write down everything she could see that could be used as a weapon or aid her in winning a fight and then study it.

It took her more than two hours to walk through the school and write down everything she could use as a weapon. At times, she had to skip a room and return to it because someone was inside, but by the time she finished, she felt accomplished. She returned to Victoria's room just in time to hide her list under her mattress and pretend to be studying before her cousin walked in.

"You're back early tonight," Victoria said as she took off her shoes.

"Yeah, my instructor said since I had been working really hard, he would let me go."

"Mm," Victoria hummed in a curious tone.

"What's mm mean?" Tennly asked.

"If you ask me, I don't think it's your instructor that's working you too hard. Don't think I haven't noticed a limp and that you keep holding your side. I know something's wrong. When you're upset, angry, sad, you bury yourself in your workouts. But you've never worked out to the point that causes you to groan when

you get out of bed in the morning. So, what
is it?"

Tennly took in a deep breath and said,
"I just miss him, Vicki."

"So, the solution to that is to work
out so much that you end up hurting
yourself?"

"It gets my mind off him and makes me
feel better."

"Pain?"

"Yeah," Tennly answered. Even though
getting hurt was a side effect of her
training, she liked it. With every hit,
punch, or cut, it sent endorphins through
her body and made her feel better. If the
physical pain hurt enough, it helped keep
the emotional pain from being so bad.

"Well, I'm worried about you."

"I'll be ok. I just need to work some
things out in my head."

The next morning, Tennly waited for
Victoria to leave the room before she got
up. She needed to retrieve the list from
under the mattress so she could study it
throughout the day. In between classes and
during any downtime, she looked at the list
and ran various scenarios through her mind

to prepare for her training later that night.

After school, she hurried outside to the front entrance to catch her ride to the house. It seemed unusual that Nigel had a driver pick her up, instead of himself, and assumed it was because he had something planned. After she was dropped off, she braced herself for some form of ambush, but no one was there. She went through the downstairs, checking each room before heading up to the second floor. Grabbing a large, heavy candlestick, she made her way upstairs. She needed to carry anything she could find because Nigel had insisted that she leave her throwing knives at the school, wanting to test her resourcefulness for any situation where she might be without them.

She checked every room on the second floor but found no one, so she decided to go back downstairs. Halfway down, she was confronted by two of Nigel's men. She turned to run back up, but two more men were positioned at the top of the steps. She realized what Nigel had done; he had led her to believe that every fight would occur in a perfectly arranged space where she could find weapons. By trapping her on the stairwell, he demonstrated that it wouldn't always be that easy.

She didn't have much time to decide
what to do. Since she had considered
grabbing the candlestick on her way up,
she found herself with a potential weapon,
but she wasn't sure how best to use it.

Feeling as if she was being
compressed as the four men moved slowly
closer to her, she looked over the side of
the banister to assess the height. As the
men closed in, she swung the candlestick
at the nearest man and then leaped over
the banister, landing on the first floor.

When she arrived in the foyer, she
seized the vase perched on a bow-front
chest and hurled it at the men giving her
time to escape. Making her way to the
kitchen, she quickly grabbed two knives.
From there she went to the living room and
hid behind the couch. Hearing footsteps,
she peeked underneath to see how many men
were present, there was only one. Quietly,
she crawled around the couch just as the
man stepped beside it and managed to slit
his left Achilles tendon. The man fell to
the floor writhing in pain, which told her
she had to get out of there before it
alarmed the others to her location.

To prove she could have killed him,
she took the knife, held it to his neck
and said, "You're dead." If it had been a

real-life situation, she wouldn't have hesitated to cut his throat. She dragged the knife slightly around his neck, just deep enough to draw a little blood, and to mimic a real cut. "Get out!"

She dashed out of the living room and quickly made her way around the first floor, searching through every room. Hearing movement down the hall, she darted into the bathroom. Grabbing the toilet bowl lid, she stepped behind the door to wait. She closed her eyes to focus on her sense of hearing and took a deep breath to steady her heartbeat. When the man stepped into the bathroom, she swung the toilet bowl lid and slammed it into his chest, causing him to fall to the floor.

She then bent over him and said, "If this were real, I would have smacked you across the face and then slit your throat. Don't come after me."

She paused before leaving the bathroom, inhaling through her nose and exhaling through her mouth to steady her heavy breathing, as she closed her eyes, so she could listen. Not hearing anything, she slowly opened the door and tiptoed down the hallway, where she encountered the third man. He was stealthily moving through the foyer, searching the first floor.

She knew she could have thrown the knife and pierced his heart, but not wanting to kill him, she wasn't sure how to convey that he was already dead.

"Boo," she said. As soon as he turned around, she threw the knife, hitting the center of the clock hanging to the right of the front door. "You're dead."

The man smiled, nodding to acknowledge that he understood her intentions, and then walked out of the house.

By that point, she had gained so much confidence that instead of being the hunted, she had become the hunter. She found the fourth man in the kitchen, standing between the island and the refrigerator, just inches away from the butcher block.

"You guys don't talk much do you?" she asked as she walked in slowly and tried to get him off guard.

"No need," the man said as he moved his hand closer to the butcher block.

"Nigel must pay you an awful lot to be beaten up like this all the time," she assumed, keeping her eyes on his hands.

"Yep," he replied, grabbing the largest knife he could find.

"Maybe when we're all done," she suggested, still trying to distract him. "We can sit down and get to know one another."

"Sounds good," he confirmed as she took another step closer.

By then they were close enough, that he lunged the knife at her, trying to stab her in the left shoulder. She was able to dodge the attack by taking a step to the left and then jumped up on the island. She turned around quickly and kicked the guy in the chest, causing him to stumble backward. Then in one smooth movement, as the man came after her, she grabbed a pan hanging from a rack and pretended to pound him across the head.

He smiled at her, knowing that if she really would have, it would have killed him. He helped her off the island and together they walked out of the house and up to Nigel who was standing by the car.

"That's how you win," Nigel congratulated as Tennly reached him. Each man she had defeated had gone to Nigel to explain how she managed to take them down, so by the time she arrived, he had a good understanding of what had happened. "How does it feel?"

"Empowering," she replied.

"Good," Nigel said, opening the car door and gesturing for her to get in. After they arrived at the school, they sat in the car for a moment as Nigel told her he would see her in the morning at the gym located across from the school.

"They took it easy on me, didn't they?" she asked.

"They did. But you did well. They had to take it easy on you, Tennly, because you were taking it easy on them. Not being able to kill in practice makes it difficult to know exactly what will happen in a real-life situation. But if you keep practicing... when the time comes for you to not hold back, you will be ready."

CHAPTER 19

Conner went to school every day during the first week that Tennly was gone, hoping she would show up. Although he wasn't sure what he would say to her, he needed to explain why he had taken the money. However, after the first week passed and it became clear that she wasn't coming back, he stopped attending school and reverted to his old ways. To punish himself for hurting Tennly so much, he drank excessively and randomly picked fights with anyone willing to hit him back.

His friends did everything they could to prevent him from fighting, but none of their efforts were successful. It wasn't until three weeks after Tennly left that things finally changed. Conner had been at the warehouse, completely drunk and behaving obnoxiously, picking fights with everyone he encountered. Fortunately, no one at the warehouse engaged with him, which only made him angrier, and he eventually stormed off.

Dante called Riley to express his concern, fearing that Conner might end up getting arrested. Riley, Sam, and Joel rushed downtown, searching every street for him. Finally, they found him at the end of an alley, beaten. They managed to get him back to Riley's house, cleaned him up, and let him sleep off the effects of whatever he had taken.

When Conner woke the next morning, he could hardly move. He managed to make his way to the living room, where his three friends were waiting, anxious to see if he would be okay. When Sam and Joel saw that despite being pretty banged up, he was going to be fine, they left so Riley could talk with him.

"I know what you're going to say," Conner said before Riley had the chance to speak.

"I don't think you do," Riley responded. "So, you need to listen very carefully. I'm not going to sit around and watch you kill yourself. If you're going to insist on living like this, then I'm done. I love you man, but I can't..."

"I'm not trying to kill myself... I just... It helps to forget about her."

"She's not going to be gone forever. I thought you said they're spending Christmas here and she'll likely be back for the summer."

Shocked, Conner turned so that he was facing Riley. He couldn't believe that the friend who had once hated her and had adamantly told him to stay away from her was now suggesting that he pursue her. "What are you getting at?"

"If you want her, fight for her."

"What happened to that being a bad idea?"

"Look, I don't know if it is or isn't," Riley vacillated. "But anyone willing to get you out of jail, is worth a chance. She is different than most rich people. I'll give her that. And she makes you happy."

"But what if... my life is... shit. What if I hurt her?"

"But what if you don't?" Riley remarked, not believing he was pushing him to give it a try. Then when Conner didn't answer he asked, "So, what are you going to do?"

"I don't know. I just want her to know that I never sold out to her father. I want her to know that she is priceless."

Tennly had four days left in her training before she needed to decide whether to go to Ireland for Thanksgiving Break with her family. She had dedicated so much time and effort to learning everything she could to become the best leader, that she had overlooked the upcoming break.

Nigel had her on a rotation to practice everything he had taught her, ensuring that she would continue to improve. She alternated between hand-to-hand combat training with the men, swimming practice to enhance her breath-holding ability, basic weightlifting and workouts to increase her stamina, and various memorization and intelligence exercises.

Two days before the jet was scheduled to arrive for her and Victoria, Nigel decided to stage a mock incident; as one last exercise to make sure she knew everything he had taught her. He convinced Headmistress Novakova to take the entire student body on a field trip, which allowed him to orchestrate the faux invasion. Tennly pretended to be sick, and with Headmistress Novakova's assistance, she was allowed to stay behind while the others went on a day trip, not to return until 11:00PM that night.

Tennly was aware of the mock invasion but was not informed about the exact time it would occur. Nigel had given her five paintball guns, three airsoft rifles, three air pistols, and two crossbows with five round-headed paint arrows. In addition, there were ten faux throwing knives that dispersed colored powder upon impact. She carefully hid the fake weapons throughout the school in various concealed locations, ensuring she could reach them when there were no other objects nearby.

At 4:00 PM, while she was eating dinner in Victoria's dorm room, she heard something out in the hall. Slowly, she grabbed her two real throwing knives, placing one in her thigh holster and the other on her belt. Coming face to face with an intruder as she stepped out of her room, she threw a faux throwing knife hitting him directly in the chest as he shot an air rifle bullet at her, barely nicking her left arm.

She shook her head, informing him that he was dead, and then walked toward the back stairwell that led to the science lab. Before she could descend the stairs, she heard footsteps approaching from above. Quickly, she grabbed the crossbow that she had hidden behind a bow-front chest at the top of the stairwell and pressed her back against the wall.

As the man reached the top of the steps, she shot him in the back with one of the fake arrows, striking him right where his heart would be. She walked over to him, put her hand up to her mouth, and made a shushing sound. Then she quietly descended the steps.

She didn't run into another person until she got to the music room. When she arrived, two men were waiting for her. She fired arrows at both of them, hitting one in the leg and the other in the stomach.

Neither shot was fatal, so they continued to advance toward her.

They used their fake pistols and shot at her, grazing her left shoulder. She ran and slid behind the piano, then fired another arrow, striking the man she had previously shot in the stomach right in the chest. Defeated, he walked away as she tossed down the crossbow, realizing she no longer had any arrows left.

Next, she lifted the seat of the piano bench and retrieved the air pistol she had hidden there. Taking a deep breath, she turned toward the sound of the second man approaching and shot, hitting him in the right shoulder. When he saw her, he fired at her twice but missed both times as she ducked behind the piano.

The man ran toward her, slid over the top of the piano, grabbed a hold of her by the neck and pulled her over the side. She screamed in pain as she felt the corner of the piano grate down her back from the nape of her neck in between her shoulder blades.

While he held onto her, she lifted her legs and fell to the floor, causing him to tumble over her, giving her the leverage to kick him in the back as he rolled a couple of feet away. He turned around quickly, before she had a chance to stand up, and started to come after her.

Before he was able to get to her, she shot him directly in the middle of his forehead, causing him to scream as the pellet lodged into his skin. She gestured to let him know he was dead and then left the room. As she walked down the hallway, she felt the pain in her back intensifying, prompting her to stop in a restroom to check on her injury.

Carefully entering, she made sure no one was inside before approaching the full-length mirror on the far wall. Lifting her shirt to examine her back, she noticed a two-inch triangular gash right on her spine, just below the nape of her neck, between her shoulder blades. It was difficult to see due to all the blood, but the gash extended into a one-inch-wide scrape that continued an additional five inches down her back.

Pushing through the pain, she stepped into the hall, and was struck in the chest, knocking her to the ground and causing her to drop the pistol she was holding.

She had done the one thing that Nigel had warned her against: never go anywhere unless she knew it was safe. After the man kicked the pistol out of her way, he grabbed her by the shoulders and slammed her against the wall. She screamed out in pain as it felt like her back was being filleted open.

At that point she didn't feel she had a choice; she had to use her real knives. She reached down and grabbed the one that was in her belt holster. She didn't want to seriously injure the man, so instead of stabbing him in the chest, she slashed his right forearm. Then she turned around and pretended to slash his throat.

Not wanting to repeat the same mistake as she headed toward the classrooms, she stopped just before the entryway to the dining hall, on the right. Thinking it would be the perfect place to ambush someone, she quietly stepped back, took a deep breath, and then sprinted as fast as she could toward the entrance. Just before reaching the door, she dove to her side and slid past it, believing that if someone were waiting inside, they would shoot high. As she slid down the hall past the dining room, she spotted a man standing ten feet inside. Without hesitation, she pulled the trigger of her air pistol and fired six shots, as additional pellets whizzed above her. Seeing she hit the man, she nodded as she stood and walked toward the natatorium.

There wasn't anyone in any of the rooms along the way and at first, she didn't see anyone in the natatorium either. Suddenly, a man appeared from behind the bleachers on the opposite side of the pool at the same time another man emerged from one of the dressing rooms. From her current angle, she didn't have a shot at either one.

She knew she didn't have much time before she would be surrounded with no way out. So, she ran the ten feet to the edge of the pool and leaped in as the men shot at her. She felt a pellet hit the back of her right calf as she went under the water and could see blood flow from her leg up to the surface. She disregarded the pain and swam underwater to the deep end, where she surfaced beside the diving boards.

Without hesitation, she jumped out of the pool, like a great humpback whale, as the men ran toward her. Grabbing the two fake throwing knives she had hidden under the right diving board, she threw the first knife to her left, hitting the man approaching from that direction in the chest. Just as quickly, she rolled over the board and threw the second knife to her right, striking the other man in the throat.

When they gave her a look that signaled her victory over all of them, she let out a deep tiresome sigh and sat down on the diving board step. As she inspected her leg, noticing a pellet embedded about an inch deep in her calf muscle, one of the men she had just fought, came up to her, telling her that Nigel was waiting for her in the headmistress's office.

Nigel sat in the same chair he had occupied when Tennly first saw him. He instructed the other men to go around the school, clean up anything that had been destroyed, and ensure there was no evidence of what had happened that night.

"You did good," Nigel praised after the men left the office.

"But...?" She asked.

"There will be times when you need to just walk away... Live to fight another day, especially if you are already injured. Does that make sense?"

"Yes."

"I have nothing more to teach you. I'm leaving in the morning."

"But there's so much I feel I don't know."

"You have everything you need. Just continue to practice and use all that you've been taught. But mainly use your instincts. Those have served you well so far."

"Will I ever see you again?"

"I have a feeling," he said with a mischievous grin that caused her to question its meaning. Before she could ask him about it, he asked, "Why don't you want to go home?"

At first, she wasn't going to tell him, but they had grown close, developing a personal relationship. She was quite fond of him and thought that maybe sharing her story would lead to some good advice. So, she began to recant her entire relationship with Conner, including the incident where he took her father's money.

"I don't know what to tell you about your father and your friend, but I can say this: you are like a caged animal here. You might manage to stay tame and domesticated for a while, but eventually, it will become suffocating. When that happens, one of two things will occur: either you will emotionally wither away, or you will lash out and end up hurting someone."

She considered his words and recognized their truth. She could feel the stifling atmosphere of conformity all around the school and knew it was only a matter of time before the wildness within her would be broken.

She nodded to indicate her understanding, and then Nigel called for the doctor to tend to her wounds. These procedures were much easier than the stitches she received on her side. She lay down on the couch, grateful that the doctor had numbed the two new areas before placing the seven stitches in her back and two in her calf after removing the pellet.

Jimmy and John owned a shared residence in Ireland: a 40,000-square-foot stone mansion designed in the Norman architectural style of the 12th century. The façade featured large, five-foot round pillars evenly spaced across the front, supporting the second and third floors and creating a portico that spanned the entire length of the building. Two square turrets flanked the front corners, helping to separate the two wings of the mansion.

Behind the mansion there were gardens with a variety of flowers and plants, including fountains and hedge mazes that the children always enjoyed. To the left of the gardens stood a century-old garage that had been modernized and expanded to accommodate more vehicles.

Daniel owned an estate that he shared with the entire O'Brien family from the United States during their visits to Ireland. The domain was a three-story, 35,000 square foot mansion designed in a Palladian style, featuring Greek and Roman influences. The outer walls of the mansion were made from chiffon ivory-colored stone, with a light-yellow section surrounding the main entryway.

Four eight-foot round pillars supported the triangular roof, which displayed stone statues intricately engraved throughout. Like the Connolly mansion, there was a portico that extended the entire length of the front; however, instead of stopping at the corners, it symmetrically extended on both sides, leading to smaller outbuildings.

On the left side of the mansion was a pool house that included a fully equipped three-bedroom apartment. It featured gardens behind it that were like those at the Connolly estate, although they were not as expansive.

The vastness of both estates allowed Tennly the luxury to avoid her father for the first two days of her Thanksgiving break in Ireland. However, on the third he informed her that there was somewhere he had to take her. The prospect of being included in the family business sparked her imagination, and she eagerly anticipated the trip.

They arrived at a centuries-old cobblestone cottage right outside Dublin, with vines and moss growing over its weathered exterior. The lawn was overgrown but had a narrow cobblestone walkway that peered through and led to the front door. Inside, the walls were covered in wallpaper with bold patterns that was worn and tearing. Hardwood floors stretched throughout the house, accompanied by tattered area rugs under the aged furniture.

Upon entering, they were greeted with a large living room featuring a fireplace at the far end, a mantle cluttered with various sizes of candlesticks, portraits lining the walls, and a set of four antique claw-leg couches at the center.

Jimmy and John were already inside, along with four of Tennly's Connolly family members who were native to Ireland. Her great uncles, Seamus and Grady were in their late sixties and bore a strong resemblance to her grandfather. They had light brown hair, blue eyes, and were physically fit, apart from a slight belly. Sean and Jameson, the sons of Grady, were in their early thirties, both looking like their father.

It was evident from the skeptical looks exchanged among her family members that they had reservations about her being there. They voiced their concerns, prompting Daniel to remind them that his wife, their niece, had been the same age as Tennly when she first became involved in the family business.

"And look where that got her," Grady remarked.

"Anyone one of us..." Daniel began to respond but was interrupted by a voice coming from the entryway.

"She's ready," the voice said. "Give her a shot. She'll prove to you she's worthy."

Tennly's jaw dropped as she became confused when she saw Nigel standing there. Even more puzzling was that he didn't have his usual English accent; instead, he spoke with a strong Irish lilt.

Nigel smiled at Tennly, as he continued, "Her training is done and further along than where Leeny was at her age.

The more Nigel spoke, the more confused Tennly became. Only the members of her Connolly family called her mother Leeny, and she couldn't understand how he knew her by that name. She wanted to ask him questions, but instead, she just sat there tongue-tied.

Her uncle Seamus looked at her father, Uncle Jimmy, and John, and asked, "Do you feel comfortable with this?"

After nodding to each other, Daniel replied, "We do."

They explained to Tennly that Seamus was the head of the entire Connolly mafia family in Ireland. When she eventually took over the U.S. faction, she would need to report to him. She listened attentively as the men spoke but couldn't shake her thoughts about how Nigel fit into all of this. She kept staring at him while the men continued to discuss the intricacies of the business.

Once the meeting concluded and they were about to leave, Nigel walked over to her and whispered, "Last lesson: never tell anyone things you don't want to get out." At that moment, she remembered confiding in him about her relationship with Conner and wondered if he had mentioned it to her father. He winked at her and added, "Don't worry, your secret is safe with me."

As they drove back to the estate, Tennly wanted to ask her father about Nigel, but her anger that she still harbored for her father, prevented her from speaking. They pulled into the garage, and just as Tennly was about to get out of the car, Daniel stopped her.

"What?" she spat; her voice filled with irritation.

"He gave the money back," Daniel confessed.

Tennly felt conflicted about this revelation. Knowing that Conner returned the money only fueled her anger toward her father. "He should have never been put in that situation to begin with."

Despite that Thanksgiving wasn't an Irish holiday, the Connollys from Ireland enjoyed the gathering and spending time with family, so they always participated. The women and older girls baked desserts and prepared the turkey and other dishes, the men congregated in the parlor while the younger kids played in the playroom.

Things were going normally until a thunderous laughter and voices echoed down the hall from the kitchen, growing louder as they approached the women. Emerging from the men was Nigel, who went straight to Seamus' wife, Hannah and gave her a hug. Tennly felt her breath escape as her eyes widened, waiting for Hannah to introduce Nigel, or whoever he was, to everyone.

When he made his way over to Tennly, they locked eyes, and he saw mixed emotions reflected in hers. She was happy to see him again but also angry with him for not letting her know he was connected to her family, leaving her feeling confused overall.

"Tennly, this is Duncan," Hannah said. "You probably don't remember him; you were so young when he left."

"Donut?" Tennly replied, half asking but already knowing the answer. She had started calling him Donut when she was three years old, having associated his name with a local donut chain in the States, which she found amusing.

Duncan smiled at her and said, "Aye."

Duncan had left Ireland ten years ago to establish an Irish mafia faction in England. He had gone under the guise of joining MI6. He was accepted into the program and trained to be a spy in his second year. Stationed in London, he helped set up the family business there while executing various assignments around the world, all while continuing to work and train soldiers for the family.

Once Duncan finished Tennly's training, he called to let them know and mentioned that he was finally coming home.

While everyone doted on Duncan, Tennly quietly slipped away to her bedroom. She had just spent a month with a cousin whom she wasn't supposed to know; he had trained her so intensely that she felt like she nearly died and wasn't sure how to process those experiences.

While in deep thought, she heard on a knock on her door, "Can I come in?"

He could tell she was upset with him, so he waited for her to speak. "Why didn't you tell me who you were?"

"If you had known I was family, you wouldn't have pushed yourself so hard. You would have expected me to take it easy on you."

"I thought you knew me better than that."

"I didn't when we first met. By the time I realized it, we were too far into it, and revealing my identity would have only hindered your progress."

After drilling her on everything he had taught her, she asked him about his memories of her mother, and to her surprise, he had more stories about her than she expected, given their fifteen-year age difference. She listened intently as he spoke, trying to remember everything she could about her mother.

During their conversation, she revealed that Conner hadn't kept the money, and this revelation, combined with his earlier comment about feeling like a caged animal, made her conflicted about returning to Prague. He assured her that if she decided to go back to Marinsburg, he would arrange for a personal trainer for her to spar with and would fly in from time to time to check on her. By the time they were called to the great room to start their Thanksgiving Day festivities, they were laughing and enjoying each other's company, despite her uncertainty about her decision.

She wasn't one hundred percent sure what she was going to do until they were on the jet heading back to boarding school. She sat, thinking about everything Duncan had taught her and with the promise of a trainer if she went back to Marinsburg, by the time they landed in Prague, she knew what she had to do.

As the jet came to a stop, she watched Victoria get up, walk around, and give all their Connolly family members a hug goodbye. Everyone noticed that Tennly was acting strangely, especially as she walked Victoria to the door.

Victoria turned to Tennly and immediately understood that she wasn't coming with her. She smiled and said, "I'm going to miss you."

"I'm going to miss you too," Tennly replied. "But I have to go."

Victoria leaned in, gave her a hug, and whispered, "Don't give up on him."

Tennly smiled, nodded, and watched her cousin walk down the steps and into the school's limousine. The driver, who had driven Tennly around for years, noticed she wasn't following and waved at her. She returned the gesture and then took a deep breath before turning to face her family.

With everyone looking at her, curious about what she was doing, she smiled and said, "Let's go home."

Scane QR Code to link to my webpage to get 'Worlds Collide' as well as the 3rd book of the series and future books.

If you enjoyed 'Worlds Apart,' please consider leaving an honest review on Amazon or your preferred media platforms. I would greatly appreciate it. Thank you for entering my world! I hope you found it enjoyable!

MAP OF NEIGHBORHOOD

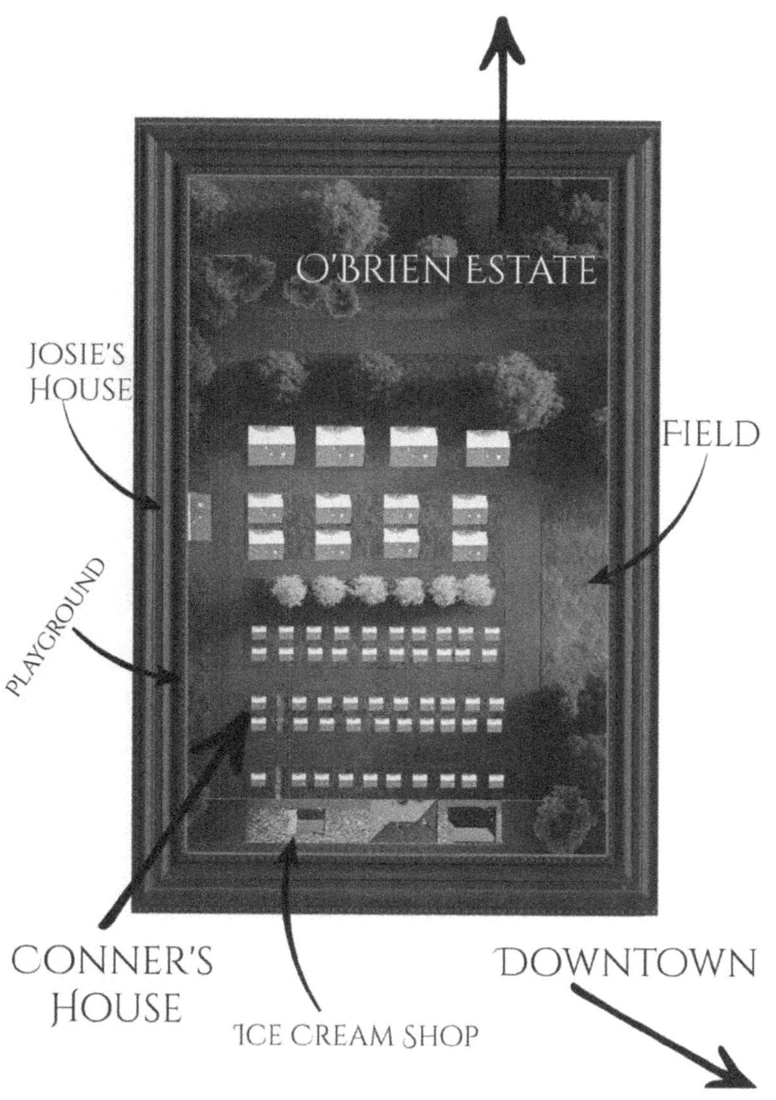

MAP OF MARINSBURG

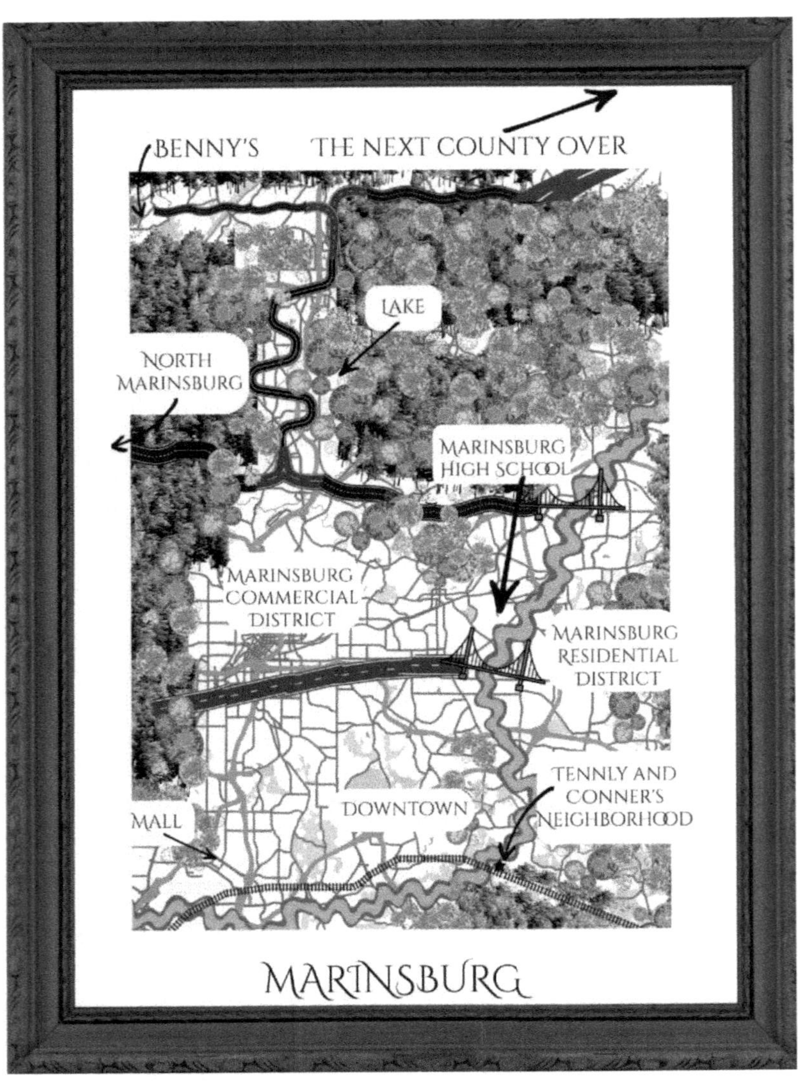

www.ingramcontent.com/pod-product-compliance
Lightning Source LLC
Chambersburg PA
CBHW061112100726
47911CB00013B/508